MARGUERITE'S LANDING

Other Books by
JUNE HALL McCASH

The Boys of Shiloh

The Thread Box: A Collection of Poems

A Titanic Love Story: Ida and Isidor Straus

Plum Orchard
winner of 2013 Georgia Author of the Year Award for Best Novel

Almost to Eden
winner of 2011 Georgia Author of the Year Award for First Novel

The Jekyll Island Club:
Southern Haven for America's Millionaires
(co-author William Barton McCash)

Jekyll Island's Early Years:
From Prehistory Through Reconstruction

The Jekyll Island Cottage Colony

The Jekyll Island Club Hotel
(co-author Brenden Martin)

The Cultural Patronage of Medieval Women
(edited by June Hall McCash)

The Life of Saint Audrey: A Text of Marie de France
(co-edited and co-trans. with Judith Clark Barban)

Love's Fools: Troilus, Aucassin, Calisto and the Parody of the Courtly Lover

JUNE HALL McCASH

MARGUERITE'S
LANDING

A NOVEL
OF JEKYLL ISLAND

TWIN
OAKS
PRESS

ISBN 978-1-937937-09-6 (hard cover)
ISBN 978-1-937937-10-2 (soft cover)
ISBN 978-1-937937-18-8 (ebook)

First Edition

Printed in The United States of America

Twin Oaks Press
twinoakspress@gmail.com
www.twinoakspress.com

Cover and Interior design
by GKS Creative
Cover painting by Sir Joshua Reynolds
Maps by Art Growden

To Katy, Abby, and Beth

MAJOR HISTORICAL CHARACTERS IN THE BOOK

Marguerite's first marriage:

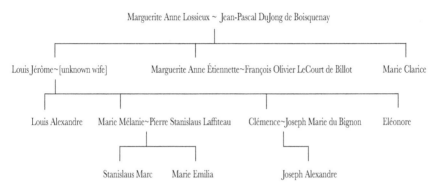

Marguerite's second marriage

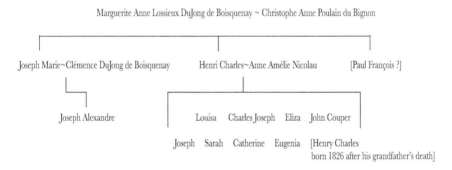

The Sapelo Company Partners (5 shares):

François Marie Loys Dumoussay de la Vauve

Julien Joseph Hyacinthe de Chappedelaine

Christophe Anne Poulain du Bignon

Charles-César Picot de Boisfeuillet

Pierre Jacques Grandclos Meslé (1/2 share)

Nicolas-François Magon de la Villehuchet (1/2 share)

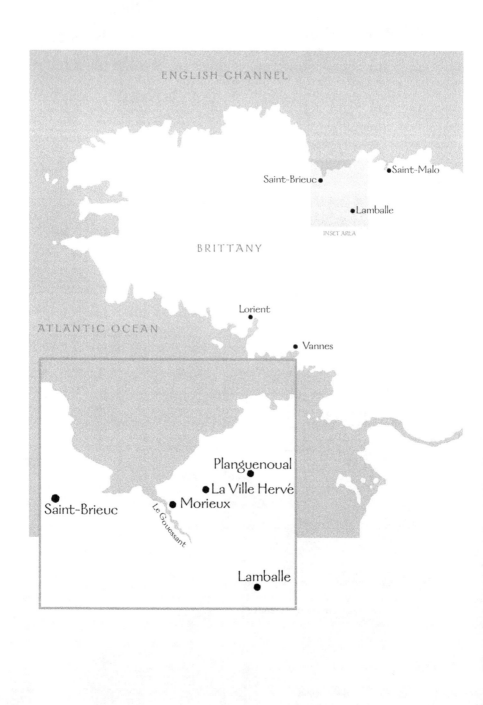

Ogeechee River

Savannah
.

————Tybee Island

————Ossabaw Island

————St. Catherines Island

———— Sapelo Island

Darien
.
Altamaha River

——— Little St. Simons Island

——— Long Island (modern Sea Island)

Brunswick
.
——— St. Simons Island

—— Jekyll Island

Satilla River

——— Little Cumberland Island

St. Marys
.
St. Marys River

—— Cumberland Island

"The incomplete joys of this world will never satisfy the human heart."
—ALEXIS DE TOCQUEVILLE

Acknowledgments

ANY BOOK I WRITE ABOUT JEKYLL ISLAND, including this one, has benefited from the continuing help and support of the wonderful staff at the Jekyll Island Museum, especially Gretchen Gremminger, Andrea Marroquin, Clint Joiner, and the former museum director, John Hunter. I am grateful for all their hard work on behalf of the historical heritage of the island. In this context, let me point out that the spelling of the island's name from *Jekyl*, which I use in the book, to *Jekyll* was changed by the Georgia legislature in 1929. The name du Bignon is also spelled various ways (e.g, DuBignon). I have chosen to use the original French spelling. One more minor name change was that of the French East India Company to the later French India Company. It was the former that actually laid claim to the island of Mauritius in 1715 after it was abandoned by the Dutch. By the time of our story, it had become the latter, a name which I use throughout to avoid confusion.

I appreciate very much the personal tour of Cannon's Point Preserve given to me by Stephanie Knox and Myrna Crook, and I thank Dion Davis of the Jekyll Island Foundation for making the arrangements. It was like a step back in time. I would also like to express my appreciation to the St. Simons Land Trust for saving this very special 600- acre tract of maritime forest, salt marsh, and tidal creeks from development.

I acknowledge here the importance of the scholarly work of Martha Keber and Kenneth H. Thomas, which I discuss in greater detail in the "Author's Afterword." Their work has been invaluable to me.

Thanks to Buddy Sullivan and Amy Hedrick for answering all my questions and helping with occasional obscure details. The historical research and publications of Buddy Sullivan of the coastal area and especially McIntosh County, where Sapelo Island is located, has been an important resource to me for years, as is the constant research and genealogical data gathered by Amy Hedrick for Glynn County. I am also grateful for the work of T. Reed Ferguson and his book *The John Couper Family at Cannon's Point* (Mercer University Press, 1994). Wendy Melton, curator at the Ships of the Sea Maritime Museum in Savannah was also helpful with nautical details.

No acknowledgments would be complete without a special word of appreciation to others who read all or part of the manuscript at various stages and gave me such helpful comments. Among them are Debbie Conner, Claire Curcio, Kathleen Ferris, Mary Growden, Emily Messier, Ron Messier, Margaret Ordoubadian, Cathy Sniderman, and the members of the Murfreesboro Writers Group, especially Julie Fisher.

I would also like to thank the many people in Brittany who provided information and help. Though she may never read this book unless it is translated into French, I would especially like to acknowledge the invaluable help of Cécile Pestel, a delightful woman whom I met in her driveway in Brittany. She had the trust and kindness to loan me, a total stranger, her detailed map of the area where La Ville Hervé is located. We would never have found it without her assistance. There were many other kind and generous people in Brittany whose names I failed to collect along the way but who provided assistance in my efforts to retrace the steps of the du Bignon family through Brittany.

A word of thanks goes to my son, Brenden Martin, for his continuing help in light of my technological inadequacies; to my grandson, Noah Martin, for accompanying me to Brittany and acting as my research assistant and navigator; to Michelle Adkerson, my editor, whose suggestions are always welcome; to Art Growden for designing the maps; to Gwyn Snider for her beautiful book design; and again to Ron Messier for his unfailing encouragement.

Finally, I want to thank all the readers of my previous books who have contacted me with their thoughts and reactions as well as those who have reviewed the books on such sites as Amazon and Goodreads. Readers must never underestimate their importance. If it weren't for you, there would be no point in writing at all.

Prologue

November 14, 1825

Jekyl Island, Georgia

A GRAY CLOUD BLOCKED THE SUN, as Marguerite gazed out over the amber spartina grass of the autumn marsh. Her heart felt heavy and uncertain, as she absently watched a black skimmer swoop low over the tidal creek and scoop up a small fish for its breakfast. She was only faintly aware of the wind lapping the water against the pluff mud of the banks, sights and sounds that had always delighted her, ever since she'd come to this barrier island so many years ago. Now she barely noticed them.

Instead, she let her thoughts drift where they would among the various shoals and swells and storms of her life—to her husband and children, to a country left behind in turmoil, and to that other island so far away, off the coast of east Africa. It floated only distantly in her memory now, having been replaced for so many years by this smaller island in Georgia, the one that had become her home, her destiny, the place where she and her husband had left their imprint—of that

1

she was sure—and even their names. This navigable creek, where for decades her family had loaded cotton for the Savannah market and brought in supplies from nearby Brunswick, everyone called *du Bignon Creek.*

She almost smiled for a moment, remembering that this dock on which she was standing even bore her own name—*Marguerite's Landing*—a name her husband had given it when they'd first arrived more than thirty years ago. Had it really been so long? And fifty years since she'd met Christophe? The memories of that long-ago night—the music, the flickering candles, the swishing of silk as they danced, and the heady scent of gardenias— all flashed, sudden and vivid, through her mind, so that she almost forgot the unfallen tears still clinging to her lower lids.

Chapter 1

August 1775

Port Louis, Isle de France (Mauritius)

MARGUERITE WHIRLED ONCE IN FRONT of her full-length mirror, assessing her reflection. She lifted her eyebrows in an unspoken question as she looked toward her maid.

"*Très belle, Madame,*" Sylvie said, admiring her mistress's appearance.

"*Merci, Sylvie.*" Marguerite accepted her maid's flattery with a grateful smile. She had not felt beautiful for a very long time.

She glanced again in the mirror and her reflection was smiling back. *I do look nice,* she thought. She was not usually vain, but it had been so long since she had felt at all attractive. For more than a year she'd worn those awful black dresses and, whenever she left home, a veil of mourning for her sea-captain husband, who now lay at the bottom of the Indian Ocean. It felt good to wear regular clothes again, not that this elegant dress was her everyday attire by any means.

It had taken more than a month for news of Jean-Pascal's death to reach Lorient, the port town in Brittany where they were living at the time. She'd been distraught with grief. Although their marriage, arranged by her mother when she was only thirteen, was one of convenience at the beginning, Marguerite had learned in time to love him. Now, after scarcely more than a dozen years of marriage, she found herself a widow in her mid-twenties, with more debts than assets and three children to support. But his death helped her to understand for the first time why her mother had married her off so young. Like her daughter, Madame Lossieux had been left the impoverished widow of a sea captain—but with *seven* daughters to support. Marguerite's marriage meant one less mouth to feed and one less body to clothe. Thus, when the opportunity came, her mother seized it without hesitation. Marguerite might well have done the same thing had she been in her mother's situation. It was not so much a matter of choice as of necessity. And it had been for her own good.

Although she missed her husband, Marguerite had grown accustomed to being without Jean-Pascal even before his death. As a ship's captain with the French India Company, he was frequently absent for long periods of time. But there was always the expectation that he would return. And when he did, he would fill their home once more with his carefree, sometimes irresponsible, spirit and try to make up for lost time by loving her all the more and spoiling her and the children with trinkets and gifts—even fabrics for new gowns—he had bought in foreign ports.

A Breton nobleman with the impressive name of Jean-Pascal DuJong de Boisquenay, he'd come from a family that was neither wealthy by inheritance nor great landowners, but rather of the merchant nobility, which had to *earn* its living. After their marriage in Port Louis, he had taken her to live in Brittany, in the seacoast town of Lorient, the Company's major trading center in France. It was there that their children were born—a son, Louis Jérôme, and two daughters, Marguerite Anne Etiennette, called Margot, and the youngest, Marie Clarice. They did well enough financially until the Company's collapse and dissolution in 1769. After that, things became harder for the captain and his family, but he still found work on various private ships and they managed.

Now that he was gone, her only income was a small pension and a tiny inheritance Jean-Pascal had left for the children, which she managed with great care to stretch the funds as far as they would go, but they were insufficient for a decent life in France. Thus, she and the children had moved back to the Isle de France off the east coast of Africa to live once more in Port Louis with her mother, who by then had succeeded in marrying off the rest of her daughters. Together the two widows were able to live better, sharing expenses, than they could have done in separate households. They could even afford to hire one serving girl, Sylvie, who now stood beside Marguerite, admiring her mistress and helping her with last-minute touches to her makeup as she prepared for the *soirée*. This was to be her first real social event since Jean-Pascal's death more than a year ago.

"*Ça suffit, Sylvie*. That's enough," Marguerite said to the girl, who was only seventeen, as she tried to add more color to her mistress's cheeks. Marguerite did not much care for the pale makeup and excessive rouge so popular at French courts. She preferred a more natural look, though she did redden both her cheeks and lips to some extent.

She touched her chestnut-colored hair, carefully arranged in a stylish pouf, augmented with long shoulder-length curls dangling from the left side. Sylvie had powdered her hair carefully before Marguerite put on her dress, and her mistress was pleased with the effect as she examined her coiffure front and back with her hand mirror. She wanted to look her very best, for tonight Marguerite was emerging from her formal period of mourning, like a butterfly escaping its tight, colorless cocoon.

The blue silk of her dress flowed around her like the waters of the sea. The gown was not new. It had been made four years ago in France and was one of the few extravagances during her marriage. Although she was thrifty out of necessity even then, she had not been able to resist hiring an excellent seamstress to create this magnificent garment from the gossamer fabric that Jean-Pascal had brought her from India. She touched it gently, remembering the first time she'd put it on for that captains' ball in Lorient three years before her husband's death. She had felt like a princess. Now, in Port Louis, she knew it would impress the other ladies, who had to depend on whatever fabrics were imported to the island.

The fact that Jean-Pascal's brother, Guillaume, was the host of the evening's event made it seem to her like a coming-out party, with his family's sanction. They all knew she missed Jean-Pascal, but they also seemed eager for her to get on with her life, in part, she suspected, because they did not want to feel responsible for her and her children. They had already taken every recent opportunity to introduce her to unmarried men capable of supporting her. To some extent, it annoyed her, but she knew she should be grateful. Her brother-in-law was the port director and well acquainted with the best sea-faring families in Port Louis. He would see that she met only acceptable gentlemen.

How good it feels to wear silk again, she thought, as she touched her wide, diaphanous skirt puffed out at the hips by a stylish whalebone pannier. For the first time in more than a year, she felt almost happy again.

Her mother, less fashionably attired, would accompany her to the party as chaperone. As she reminded Marguerite frequently, "A widow can't be too careful if she hopes to remarry."

Once they were finally ready to leave, Marguerite gave last-minute instructions to Sylvie, who would stay behind with the children. Little Marie-Clarice stood with her at the door to see them off, her large blue eyes shining in wonder.

"You look so pretty, *Maman*," she said. Marguerite knelt down to give her daughter a farewell kiss and inhale the sweet smell of her fresh-scrubbed face.

"*Merci, ma chérie*," her mother said. "*Sois sage*. Be good for Sylvie. And don't ever forget I love you."

"I won't, *Maman*. I promise to remember *always*." She smiled her merriest little smile and stretched out her arms to give her mother and grandmother a final hug.

Marguerite left the house, basking in the admiration of her smallest child and feeling as though she had already had her first glass of champagne.

CHRISTOPHE SAW HER THE MOMENT she entered the *salon*. Light from the gilded sconces on each side of the door and the crystal chandeliers that graced the ceiling reflected in her eyes and on the auburn highlights of her hair. An uncertain smile played on her lips as she glanced around the crowded room. The combination of poise and hesitation gave her a stunning vulnerability and aroused his curiosity. She was as beautiful as any woman he had ever seen in France. The port director, who had so graciously invited Christophe to the evening's festivities, immediately greeted her. *Who is she?* he wondered. An aging woman at her side appeared to be her only companion.

Suddenly his host was leading the younger woman through the crowd toward him. Now she was standing just in front of him, as Monsieur de Boisquenay introduced them.

"Marguerite, I would like to present Captain Christophe Poulain du Bignon, whose ship the *Merger* is currently gracing our dock for repairs."

She curtsied as he bent forward to kiss her hand.

"*Enchanté, Mademoiselle,*" he said warmly, rising to gaze into remarkable eyes that reflected all the colors of the sea.

"*Madame,*" she corrected him gently. He felt a surge of disappointment.

"Madame de Boisquenay is the widow of my late brother," his host said, and Christophe could not help but smile at the words. His long, weathered face could give a sullen appearance, but when he smiled, it broadened boyishly, and his eyes lit up like candles. He tried quickly to take on a more sober countenance as he nodded, "I am so sorry for your loss, *Madame.*"

"*Merci bien.*" Her eyes clouded over for just a moment.

Their host nodded and left them together, while he moved away to greet other guests.

"I hope your life has not been too difficult since your husband's death," Christophe said.

"I have managed to survive, Captain. And tonight for the first time I feel as though I am returning to life." He followed her gaze as she looked around the brightly lit room, where the reflection of hundreds of tiny flames sparkled in tall, gold-framed mirrors. Large-paned casement doors stood open to the evening air, and people strolled in and out like splashes of color on a canvas.

"I'm happy to be here to witness that return," he replied. "Widowed so young. It must seem terribly unfair."

"Indeed it does. My husband was a sea captain like you. But my mother, also a widow, tells me life must go on."

"And she is right," he added with a smile.

The string quartet was playing a stately Bach minuet, and two couples began to dance at opposite ends of the room.

"Do you feel that you could dance?" he asked uncertainly, wondering whether it was an appropriate question to ask a young widow.

She hesitated for a moment, glancing toward her mother, who had taken a seat across the room and was chatting with the woman seated beside her, before she replied.

"Tonight I feel like a bird freed from its cage, and I would like very much to dance," Marguerite said, lifting her chin.

He took her hand and led her to the center of the room. The minuet in a minor key was slow and dignified, *suitable for a widow's first dance*, Christophe thought. He had never been an extraordinary dancer. In fact, he didn't even care for dancing very much, but tonight his *pas menus* and bows felt just right. The next dance was a livelier *gavotte*, to which she also assented, this time without a pause. However, when the quartet began to play a waltz, the new dance so popular in Vienna and sweeping through Europe and the colonies, she looked again toward her mother and demurred. Even Christophe could see her mother's frown of disapproval from across the room. It would be unseemly, he surmised, for a young widow to dance with a gentleman in such an intimate way, to let him put his hand on her waist.

"Would you care to get some fresh air?" he asked, motioning toward the wide-flung doors, beyond which stretched a large terrace and a garden. "It's a lovely evening."

Noticing several other people on the terrace, she nodded. "It's a perfect night for such an event, don't you think?"

He agreed. The Isle de France, as the French India Company had renamed Mauritius when they took it over after its abandonment by the Dutch sixty years earlier, enjoyed a delightful year-round climate. It could be quite warm and humid in the summer months of January and February, but August was one of the more pleasant and temperate months of the year. Christophe always marveled at the fact that when it was summer in France, it was winter, or what passed for winter, in Mauritius, as most seafarers still called the island. He felt fortunate to be here on this extraordinary evening and to spend it with the only woman who had caught his eye in a very long time. He was thirty-six years old and, if he was ever to start a family, it was time for him to take a wife, though that particular thought crossed his mind only fleetingly that evening. He merely found her to be an extraordinarily attractive woman.

WHEN MARGUERITE LATER RECALLED THAT FIRST *soirée* they spent together, she remembered the swirling and swishing of her silk skirt as they danced, and how a few strands of her hair came loose and curled around her ears as the evening wore on. Christophe told her how attractive it was and how he loved the natural look it gave her. She remembered her sapphire earrings dangling jauntily against her bare neck and the sweet smell of the night air. She recalled the depth of his eyes as he gazed into her own, as though trying to look into her very soul. For the first time since Jean-Pascal's death, she felt her heart stir. The captain seemed to find her enchanting. He brought her a silver cup filled with champagne punch and tidbits of hors d'oeuvre, which he fed her as they sat in the gardenia-scented garden.

She found him not only attentive, but also attractive. He was not tall or particularly handsome, but there was something compelling about him. His dark blue eyes were intense and demanded attention. His skin was ruddy, tanned from his days at sea, and his face was angular and serious, except when he smiled. Then it seemed to light up the world around him. His hair was brown, but burnished by the sun, which gave it reddish tints, not unlike her own. She wondered at first if his special charm might come from the fact that he was the first man to show her such undivided attention since her husband's death. But she knew it was more than that. She felt drawn to him in a way she had never felt before. And before the magic evening ended, she introduced him to her mother, who smiled her approval.

"HOW LONG WILL YOU BE IN PORT LOUIS?" her mother asked the first time Christophe came to call on her daughter.

"As long as possible," he replied with a grin and a quick glance toward Marguerite. "I have a brother here. Perhaps you know him— Ange du Bignon. He's a seaman like me, who makes his home in Port Louis. It's a wonderful opportunity to spend some time with him," he claimed. But he made it quite obvious, as his eyes frequently sought Marguerite's face, that visiting his brother was not the only reason he was reluctant to leave.

Almost every day for the next six weeks, as the *Merger* was having her hull repaired from its hazardous encounter with an uncharted rock in the Indian Ocean, Christophe and Marguerite managed to meet. They took leisurely walks along the quays or the beach, laughing at the antics of the gulls and the winds that snatched at Marguerite's bonnet, though really paying less attention to their surroundings than to each other. He came to tea or dined with her family on several occasions. He dropped by to borrow or return a book, always looking crisp and smart in his captain's cap. And he befriended her children, most of all Louis, her twelve-year-old son, who quickly became his greatest admirer. Christophe often appeared at the front door to invite the boy, who was always eager to go, on an outing along the harbor or down one of the dusty roads that led toward the small volcanic mountain called Le Pouce. Sometimes all the children went along, and their mother packed a picnic lunch and accompanied them. Marguerite thought they must look like a family as they walked together. Only the little girls, both of whom were blond like their father, had a somewhat different appearance. Louis's hair was a shade darker than his mother's, but had burnished highlights like Christophe's.

THE BOY WANTED TO BE JUST LIKE HIS FATHER, to sail the seas and travel to foreign lands. Christophe, although he looked nothing like Jean-Pascal, was nevertheless enough like him to captivate the child. Occasionally Christophe would touch the boy's shoulder and call him "*mab*," the Breton word for "son," as his *papa* used to do, and Louis could hear the echo of his father's voice. Both men were from Brittany, where Breton was a more common language than French, though as captains, they had to speak French as well. Warmth flooded through him when he felt the affectionate touch of Christophe's hand on his shoulder, and a sudden, secret thought was born—one he dared not say aloud—that Christophe might become his new father. He couldn't think of anyone better.

"Would you like to go aboard my ship?" Christophe asked the boy as soon as the *Merger* was back in the water, fresh from her repairs.

Louis nodded with excitement. Once aboard, the boy breathed in the salt air, feeling exhilarated by the stiff breeze against his cheek as he looked around at the ship's freshly scrubbed wooden deck, its sails folded like great wings in wait, its masts swaying in the wind.

"I want to go to sea some day," he offered hopefully.

"Perhaps you'd like to return with me to the seafarers' school in Vannes. It's in Brittany, not too far from Lorient where your mother tells me you were born. You could act as my personal cabin boy on the return trip," Christophe suggested.

To the eager child it sounded like a dream come true. He would miss his family, of course, but Christophe told him how, when he was only ten years old, two years younger than Louis himself, he'd left his family's home in Lamballe, Brittany, to go to sea as a cabin boy and what an adventure it was.

"It's the best way to learn the skills of seafaring … to start when you are young," he told the boy.

"Do you think my mother would permit me to go?"

"I don't know. Why don't we ask her?"

MARGUERITE WAS HESITANT AT FIRST, fretting over her indecision. Although in recent years both her older children had grown less overtly affectionate, as children do when their world widens and they begin to explore their own interests, she would miss them terribly if they were not all together. And could she trust Christophe to keep her son safe at sea? She'd already lost both her father and her husband in seafaring disasters. But Christophe was reputed to be a competent captain, and she was well aware that the boy was fond of him and wanted desperately to go.

"Please, *Maman*," he begged day after day.

"I'll take good care of him, Marguerite. I promise," Christophe assured her.

She knew she would never be able to keep her son away from a seafaring life, and this might be the best and safest chance he would have to launch his dream. It might even bring Christophe back to Port Louis or at least cause him to write to her. Finally, his urging and the boy's pleading won out, and she consented.

ON THE OCTOBER MORNING OF THE *Merger's* sailing, Marguerite, with her mother and two daughters, stood on the dock buffeted by the steady wind to wish the pair a *bon voyage*. Louis and Christophe, side-by-side on the poop deck, waved an enthusiastic farewell. Holding tightly to the small hand of Marie Clarice while her other arm held Margot close, Marguerite could see her son's broad smile and his eyes gleaming with excitement. Christophe was standing behind him now, his two hands on the boy's shoulders, gazing intently at Marguerite. They looked like father and son standing there. *Oh God,* she prayed, *keep them safe, and please let my decision be the right one.*

Long after her mother and daughters returned home, Marguerite still stood on the dock, brushing away tears and watching the white sails of the *Merger* slowly fade into the misty horizon.

MONTHS PASSED SLOWLY WITH NO LETTERS from either Christophe or Louis. In the afternoons Marguerite would walk the beaches with her two daughters, gazing toward the horizon for the sails she knew were still far away. But it made her feel closer to both Christophe and her son to think they might be looking at the same ocean, watching the waves as restless as her heart. When would she ever see them again?

Marguerite was still not sure that her decision had been the right one or even that she had made it even for the right reasons. She feared that she'd given into her son's desire in part because of her own. She'd come to care deeply for Christophe, and Louis had become, in a way, their bond. But she was still not sure Christophe felt as strongly about her as she did about him. She missed his touch, his arms around her, the kisses they had shared whenever they could steal a few moments alone. She had even let him fondle her breast the night before he sailed.

The children were in bed, and her mother had left the room to fetch a cup of warm milk, when he reached out to take her in his arms. She had not resisted. She'd heard his sharp intake of breath and sensed his body's strong response as his hand slipped inside her bodice. She felt her nipple hardening in urgent need of his fingertips. The moment, all too brief, had left her longing for more as they heard her mother's returning footsteps. The yearning she'd felt after his departure was stronger than anything she'd ever felt for Jean-Pascal.

Christophe seemed so perfect for her, yet he had not asked her to be his wife. He'd hinted on occasion that he was thinking of it. He'd never been married, but he said he wanted to settle down. He had begun to express his need for a wife and family quite openly, and he had let her know that he had quite a little nest egg set aside from his adventures at sea. Money would be no problem, he assured her. She wanted so little—a stable life and a loving family. If fate could provide

MARGUERITE WAS HESITANT AT FIRST, fretting over her indecision. Although in recent years both her older children had grown less overtly affectionate, as children do when their world widens and they begin to explore their own interests, she would miss them terribly if they were not all together. And could she trust Christophe to keep her son safe at sea? She'd already lost both her father and her husband in seafaring disasters. But Christophe was reputed to be a competent captain, and she was well aware that the boy was fond of him and wanted desperately to go.

"Please, *Maman*," he begged day after day.

"I'll take good care of him, Marguerite. I promise," Christophe assured her.

She knew she would never be able to keep her son away from a seafaring life, and this might be the best and safest chance he would have to launch his dream. It might even bring Christophe back to Port Louis or at least cause him to write to her. Finally, his urging and the boy's pleading won out, and she consented.

ON THE OCTOBER MORNING OF THE *Merger's* sailing, Marguerite, with her mother and two daughters, stood on the dock buffeted by the steady wind to wish the pair a *bon voyage*. Louis and Christophe, side-by-side on the poop deck, waved an enthusiastic farewell. Holding tightly to the small hand of Marie Clarice while her other arm held Margot close, Marguerite could see her son's broad smile and his eyes gleaming with excitement. Christophe was standing behind him now, his two hands on the boy's shoulders, gazing intently at Marguerite. They looked like father and son standing there. *Oh God,* she prayed, *keep them safe, and please let my decision be the right one.*

Long after her mother and daughters returned home, Marguerite still stood on the dock, brushing away tears and watching the white sails of the *Merger* slowly fade into the misty horizon.

MONTHS PASSED SLOWLY WITH NO LETTERS from either Christophe or Louis. In the afternoons Marguerite would walk the beaches with her two daughters, gazing toward the horizon for the sails she knew were still far away. But it made her feel closer to both Christophe and her son to think they might be looking at the same ocean, watching the waves as restless as her heart. When would she ever see them again?

Marguerite was still not sure that her decision had been the right one or even that she had made it even for the right reasons. She feared that she'd given into her son's desire in part because of her own. She'd come to care deeply for Christophe, and Louis had become, in a way, their bond. But she was still not sure Christophe felt as strongly about her as she did about him. She missed his touch, his arms around her, the kisses they had shared whenever they could steal a few moments alone. She had even let him fondle her breast the night before he sailed.

The children were in bed, and her mother had left the room to fetch a cup of warm milk, when he reached out to take her in his arms. She had not resisted. She'd heard his sharp intake of breath and sensed his body's strong response as his hand slipped inside her bodice. She felt her nipple hardening in urgent need of his fingertips. The moment, all too brief, had left her longing for more as they heard her mother's returning footsteps. The yearning she'd felt after his departure was stronger than anything she'd ever felt for Jean-Pascal.

Christophe seemed so perfect for her, yet he had not asked her to be his wife. He'd hinted on occasion that he was thinking of it. He'd never been married, but he said he wanted to settle down. He had begun to express his need for a wife and family quite openly, and he had let her know that he had quite a little nest egg set aside from his adventures at sea. Money would be no problem, he assured her. She wanted so little—a stable life and a loving family. If fate could provide it, she also silently longed for a fine home and a few servants. But a loving, harmonious family was her most important goal. *We seem to want the same things,* she thought. He obviously found her attractive and enjoyed her company. But he had not asked her to be his wife.

A FULL YEAR PASSED WITH NO WORD from either of Christophe or Louis. Then on the afternoon of the first day of February 1777, there was a loud knock on the front door of the modest house Marguerite shared with her mother. Sylvie opened it and accepted a sealed message from a boy sent by the port director. She took it to her mistress, who was sewing in the parlor with her mother, Madame Lossieux, and her younger sister, Marie Françoise.

Marguerite broke the seal, unfolded the note, and read it quickly. With a sudden intake of breath, she dropped her sewing basket to the floor and rushed to the door. Snatching her shawl from the coat rack, she reached for the knob.

"What on earth …?" asked Madame Lossieux.

"The *Merger*! The *Merger* is docking at the port!"

"My dear," said her mother, "don't you think it would be more seemly to …"

Marguerite did not wait to hear the rest. She bounded out the door and raced down the cobbled street in the direction of the wharf.

One block from the dock area, she rounded the corner of a narrow lane and almost collided with Christophe and a grinning Louis.

"*Maman!*" Louis shouted, throwing himself into her arms, as he had when he was a little boy.

She smothered him with kisses until he pulled away, his face red from embarrassment.

"I'm a student pilot, now, *Maman*, on Captain du Bignon's ship," he said in a voice that had changed from that of a child into the uncertain voice of an adolescent in all the months he was away.

Marguerite, her face wreathed in smiles, turned to Christophe, who was patiently waiting his turn for her attention. "*Vraiment?* Really?" She had assumed the boy would have to serve for several years as a cabin boy before beginning the serious training required to become a captain, the first step of which was that of student pilot.

"Really," Christophe replied. "And he's an apt pupil. A born seaman. I made a special request for him to accompany me on this voyage." His face reflected both the afternoon light and his obvious delight at seeing Marguerite again.

"But the *Merger* was not scheduled to come here." She flushed, aware that he would realize that she regularly checked with her brother-in-law for any news of the *Merger's* whereabouts and itinerary. "What did you … ? How did you … ?" Her voice was incredulous. She seemed incapable of forming a coherent question.

CHRISTOPHE TOOK A DEEP BREATH, hoping to explain in a way that she would fully understand why he had come, without his having to spell it out in front of her son.

"By some miracle," he began in a playful tone, "we were on our way to India, when we seemed to be running out of water. We couldn't possibly continue our voyage without refilling our supply, so I ordered the ship to put in to the harbor here for that purpose." His eyes crinkled with humor as he told her his ruse. "Besides, Louis was feeling homesick and ..." He hesitated, then continued, "The fact is, I … we … simply couldn't come this close without stopping to see you." His voice was husky with emotion.

Crew members who had been on his ship a year and a half earlier had easily seen through the ruse and noticed that the water barrels were still more than half full from an earlier stop in the south of Africa.

They were well aware of what attracted him back to Port Louis and actually dared to tease him, "*Absolument.* We absolutely need to fill the tanks, *monsieur le capitaine. Nous comprenons*, we understand," they said, with smirks and mock salutes. He couldn't be angry with them, for he knew they were right. But they made him feel like a schoolboy.

In fact, Christophe had not ceased thinking of Marguerite since his departure, and he gazed at her now as though he saw the face of an angel.

Smiling her welcome to them both, she slipped a hand in each of theirs to walk them home.

Chapter 2

LATER THAT EVENING, WHEN THEY WERE ALONE TOGETHER in the darkness of the small garden behind her mother's house, Christophe whispered to her, "The whole time I was away, all I could see was your face in the sea and the sky. *Je t'aime*, Marguerite. I love you."

She had learned already that Christophe was not by nature a demonstrative sort, and his sudden declaration was a delightful surprise. Perhaps there was a romantic streak in him after all.

"I have thought of you as well," she murmured between kisses. "And I ... I love y..." He stopped her words with another kiss. She accepted it with the same hunger he offered it.

"I had to come back," he said. "I couldn't wait any longer to hold you in my arms again and ask you to be my wife."

Her heart lurched with joy. These were the words she had wanted to hear before he sailed away in the first place, words she'd feared she would never hear.

"I would be honored to be your wife," she said, holding him close and offering her lips once more for one of his hungry kisses.

IN THE DAYS THAT FOLLOWED, Christophe seemed to slide easily into the empty places in her life. In some ways he was much like Jean-Pascal. They were almost exactly the same age—both nine years older than Marguerite. They even wore the same size clothes, except for length, for Jean-Pascal had been about five inches taller. But she fit more securely in Christophe's arms, and their lips could meet on almost equal terms. She felt a warmth and a rightness when he held her that she had never felt before. There was a maturity and a protectiveness about him that made her feel safe. He didn't laugh as often as her carefree husband had. He was calmer, more serious, and seemed more responsible, more caring about their future security together. Unlike Jean-Pascal, he was actually *planning* for the future. He had no intention of being a sea captain for the rest of his life.

"I intend to remain at sea only long enough to amass sufficient funds to buy a fine manor house somewhere in Brittany and live the life of a country gentleman with a good family from that time on. Would you be willing to live a life like that?"

She laughed with delight. He seemed to be giving voice to her own unspoken desire to live just such a gracious and stable life, away from the ever-changing sea. It had always seemed far beyond her reach. Jean-Pascal had never had such lofty goals, and when he died, he had left her and the children with many debts. But now, here was Christophe, sharing her dream and eager to live it with her. He looked into her eyes with such intensity that she felt as though he were seeing straight into her soul. It made her desire him in ways she had never desired Jean-Pascal.

Christophe embraced her three children warmly and without hesitation, carrying three-year-old Marie Clarice on his shoulders whenever they walked together on the beach, and holding the hand of her older sister Margot. He'd already taken Louis under his wing and promised to do everything possible to launch him in his new career. So far he'd kept his promise. And the boy, who so desperately wanted a father, clearly adored him.

The four days they spent together in Port Louis were filled with sunlight and joy, as the newly declared couple made plans for their future together. But all too soon, Christophe and Louis had to set sail again, leaving Marguerite behind to make the necessary arrangements to join them in France where the couple had decided to marry and where they would reside.

EVEN THOUGH SHE'D ALREADY lived through more than a decade of marriage, Marguerite felt like a young bride as she prepared her clothing and linens for the trousseau she would take to Brittany. She was in no hurry, for voyages of sailing ships like the *Merger* took many months and, as yet, they had set no specific date for a wedding, so uncertain was the life of a seaman. With her mother and sister, she sat daily by the parlor window with Marie Clarice snuggled at her side as she happily embroidered *deB* on the pillowcases and sheets she would take with her to France, bedding items she and Christophe would share in the years to come. She felt a frisson of anticipation, making her miss a stitch that she had to do over again.

THE FIRST LETTER DID NOT ARRIVE until late September, more than seven months after his departure. It came from India, bringing welcome expressions of affection, but also bad news.

August 22, 1777

Ma très chère Marguerite,

Louis and I both send loving greetings from Chandanagore, where we have met with a rather serious misadventure. Alas, our ship, the Merger, is no more. As we approached Bengal through an always-treacherous route up the waterways of the Ganges, our incompetent pilot, a local man I was forced to hire since no French pilots were available, steered us quite suddenly into a rocky shoal. Louis could have done better. Everyone aboard was thrown violently to the deck, and several members of the crew were badly injured. Two of them later died. But I am happy to say that Louis and I are both fine.

Unfortunately, the ship did not fare so well. A huge gash in the hull doomed her, and the treacherous current finished her off, breaking her apart quite completely. All this happened on June 21, and I have spent the last two months dealing with the aftermath, filing reports and making sure my men were taken care of. I had not wanted to write you until I had better news to report, for fear you might despair of our safety and even our future together. I did encourage Louis to write, but I fear that he has been as lax as I in putting pen to paper.

Now I am happy to report that I finally have good news. I have been given another ship, the Ville d'Archangel. The captain, a Frenchman, has fallen ill and been compelled to give up his command, which he's offered to me. Needless to say, I accepted without hesitation. We are set to sail once more on the first of September. I won't bore you with the details of the cargo and crew, except to say that Louis will join me on board. But I will share with you the most excellent news that we are scheduled to arrive at Port Louis sometime in December. Perhaps then you and I can make our wedding plans, as I will soon be returning to France, where I expect you to join me.

I assure you of my most faithful and abiding love, and I long for the day when we can be together again for always.

Je t'adore, ma chérie,

Christophe

Marguerite read the letter with mixed emotions, distress to hear of the lost ship, which went against a captain's record, but delight to know that he planned to set sail again so soon and was bound for the Isle de France once more.

SHE DID NOT HAVE LONG TO WAIT. The *Ville d'Archangel* arrived at Port Louis right on schedule, like a big, brown swan, sailing into the harbor on December 14, where foul weather would keep it until after Christmas. During those short weeks, Christophe and Marguerite took the time to finalize their marriage plans. They decided against holding the wedding in the Breton port of Lorient, where she'd once lived with Jean-Pascal. Instead they would rendezvous in the nearby coastal town of Vannes, where Christophe had passed his examinations to become a captain, which gave it happy associations, and where they would begin their new life together.

Neither of them was satisfied by now with mere kisses. In their cravings they sought out dark corners and shadowed places where they might touch each other with greater intimacy, still short of that final act they both desired. When he left once more, it was wrenching, as though he carried a part of her body and soul away with him. In her longing following his departure, she could hardly wait to leave for France.

Vannes (Brittany), France, August 1778

THE SHIP THAT CARRIED MARGUERITE and twelve-year-old Margot glided through the early-morning mist that hovered over the glassy waters of the Gulf of Morbihan and into the sheltered port of Vannes. The town, which had sprawled well beyond its original medieval walls, lay tranquil with the morning sun beginning to settle on its dove-gray rooftops. The Breton air was cool, fresh, and familiar, but Marguerite could tell that the day would be warm.

The only thing that marred their arrival was the absence of her youngest child, Marie Clarice, who at age six was still sweet and delicate as a porcelain doll. Although Margot had clung to her mother throughout the voyage, Marguerite still felt an ache inside at having left Marie Clarice behind, something she'd never wanted to do. But before their planned departure from Port Louis, the child had become more and more withdrawn and begun to cling to her grandmother's skirts.

"What's wrong, *chérie?*" her mother asked, pulling her close and stroking her golden hair. Marie Clarice burst into tears and hid her face with her tiny hands. By the time Marguerite realized that the child's grandmother was planting fears in her head about the sea voyage and about leaving her alone, it was too late. "*Papa* died at sea," the little girl finally confessed. "I want to stay here with *grand'mère.*"

"I'm getting old," Madame Lossieux complained. "Who will look after me in my old age? Monsieur du Bignon is a sea captain—gone more than half the time. Why can't you live here instead of Brittany? What difference would it make?"

"It's all decided, *Maman*. And I can't leave Marie Clarice behind. You have other daughters here."

"But they don't live with me," her mother replied. "She'd be so much company."

Some of what her mother said made sense. Sea captains *were* often absent for months, even years, at a time. But Christophe was adamant that he wanted his family in Brittany. He hoped to see them, if not more often there, then at least for longer periods of time. He had inherited a small amount of property to the north near Lamballe, where he was born, and that was where he had promised Marguerite they would one day acquire a fine manor house when he retired—a day, he swore, that was not long in the future. Mauritius was not a good place to raise a family, he argued. It had been a pirate lair before the French India Company came, and it still attracted all sorts of wastrels and riff-raff to its shores. There were few opportunities there. So many reasons.

It was a heart-wrenching decision, but after much painful soul-searching and to pacify both her daughter and her mother, Marguerite had finally agreed to allow Marie Clarice to stay behind either in her grandmother's care or to help care for her grandmother, whichever was required, but just for a while until she and Christophe were able to buy the property they wanted and settle there permanently. Then perhaps her mother and Marie Clarice could both come to live with them, if she could persuade her mother to leave Port Louis. The child had always been Madame Lossieux's favorite. But Marguerite missed her daughter desperately. Marie Clarice was her only child still young enough to climb into bed with her mother in the mornings for a snuggle or to run to her arms whenever there was a thunderstorm.

Even now in her mind Marguerite could see her daughter, nestled in her lap as she brushed her shining hair or read her a story. The decision to let her stay, which the child begged to do, had been a painful one, but it seemed all that would settle the matter. And Marguerite knew that her sister, Marie Françoise, for whom little Marie Clarice was named, and her husband Louis de Chermont, would look after the child as though she were their own. And it was only for a little while.

"You will write often?" Marguerite, still anxious, asked.

"I will send a letter on every ship sailing for Brittany. I promise," Marie Françoise assured her with a hug. "Don't worry. She'll be fine. And she will soon be with you again."

"You will tell me everything, every detail, every change in her life, won't you?"

"Of course, dear sister. Please don't worry. Louis and I will take good care of her."

With these assurances, Marguerite reluctantly set sail without her youngest daughter. But she missed her terribly. A second marriage was so complicated.

AS THE SHIP DOCKED IN VANNES, Marguerite anxiously scanned the faces on the dock. None looked familiar. She and Margot hurried down the gangway, hoping that Christophe would be waiting among the teeming crowd of passengers, greeters, dockworkers, and baggage handlers. But he was not there. All she could do was hire a carriage to take her, Margot, and their luggage to the boarding house outside the old city where Christophe had promised to reserve a room. A message was waiting for her there.

"It arrived almost two weeks ago," the concierge told her as she handed over the heavy, brass key to the room, along with a sealed letter. Once inside, Marguerite ripped open the letter with anxious hands and read it twice.

Ma chérie,

I sincerely regret that I am unable to be waiting for you in Vannes upon your much longed-for and anticipated arrival. When my ship landed in Lorient in late June, I was quite ill with a malarial-type fever. Louis, dear boy, helped me get to Saint-Brieuc, where my youngest sister, Angélique, is a nun with the White Sisters, as most people call the Daughters of the Holy Spirit. I have told you about her. Her name suits her well, and she is as close to a saint as any in my family. The Sisters of her order care for the sick, among their many good works, and I knew they would take me in and nurse me back to health in time for our wedding. I was quite weak from the ordeal. I'm happy to report that I am now almost fully recovered and eager to join you.

However, an important matter has arisen concerning my sister Jeanne, who, as you recall, is a spinster and lives alone in Corseul, not too far from Saint-Malo. She needs my help, and I could not turn her down. Nonetheless, Louis and I should arrive very soon, and I look forward to seeing you again and holding you in my arms.

As always, I am yours,
Christophe

Marguerite was determined not to be upset by the delay. They had known each other for three years by now, and she trusted him. She would use the time to plan the details for their marriage.

As Margot opened the windows to let fresh air into the stuffy room, Marguerite gazed about her. The room was plain, with two single beds, both with sagging mattresses, lined up on opposite walls. There was a small fireplace, intended to provide their only heat on cool evenings, which often occurred even in August. A washstand held a white basin and pitcher. It was simple but adequate. Once she and Christophe were married, they would find something larger and more suitable.

She was glad they had chosen Vannes for their wedding rather than Lorient, where she had once lived with Jean-Pascal. Vannes was a charming town with few previous associations for her. It represented a fresh start. There would be no family members at their wedding, except for Louis and Margot, but they would do. It would be a small ceremony for them alone, with only required witnesses and the priest who would perform the ceremony.

AFTER A GOOD NIGHT'S SLEEP, Marguerite and Margot began the very next morning to explore the various churches where the wedding might take place. They went first to the nearby parish church of Saint-Salomon. It was quite splendid, built in the shape of a cross and enriched by many small chapels and altars.

"But it's so big," Marguerite said to her daughter. "And the wedding will be so small."

"And there's a graveyard all around, *Maman*." Margot pointed out. "I think that's a bad omen." It was late in the day, and the shadows of the tombs had grown long and almost sinister. Margot shuddered.

"You're right, *chérie*. Let's find something else."

As they walked down the narrow streets, the sound of women's voices singing vespers drifted into the rue St-Yves.

"How lovely," said Marguerite. "Do you hear it, Margot?"

They paused to listen, until the short service came to an end.

"There must be a church behind these walls," Marguerite said. "Let's find it."

The entrance to the convent was closed with an iron gate. Marguerite rang the bell and waited patiently as she heard shuffling footsteps approach.

"*Oui, Madame?*" an elderly nun, dressed in a black habit, a rosary hanging from her belt, peered through the gate.

"We heard your singing of vespers. Could we come in and talk with the Mother Superior?"

The old nun peered out, appraising Marguerite and the girl standing beside her.

"*Mais oui, Madame.* Right this way." She smiled, unlocking the gate. It creaked as she swung it open for them to enter.

And there, in the Convent of the Visitation, Marguerite found the site of her wedding—the little church, built high off the ground, where the nuns marked the hours and held their services. Located between the rue St-Yves and the rue de la Vieille Boucherie, it was small and intimate, with only a few rather simple stained glass windows reflected in puddles of colored light on the stone floor. Over the entrance was a little rose window depicting the Virgin Mary, surrounded by smaller rounded panels of winged cherubim. The nuns, with the Mother Superior's approval, were excited about helping to plan such a rare thing as a wedding for their little chapel. Few people ever married at the convent. The ceremony would be ever so plain, but Marguerite knew it would be perfect.

By the time Christophe finally arrived in Vannes, preparations for the ceremony were virtually complete. He made no complaint that Marguerite had taken care of the arrangements without him, for despite the protestations in his letter, he was still a bit weak from his illness and, she thought, rather nervous at the prospect of marriage. They had only to post the banns and meet with the priest from Saint-Salomon, who would perform the ceremony.

Saturday, August 29, 1778

On the day of the wedding, the little stone church was cool, while the air outside was quite warm. The nuns were all aflutter to have a bride to dress, though the gown was not elaborate, just a becoming rose-colored muslin. Marguerite felt that one of her finer gowns, few though they were, would be out of place in this simple setting. She marveled that this day was finally here. They'd waited so long—an eternity it seemed. In a festive mood, she'd added a tiny touch of rouge to her cheeks, hoping that the nuns would not notice or would assume her heightened color was caused only by excitement.

Just before the marriage ceremony began, one of the nuns, Sister Elisabeth, placed a wreath of white roses like a crown on Marguerite's head and gave her a hug as she held out a small bouquet to match. Sister Jeanne put a basket of rose petals in Margot's hand so that after the ceremony she could scatter them before the couple for good luck.

Outside the door of the sanctuary, where the wedding vows were to be exchanged, Christophe waited, smiling with relief when he caught sight of Marguerite climbing the stone steps to meet him. With Christophe stood the wizened old priest, Father François from Saint-Salomon, who served as confessor to the nuns. His hands shook with palsy. Margot in her best dress, her golden curls floating around her shoulders, and Louis, looking uncomfortable in his tight-fitting suit, stood aside with the nuns to witness the little ceremony. Marguerite blinked back tears of joy as she approached her sober-faced fiancé and waited to be joined to him for a lifetime.

It was all so brief—a declaration of intent and an exchange of vows that took no time at all. The priest made the sign of the cross to bless them as he intoned, *"Ego conjugo vos in matrimonium, in nomine Patris, et Filii, et Spiritus Sancti. Amen."* Marguerite felt the drops of holy water fall on her hair and face as he sprinkled a blessing upon the couple and then on the gold ring, which he handed to Christophe. With instructions from the priest to help him, Christophe nervously slid the ring partway onto her thumb as he said, *"In nomine Patris,"* then on her index finger, *"et Filii,"* and her middle finger, *"et Spiritus Sancti,"* before placing it firmly on her ring finger with the word *"Amen."* A short ritual prayer from Father François concluded the ceremony. After years of anticipation, it took less than ten minutes to complete. They were married.

Christophe, holding Marguerite's hand, brought it to his lips, and the two trailed the old priest into the sanctuary for the nuptial mass. Marguerite could feel Christophe's fingers trembling almost as much as those of the palsied priest. She smiled to reassure him. He was far more tense than she was. After all, he was getting married for the first time—at age thirty-nine. She gently squeezed his hand to steady him, as they approached the altar, where the priest was now waiting to give them their first communion as husband and wife.

When the wedding party left the church, Margot smiled and tossed her pale hair self-consciously as she led the way, spreading her rose petals before the new couple as they walked the short distance to the convent refectory, where a simple meal of fruit, bread, cheese, and wine, offered by the nuns, awaited them. Thus, with little fanfare, the marriage began.

FOR A SHORT WHILE, THE FOUR OF THEM, Christophe, Marguerite, Louis, and Margot remained in a jovial mood—aware that they were now a real family as they got to know each other better in the close quarters of the four-room apartment Christophe had rented for them in Lorient.

As days went on, however, the little apartment seemed increasingly small. Christophe, unaccustomed to living daily with a family, especially Marguerite's children, seemed less patient than he had been during his courtship of their mother. Although he had been with her son daily on the ship, there he had his own private quarters. Besides, Margot and Louis were hardly children any longer at twelve and almost fifteen. Like most young people, they were beginning to strain against parental authority, particularly against a man who was not their real father, as he tried to establish paternal prerogatives in the household. Given the thin walls of the rooms, their very presence in the apartment seemed to irk him at times and even constrained his lovemaking. Marguerite believed that, as time passed, they would all adjust. At least she hoped so.

One afternoon, when Louis returned from the port, where he spent much of his time, he was grinning from ear to ear.

"I've been offered a job on a merchant ship," he announced, seemingly pleased to be released from the tutelage of his stepfather and to have found the job on his own. "We sail next week." He puffed out his chest with pride.

Marguerite, trying to absorb the news, glanced at Christophe. His face was a complicated mask. She thought she sensed a note of relief, but there was something else as well. Annoyance? Irritation? Was it because Louis had made plans for his future, while his stepfather was still unsure of his own? Perhaps, she thought, her husband was only surprised. She knew that he, too, was eager to get back to the sea, for the sooner he could sail, the sooner he would have sufficient funds to fulfill his lifelong dream. He had informed her that he intended to take advantage of a new war between the British and the Americans to build his fortune.

"I've heard that the king has signed a treaty with the Americans and gotten France involved in that conflict. I think it was a foolish move, but I'll find a way to make it work in our favor," he'd declared. She did not yet realize what he had in mind.

Chapter 3

December 21, 1778

Lorient, France

CHRISTOPHE HAD LEARNED THE NEWS about France's involvement in yet another war even before the wedding. Rumors of it had been rampant among the dockworkers when he first arrived in Vannes, still weak from the malaria that had attacked him shortly after a stop for water off the coast of West Africa. At first he was incredulous, taking it as a bad joke.

"But it's true," the dock master assured him. "Everyone's been talking about the king's treaty with the Americans for months. Now the British have declared war on France again." But Christophe saw no warships in the Vannes harbor. It had to be just silly gossip. Barely recovered from his illness, he was impatient with such absurdity.

"The king may be foolish," said Christophe, "but surely he's not foolish enough to join a bunch of roughneck colonists against the best-trained military in the world." Everyone in Lorient and every other port in France knew that the navy of George III was the most powerful on earth.

For a time he was able to put the rumor out of his mind, but everywhere he went he heard the same story. He and Louis had taken a carriage to Saint-Brieuc, where his sister Angélique was a nun. The boy was a godsend to him in helping with bags and caring for him throughout the arduous trip. However, once they arrived in Saint-Brieuc, the White Sisters had taken charge, putting him to bed and fussing over him until he began to regain his strength. Even there the nuns fretted over the possibility of an English attack.

"They are such *brutes*, those English sailors. They pillage and loot and rape …," the Sisters prattled on and on, expecting the worst any day now.

Can it be true? Christophe had wondered, as his health slowly improved and he began to regain his strength. *Have the king and his ministers really lost their minds?* Yet everyone he met hammered him with new details, so compelling and convincing that he was finally forced to believe them.

The French government, it turned out, had signed not one, but two agreements with the Americans—both on February 6 at the Hôtel de Crillon in Paris. One was a treaty of alliance with the revolutionaries, certain to enrage the British, and the other a treaty of amity and commerce. In short, the king was informally recognizing the rebellious colonies as the independent country they proclaimed themselves to be and evidently saw a bright future of trade with the new nation, if they succeeded in breaking away from England. Or else he merely wished to antagonize the British. Whichever it was, Christophe thought, it was foolhardy. France had already lost vast territories in the New World to England in the last war more than twenty-five years ago when Louis XV was still king. Why would his grandson, Louis XVI, want to challenge the British yet again?

He had tried to put thoughts of the war aside to celebrate the beginning of his married life with Marguerite. Once wed, however, and having new financial responsibilities for a family, he was compelled not only to face the unwelcome news of war, but also to determine how he might make it work in his favor. One thing was for certain: he had no intention of sailing a slow merchant ship through hostile waters. *But perhaps*, he thought, *there was another possibility*. It was a possibility he did not share with Marguerite until after their marriage.

MARGUERITE, THOUGH SHE PAID LITTLE attention to politics, agreed with him that another war with the British made no sense. She knew from life with her father and Jean-Pascal that war was bad for the shipping trade, and she could understand why Christophe didn't want to sail a vulnerable merchant ship in hostile waters. However, she didn't like the alternative he was proposing. Not long after their wedding and Louis's departure, Christophe announced his intention to apply for one of the king's letters of marque, which sanctioned privateering against British ships. She was shocked.

"Sometimes it's better to be the predator than the prey," he told her.

To her repeated objections, he replied, "It's my chance to make a real fortune, Marguerite. And it will be easy." He told her that captains with letters of marque who plundered rich ships on the high seas and brought them to port to be sold, along with their cargo, earned a substantial share of the profits.

"Merchant ships are slow and not well-armed," he explained. "A swift corsair with sufficient guns can easily overtake them. The trick is to find a ship owner willing to convert his vessel into a corsair and make me its captain."

Marguerite argued vehemently against the idea. "But it's so dangerous. Surely merchant ships have some guns, at least. Won't they be trying to protect themselves? And it's immoral, stealing like that. Why, you would be a virtual pirate."

"Not a pirate," he protested. "A legal privateer with the king's blessing."

She was not convinced it would be as easy as he seemed to think, but he ignored her protests. To her dismay, it didn't take him long to find what he was looking for. His main chance was waiting in Lorient with a willing company that bore the name of its owner, Monsieur Lavaysse, and a ship, soon to become a corsair, named the *Salomon*.

It felt as though time had reversed itself. Marguerite, once again the wife of a ship's captain, stood on the dock in Lorient to wave farewell to her husband, as the last tether of the ship to the dock was removed. The dark shape of fear once again formed itself in her breast, as she listened to the screaming gulls overhead and watched Christophe's new ship sail away from the safety of the solid port into the blue vastness of the open sea. How many times had she done this, with Jean-Pascal, and now with Christophe and Louis? Even as a child, she had stood waving from the dock in a stiff breeze as her father sailed away.

But this time it was different. The cargo the *Salomon* carried was only means to an end. Christophe, letter of marque in hand, was sailing to Port Louis to sell the goods for enough money to outfit the ship as a corsair. She was appalled and frightened at the prospect. *He might call himself a privateer*, she thought, *but it's piracy, whatever he wants to call it*. Although he seemed sure it would be more lucrative than sailing a merchant ship, it was also far more dangerous. As much as she longed for a wealthy future, she wasn't convinced it was worth the risk. Or that it was an honorable profession for one who hoped soon to retire and live as a nobleman and member of the landed gentry.

Once again Marguerite found herself with only Margot and her new maid, Nanon, hired by Christophe to look after her and keep her company, waiting in dreary rented rooms for her husband's messages and his eventual return. It was the life of a sea captain's wife—this waiting. When his letters arrived, usually many months apart, they were packaged in oiled sailcloth to keep them dry. She would open each one reverently as though it contained Holy Scripture and read it aloud to her daughter. The first one did not reach Lorient until mid-October, and as she read it, first to Margot and then to herself again and again, the little coal-burning fire in the grate seemed more cheerful.

August 20, 1779

Ma chère Marguerite,

I thank you for your welcome letters, which arrived before we did, and were waiting for me when I reached Port Louis in June (following many stops along the way). There I saw Marie Clarice and can assure you she is safe and growing rapidly, though, as always, she seems a bit frail. Your family, however, is looking after her very well. She, your mother, and your sisters send their love.

I also saw again my dear brother Ange, who, I am happy to say, has agreed to join me in my expedition as second captain. (By the way, he also has an attractive new lady he is courting. Her name is Félicité Morel.) Together Ange and I have hired additional crew members, both white and black, some of them slaves sent by their masters. We've begun to outfit our ship for its new role as a corsair. I have, by the way, taken on a fine African valet called Mustafa, who will no doubt return with me to France.

When I first arrived in Mauritius, I contacted one of your brothers-in-law, Robert Pitot, who generously expressed a willingness for his company, Pitot Frères, to outfit the Salomon as a corsair. He and his brothers are doing quite well, as you no doubt know. He was a bit cautious at first, for he does not want to overextend himself or his company, but he's already sent out one corsair and fully understands both the risks and the investment potential.

However, before we concluded anything, I met another prominent ship-owner whom you may also know, one Pierre Paul de La Bauve d'Arifat. He was very interested in the Salomon and our proposed expedition. Before long, he was offering to buy the vessel outright and fund our enterprise himself. Monsieur Lavaysse had expressed to me before our departure his need for capital and gave me carte blanche to raise it however I could, even if I had to sell the ship. So I decided to take Monsieur d'Arifat up on his generous offer of two hundred thousand livres. Robert Pitot can still invest in the expedition if he so chooses.

Although, as you know, I already have the king's letter of marque for the Salomon, I am still awaiting the authorization of Governor Souillac. It is, I think, but a formality, but we cannot sail without permission from the governor of the Mascarene Islands, of which, alas, Mauritius is, and will always be, one. As a new governor, he is, I think, unduly cautious.

As I wait, I think of you daily and miss your kisses, my beloved. I remain, your faithful and loving husband,

Christophe

The letter made no mention of their first wedding anniversary, Marguerite noticed, even though he wrote it only nine days before the event. She was not really surprised, for she knew that men cared little for such sentimentality. Still, she felt a tiny pang of disappointment. But another of the letters, which arrived in early February, gave her hope that, when her husband finally did return, he would be coming home to stay.

December 28, 1779

Ma chère Marguerite,

Monsieur d'Arifat must now be quite happy that he invested in what has proven to be a most lucrative opportunity.

We finally set sail on August 23, as soon as I received the governor's authorization. D'Arifat sent with us another ship, the Sainte Anne, which proved to be little more than a nuisance most of the time. We had a number of false hopes in the beginning, but on October 5, little more than three weeks ago in the Indian Ocean, we captured a British ship called the Merchant of Bombay. She was a slow vessel and did not at first try to evade us, for we were flying the British flag.

When we captured her, she proved to be a real treasure ship, loaded with diamonds and pearls, gold and silver, and sacks and sacks of money. We found at least sixty bags of silver coins. Even three fine Arabian horses on their way back to England for some English gentleman's stables. The entire crew was ecstatic. We have now sent the Merchant of Bombay back to Mauritius, where, no doubt, Monsieur d'Arifat is rejoicing.

Marguerite, if you ever doubted the value of this venture, you may now rest assured that it will be worth it. Soon I will have enough to retire back to France and to give up my sea-faring career and dedicate myself to being your devoted husband.

I am so very sorry that we must be separated this long so early in our marriage, but I will make it up to you in diamonds and pearls, my love. We will soon spend the rest of our lives together on our own lands in Britanny.

Je t'aime de tout mon coeur,

Christophe

Marguerite could not contain her smile at her husband's sweet expression of love at the end of the letter and at the thought of his success. Nor did she really try. Margot was especially delighted with the news of his good luck. After all his promises, she dreamed of being a rich young noblewoman, which she hoped would help to launch her social life.

"Just think of the pretty gowns we can buy and the jewels he will bring home," she said to her mother with a laugh. Her eyes sparkled as she gazed out the window toward the rooftops that obstructed their view of the wintry sea. They went back to their sewing, but somehow their cramped rooms in Lorient seemed a bit less somber as they thought of their bright future.

Seeing Margot's joy, Marguerite wondered if God would forgive her husband for his sin of piracy. *Perhaps he's right after all,* she thought. *If the British are our enemy, reducing their resources by any means possible can only help end this war sooner.* Instead, she should no doubt consider herself fortunate to have found such an enterprising husband. If he came home a wealthy man, she would hold him to his promise to give up the sea. They could settle down once and for all in the manor house they planned to buy and assume their place as noble landowners. They would have servants to attend them. And she would plant roses, roses of all colors, in the garden. And irises. And lilacs. She could already smell their fragrance.

With happy thoughts in her heart, she began to leave her rented rooms more often and go out to enjoy the brisk days of autumn, even to seek out some of the other captains' wives in Lorient. Before, her only *sorties* had been for essential shopping and to go to mass. Now, for the first time, she began to permit, even encourage, Margot to attend the occasional *soirées* enjoyed by Lorient's young people—but only if she went along as chaperone. She knew Margot's flighty ways and feared that she might not always show the best judgment if left to make her own decisions. But the girl would be fourteen her next birthday, and her mother realized they must begin to think about her future.

Two more letters from Christophe arrived—one in the spring and one in the summer of 1781—all from foreign ports, small ones, she presumed, for she did not recognize the names. He had been gone for two and a half years now, and she was afraid he would be like a stranger when he returned. He assured his wife that he was well, but sent little more news, except his reassurance of his love for her, which she was always happy to read. Still, he was beginning to seem more and more distant.

Finally, in late autumn she received a much longer letter. It looked as though it had passed through many hands before reaching hers. The sailcloth in which it was wrapped was dirty, and the frayed string that held it together looked as though it had been untied and retied many times. But the letter's seal remained unbroken. This time his message came from Port Louis. Marguerite began to read it eagerly, but her heart lurched with the first three sentences.

October 1, 1781

Ma chérie,

How can I write you such a letter? When I think of the joy with which I wrote to you so many months ago, I am dismayed to report the latest news to you, lest you think ill of me. But as husband and wife, we must share the bad with the good.

I have been dismissed as captain of the Salomon. Ange has been assigned the captaincy in my place.

It is hardly my fault that the rest of the expedition went so badly. Despite the albatross of the Sainte Anne, which was never where it was supposed to be at any given time, and the incompetence of its fool captain, a man named Champdeuil, we captured a number of other English vessels in the Bay of Bengal and other areas. But I could never tell what the cargo would be until we boarded the ships. Unfortunately, these did not carry gold and silver, but rather such mundane items as rice or coconuts. The cargo of one ship was even a load of sand. Utterly worthless, and, while the ships themselves may have been of some value, we were forced to torch most of them for various reasons.

The capture of the Merchant of Bombay, however, was enough to reward the investors with a 50 percent profit on the enterprise. But do you think that was enough for them? Oh, no. They have complained bitterly and criticized me harshly. The worst critic among them is your brother-in-law Pitot, who has publicly made scathing remarks about my lack of integrity and bad manners, which you know well to be false. I did not take kindly to his remarks, and I almost challenged him to a duel. However, since he is the husband of one of your sisters, I have refrained—so far at least.

The investors were angry that we did not continue our expedition and bring back more booty, but Champdeuil had babbled about the Salomon in every port he entered, to the extent that everyone could recognize our vessel from a great distance, regardless of what flag we were flying, which gave them ample time to escape. Thus, it seemed useless to continue. It is entirely his fault that the expedition ended so badly, and I have so stated in my official report.

I have also been criticized by Monsieur d'Arifat and even by Governor Souillac, who has withdrawn his approval of future privateering expeditions for the Salomon. I am quite fed up with the entire affair.

There are two bits of good news, however; I served as witness at the wedding of my brother Ange to Mlle Morel—who is now, like you, Madame Poulain du Bignon. They seem very happy.

The other bit of good news is that, despite a great deal of bickering over the division of proceeds from the expedition, with investors claiming that the slaves they sent on the voyage should receive a full share, we have prevailed. Maritime law clearly gives only the captain and crew the right to decide on how the profits will be distributed. The slaves' share is to be only one-third of the free men's. My share is 17,500 livres, in addition to my salary, of course. It isn't what I had hoped for, and certainly not enough to let me retire entirely from the sea, but it is substantial nonetheless.

Perhaps the best news of all, my dear wife, is that I am coming home as soon as all matters here are settled and I have finally received my share of the earnings from the Salomon expedition. With any luck I should be home not long after the first of the year.

I hope you will find it in your heart to receive me with open arms and as much love as I feel for you.

Yours,
Christophe

Chapter 4

Summer 1781

Lorient, France

MARGOT SULKED FOR DAYS AFTER THE LETTER CAME, her dreams of becoming a wealthy man's daughter fading with each soulful sigh as she stabbed at her needlework. She tossed her curls in disdain at the mere mention of Christophe's name. Marguerite, too, was disappointed to know that his retirement would have to be delayed, but she was happy to know that her husband would soon be home again. To Margot that made no difference.

"He'll still return with wonderful gifts for us both, Margot," she said. "Try to welcome him with an open heart."

"Hmph," Margot snorted. "So many promises. So little delivered."

"A person's value has nothing to do with money," Marguerite said to her daughter, "He's doing his best and taking many risks to provide a good life for us. He's a good man. And he *is* your stepfather. You must show proper respect."

Margot refused to look at her mother as she shot her embroidery needle sharply through the green petal she was stitching. A drop of blood appeared on the fabric.

"*Merde*," she said.

"Margot! Such language. I will not have it." *Perhaps it would have been better to remain a widow*, she thought. Merging two families into one was more difficult than she had imagined. Human interactions, she had discovered, were fraught with unforeseen conflicts. And she was still making an effort to pay off some of the debts left by Jean-Pascal with her meager pension, not to mention debts her children had incurred by buying things they did not need or, in the case of Louis, in the taverns he had begun to frequent with the other sailors. Just after their marriage, Christophe had paid some of the bills without complaint, but there were still others he didn't know about that were well beyond her ability to pay, and the interest was mounting. Sometimes she felt trapped in a whirlpool. She looked across the room at her daughter, who sat sucking the tip of her finger and pouting like a little child, as Nanon served tea and discreetly disappeared, leaving behind the tension in the room.

Mother and daughter worked side-by-side in silence for the rest of the afternoon.

WHEN HE FINALLY CAME HOME, Christophe's promised diamonds and pearls were a pair of small pearl earrings with one tiny diamond in each for Margot and for her mother a fine strand of matched pearls. Both were magnificent, and pearls were so rare that only the wealthiest wore them. But Margot expressed only disappointment.

"I thought surely there would be more than this," Margot grumbled.

Marguerite, quite satisfied to have her pearls and her husband home again, tried to shush her, but Margot wouldn't give up.

"At least with all that money you say you made on this trip, surely you could spare a few *livres* for some of the things I need."

Christophe bristled at her impertinence, but he refused to spend the funds he'd earned from his share of the *Salomon*'s expedition on the lavish new gowns and the fancy frivolities Margot wanted. Instead, he chose to deposit it in a bank at the modest rate of five percent toward the time he and Marguerite could buy the manor house he still longed for near his birthplace in Lamballe.

"It won't be long now, *chérie*," he promised his wife. "One or two more voyages, and we'll surely have enough for me to retire from the sea."

But the news of Christophe's troubles with the *Salomon* followed him to Lorient when he returned in early 1782. Given that, and coupled with the earlier loss of the *Merger*, it was not easy to find work again. Many owners of merchant ships were also unwilling to put their vessels in danger while the country was at war, though warships were being built at a rapid rate. Louis, now eighteen, had joined the royal navy and was constantly at sea, while Christophe sat waiting for new commercial offers in the port of Lorient.

"Perhaps you too could join the navy," Marguerite suggested.

"I am not a military man by temperament. And in my mid-forties, I think it's too late for me to change. You know I would not last long under military discipline."

Marguerite knew he was right. He needed a ship of his own. She tried to console him with her kisses and their lovemaking, which she desired more than ever. But his temper grew shorter with every passing day, and tensions increased in the dark, rented rooms. Margot proved to be a special source of contention. Christophe grumbled about her constant demands, her desires to go to parties and buy new dresses. She was restless and sulked at being what she called "locked up again in this dreary apartment," for her stepfather thought her too young and undisciplined for an independent social life.

As months went slowly by, Christophe complained that his earnings were being gobbled up by the expenses of daily life. They rarely went out, for he no longer seemed to enjoy *soirées* like the one where he and Marguerite had met in Port Louis. He didn't relish conversations with other captains, who inevitably asked questions about the *Salomon*. Marguerite tried to understand, but she believed he would have a better chance at getting the captaincy of another vessel if he mingled more with the seafaring community. Finally in July a rumor began to circulate in Lorient that ship captains were desperately needed in Portugal.

At first Christophe scoffed at the idea. "Portugal is ruled by a woman—Queen Maria—whose husband is little more than a consort. France would never tolerate a female ruler." He paused for a moment and then added, "I can't fathom how any man of noble blood could take on such a secondary role to a woman."

"Be that as it may," Marguerite said, "there aren't many other opportunities here at the moment. I doubt that most of the ships are owned by the queen anyhow." Given his mood of late, although she would miss his caresses, she would not be entirely reluctant to see him go.

He stared at her for a moment as he thought about her comment. Then he brightened. "You may be right," he said. "I expect most of the ship owners are honest businessmen, and good Christians who feel as I do." It was certainly better than nothing, he agreed, and, unlike France, Portugal was not involved in the war. A Portuguese ship could trade with anyone.

"It might be a good change," he concluded, and Marguerite was glad to know that he would no longer be a privateer.

WHEN CHRISTOPHE LEFT FOR LISBON in late July, Marguerite no longer had even Margot for company. The girl's daily petulance had annoyed Christophe so much that, in the absence of any prospective husbands he could marry her off to, he had finally insisted that she be enrolled at the Ursuline convent school in nearby Le Faouët. The Ursuline order was known for its teaching of girls and certainly seemed to both Christophe and Marguerite the best option available. Margot didn't resist—at least not at first.

"Anything," she grumbled, "even a convent, is better than being cooped up in these dreadful rooms." Once she had experienced a real social life while her stepfather was away, she was even less tolerant of being so confined.

Not long after Margot left for school, however, she began to bombard her mother with letters of complaint. She was unhappy in Le Faouët. Marguerite sighed as she read each note, wondering if her daughter would ever be happy anywhere. The Ursulines provided the best possible education for a girl like Margot—one that emphasized Christian living in the home, which, Lord knows, Margot needed.

"*Maman*," her daughter pleaded in her letters. "Please, let me come home or find me something else. The Mother Superior hates me and belittles me all the time. She singles me out for punishment, when all the girls are guilty of something. I hate it here; I am very unhappy."

After receiving six such letters in three weeks' time, Marguerite finally packed her valise and made a trip to the convent to talk with the Mother Superior, who assured her that she treated all the girls the same. Still, Margot claimed to be miserable, so her mother began to search for other schools for her. Perhaps one closer to Lamballe, in the area where she presumed they would eventually be living. She found an opening at another well-respected Ursuline convent school in Guingamp, near Saint-Brieuc, and she took Margot to visit it. Margot argued with her mother throughout the journey.

"Not another convent! Do you want me to be a nun?" Margot pouted.

"No, I want you to be a well-bred young lady, suited to your station in life and suitable for marriage, once we've retired to the manor house."

Margot laughed bitterly. "And when, pray tell, will that be?"

Even to Marguerite, her words sounded hollow. When indeed? But she was trying to maintain her faith in Christophe, determined to expect nothing, but still hoping for everything.

Guingamp proved to be a pleasant town on the banks of the Trieux River, which flowed through a gentle wooded valley dotted with dark, cultivated fields. Women in high white muslin caps and dark dresses sat busily knitting or making lace outside their front doors in the open spring air. The convent, on the rue de la Trinité, was airy and pleasant and had a lovely little chapel.

The Mother Superior was fairly young and greeted them with enthusiasm. Margot seemed, if not pleased, at least resigned.

"It can't be as bad as Le Faouët," she conceded.

Her mother, taking this as acquiescence, enrolled her at once, before she could change her mind.

MARGOT DID SEEM HAPPIER at Guingamp, and her letters of complaint, though they still came, were fewer and farther between. Although she still did not like being confined at a convent school, she seemed to get along well enough with the nuns and the other girls. *Perhaps*, Marguerite thought, *things will be better now.* In fact, things did seem better. Months went by now between her daughter's petulant letters. And tensions in Lorient eased after the signing of the Treaty of Paris in early March 1783, officially ending the

American Revolution. To Marguerite's amazement, the colonists had prevailed and formed a new country, independent of England.

Louis, no longer needed by the navy, returned to Lorient, arriving unexpectedly and bursting into the room where his mother was having her afternoon tea. She hardly recognized him. He sported a small moustache, and when she stood to greet him, she was shocked at how tall he had grown. He gave her a perfunctory hug, and she could smell tobacco on his clothes.

"I'm so glad you're home again. It's been lonely here."

"Where's Margot? Did she finally find a husband?" His mother laughed.

"She's still far too immature for marriage. She's in a convent school, where I hope she'll learn the skills she needs. But it will be good to have my son at home for a while."

"We'll see a lot of each other, I'm sure, *Maman*, but I've taken a room at a boarding house nearer the docks."

"But why?" she asked.

"*Maman*, I'm a man now, and I need my privacy. I need to be independent. And I'll hear more about jobs that might arise."

She looked at him in disbelief. "But the cost ..." Surely he could understand, but she had never shared her financial worries with her children.

"I have a little savings. There's not much to spend money on in the navy, and I have the income from my inheritance." He had no idea how little that income was or how many debts of Jean-Pascal she still owed. But he would not change his mind, wanting to be on his own and not under his mother's roof.

As MARGUERITE FEARED, his small savings were used up in a matter of months. She felt compelled to pay for his rented room and board, trying to stretch her small pension and the monthly allowance

Christophe had arranged for the bank to send to her to cover her expenses while he was away. She only hoped that her son would soon find work.

A LETTER FROM CHRISTOPHE arrived indicating that he had finally found a Portuguese ship named *Notre-Dame de Lampedusa* to captain. The need for captains in Lisbon had not been so great as rumors in Lorient had led them to believe, but he was finally sailing to Calcutta to buy Indian silks and other fineries Portuguese merchants desired. He was planning to stop in Mauritius on his way to persuade his brother Ange once again to be his second in command. *At least,* Marguerite thought, *the waters will be safer now that the war has ended.*

He'd promised in his letter that this trip would be his last, but she had heard it all before. *Best to expect nothing. That way I won't be disappointed again,* she thought. Who knew how long her imagined flower garden, the manor house they had dreamed of, and a steady life with her husband must wait? For now she had other things to worry about.

At least it was spring, and she was able to fling open her casement windows on sunny afternoons to catch the breeze and the fragrance of the flower market in the street below. She had become accustomed to being alone and was almost beginning to enjoy the freedom to do whatever she wanted whenever she wanted. Nanon was always there when needed, of course, but made a point never to be underfoot.

Finally, one morning in mid-May three letters arrived for Marguerite, all coming on the same vessel, one from her sister and two from Christophe, written only days apart. She kissed the seals on each one and nestled in her chair by the window, prepared to enjoy the cup of steaming tea Nanon placed at her elbow and her veritable feast of letters. In high anticipation, she opened the one from her sister first.

March 26, 1784

My dear sister,

It is with heavy heart that I write these words. Would that I were there to put my arms around you and absorb some of your grief, though I bear much of my own. There is no way to tell you without breaking your heart, so I will tell you straight out. Marie Clarice is now with God. As you know, she was like a daughter to me and my husband. We loved her as if she had been our own child, and we would have given anything to save her.

She took ill more than a week ago, and we called in every good doctor in Port Louis, but there was nothing they could do. She was always a frail child, and at thirteen she seemed to grow even thinner and frailer. When she was struck by malarial fever, it took all her energy and finally her life. But yesterday she died peacefully in my arms, with all of us around her, loving her and praying for her. I know she is now in Heaven with the angels, where her sweet spirit watches over us all.

We miss you so much, my dear sister, and long for your return to Port Louis one of these days. I trust we will meet again sometime in this life. If not, we will surely meet in Heaven, where we will all join Marie Clarice one day.

Your loving sister,
Marie

The ink was smeared here and there as though a teardrop had fallen on the page. *Marie Françoise must have been crying when she wrote these awful words,* Marguerite thought, trying to imagine her sister's face. Then she realized the tears were hers.

She stared at the letter in stunned disbelief. *How could this happen? Did I make a mistake? Would God have let her live if I'd kept her by my side?*

Was this a mother's punishment for leaving her daughter behind, however well-intentioned her reasons might have been? She had written to the child every week, but the replies had come not from Marie Clarice, but from Marguerite's sister or mother. Only rarely would her daughter scrawl a personal note at the end of a letter. The thought that Marie Clarice died without her mother's loving arms around her was like a knife in Marguerite's heart. She could almost feel the warmth of the little girl nestled in her arms as she snuggled against her mother's breast. Marguerite sat for a while, staring at the wall, unable to catch her breath, before reaching for the next letter. It too had come from Port Louis. Perhaps Christophe was telling her it was all a mistake. It had to be.

Her hands were shaking as she unfolded the oiled cloth in which it was wrapped. It had been written only a few days after the letter from Marie Françoise.

March 29, 1784

Ma très chère Marguerite,

I arrived day before yesterday in Port Louis and learned the dreadful news of Marie Clarice's death just four days ago. I hate to be the bearer of bad news and I know it will grieve you. They think it was malaria that caused it. But apparently there was nothing anyone could do to save her. She was buried on Saturday, the day before I docked. I wish I could have been there. I am so very sorry, my dearest, and I hold you in my arms.

As for me, I am finding things much changed in Port Louis. Now that the war is over, there is a great deal of buying and selling here on Mauritius, and Ange thinks there is much profit to be made in selling our goods and perhaps remaining here to trade a bit more. I am thinking it over and may stay here for a while, though the ship must be on its way. There is a Captain Razot here who is interested in taking over the captaincy. To abandon my duty in such a manner would surely go against my record, but since I plan to retire when I return to Lorient anyhow, I would likely be better off following Ange's lead to greater wealth than merely to sail the ship back to Lorient. I haven't decided yet, but I will write to you as soon as I do.

With my love,
Christophe

The letter left Marguerite with disbelief that he could even think of profit after such devastating news. She stared at Christophe's second letter as though it were a dead thing in her lap. Then, automatically, with unfeeling fingers, she ripped away the seal and unfolded it. It had been written two days after the first one and merely confirmed his decision to remain for a time in Port Louis. It told her he would be coming home to stay as soon as possible.

At the moment she felt only numb at the prospect of his return. It seemed inconsequential alongside the news that her daughter was dead. Her little flaxen-haired girl, her sweet Marie Clarice, the child she had held in her arms at night when she said her prayers, was gone from the earth. She no longer existed. She was dead, *morte*—such finality to the word. She would give up all of Christophe's profits to hold the child once more. Marguerite's silent tears gave way to heaving sobs, and she wept inconsolably—for how long, she had no idea. By the time she was too exhausted to weep any more, she was oblivious to the sunset that reddened the sky and announced the coming night.

NANON, YOUNG AS SHE WAS, had never witnessed such profound anguish in her life. She could not persuade her mistress to get up in the mornings or eat any of the meals she brought to her. Now Marguerite had locked herself in her room and would not answer the door. Nanon went to find Louis, not knowing what else to do, but he seemed never to be at his hotel. After Marguerite remained locked in her bedchamber without eating for three days, Nanon was fearful she would die. Finally she sought the help of the concierge, Madame Aubain, who had keys to all the rooms. Concierges, by and large, had a fearsome reputation, and calling on her was a last resort. But the older woman climbed the steps with Nanon without complaining about the trouble she was being put to.

When they unlocked the bedroom door and the concierge saw her tenant's ravaged face, etched with grief and the shadow of death, her eyes widened in shock. She stared about the room. The smell made her recoil, for the chamber pot had not been emptied for days, and Marguerite had clearly not changed her clothes in all that time. It was clear something had to be done.

"You did right to call me," Madame Aubain assured a nervous Nanon.

The concierge, accustomed to taking charge, brought a basin of water and washed Marguerite's face with a damp cloth. Together Madame Aubain and Nanon made her stand, and, one on each side supporting her weakness, they stripped off her filthy garments, sponged her body, and helped her into a clean warm robe. Then they led her to a chair beside the fireplace.

"Sit down here" Madame Aubain ordered. "You stay with her, Nanon. I'll be right back."

The concierge returned a short time later, with a bowl of fish-and-leek soup, half a baguette, and a glass of stout red wine.

"Eat this," she insisted. "It will give you strength."

Marguerite obeyed, for she no longer had a will of her own. Madame Aubain sat with her, at times even holding her hand, until she could get Marguerite at least to acknowledge her presence and speak. Although Marguerite had not eaten for days, she had no recollection of being hungry. Madame Aubain, whom Marguerite had never thought to be a friendly person, visited her every day, sometimes twice, until the concierge thought her tenant was on her feet again and able, with the aid of Nanon, to take care of herself. Then she disappeared once more.

Gradually, Marguerite forced herself back into a daily routine. But grief was a persistent beast, always lurking in dark corners and ready to pounce when she least expected it.

Chapter 5

1784

Lorient, France

FOR A LONG TIME THERE WAS ONLY DARKNESS. Then, little by little, Marguerite began to notice the daylight again. One day she opened a window to let in the bright rays of late summer sunshine. Eventually she walked outside among the falling leaves of autumn and noticed the red and gold fluttering around her. By the end of November she was making her way to the *boulangerie* to buy croissants for her breakfast. Then one afternoon, feeling the crisp air as she left the bakery, on a whim she ducked into the warm, sweet-smelling pastry shop next door for a cup of tea and an éclair. The familiar taste of the tender pastry, with its cream filling and thin chocolate coating flooded her with an almost forgotten sense of joy. It was more than she deserved, she knew, but she ate it slowly, savoring every bite. The process of coping with her grief had been and still was a slow one, but at that moment she realized that, although she would always carry

Marie Clarice in her heart, she could somehow manage to survive and face life again.

In January 1785, Christophe returned to Lorient. He sent word from the dock that he would arrive at the apartment as soon as he made arrangements to store the goods he had brought home. Marguerite read the note with a flutter of excitement and anxiety. Then she hurried to her dressing table to brush her hair and hide her pallor with a touch of rouge, preparing to welcome him home without letting him see the sorrow-ravaged face she had worn for so long. When she was ready, she waited by the window for his approach for what seemed like forever. Then she saw him coming, a sea bag tossed over his shoulder. Rushing to the door, she held her breath in anticipation, preparing to greet him with a smile and what she hoped was an enthusiastic kiss, for she was truly grateful to see him, grateful that he would hold her in his arms once again.

"Welcome home," she said, opening the door wide when she heard his footsteps on the stairs. He looked older, as though he had seen much, done much, and learned from it all. But his blue eyes were as intense as ever.

"Home to keep my promise," he said. "Home for good this time, *chérie*." He dropped his sea bag and reached out to gather her in his arms. "I have finally saved enough to retire and buy our estate," he whispered into her ear before he gave her a hearty kiss. He did not mention Marie Clarice's death. In a way, it was a relief, for Marguerite was not sure she could have kept from weeping. His arms holding her close were consolation enough.

Over the next several hours, he revealed with enthusiasm the tidy profit he had earned from his trading in Mauritius, as he always called the Isle de France. Along with his savings and the booty from his privateering days, he assured Marguerite, they finally had sufficient resources to feel confident about their future. He was eager to begin looking for their new property—a real manor house near Lamballe, not far from the northern coast of Brittany.

"We will finally be landed aristocrats," he announced. The destiny they had long planned was about to begin. Spurred by his excitement, he would have left for Lamballe at once, had Marguerite not begged him to wait at least a week or two.

"It will give you time to get your land legs and a little rest before we set out in a cold *diligence* in the middle of winter," she whispered, evoking a chilly stagecoach, by contrast to their mutual warmth as she snuggled in his arms before the blazing fire. They needed the time to become reacquainted. She'd given Nanon three days off in order to be completely alone for the first time with her husband. Even on their wedding night, they were both keenly aware that her children, Margot and Louis, slept in adjacent rooms. The once-cramped apartment now seemed cozy and almost cheery with just the two of them.

Marguerite had not realized how much she'd needed him. Although she tried not to burden him with the grief she still felt, having his comforting arms around her helped fill the terrible void and brought them closer together. Any earlier tensions between them melted away with their new privacy and their first real kiss since his return. She needed to live again, and it was good to have something positive to think about.

"Please," she begged. "Let's stay here for at least a week before we go to Lamballe." She was reluctant to give up this new intimacy.

He acquiesced almost at once to her request, as he held her close. He'd almost forgotten the sweet smell of her body and the softness of her breasts during his long days at sea with only rough sailors for company. One night at home was enough to remind him of all he had missed. Now, able once more to indulge himself in her embraces, he welcomed the long nights and the sensual mornings they spent together. He would have welcomed an even longer delay, had she not promised to accompany him to Lamballe.

MARGUERITE'S CHEEKS WERE ROSY from the cold as they set out in the coach, even though she and Christophe were dressed warmly and wrapped together from the waist down in a blanket. It was a difficult three-day trip over rough roads to cover the seventy-five miles to Lamballe. The first day was the hardest, as the stagecoach pushed on almost to Pontivy before it stopped for the night at a small inn. The second night, about ten miles north of Loudéac, they stopped once more at a country inn for a welcome hot supper and separate, uncomfortable beds shared, as was the custom, with other passengers of the same sex. Stagecoach passengers, regardless of rank, were compelled to observe the same practice as everyone else. Otherwise they had to travel in private coaches. It was a relief finally to reach Lamballe and an inn with a proper room for the two of them.

While Marguerite rested, reading a book she had brought with her, and enjoying the comfort of the inn's four-poster bed, Christophe began the very morning after their arrival to scour the countryside for properties that might be bought near his childhood home, which seemed especially important to him, for he wanted to restore his family's former prestige in the area. He was accompanied by René Peltier, his *notaire*, a lawyer who specialized in contracts and real estate transactions. Christophe would make no move without him and trusted him completely. Peltier was not only Christophe's legal representative, he was also his friend. The two had known one another since childhood.

In the afternoon, while the men continued to look at properties, Marguerite strolled the town's narrow streets, shaded by tall houses and shops made of stone, some half-timbered in the Norman style. It was a lively town, with more than three thousand residents and still growing. She liked it at once. It was so different from the seacoast town of Lorient, where everything centered on the shipping trade. She could imagine Lamballe in the spring bursting with flowers and in late summer and fall with its wide outdoor market abundant with fresh fruits and vegetables. The only waterway in the area was the narrow Canal du Gouessant, built only a few years earlier in an effort to contain the small river that threatened to overflow its banks each spring. *Yes,* she thought, *this would be a delightful place to live.* When they bought their new property, she decided, she would bring Margot home from the convent. The girl was almost nineteen now, the oldest student still in the school. Her mother only hoped she had matured under the nuns' strict influence. She felt sure it would be easier for them to live all together in a large house rather than in a cramped apartment.

When Christophe returned that first night to the inn in Lamballe, he looked tired and a bit discouraged.

"There isn't much for sale at the moment," he told her, as she rubbed his shoulders to help him relax. "But Peltier tells me that there will be more properties in the spring and urges me to wait. He says he'll keep his eyes open for us." Peltier had represented the Poulain du Bignon family in such legal matters for almost two decades now and had overseen the welfare of Christophe's sisters during their brother's long absences. Although neither Angélique nor Jeanne lived in Lamballe, Peltier kept in touch and oversaw their affairs by post. He had never let the family down. But Christophe was impatient and disappointed to have to return to Lorient and wait. Unlike his wife, waiting was not something to which he was accustomed or able to do with patience or grace.

WITHIN A FEW MONTHS after their return to Lorient, Marguerite began to notice the swelling of her breasts and her late-morning queasiness. She had experienced it all before and was certain she must be pregnant.

"A baby! *Enfin un fils*, finally a son," Christophe's face lit up like a torch when she told him. "*Grâce à Dieu*, Thanks be to God," he said, making the sign of the cross. He was already forty-five years old, and she was in her mid-thirties. If they were going to make a family together, it was high time.

"There is no guarantee it will be a boy," Marguerite reminded him. They had been married more than five years already, but she was glad she had not given birth during his long absences. A baby would have kept her occupied, she supposed, but it would have been harder in the rented rooms in Lorient.

"*Bien sûr*, certainly, it will be a boy." He was more eager than ever to find their new home. They must have spacious quarters and a safe place for his son to play.

IN LATE JUNE CHRISTOPHE received a letter from Peltier listing several properties now available, properties he deemed suitable for a man like Christophe—with noble blood and sufficient funds. This time, Christophe decided to rent two rooms at an inn in Lamballe, one to be used as a bedroom and another as a sitting room, where they would remain until they bought their new home. Marguerite was almost six months along in her pregnancy now and did not need to be bouncing around in a stagecoach back and forth between towns separated by a three-day journey. He did not want her to risk losing the child.

It didn't take him long in his eagerness to find just what he was looking for. On their fourth evening there, just after dark, he burst into their sitting room, a smile beaming on his face.

"I've found it, Marguerite. The perfect manor house." He hugged her as though she were made of porcelain and as gently as his enthusiasm would permit. "I think you'll love it." It was exactly what he'd had in mind, he told her, all that he'd promised her when they married. The lamplight flickered, as he described the manor—a fine house of noble character and in good condition. His eyes gleamed with satisfaction.

"Have you bought it already?" she asked. "Tell me about it."

"It's called La Grande Ville Hervé. They call it *grande* only to distinguish it from a nearby property called La Petite Ville Hervé. But it *is* quite large. It's a well-established domain with almost twelve hundred acres near Planguenoual, just north of Lamballe, and it's in an area with many grand estates. We'll have fine neighbors, I'm sure. I haven't bought it yet, but I've made an offer of just over 31,000 *livres* that Peltier thinks will suffice." His words came pouring out with hardly a breath in his excitement.

Christophe was especially eager to close the sale before their child was born. He wanted his son (and he was unshakeable in his certainty it would be a boy) to be born in the new manor house, as a young nobleman should. When all negotiations were complete and his offer accepted, all that remained were the signing of papers and the transfer of money, which he and Peltier took care of on August 10. La Grande Ville Hervé was theirs.

WHEN CHRISTOPHE TOOK MARGUERITE to see the house for the first time, she could tell he was almost bursting with pride. He had rented a carriage, which he drove himself for the occasion.

He wore a broad smile as they drove down the long *allée* overhung with beech trees, past a small, shady pond. Suddenly they were in an open area, at the end of which stood the distinguished two-story manor house. The shutters had been flung open to let in the light.

"Well, *ma chérie*, here it is," he said, triumph in his voice. It was everything he'd promised and what he'd worked so hard for—to return to Brittany, have his own estate, establish his lineage, and live like a true aristocrat for the rest of his life. It was the manor house they had dreamed of.

"It's perfect," she said, both hands on her cheeks to contain her smile. "Just perfect." She loved it at once, this splendid property, the house and gardens surrounded by woods with fields beyond them. There was plenty of acreage, he told her, to farm or hunt. She could already envisage their child sailing miniature boats in the little pond, where a paddling of ducks now waddled around the edge, some floating idly on the water. A profusion of pink roses climbed a trellis by the carriage house. Servants' quarters built of stone stood not far from the house, which looked to Marguerite like a small *château*.

"It's not far from the sea," Christophe said, referring, she knew, to the *Mor Breizh*, as the Bretons called the channel that separated Brittany from England. "I don't intend to go back, of course, but if we ever need anything, there's a small port called Dahouët nearby. It's mostly a fishing village with only a modest shipping trade, but it has a nice little dock." She smiled, understanding that it would be there when moments of nostalgia drew him to the sea.

Christophe helped her gently down from the carriage and led her to the house. They wandered hand-in-hand through the splendid rooms, which, after weeks at the inn, seemed cavernous with their ample proportions and high ceilings. It was all she had ever wanted. Until now her whole life seemed to be one of waiting for just this moment, when she and her family would come into their own. She was eager to begin, to move in and select furnishings, proper draperies, and add those touches here and there that would transform the large, empty house into a real home for her family.

As they explored the upstairs bedrooms, Marguerite turned to her husband and put her arms around him. "My dearest, I must say it once more. It's just perfect." He kissed her with deep longing. They had not made love for more than a month, now that her pregnancy was so far advanced, but she sensed his hunger, which matched her own. The next time they did, she knew, it would be in this house, perhaps in this very room.

WITH CHRISTOPHE'S PERMISSION SHE SENT for Margot, who was delighted to be out of the convent school. The three of them spent the last six weeks of Marguerite's pregnancy making decisions about carpets, the placement of furniture, and the hanging of paintings. Given her condition, she did not go out, and Christophe did all the buying. Whenever possible, he had merchants bring items home for her approval. In the end, however, most of the furniture and fixture decisions were his. But from dawn to dusk the house seemed abuzz with people coming and going, decorators laying out fabrics and paint samples, paper hangers, carpenters repairing staircase spindles or hanging shelves, artists' representative showing their paintings, and wagon drivers delivering furniture.

Christophe selected armchairs of gilded beechwood, covered with a wool and silk tapestry fabric from Beauvais and a rose-colored velvet sofa with cabriole legs for the *salon*. On the mantle stood a gilded bronze and enamel clock with matching candlesticks. Damask draperies, selected by Marguerite to match the bisque color of the walls, hung at the windows. The dining room, lined with gilt mirrors and wall sconces, was furnished with equal elegance—a magnificent sideboard with a marble top, a polished mahogany table that could seat twelve guests, and gilded oval-back chairs covered in blue brocade.

Through the years Christophe had brought back from his buying trips in exotic ports splendid carpets made in Persia and India. Now he rescued them from the warehouses in Lorient where they were stored, and Marguerite parceled them out to various rooms. She could tell that her daughter was impressed with the fine and fancy furnishings in the public rooms. The one thing Christophe and Margot seemed to agree on was their taste in elegant furniture. And, in the excitement of furnishing the spacious new house and preparing for their new life in the country, the two seemed to get along quite well.

Unlike them, Marguerite preferred a simpler look, without all the gilt and elaborate carving so popular in Paris. But only in the bedrooms was she permitted to indulge her own "provincial tastes," as her husband jokingly called them. The house had six sleeping rooms, but for the moment, to cut costs, they furnished only three—with beds and armoires made of natural walnut and other native woods. For bed covers she chose toile and ticking and pillows ornamented with her own and Margot's embroidery work. She thought they looked homey, warm, and welcoming. Christophe did not complain, for these were far less expensive than the items in the *salon* and the *salle à manger,* where they expected to entertain the fine, new friends they would make. Only Margot pouted a bit that her mother did not allow her to furnish her room with the pomp and elegance she wanted, but it would have to do.

In addition to Mustafa and Nanon, Christophe and Marguerite also hired a new cook, Bernadette, and a gardener, Pierre, whose job was to tend the grounds and plant Marguerite's rose garden in front of the manor house before the warm season ended. Christophe required reliable farm workers as well, but Marguerite was not involved in their hiring.

As she surveyed the finished rooms of the house and looked over the newly planted rose garden, she thought, *this would have been the moment when I would send for Marie Clarice and Maman.* She tried with all her might to brush aside her feeling of loss and focus instead on what she had and on the baby she was expecting. Her husband and older daughter were here with her, to live out their lives in this magnificent manor house and just in time, for within a matter of weeks after they had fully settled in, she knew she was in labor.

ON THE CRISP MORNING OF OCTOBER 26, barely nine months after his father's return to France, Joseph Marie Poulain du Bignon, the boy Christophe had predicted, was born. His father had paced outside in the hallway much of the night, knocking several times on the door for reports. Finally Margot, who had been trying to comfort her mother, slipped out of the room to make him coffee and sit with him in the hall to keep him calm. Once the baby came, however, the midwife hardly had time to clean up the afterbirth and change the linen before an impatient Christophe burst into the room, a broad smile on his face.

"Let me see him! Where's my son?"

Marguerite, exhausted, her hair still wet with perspiration from her efforts, managed to smile and pull back the blanket to display the baby, sleeping peacefully in the crook of her arm. Her husband sat down on the edge of the bed to get a closer look.

"He's a handsome lad, isn't he, Marguerite? Do you think he looks like me?" He didn't wait for an answer before he reached out to take the baby in his arms. Mesmerized by the child, he grinned with pride as little Joseph, startled awake, grasped his father's index finger. "Such a strong lad," he boasted. He held the baby in his arms, rocking him gently and gazing into the dark blue eyes, so like his own, until they closed once more with contentment.

"Shhhh ... he's sleeping," Christophe whispered proudly to his wife as he laid the infant in the cradle beside her bed.

THE DAY AFTER LITTLE JOSEPH WAS BORN, Christophe drove his carriage around the countryside announcing the birth of his "son and heir." He would have taken the baby with him, had Marguerite permitted, but she told him firmly that the child was too young to leave the house. Wherever Christophe stopped at their homes, the residents would smile indulgently and offer their congratulations, agreeing that the newborn must indeed be a "fine baby boy."

A few weeks later, as soon as Marguerite pronounced their son old enough, his father insisted on taking him and his mother for brief visits to nearby domains so that whoever lived there could have a first-hand look at his "son and heir," as he repeatedly described him. Marguerite had never seen her husband so exuberant, not even the day they bought the manor house. It was a joyous time for the entire household. Even Margot smiled these days far more than she frowned.

One afternoon as the baby napped, Marguerite and Christophe strolled together beside the little pond, its waters darkened by the overhanging trees. It was a lovely fall afternoon, leaves drifting down around them like golden feathers.

"People say money can't buy happiness," Christophe said as they walked. He held Marguerite's hand tucked firmly into the crook of his arm. "Perhaps not, but it certainly takes away life's anxieties, doesn't it?"

The hem of Marguerite's dress rustled along the ground through the dry leaves as she pondered his statement. She looked around her at their fine house, feeling the security of her husband's presence, and enjoying their stately walk, wondering whether even Marie Antoinette felt such contentment while strolling with the king in the gardens at Versailles.

"I can't disagree with you," she said. "But we have to remember that it's not the only thing that matters. Love is important too."

"Then we are indeed lucky, for we have both." He pulled her toward him and leaned down to kiss her. Although their wealth was relatively modest by comparison to many of their friends in the region, it was sufficient, they were sure, for everything they could possibly ever want or need.

MARGUERITE AND CHRISTOPHE were shocked to learn, before they could catch their breath and as they were still adjusting to their new son and their new home, that she was pregnant again. She told her husband as he was enjoying an after-dinner brandy in the *salon*.

"Are you sure?" he asked in disbelief.

"Quite sure," she told him.

"Well then," he laughed. "God told us to multiply and bear fruit, didn't he? We're simply obeying his command." He lifted his brandy in salute and drained the snifter with a hearty gulp.

IT WAS A HOT AUGUST 2, 1786, not yet ten months after Joseph's birth, when their second son, Henri Charles, came into the world with a lusty cry, causing almost as much excitement on his father's part as Joseph's arrival had done. This birth had been harder for Marguerite, and it took longer for her to get back on her feet, but even so, she enjoyed Christophe's pride in his two sons.

"A fine new estate and two sons in just one year. We are indeed blessed, Marguerite," Christophe would say, beaming. He saw their fecundity as a symbol of prosperity and contentment. God was smiling on their union.

As AUTUMN CAME AGAIN, they sat on the verandah on sunny afternoons with their two babies, enjoying the sweet clear air and watching Joseph learn to walk. Margot frequently joined them. Two-month-old Henri, sitting in Margot's lap, watched his brother's every move and would chortle with glee when Joseph sat suddenly on his rump and began to cry. Margot laughed at both the babies and dangled her necklace for Henri to play with, while Marguerite scooped up her older son, gave him her hand, and encouraged him to try again. Christophe merely sat back in his chair, enjoying the little domestic scene and congratulating himself on his good fortune.

Whenever the babies needed to be fed or changed, Marguerite tinkled a little silver bell to call for Nanon, who took over the role of nursemaid whenever Marguerite and Christophe wanted simply to relax and enjoy themselves. Margot played with the babies whenever it suited her ever-changing moods. But to Marguerite her little boys were the joy of her life, as all her babies had been.

On other afternoons the entire family would take carriage rides through the rolling hills that surrounded the property. Even the little ones sat up and paid attention as the abundant landscape rolled by.

"*Tu vois le dada?* You see the horsie?" Marguerite would point Joseph's attention to the animal munching grass in a pasture.

Joseph would clap his hands and repeat, "*Dada.*" Little Henri too looked where she pointed, drooling in bewilderment at all the new animals and trees his mother named, until finally the rocking of the carriage lulled him to sleep.

THE CHILDREN WERE NOT THEIR ONLY happy preoccupation. The du Bignons were occasionally invited to dinners at nearby manor houses. Christophe's unorthodox announcement of Joseph's birth had made him known to almost everyone in the area, and they often encountered their neighbors at Sunday mass in a nearby parish church. Margot was most often included in the invitation as well. The fact that Christophe's family had once been prominent in the area made those from nearby domains receptive to establishing a friendship.

Finally, when another summer came, Marguerite and Christophe decided it was time for them to hold a dinner party on their own estate. They chose to invite two families they particularly liked for this first social occasion in their new home. The families were distantly related to each other by some obscure marriage a century ago and seemed to get along well enough. Monsieur and Madame des Vauhéas had a married son and daughter-in-law who were also invited.

The other family consisted of Monsieur and Madame de Quélen, as well as Monsieur de Quélen's widowed mother, a rather stiff old lady who lived with them, accompanied them everywhere, and made certain that everyone knew that the well-known archbishop of Paris was their kinsman. Otherwise, the family was congenial and easy-going. The younger Madame de Quélen was an attractive woman about the same age as Marguerite, and the two got along well. The family also had a daughter, Jacquette, only a few years younger than Margot. To fill the twelfth place at the table, the du Bignons decided to invite the affable, middle-aged parish priest.

The role of hostess in a grand house was new to Marguerite, but since she and Christophe did not expect to entertain too often, they wanted to make this first time very special. She was already nervous about the affair, wanting to get everything just right, when she sat down with Bernadette in the cluttered kitchen to plan what she hoped would be a splendid meal.

"Do you have any suggestions, Bernadette?" she asked the portly, round-faced cook, who had once worked for a wealthy family in Saint-Brieuc.

"My specialties are *sole meunière, coquilles Saint Jacques*, and *blanquettes de veau*," the cook offered proudly.

"*Coquilles Saint Jacques* seems like a lovely choice for a fish dish," Marguerite said, grateful for the suggestions. "What about the *blanquettes de veau* as a main dish?" As one who had grown up eating such simple fare as *potage, ragoût,* and *pot-au-feu*, she felt almost overwhelmed by the elegant choices and even a bit pretentious at making such suggestions. But she knew that these were the kinds of dishes everyone would expect, and, in Bernadette's hands, she was sure they would be delicious.

"Excellent selections, *Madame*," Bernadette assured her. "I can plan the side dishes to go with them."

"*Très bien.* And what about a dessert?"

"I think regional dishes like *far Breton* or *clafoutis aux cérises* would be delicious. They are simple desserts, but always well received. Or for something a bit fancier, perhaps a *cotillon chocolat*?"

"Why don't you prepare them all for the family in the next few days. We'll try them out and then decide."

Bernadette nodded. "I'll make the *clafoutis aux cérises* for tomorrow evening. The cherries are especially good this season."

Marguerite had no doubt that the food would be excellent. They had been very fortunate in finding such a good cook. She was less certain, however, about the table service.

Because their evening meals tended to be informal, Christophe had elected not to hire footmen as some wealthier households had done, but clearly footmen would be needed for this occasion. As a solution, he decided to train Mustafa and the gardener Pierre to do double duty and serve the various dishes. For several days before the social event, the two were assigned to practice at family dinners. Mustafa took to his new role with alacrity, but Pierre could never fully acquire the skill of serving with the dignity that Marguerite hoped for. To her dismay, he would frequently spill a drop of soup or sauce on the tablecloth or carpet. Fortunately, both men wore gloves when they served, for Pierre could never seem to get all of the garden soil from under his fingernails. By the night of the dinner party, his mistress could only hope they were ready.

Marguerite examined the dining room to make certain everything was in place. The centerpiece of roses from her garden that graced the table was stunning and fragrant, composed as it was of pink Damask roses, white Albas, deep red Gallicas, and Tuscany velvets. The entire table was inviting, set with shining silverware, sparkling crystal, and the china Christophe had ordered from Limoges, all of which reflected the flickering light from the four-armed silver candelabras placed at each end. By the time the *vichyssoise*, Bernadette's choice of soup, and *coquilles Saint Jacques* had been served, most of their guests were mellowed with the fine wines selected by Christophe and were in good spirits. The conversation was flowing well, and, fortunately, the formalities so essential in Paris were hardly observed here in the countryside. Guests simply relaxed and enjoyed themselves. Thus, when Marguerite noticed in horror that Pierre had managed, despite her warnings, to spill a drop of sauce from the *blanquettes de veau* on the coat of Monsieur des Vauhéas, the guest merely brushed it off with his napkin as though it were nothing and kept on talking to Christophe.

"Can you imagine the king wanting to tax the lands of noblemen? How absurd! It's never been done," he was saying loudly.

"And that controller-general, the one the king dismissed ... what was his name? ... Monsieur de Calonne, I believe ... even wanted to sell Church property," the priest added, scooping a morsel of veal into his mouth..

"Equally absurd. The royal family should learn to live on the taxes the common people already pay," Christophe responded. "It's all these wars, especially the one in America, that have gotten him into such a mess."

"More like the high living at Versailles," Monseiur de Quélen suggested, tugging at his full, brown mustache. "That Austrian woman the king married is part of the problem, I hear. Her fancy balls and insatiable appetite for jewelry have contributed their share. At least that's the rumor."

The gentleman's mother drew herself up and, with a haughty lift of her chin, fixed her sharp, gray eyes on her son, and held up her hand to silence him. "One should not talk about the king and queen in such a way. They are our monarchs, you know." He glanced at her and nodded, taking a swallow of wine.

Monsieur des Vauhéas, however, frowned and ignored her comment. "Can you believe the king resurrected that old Assembly of Notables? No one has heard of it for well over a century. Most people didn't even know it existed."

"Well, at least they held their own and refused to submit to the king's demands," Christophe offered.

"But then the king dissolved them. They never had any real authority. But I suspect it's not over yet," Monseiur de Quélen chimed in again, glancing at his mother, but careful not to say anything disrespectful about the king.

The other ladies ignored all the political talk, instead expressing their enthusiasm for Marguerite's roses, Bernadette's delicious dishes, and the fine way in which the du Bignons had furnished their public rooms. Marguerite basked in their admiration, enjoying herself immensely, and aware of the warm ambiance created by the sweet fragrance of the roses and the candlelight. She knew that the evening was a huge success and was almost certain that they had made fine friends for the future.

FOLLOWING THAT EVENING, JACQUETTE DE QUÉLEN and Margot became fast friends, and Jacquette often invited Margot for visits and excursions to Saint-Malo or Saint-Brieuc with her and her family. It was a joy for Marguerite to see her daughter smiling now so much of the time. On occasion she and Margot would also take little mother-daughter outings, leaving the children behind with Nanon and asking Mustafa, who also sometimes doubled as carriage driver, to take them in the carriage to nearby Planguenoual or Morieux for afternoon tea.

CHRISTOPHE SPENT HIS TIME INSTEAD ENJOYING the life of a landowner, riding across his wide expanse of fields and about the countryside, always on the lookout for a new piece of property to buy or a new income-producing crop to plant. At the same time, he kept a keen eye open for other opportunities as well. As he explained it to his wife, while he had faith in the long-term value of his land purchases, he also believed in the platitude *de ne pas mettre tous les oeufs dans le même panier,* of not putting all one's eggs in the same basket. He was also well aware, as one who had engaged in the shipping trade throughout his working life, that money could be made more quickly by taking greater risks and investing in more commercial activities. He kept himself busy scouting out new types of investments, including a china factory in Nantes, for which he lent money at a good rate of interest. He even decided to back a slaving expedition. But he was a cautious man at heart, seeking to put his money only where he was reasonably sure it would pay off.

Despite his caution and careful planning, however, he would soon learn that some things were beyond his control.

Chapter 6

Autumn, 1787

La Ville Hervé

MARGOT, FREED FROM THE RESTRICTIONS of the convent, continued to be delighted with her new life. She thrived on the excursions with Jacquette and her parents. Whenever she returned, she was overflowing with enthusiastic tales of her trips and the social events they attended, occasionally showing her mother some trifle she had purchased and charged to the family's account—a new pair of gloves, a lace fan, a pair of satin garters. Marguerite was pleased to see her daughter in such a happy frame of mind.

Then the bills began to arrive. Marguerite paid them at first without comment, but their numbers were increasing. Soon there were so many that she could no longer cover them from her daughter's inheritance or her own small pension. She made it a point of pride not to burden Christophe with her children's frivolities, though he took care of all necessities. She had still not managed to pay off all of her son Louis's bills from his time in Lorient. Thank God, her son was finally working again on a merchant ship and had ceased to drain the family coffers, but she'd been appalled at the considerable sums he had spent while he was out of work.

Little by little she realized the debts were overwhelming her. Many remained unpaid, and the interest mounted. She'd never be able to pay them off. *I should have reprimanded her sooner,* she thought as she finally approached Margot's room, intending to speak harshly with her about the situation.

As she entered, Margot was sitting at her dressing table brushing her hair and gazing at her reflection in the mirror. She turned around to look at her mother, but she did not rise.

"Margot," her mother said in a tense voice, "we must talk about all these things you've been charging to our account. We can't afford so much extravagance, so many unnecessary expenses. The bills keep growing." Margot's face showed little remorse.

"They're things I needed," she said, turning back to her mirror and smoothing her eyebrow with her fingertips. Marguerite studied her daughter's carefully composed face—the feigned innocence of her blue eyes, her pouting lips—looking for sincerity. She wasn't sure she found any.

"They have to stop," Marguerite said firmly. "Any future expenses must have my permission. Is that understood?" Margot sighed loudly, moved her head slightly in what Marguerite took for agreement, but said nothing as her mother left the room, closing the door firmly behind her.

The growing indebtedness was a constant anxiety that, for a time, Marguerite fretted about only in silence, using any ploy and making every effort to stave off the creditors without worrying Christophe. But it was becoming increasingly difficult. She settled all the debts she possibly could without her husband's knowledge. On several occasions creditors from Saint-Brieuc and Saint-Malo were audacious enough to show up on the doorstep of the manor house, insisting on being paid. So far they had only come when Christophe was away, but she knew she couldn't count on that forever.

Christophe was well aware that his wife paid her children's bills.

"You indulge them without any restraint," he said. "You should set limits on them." He had reproved her more than once, but always in a loving manner. He didn't really worry, assuming she took care of their expenses with her limited income, particularly since he was paying all the other bills. He knew that Marguerite's first husband had left debts, and shortly after their marriage, he'd paid some of them off. But at the time, Marguerite assured him she could handle the rest—and she could have, but for the continued spending by her children.

She didn't want to upset Christophe, but the day came, all too soon, when she could no longer bear the burden alone. She felt she had no choice but to ask for his help. Thus, with a quiet prayer, one afternoon she arranged the stack of bills neatly on her husband's desk, where he could not help but find them. She would never forget the reaction when Christophe came home late that afternoon after inspecting his fields. When he saw the pile of her daughter's accumulated bills lying on his desk, he blanched.

"What are these?" he asked, clutching the merchants' duns in his fist as though crushing them would make them disappear. His hand was shaking with fury as he held them out to his wife. "What are these?" he repeated.

Marguerite bit her lower lip. "I'm sorry to say they're exactly what they look like, Christophe," she replied as steadily as she could. "I've spoken with her. She won't do it again. They accumulated before I realized …." She could see in his rigid face that he was unsympathetic. "I thought I'd taught her better. I thought her education at the convent would help."

His eyes were dark and steely. "I can't have this, Marguerite. I'm not made of money. Look at these frivolous charges … corset lace? satin garters? Seventeen yards of black silk? *Seventeen yards?* Why in God's name does she need so much black silk? Is she going into mourning?" Most of them were small things, but there were many of them. Far too many. He could afford to pay them, certainly, but she knew it was not what he intended to spend his money for.

"I know," she said quietly, wringing her hands. "It won't happen again." At least she hoped not.

Christophe fumed and cursed off and on throughout the afternoon, but to keep the interest from mounting further and to his wife's relief, he agreed to pay the bills. By evening his tone had softened, and he even told her that he would settle the rest of Jean-Pascal's debts, which she now confessed as well, just to get them off her mind. But it was obvious, when he began to talk about finding a suitable husband for Margot, that he was beginning to wonder whether his stepdaughter would remain a spinster and be a burden on him forever.

FINALLY, IN THE EARLY SUMMER OF 1789, the young woman received an offer of marriage from a Saint-Malo nobleman by the name of François Olivier LeCourt de Billot, whom she had met at one of the *soirées* she had attended with Jacquette.

Marguerite was skeptical, arguing that Margot's suitor must be a rather self-absorbed widower to have both his children named for their father—a son François and a daughter Françoise. "Besides," she said, "we hardly know him."

"Nonsense," her husband argued. "He's a fine man, and he can provide well for Margot."

Marguerite's concerns stemmed not only from her doubts about the perceived character of the suitor. Given Margot's immaturity, she also questioned whether or not her daughter was up to the task of being a wife and raising two young children that were not her own.

"It's a good match, Marguerite," Christophe argued. "We should give our approval without delay."

"I don't know … " she hesitated.

"Margot is already twenty-three, well past the age when she should have been wed, and there might not be another chance. I only want her happiness," he told his wife, without meeting her eyes.

But Marguerite was not fooled. She was well aware that he saw this as his opportunity to get her daughter out of his house, to make her someone else's responsibility. Yet despite her concerns and hesitation, Marguerite knew that her own reservations would never be sufficient to overrule her husband and prevent the marriage. And perhaps he was right, for Margot seemed equally determined. It was one of those rare occasions when she and her stepfather were in agreement.

Thus, the nuptials, with moderate splendor, took place in Saint-Malo on September 7. For once, Christophe beamed his approval, paying the bills and even providing a small dowry without complaint.

ONLY A FEW MONTHS PASSED BEFORE the real reasons behind the marriage offer became apparent. In January, a letter arrived from their new son-in-law's lawyer, addressed to Madame du Bignon, a letter accusing her of mismanagement of her children's inheritance. LeCourt de Billot had taken Margot to be the daughter of a wealthy nobleman, an heiress. He'd not complained about the meager dowry provided by her stepfather, for he'd come to believe that her inheritance from her father's estate provided significant income. Her extravagances and profligate spending had only encouraged him in his expectations.

Now he was angry, for he had finally learned the truth and persuaded his bride to join him in his accusations. To both Christophe's and Marguerite's surprise and dismay, the name of Margot's brother

Louis also appeared on the legal demand for an accounting.

"*Sacré bleu!*" Christophe cursed when he read the letter addressed to his wife. "*Mordieu!*" He waved the letter around, pounded on his desk, and ranted for almost an hour before he was finally calm enough to sit down and draft a letter to his attorney.

"The income from my stepchildren's inheritance is a pittance compared to all the bills *I've* had to pay," he fumed to Peltier, who would prepare the du Bignons' response. Fortunately, Christophe had kept a careful record of all of his expenses on behalf of Margot and Louis, which he presented, along with statements reflecting the small inheritance income. Unfortunately, Marguerite had been less careful in her accounting, and there were many expenses for which she had no evidence. Nevertheless, Christophe informed Peltier, "Margot and her brother in fact owe money to their mother and me to reimburse us for all our expenses on their behalf."

Despite her love for her children, Marguerite could well understand her husband's reaction, especially when he saw Louis's name as well on the document submitted by LeCourt's attorney. She remembered Christophe's efforts before their marriage to befriend her son. She'd loved him all the more for embracing Louis as though he were his own son and trying to help launch him on his career. He'd seemed, in fact, quite fond of the boy and looked upon him as a protégé. Until now.

How could they do such a thing? Her own children questioning her scruples and those of their stepfather? She knew it cut Christophe to the quick, as it did her. She would always love them, no matter what, but she wondered if their stepfather would ever be able to forgive them.

The matter was finally settled out of court, though not without acrimony on both sides. Marguerite and Christophe easily proved that their expenses for the children far exceeded the income from their inheritance. In fact, they were able to show that, on the contrary,

Margot and Louis owed them money, some of which Christophe was determined to collect as a lesson to them both. Marguerite would have preferred to forgive such debts, but she said nothing, realizing that the entire incident left a bad taste in his mouth and not wanting to make things worse.

She was grateful that her husband didn't dwell on the matter as long as he might have done, at least not overtly, but she suspected it was only because he was distracted by other even more serious matters that were threatening to disrupt their well-ordered world.

THE HARVEST OF 1788, one in a series of poor yields, had been a disaster, and the price of wheat had skyrocketed. Things were bad enough for landowners who could at least compensate to some extent by charging more for the little they produced. But among the peasants of France, who could not afford the higher prices of wheat and grain to make their bread, it was critical. Their children were hungry. And they were growing angrier and more desperate by the day.

Marguerite and Christophe observed their fury first-hand one early August morning as they were setting out for a leisurely drive in their brand-new *calèche*, the small carriage pulled by a single horse. Christophe himself was driving. He refused to hire a coachman, less because of the expense than because he liked to control the horse himself. He also wanted the privacy to be alone with his wife and to say whatever he liked without a servant in hearing distance. And there was always Mustafa if they ever really needed a driver.

As they emerged from the long, tree-lined *allée* of La Ville Hervé and turned onto the main road, they were confronted by a crowd of angry peasants waving pitchforks and axes and shouting foul slogans as they marched in the direction of the little port of Dahouët. The du Bignons were both startled by the noisy clamor and the mob's curses, some of which seemed to be aimed in their direction. They could not understand everything the people were shouting, but it was easy to see that they weren't a friendly lot. Marguerite recoiled in fear when one bitter-faced old man shook his axe and spit at them. Christophe stood up in the carriage, flicked the reins vigorously, and whipped the little horse in a frenzied effort to make it move faster away from the hostile peasants. When they were far enough down the road, he sat down again, stopped the coach, and put his arms around Marguerite, who was beginning to cry. She was visibly shaken by the incident. Christophe too was disturbed by what had happened.

"We're safe now, *chérie*. Please don't cry. I won't let anyone hurt you."

But they did not continue their drive. As soon as the peasants were completely out of sight, he turned the rig around to take her home.

Only later did she and Christophe learn that the shouting horde—men and women alike—had tramped all the way to Dahouët, broken down the door of a warehouse filled with grain, stored for intended shipment to England, and stolen all the wheat they could carry. The rest they defiled with excrement and urine.

THE NEXT MORNING, AS HE WAS DRESSING for the day, Christophe told his valet of the incident, expressing his disgust at the mob's unruly behavior as Mustafa was brushing his jacket. His valet replied in a matter-of-fact manner, "They are hungry, sir." His words made Christophe uneasy, for Mustafa seemed to side with the peasants.

Although it was the first time Christophe and Marguerite had personally witnessed such behavior, they had heard of it in other parts of the country. Things had grown much worse since the dissolution of the Assembly of Notables in May of 1787. The political upheavals and the struggles between the Paris Parliament and the king had grown worse the following year, with new ministers being appointed to solve the problems and then dismissed in failure. Two members of parliament had even been arrested and imprisoned. Finally the new minister of finance, appointed to replace Calonne, realizing that the royal treasury was virtually empty, recommended that the king call together the Estates General, another little-known body that had not been assembled for more than a century and a half. The minister then resigned. A man by the name of Jacques Necker had been his replacement.

None of this was good news for the nobles of the land. The Estates General, unlike the Assembly of Notables, was composed of members of all three estates: clergy, noblemen, and commoners, which included both peasants and members of the bourgeoisie. Believing that members of the first two estates would stand together, Necker decided to balance the scale by doubling the number of representatives from the Third Estate. Meeting together the three groups were to be given the task of resolving the country's financial woes.

Noblemen like Christophe were outraged. Word spread rapidly, and a group of Breton aristocrats agreed to meet in the Church of the Cordeliers in Saint-Brieuc on April 16, 1789, to discuss the matter and choose their representative. When Christophe arrived, he was surprised by the size of the group. There must have been seven hundred people or more there, not counting the handful of clergymen present. The meeting was in an uproar, with voices shouting to be heard.

"The Estates General? What's that?" one of the younger men spoke as loudly as he could. "Who knew it even existed?"

"It's a relic from the Hundred Years War. They say it didn't work very well even then." A dapper man in a powdered wig shouted.

"What on earth is the king thinking?" asked another old man, shaking his silver cane in the air.

"He wants to tax the nobility like we were peasants," the man in the powdered wig offered, trying to be heard over the crowd. Everyone seemed to be talking at once in competing, angry voices. Christophe could make out only the words of those nearest him. Their comments reminded him of what his friends had said about the Assembly of Notables at the dinner they had held. The new assembly, however, was to include the common people as well.

"*Mordieu*, we've been exempt from the *taille* from the beginning of time ... at least for as long as anyone can remember."

"The whole thing is absurd."

"The king is bankrupt from all that high living at Versailles. Now he expects us to pay his bills."

"He's even robbing the Church."

"We shouldn't even stoop to respond."

"I agree."

"So do I."

A great shout of acclamation went up and grew as the idea spread.

And so it went. In the end, the furious Breton noblemen chose not to send a representative at all, as though their scorn for the Estates General would somehow weaken the authority of the meeting, which began on May 5. It did not.

CHRISTOPHE AVIDLY READ THE BROADSIDES that circulated around the countryside, as well as the journals he received from Paris. The news was all very upsetting. The so-called Third Estate, he learned, *did* send representatives to the Estates General at Versailles, as did nobles and clergymen of other regions. The absence of those from his region of Brittany had scarcely been noticed.

After much bickering and a major disagreement over voting procedures, it appeared that the Third Estate took vigorous control of the meeting and then broke away from the Estates General on June

17 to draw up their own constitution, declaring themselves to be "the National Assembly."

There was so much going on in Paris and Versailles that Christophe could hardly keep up with all the upheaval. He was, however, surprised but pleased to learn that on July 11, the king had once again dismissed the finance minister, this time Jacques Necker, allegedly for his refusal to attend a meeting of the Royal Council. His removal from office was applauded by the representatives of the First and Second Estates, there to speak for the nobles and the clergy. However, members of the Third Estate viewed Necker as something of a protector and were enraged by his dismissal. It was a tipping point for the people.

Stirred up by their fury and by the inequalities of the past and tasting for the first time a bite of power, they began to protest openly. Riots broke out, and on July 14, just three day's after Necker's dismissal, the people of Paris stormed an antiquated royal prison called the Bastille. They were in search of ammunition for the almost three thousand weapons they had looted earlier in the day from the basement arsenal of Les Invalides, a hospital for wounded soldiers founded by Louis XIV. In the process the rioters released the seven prisoners inside the Bastille, killed the guards, and beheaded the prison governor, whose head they placed on a spike and paraded around the streets of Paris for all to see.

Learning of the events of that day sent a chill through Christophe. Paris was a long way from Lamballe, and until now things were still relatively calm around La Ville Hervé. But the riot of the peasants in Dahouët the previous August was a clear manifestation of the people's fury and potential violence, even into their little corner of France.

For the first time, Christophe was seeing all too clearly the cracks that were forming in his small, perfect world. Most of the time he tried to ignore them, but despite his efforts to shield his wife and protect her, even Marguerite could also see that there were good reasons to be apprehensive about their future.

At first they went about their daily lives as though nothing had changed. They did not openly discuss the situation, and Christophe made every effort to tuck away the copies of the *Journal de Paris*, which arrived in Brittany only days after their publication. He didn't want Marguerite to see them and be upset about all that was happening. But he could not hide them all, and she had learned enough to realize that, in some parts of France, life was changing dramatically. She could also sense Christophe's misgivings.

One evening in the *salon*, after they had kissed their little boys goodnight and Nanon had taken them upstairs to tuck them in, Marguerite laid down her needlework and turned to her husband, "What do you think will happen here, Christophe?"

"What do you mean?" he asked.

"I'm talking about all this unrest among the commoners," she said. "The riots and violence you don't want me to know about. How will it affect us?" Her eyes were fixed on his face. He stared into the empty fireplace, took a swallow of brandy, and set down the glass on the little table beside his armchair. Only after a deep breath did he let his eyes meet hers. He looked at her for a long moment, shaking his head, as he thought about her question.

Finally he replied, "I wish I knew, *chérie*. ... I wish I knew.

Chapter 7

October 5, 1790

La Ville Hervé

IT WAS ONE OF THOSE BRIGHT DAYS WHEN Marguerite refused to worry about the world outside and focused instead only on the present. She'd spent the earlier part of the day discussing the landscaping with her gardener and supervising the pruning of the roses planted several summers ago. They had bloomed throughout the season in magnificent splashes of color. She loved to relax there on warm days to enjoy the sunshine, smell the fragrance, and admire her garden's centerpiece—a splendid sundial in the shape of an orb to record the sun's movements.

Although it was still early October, the leaves were already beginning to change to their autumn gold and red, and a winter chill threatened the late afternoon. Now, just before dusk, she sat drinking a cup of tea and reading beside her bedroom window overlooking the garden, a woolen shawl wrapped around her shoulders and a new-laid, crackling fire in the grate. She read more than usual these days, for it kept her mind occupied and away from the terrible things happening throughout her country. She was totally absorbed in her book, *Paul et Virginie*, a popular novel she was particularly enjoying, for it was set on the island of Mauritius.

Suddenly she heard a clamor downstairs. Christophe burst into the manor house and called in a loud voice, "Marguerite! Where are you?"

She almost turned over her teacup, for she hadn't expected him back until the next day and she was unaccustomed to such noisy exuberance from anyone but the children, who had already been put to bed. She rushed downstairs, though with care for she knew she was pregnant again, and into the *salon* to find out what was wrong. His face was flushed from a combination of the two-day ride back from Saint-Malo in the brisk wind and his unconcealed excitement. He was virtually dancing as he took off his redingote and tossed it onto one of the chairs. He picked her up, swinging her around the room until she laughed and begged for mercy.

When he finally put her down, he kissed the tip of her nose. Then, with great relish and broad gestures, he poured a snifter of brandy and sat down before the fire to warm himself.

"Brandy before dinner?" she said. "What on earth?"

He took a sip of the amber liquid and set the glass on the table beside his chair.

"Marguerite. God is still smiling on us. I have some amazing news!" he said, rubbing his hands together and stretching them toward the blaze. She lowered herself into the armchair facing his and held her breath to see what was coming. He swirled the brandy in his glass and took a bold swallow as he leaned toward her.

"I just came from a most extraordinary meeting in Saint-Malo." Marguerite listened, watching him carefully as he told her about the young man he'd met there—Julien de Chappedelaine, a native of

Saint-Brieuc, who had just returned from a prolonged visit to the United States.

"He did all sorts of things there—even visited the new American president, George Washington. They went hunting together. And during his travels he met a fellow countryman, an adventuresome fellow, a nobleman of course, named François Dumoussay."

"Oh?" Marguerite listened, curious as to where his excitement was leading. *What does all this have to do with us?* she wondered, but she kept silent, waiting for him to reveal whatever it was that he obviously wanted to tell her. He didn't seem to be calming down, but went on breathlessly with his story.

"Dumoussay has found a private island for sale off the coast of the colony ... I mean, the new state of Georgia, and he and Chappedelaine have proposed that a small group of compatible French investors can buy it together and make a fortune." Christophe rarely talked so much or with such animation.

"And best of all," he announced finally, "they want us to be part of it."

Christophe was not an impetuous man. Usually he acted carefully and with forethought, especially when it involved investing his money. But now Marguerite saw his eyes gleaming with the visions he described.

"It's our chance, Marguerite, a chance to leave behind all this madness that's going on in France." She knew he worried constantly about his new estate and the safety of his family. He scoffed at the revolutionaries' slogan of *Liberté, fraternité, égalité.* Some of their publications even added "*ou la mort.*" Liberty, brotherhood, equality—or death. He bristled at the implied threat. No aristocrat, not even members of the merchant nobility to which Christophe and his friends belonged, could accept the idea of a crude peasant as their equal. But by now unruly mobs of ruffians were roaming the countryside, setting fires to *châteaux,* and wreaking havoc in some of the large cities. So far they had not bothered rural manor houses like La Ville Hervé, but Marguerite had heard her husband express fears that it was only a matter of time. She too remembered vividly the shouting crowd of peasants they'd met that day on the road to Dahouët. No doubt he was right to be worried, both for his family and for the modest fortune he had so laboriously acquired. Still, this sounded like an impetuous idea.

She tried her best not to think of all the unrest, but she knew it was always on his mind. *It's so unfair*, she thought. They had waited so long, and he had worked so hard to achieve the life they'd both always wanted. They'd been so happy to live on this fine Breton property and start a family. Now, after only a few short years, it could already be coming to an end.

"It's the answer to a prayer, Marguerite," he said. "It's likely our best chance to escape this craziness that's destroying France and preserve what little we can until it's over."

His eyes were shining for the first time in many moons, reflecting the firelight as they had in 1785, when he first retired from the sea, eager to establish his new life as a landed aristocrat. *Only five years ago?* Marguerite thought. They had barely settled into their new world, and it seemed as though their lives together had only begun. And now, already, it looked as though it could end in a heartbeat. It had all happened so quickly. She'd invested so much energy in her home and garden these past few years that she could hardly bear the thought of leaving them behind. She knew her husband must feel the same way about all his efforts.

"It's worth thinking about, I suppose," Marguerite said, though as yet, she was not prepared to do anything more than consider it as some remote possibility, not as a present reality.

"I've already done it, Marguerite," he said with a sheepish smile. "I've invested in the *Société de Sapelo*, the Sapelo Company, as it is to be called."

Marguerite's eyes widened in disbelief. "What? You've done it? You've invested in an island on the other side of the world, sight unseen? How could you do such a thing?" It was so unlike Christophe, who was usually very careful about his investments.

"But, *chérie*, I was forced to seize the opportunity on the spot, or else they would have offered it to someone else. Surely you understand. They're accepting just a few investors. It was our only chance to be a part of it."

She said nothing, only shook her head in dismay and turned toward the staircase that led to their bedroom.

CHRISTOPHE WAS TAKEN ABACK by her shocked reaction. They took dinner together that evening in complete silence, and she was already in bed, pretending to be asleep, or so he thought, when he finally went upstairs.

As he dressed for bed, he was beginning to have second thoughts. *Was this really such a good idea?* He rarely did anything so impulsive. But in fact, it wasn't as impulsive as Marguerite thought or as he had perhaps led her to believe. Chappedelaine had first contacted him about the possibility in July. At the beginning it all seemed rather far-fetched, and he'd chosen not to mention it to her. He had wanted to take time to mull it over and learn more about the situation. The two men had met several times that month in the coffee houses of Saint-Malo and Saint-Brieuc. And Christophe had thought of little else during recent weeks. Perhaps he should have told her then, he thought. But he had not yet decided.

Finally, on July 20, he learned that a cautious Saint-Malo businessman named Pierre Jacques Grandclos Meslé had thought the venture sound enough to make an investment in it. Thus, with bolstered confidence, and considering both the violence spreading throughout the country and their fear and concern at having confronted a mob of angry peasants virtually on their doorstep, he'd felt it prudent to make the decision. Convinced by Chappedelaine that they could live like true aristocrats in America as well as in France, he agreed to make the investment. At the time, he had not put up any money or signed any documents. But he gave his word. He had made a payment of forty-eight thousand *livres* for his one-fifth share in late September. It was a sizeable investment, even more than he had paid for his manor house and land. Then earlier today, at the home of Chappedelaine they had finally signed the partnership papers. There was no way he could turn back now.

He raised the issue again the following morning at breakfast, after they had both had a good night's sleep and a chance to think it over.

"I thought you would welcome the opportunity to get out of France at this terrible time," he told her. "Even the king and queen aren't safe. Remember last fall how the peasants mobbed Versailles? Now King Louis and his wife can't even live there any more." She nodded faintly. Everyone knew of that occasion, when the royal couple was forced to move into the city of Paris and take up residence at the Tuileries Palace, where citizens could keep them under guard.

"The king is no long in power," he argued. "That damned National Assembly created by those fool commoners has gone insane, trying to abolish the nobility, as though they could simply erase centuries-old traditions and ranks. Even the Church is under attack. They've taken over church property and abolished monastic vows. It's insanity. Nuns and monks are being run out of their convents and monasteries. Remember when my sister Angélique had to move to Corseul to live with Jeanne. How much further can it go?"

"Perhaps if we don't protest and just remain quietly here …?"

"*Sacré bleu*, Marguerite. You think they'll just ignore us? I don't

think so. Remember Dahouët? And think of the children, our two boys and the child you're carrying. They deserve some kind of peaceful life."

While he was sure this national maelstrom would not last forever, he had no idea how long it would go on. It was not a time to be complacent. Who knew what the so-called "citizens" would do next?

"There are fortunes to be made in the new world. We just have to seize the opportunity while we still can. Peltier can look after my investments here." He paused only briefly. "You should have heard Dumoussay's description of the island: perpetual summer, lemon and orange trees, flowers everywhere. As Chappedelaine said, a veritable paradise." He went on to tell her about its pleasant year-round climate, abundant lands to cultivate, live oak trees to be harvested for timber, wild horses to be bred with donkeys, which could provide much-needed mules to farmers, abundant marshlands, and waterways to keep unfriendly or unwanted neighbors at a distance.

"It will all be ours, Marguerite. It will all belong to the Sapelo Company to rake in the profits. It will be a wonderful place to raise our children and wait out this idiocy, this vertigo, this national insanity. We'll be there with people of our kind. We can live as we do now. And then, when everybody in France finally comes to their senses, we can come home again."

"What do you know about timbering and breeding mules and this … this Sapelo, which you've never even seen?" Marguerite chided.

Her skepticism sobered him somewhat. Perhaps she was right, at least about that point. Before taking his family to this new country, perhaps he should be sure. It was too late in one sense. He'd already committed a substantial sum of money. But perhaps he should go there to make certain he wasn't going to *sauter de la poêle dans le feu*, as his mother used to say. Jump from the frying pan into the fire. Go from bad to worse. He knew that Dumoussay and Chappedelaine were leaving on a ship called the *Silvain* to go back to Sapelo at the end of the month. Perhaps he should join them. It was a chance to see the island first hand before he brought over Marguerite and the children. Then he could reassure her from his own observations.

The new baby wasn't due for another six months. During that time he could go to see this Sapelo for himself, stake out his land, and make arrangements to build a home before taking his wife and children there. Not perhaps. He would do it.

"I will go and visit the island before I take you to America. I will leave before the month is out," he informed her. He was resolute now. This trip would be necessary.

"But how will I manage here alone?" she asked.

"You won't be alone. You have servants and two sons."

"How will I manage two little boys, with me pregnant?"

"I will take them with me then," he answered. He had an answer for everything.

"What would I do without them?"

"You can't have it both ways, Marguerite. We'll split the difference. I'll take Joseph with me, and you can keep Henri here with you. It's time Joseph learned about life at sea anyhow. It's his legacy. It's in his blood."

Marguerite looked appalled. "He's only five years old. He's far too young," she said.

"Nonsense. He's a sturdy lad. He'll be fine. I went to sea on my own when I was just a boy."

"You were twice his age."

"But he'll be with his father. I wasn't."

Christophe had made up his mind, and it would do little good to argue. He had no intention of backing down. He would make this trip, and Joseph would accompany him.

Chapter 8

July, 1791

La Ville Hervé

THE NEW BABY WAS ALREADY FOUR MONTHS OLD by the time Christophe returned to La Ville Hervé. He'd sent word by courier from Saint-Malo that he had business to attend to there and would take a small boat for Dahouët that was sailing in a few days. Mustafa had learned its approximate time of arrival and taken the carriage to the small port to meet him. Marguerite was waiting with anticipation. She heard the carriage as it drove up the *allée* and hurried downstairs, the baby in her arms, to greet her husband. Young Henri, shouting with excitement, passed her on the staircase and bounded out the door to greet his father.

While Mustafa tended the horses, Christophe strode briskly toward the house, scooping the boy up for a hug. When he saw his wife standing in the doorway holding the new baby, he put the child down and held out his arms in greeting. He was alone. But before she could say a word, he scooped her up for a long kiss.

"Where is Joseph?" she asked as soon as she caught her breath, a small frown wrinkling her forehead.

"He's still at Sapelo. He's all right. I left him in the care of Julien de Chappedelaine. Mustafa told me you had given birth to another boy. Three sons now! Splendid!" He said, changing the subject and reaching out to take the new baby in his arms.

"You left Joseph behind?" She said in shocked disbelief.

"He'll be waiting for us in America," he promised. "Believe me, it was better for both of us than bringing him back again."

"What do you mean?" Her face was ashen, her voice incredulous.

"He did not fare well on the sea voyage. Seasick the whole way over. Just imagine how humiliating that was. A sailor's boy puking throughout the entire trip," he said with disgust. "He was miserable the entire way, and Julien said he would look after him. I just couldn't stand his whining for another month-long crossing. We were both miserable. It was the right decision. He'll be fine."

"You left our son behind?" She was stunned. *How could he do such a thing?*

"He'll be fine," he repeated. "He likes Julien, and Julien took a liking to him and promised to teach him English before we come back."

"Christophe, I can't believe you left him with a stranger."

"He's not a stranger. He's one of my partners, and Julien is a gentleman. He'll look after the boy and take good care of him."

She could only stare at him as she tried to absorb the shock.

Before sailing to America, Marguerite recalled, Joseph, their firstborn, had been Christophe's favorite. But now he seemed unconcerned about the child's welfare. Obviously he had not hesitated to leave the boy behind.

Christophe kissed the pale forehead of his new son, and then handed him back to his mother. "Marguerite," he said, "please stop looking at me that way. I just couldn't bear to have a sick child on my hands all the way back. As I said, he felt wretched for the entire trip and spent most of the time hanging over the rail or lying in his bunk. Believe me, it's for his own good. He's better off with Julien at Sapelo than on another ocean voyage. I hope this one will take to the sea better than his older brother," he said, as the baby nestled with contentment in his mother's arms.

"I know I will, *Papa*." Henri said, tugging at his father's coattail for attention.

Christophe ruffled the boy's hair, "I'm sure you will, son," he said. "It would be hard for you not to do better than your brother."

Tears welled up in Marguerite's eyes as she thought of her little boy so far away without any member of his family. She ached inside. She had missed Joseph immensely and had so looked forward to holding him in her arms and introducing him to his new little brother.

"Did you name the baby already?" Christophe asked, his voice hopeful, as he stood at the foot of the stairs.

"Yes, of course," she said. "I named him Paul François, for both our fathers."

"A good choice," he replied, but she could see a flicker of disappointment cross his face. She suspected he'd wanted this baby named for him, but she had so resented his absence during this most difficult part of her pregnancy that she was determined not to name the child for his father. It was petty of her, she supposed. But now, after what he had done, leaving Joseph behind, she felt fully justified.

"If you'll excuse me," he said, "I really must get some rest. The voyage was exhausting." With Henri clinging to his father's hand, the pair mounted the staircase.

It was not the homecoming Marguerite had expected and hoped for, but at least her husband was home again, and, despite everything, she was glad to see him.

IN THE NEXT FEW DAYS SHE COULD TELL BY Christophe's demeanor that he felt less enthusiasm for the Sapelo venture than he had when he'd left France the previous November to visit Georgia. He still spoke of nothing but the island's finer points, but it was without the excitement he had shown before he left. Little by little, she wheedled the truth out of him.

"*Eh bien*, things are not as well organized or quite as idyllic as I had hoped," he said. "It's devilishly hot in the summer months, and mosquitoes and sand flies can be a problem. The only women there so far are slave women, and that makes a difference. Now there are just the men—Dumoussay, Chappedelaine, and another partner, a man named Villehuchet living on the island. They live in a rather primitive fashion, and so far they don't seem to get along very well."

"Why? What's the problem?" she asked, apprehensive about the whole affair.

"Well, there are age differences. One of the investors, Villehuchet, is an old man—already over sixty—not much use as far as work is concerned. He mostly just sits around as though he expects to be waited on, as he obviously was when he lived in France. The other men are much younger and more vigorous, and they make fun of him, even to his face."

"How unkind of them," Marguerite said.

"Well, in fairness, the old man is hard to get along with. He isn't happy being there without his family, hasn't been from the beginning, and he lets everyone know it. Evidently he had no choice but to get out of France as fast as he could, and either he couldn't bring his family with him or else they refused to come."

"Why did he have to leave?"

"About a month or so after the violence broke out in Paris— maybe you remember—some of the commoners in Saint-Malo were getting stirred up by all the propaganda and started to take it out on the rich. Well, they stormed Villehuchet's home one night and started looting. They scared him and his family half to death. He tried as best he could to defend them, of course, and whether on purpose or by accident, he shot and killed one of them."

"Good heavens, what happened to him then?"

"They arrested him, but the charges were dropped when he claimed self-defense. Then he heard the widow of the dead man had made an appeal to the revolutionary government that he be rearrested and tried. He panicked. He doubted he'd get off a second time. Things have changed in France in the last year, as you well know."

"Is Villehuchet still at Sapelo?"

"He was when I left. But he was mighty unhappy. I brought back a letter of complaint he wrote to another one of our partners, who is his good friend. You've heard of him, I'm sure—a wealthy ship-owner named Pierre Grandclos Meslé. Very rich. He lives in Saint-Malo. We're lucky he's one of our partners. It shows his faith in the project, but I've learned that he doesn't really plan to move to Sapelo. It was just another investment as far as he's concerned. He split his partnership with Villehuchet, probably to help the man out when all the trouble started. To spare the old fellow's feelings, most likely, Grandclos told him he was sending him there to look out for his interests. But I don't think Villehuchet is really interested in the Sapelo Company. To him it's just a place of refuge until the troubles end in France."

"And there are no French women there at all?" Marguerite asked. "I thought you said they'd all bring their families."

"I thought they would, but Dumoussay and Chappedelaine aren't married yet, and so far the only married partner who has shown up is Villehuchet, but without his family. I presume he'll bring them sooner or later if they'll come … or if he stays," he added quietly. "As I said, he's very unhappy."

"Aren't there any others?"

"Well, Grandclos Meslé has a family, but as I said, I don't think he's planning to leave France. I hope he won't regret it. Chappedelaine has an uncle by the name of Charles-César Picot de Boisfeuillet, who plans to move to Georgia, and I understand he's bringing his family. They live in Bergerac now and needed to make some arrangements before they leave. They haven't arrived yet. But I'm sure you won't be the only woman there, at least not for long." He smiled, and the baby smiled back.

"But if you are the only one for a while, you can rule the roost," he added, his smile turning into an impish grin. "Don't worry. Boisfeuillet and his family will be there soon. And surely Dumoussay and Chappedelaine will marry one of these days."

"My goodness, that's a lot of names to remember," Marguerite said.

"I know, but you'll get used to them gradually. At least you don't have to learn their whole names. Dumoussay, for example, is François Marie Loys Dumoussay de la Vauve." He laughed.

"Good heavens," she said.

"They won't all be there at once. Don't worry. This is just a transition period, a start-up time. Things will settle down as we get our little colony organized."

But still, she thought, he didn't speak with the same tone of wonder and conviction about the island as he had before his visit.

IF CHRISTOPHE HARBORED ANY RESERVATIONS about following through with his intention to move to Sapelo, he set them quickly aside when he saw the deteriorating conditions and increasing violence in his home country. There was also no real question of not returning, because Joseph was there, waiting for his parents. There were times, he suspected, when Marguerite wondered if that was the real reason her husband had left their son behind—so that he wouldn't weaken in his resolve to return and to make certain she would come with him. Perhaps she was right.

Whatever the reasons, Christophe set about at once to make the necessary preparations to return to Georgia and to wind up any business matters he needed to tend to in France. He gave his proxy to Peltier, who, as his legal representative, would manage affairs in his absence. To raise sufficient funds for the trip, he arranged for Peltier to sell one of his most valuable Breton properties, a farm known as La Vigne. His Sapelo partner Grandclos Meslé had agreed to purchase it. It was a good arrangement, Christophe thought, because Grandclos understood the situation and, to eliminate any possibility of questions with the revolutionary government, he was willing to register the deed only after the du Bignon family had left the country. And he would probably be willing, Christophe assured Marguerite, to sell it back to him when the family returned to France—at a profit, of course.

WITH THE MONEY FROM THE SALE of La Vigne in hand, Christophe, accompanied by his new friend Grandclos, whom he'd brought along for advice, attended a November ship auction in the walled city of Saint-Malo. It was a strategic port, located on an estuary of the Rance River, which made access to England and the islands very convenient. Fortified since the Middle Ages and a haven for privateers and corsairs, especially during the wars with England, the seaport town was always filled with people, and there was never any lack of ships for sale.

The auction was crowded and noisy, but after a round of spirited bidding against the background of the city's medieval walls, the auctioneer banged his gavel down for du Bignon's purchase—a small, well-built vessel called the *Aimable Angélique*, whose name he promptly commissioned a ship's painter to change to *Le Sapelo*. It was only 140 tons, but Grandclos agreed it was a good little vessel and an excellent purchase, and it was certainly sufficient to get the du Bignon family and a few extra passengers willing to pay for the trip to America. Christophe's only irritation was that the incompetent painter misspelled the name and painted *Le Sappello* on the side of the ship.

"*Sacré bleu*, man. Look what you've done," Christophe cursed as he berated the painter for his error. He had even spelled it for the man, who evidently had limited memory. Grandclos only chuckled. "What difference does it make? It will still get you there. And you will always be able to distinguish the ship from the island in any official documents." Christophe grumbled, but he didn't want to pay a second time for the job, and as Grandclos pointed out, he should have written it down. Thus, *Le Sappello* it was.

CHRISTOPHE WAS ITCHING TO SET SAIL, for conditions in France were getting worse by the day. Violence was increasing, as peasants vented their hatred of the aristocracy. It was also becoming more and more difficult to leave the country under the revolutionary government, and Christophe worried that if they waited any longer, they might never be able to leave at all. People of noble rank who were trying to emigrate from France were now often accused of being traitors to the revolution and of trying to seek help from outside the country. They were prohibited from departing and, if they were brave enough to try at all, were compelled to do so surreptitiously. As a precaution and with the help of the crafty Dumoussay, who was quite a finagler and who always seemed to find a way to get what he wanted, Christophe had managed to obtain an American passport and residency papers during his stay in Georgia and was, thus, able to declare himself a citizen of the United States on his sailing documents.

"Why don't you come with us, Pierre?" Christophe asked Grandclos as the ship was being readied for a long sea voyage. "Things are getting dangerous here."

"I appreciate your asking, but I have far too much property and business to leave it all behind. I can take care of myself, and I don't dabble in politics."

"I hope you're right, but I'd rather take my chances in America. My lawyer is looking after my interests here."

"I hope he's trustworthy."

"Absolutely," Christophe assured him. "He has handled the affairs of my family for many years. I have complete confidence in him."

"Well, then, you're a lucky man. I have little trust in any lawyer. In fact, one of the things that attracted me to invest in the Sapelo Company was that I've heard that the colony's founders didn't even allow lawyers to practice there."

"I don't think that's the case any more," Christophe said, lifting his eyebrows, as he recalled all the legal entanglements the Sapelo purchase had created.

Both men laughed, but Christophe did think himself lucky. He had no reason to doubt Peltier's integrity. He had always been an honest and straightforward man—a friend as well as a lawyer. With the bill of sale for his new ship in his pocket and unshakeable confidence that all would go well, it *had* to go well, Christophe bid a hearty *au revoir* to Grandclos. Accompanied by the small crew he had hired, he set sail for the little port of Dahouët, where the men would load the ship with the household goods they were bringing and the many cases of fine French wines Christophe assumed he could not find in America.

IT WAS A HEADY TIME, trying to decide what to take and what should be left behind. Marguerite and young Henri were both excited, Marguerite about finally getting to see Joseph again and Henri just for the adventure. The new baby seemed upset by the disruption and all the strangers coming and going. He did not have the rosy-cheeked, easygoing disposition his older brothers had shown as infants, but was rather a quiet child who seemed most content with a simple and undisturbed routine.

ONCE LOADED AND WITH EVERYONE ABOARD, the family and crew sailed back to Saint-Malo, which was on their way, to purchase a few more supplies and pick up some paying passengers Grandclos had recommended—a family called Dechenaux, who planned to settle in Savannah. Saint-Malo would be their port of embarkation.

On the day of their sailing, Monday, the fifth day of March, Marguerite's daughter Margot, now living with her husband in Saint-Malo, came to the dock to see them off. She hugged her mother and little brothers and tried to say something to Christophe, but he turned his back and headed up the gangway, having already made it clear he never wanted to see her and her brother again. She shrugged with a studied indifference, turning instead to her mother, who embraced her once again before she followed her husband onto the ship.

Once the passengers had all boarded the *Sappello*, to join the crew of eleven, a final flurry of activity signaled that there were about to cast off. The ghost of a three-quarter moon hung in the afternoon sky, as Marguerite stood at the rail, waving goodbye to her daughter.

"A waxing moon is a good omen, Marguerite," Christophe said, once they had cleared the wharf. He brushed against her back and gave her arm a squeeze. "It's a good time for new beginnings."

She noticed two sailors exchange glances when they overheard his words. One of them made the sign of the cross, but she ignored them and turned away to watch the docks and walls of Saint-Malo recede in the distance. She still stood at the rail, waving her white linen handkerchief in farewell to Margot, even after she knew that her daughter had left the dock and started home in her carriage.

Marguerite watched the edge of the sea, like a thin fabric, tearing away from the land they left behind, from the graceful noble life she'd grown accustomed to and had hoped to continue for as long as she lived. They were leaving their beautiful manor house and the garden of roses she'd planted during the few short years they had lived there. The bushes were just beginning to show new leaves and form tight buds that would, in summer months, burst into cascades of colors. But she would not see them.

Even more important, she was leaving behind both her children from her first marriage. She thought of Marie Clarice, now gone forever, whom she'd left in Mauritius. *But this is different, dear Lord,* she whispered, *for Margot and Louis are grown now and have their own independent lives. I'm not abandoning them—not like that. Lord, please take care of them.*

She had long since forgiven her adult children for what her husband called their "presumptive greed," and they too seemed to have put the unfortunate incident behind them. But for Christophe, she feared, the damage was permanent. His was not a forgiving nature, she had observed. Only time and proximity would help heal such a wound. But now they would be separated by an ocean, and there would be little chance for healing. She feared he would carry the anger in his heart forever.

"They are nothing but gold diggers," he had said to Marguerite when she expressed her sadness at leaving them behind. Although it still hurt sometimes to remember their mistrust, the tears she was shedding now were for them, the children she was leaving behind.

"Good riddance," Christophe had muttered when he'd spotted Margot on the dock, come to say goodbye to her mother. Marguerite had overheard him and was shocked by his words, though not surprised by his feelings. Before their departure, he had insisted that she sign a document for Peltier's files declaring that none of his property in America could ever be inherited by Margot or Louis or their children, even if he died first. She did as he asked, but she felt a sense of shame at his request, as though he didn't trust her judgment any more than her older children did. It left a dark place in her heart.

Although she was hurt that they had questioned her integrity, they were still her son and daughter, and their children would be her grandchildren. Whatever affection Christophe may once have shown them, he'd obviously had little difficulty in casting it aside. He appeared to view them now only as troublesome leftovers from her first marriage. Coming to America was his way to escape not only the upheaval in France, but also his stepchildren, she thought. But for her, their mother who had loved and nurtured them for so long, it was a rupture of the heart. Marguerite wasn't sure that her husband even noticed.

Once the ship sailed, however, Christophe sought her out, led her to the captain's quarters, and took her in his arms to comfort her for whatever she was so obviously grieving. He was not insensitive to her pain.

"Don't be so sad, *chérie*," he said. "In America we will find our true destiny. We will be happy there, where we can make a new life." She could tell he was trying hard to sound convincing. Leaving France and all they had dreamed of was, she knew, as hard for him as it was for her, though for different reasons. She felt a flood of love for him as he tried to comfort her.

Resting her head on his shoulder, she whispered, "I hope so, Christophe. I hope so." After a moment, she added, "God willing."

Chapter 9

April 1792

Mid-Atlantic

Hᴇʀ ᴇʏᴇs ɢʟɪsᴛᴇɴɪɴɢ ᴡɪᴛʜ ᴛᴇᴀʀs, Marguerite watched the small, tightly wrapped bundle rock on the restless cradle of the dark sea until it sank beneath the surface.

"*Courage, ma chère.*" Christophe squeezed her shoulder as he brushed past her to return to his duties after reciting the necessary words and ordering the tiny body released into the deep. As the ship's captain, he'd conducted the ceremony himself. He knew it all too well, she thought, having been compelled to recite it once already during the voyage when one of the ship's sailors died only two weeks after they set sail from the Breton port of Saint-Malo. And who knows how many times he had performed such rituals at sea during his years as captain for the French India Company?

But this time was different. This time the body belonged to his own son. She felt that his emotions must surely be similar to hers and that this time he must have spoken with genuine feeling of God's calming of the "primeval seas" and "raging waters" and the tranquil new life promised in the waters of baptism. But she couldn't read his feelings in his voice, for it had not broken even once during the little service. She supposed that did not want to appear weak or emotional in front of his sailors.

The boy *had* been baptized, thank heaven, shortly after his birth the preceding March. In Christophe's absence, Marguerite had seen to that. The parish priest they'd invited to dinner had succumbed to her pleading and, in defiance of the new revolutionary law that forbade the sacraments and ordered the doors of the parish church bolted shut, he baptized the child in his mother's arms.

Now she stood alone beside the rail of the stern, wisps of chestnut hair blowing wildly about her bonnet in the wind, as she watched the waves swallow the body of her last child. She felt its finality in her bones. She would be forty-three her next birthday, and she had already noticed that her monthly bleedings were becoming irregular. Some women, she knew, bore children almost to their fifties, but not in her family. For the most part, she considered it a blessing, for almost thirty years of childbearing was enough to wear a woman to a nub. And she had given birth now to six children—her three sons by Christophe and a son and two daughters from her youthful marriage to Jean-Pascal. Not counting occasional miscarriages along the way.

She could still feel her baby's soft skin as he nestled in her arms. Even though he had been from the very beginning a frail child, he was beautiful, with his pale blue eyes that looked so wisely into her own while he nursed, and wispy ash-colored hair that seemed to float weightless as a halo around his head. He had been only eleven months old when they left their Breton manor. They had celebrated his only birthday aboard ship four days after they set sail.

He never learned to walk. The rolling deck of the *Sappello* would have been a challenge to even the strongest toddler, much less for one as weak as little Paul. Had they not left France, Marguerite wondered, would her baby have lived? The constant rocking of the small ship had made her sick at the beginning and perhaps, she thought, caused her milk to sour. The baby was colicky but had been soothed by the calm atmosphere of La Ville-Hervé. She had worried about taking him on this long ocean voyage, which could require as much as two months at sea. His fretfulness had grown worse with each day on the turbulent ship, and he'd begun to have trouble breathing.

Now he was gone, and she felt certain she would never rock another baby, not one of her own, in her arms. Her heart felt empty, though her breasts were full, aching painfully in their bindings, craving the hungry mouth that would suck at them no more.

She gripped the rail and watched the horizon until the glinting noonday sun blinded her eyes, forcing her to turn back toward the deck. Members of the small crew were busily carrying out the tasks they had been hired to do. The watchman never left his post, not even during the burial. He peered from the crow's nest, his rheumy eyes straining toward the flat horizon to watch for other vessels or for the land they all knew they wouldn't reach for at least another couple of weeks. Two sailors with calloused hands leaned against a bulwark, mending a torn sail while another vigorously swabbed the deck, aided by an apprentice sailor with a blue sailing ship tattooed on his forearm. The round-faced cabin boy scurried here and there, trying to look important, on whatever errand any crewmember sent him on.

Marguerite watched them work. She remembered their mutterings and sidelong glances when the first sailor had died. *Mauvaise chance,* bad luck, they grumbled. She tried to ignore them, but she knew they considered it a bad omen to have women aboard. They were outspoken about that to one another. Even worse, Christophe had changed the name of the ship from the *Aimable Angélique,* the name it bore when he had bought it at auction in Saint-Malo, and rechristened it the *Sappello,* in anticipation of their adventure in the New World.

That too, the sailors believed, was bad luck. She had scoffed at their silly superstitions. Then, when the baby died and Marguerite heard the sailors' uneasy muttering once again, even she began to wonder if there weren't some truth to their suspicions.

Nevertheless, the crew went about their work, evidently determined to make the best of a bad voyage. Everyone seemed busy except her, and she had too much time to think, too much time to remember.

"*ALLONS*, MARGUERITE. Why don't you come below and rest for a while," said a gentle voice at her elbow. It belonged to Sophie Dechenaux, the only other woman on the ship except for the servants. Sophie was the wife of Thomas Dechenaux, whose family members were the paying passengers on the voyage. Their children kept Sophie busy from morning to evening, so the two women rarely had time to talk alone. But the death of little Paul had brought them closer, and Marguerite felt that Sophie might be the only person aboard who truly understood.

Her steadiness had been a great comfort to Marguerite throughout the voyage. When the baby cried, Sophie would reach out her arms to take him from his mother and walk him on deck so that Marguerite could get some rest. Now she held the hand of his brother, five-year-old Henri, as she had throughout the ceremony, allowing the mother to grieve without distraction. Marguerite did not resist. She let Sophie lead her below to the captain's quarters, where she stretched out on the hard bunk to let the darkness close around her, if only for a little while.

HER MIND REFUSED TO REST. She had never shared Christophe's enthusiasm for this voyage, not while the baby was so small and so frail. Uproot their lives to go God knows where? But he had insisted that it was necessary *now*. They could delay no longer, he argued. The window of their past life was closing, and they must grasp this opportunity to salvage what they could of their modest estate—not the land, of course, which they hoped would still be theirs when they returned, but at least their lives and some of their assets and movable goods— from the wrath of the revolutionaries who were overrunning France.

She lay on the hard bunk in the captain's quarters and closed her eyes, but sleep would not come. Unwanted visions kept floating behind her eyelids, demanding her attention. The sweet face of Marie Clarice as it must have looked in her coffin. The still form of her baby Paul after he breathed his last. Her daughter Margot, who had come to see them off, waving from the dock at Saint-Malo. The scowl on her husband's face when he saw her there.

Things had not always been this way. At the beginning, her life with Christophe seemed heaven-sent, like a new dawn. But so much had happened in so short a time. Marguerite thought of herself as a strong woman, but there was a limit to her strength, and she felt she had reached it. Now all she wanted to do was close her eyes and sleep, sleep, sleep until they reached Georgia. Her son Joseph, now six years old, would be there, his arms outstretched in an eager greeting to his *maman*, whom he had not seen for more than a year. Their new house, which they had decided to call Bel Air, would be finished and waiting, graceful and hospitable, on the magnificent island that Christophe had once described to her as a virtual Eden and for which he had named his vessel.

Sleep. Perhaps that would cure the aching in her heart and turn her mind to the new world that lay ahead and where Christophe assured her that things would be better. She longed to blot it all out in a deep sleep without dreams. She could hear distant thunder, and with it memories flooded her mind of the tossing and turbulence of the vessel, of her sickness, of her baby's death. *Not another storm*, she hoped. *Dear God, not another storm. I can bear no more.* The thunder only grew louder. She let herself weep with grief and despair until, exhausted, she finally fell into a deep, though not dreamless, sleep.

Chapter 10

Mid-Atlantic, 1792

Aboard the *Sappello*

W HEN MARGUERITE AWOKE, IT WAS MORNING. Christophe lay beside her in the narrow bunk of the captain's quarters, his arm across her chest, holding her close. His warm body felt good beside her, though she still ached inside. She thought she could never again feel the kind of pain she'd felt those eight years ago at the news of Marie Clarice's death, when she'd learned firsthand how physical grief could be. All that time she'd kept it enclosed in a secret place inside that she allowed herself to visit only rarely and when she was alone. But now, here it was again—that incomprehensible, stabbing grief, surging from its hiding place, up from sleep and into her waking hours. In the night she'd dreamed of the body of her beautiful little son, wrapped in canvas, rocking on the waves. Marie Clarice, her face still that of the child she'd left behind, appeared beneath the waters and reached out her arms to pull her brother down into the dark sea of death. Marguerite closed her eyes again in an effort to stop the tears.

She had to get hold of herself. All those years ago, in Lorient, she had been alone, able to indulge her grief. Now, aboard ship, surrounded by people, many of them virtual strangers, she had to be stronger. *God help me endure this,* she thought. *Give me strength. And never let me lose another child. I don't think I could bear it.*

She thought of Margot and Louis, back in France with their own lives now, and Joseph waiting for her in America. She would miss them until they were together again, but she knew they were safe and alive. Nothing separated them but distance, and distance could be crossed. She was crossing it now, and soon she would be with Joseph again. She was sure she would see her children again. Except for …

No, I won't think of them. I'll think of what I have, not what I have lost. I'll turn my thoughts and my heart toward the future. Christophe and I will make a good home on the island we're bound for—on Sapelo—and we will cherish each other and what we've saved. Saved from that awful revolution that was destroying all she knew of France. She'd brought with her the china and silver purchased for the gracious manor house they'd bought near Lamballe, the miniature portraits she and Christophe had commissioned in Saint-Brieuc, and the blue silk gown she was wearing the night she met Christophe. They would create a new life in Georgia with the other French families who would be there soon.

We will *be happy,* she thought. *I will think of the coming years, not the past. I will not let myself look back on what I have lost. I will not dwell on it.* But she knew that even when the mind decided, the heart did not always obey.

Two weeks later

THE SHIP FINALLY DROPPED ANCHOR off the shore of Sapelo Island, after a brief stop in Savannah to deliver the Dechenaux family to their destination. Christophe's excitement was visible in his broad smile, his eyes crinkling with jubilation. He could hardly contain himself as crewmembers prepared to launch the little dinghy that would take them ashore. The winches creaked and the wooden boat bumped against the ship's hull as they lowered it by ropes.

Marguerite hadn't seen her husband so happy since their earliest days at the manor house in Brittany. She knew he was eager to show her the island's wonders about which he had boasted for months now, and she was eager to see them. He talked about it so much and so vividly that she felt already familiar with the live oaks, the resurrection ferns, and the majestic marshes. He was especially anxious for her to inspect the new house he'd designed himself.

"I hope you'll like it. It's rather small, I'm afraid, compared to La Ville-Hervé, but it should be comfortable. I didn't make it bigger because I wanted to be sure they could finish it before we returned. We can always add on."

"I'm sure it will be fine," she said. She was determined to like it, no matter what. Christophe was not usually so talkative, but she could hear the excitement and pride in his voice and feel his impatience with what he perceived to be the lackadaisical efforts of the crewmembers, who were bending their backs to row him, Marguerite, and little Henri to shore.

She, on the other hand, felt they were moving toward the island as quickly as the little dinghy could carry them. The late May air was soft and warm against her face, and the murky waters slapped at the sides of their boat as the crew dipped their oars into the sea again and again.

Little Henri sat in the bow, peering straight ahead through his father's spyglass, eagerly scanning the beach and watching their approach to land. Marguerite couldn't help but smile at the seriousness with which he examined the approaching shoreline. She remembered how the boy took to the sea like a veritable sailor, loving the weeks and weeks of endless ocean. In fact, he gained his sea legs almost at once and followed his father like a faithful puppy around the vessel. From time to time Christophe would take over at the helm, not usually the captain's job, just so he could let Henri help him steer. The boy's face would shine with excitement on these occasions. How alike they were—the same sharp blue eyes and narrow face, the same intensity of purpose, the same love of the restless ship.

MARGUERITE BREATHED A SIGH OF RELIEF when she was finally able to step off the boat and onto the sandy shore, littered as far as she could see with all sorts of seashells she had never seen before—some whorled and spiraled, and some flat and round, the color of sand. The land seemed to sway beneath her feet, as she tried to grow accustomed to its stillness. From a narrow road she hadn't noticed before between the dunes, a carriage was approaching with two figures side by side on the driver's seat.

"*Bonjour et bienvenus*," a young man, his skin tanned and his dark-blond hair and beard unkempt, called out as he jumped from the dusty, run-down carriage and waved his straw hat. "Welcome to Sapelo!"

"Marguerite," Christophe said, once the two men had greeted one another with kisses on both cheeks, "I would like to present Julien de Chappedelaine."

Marguerite held out her hand. Julien was not the dapper French nobleman she'd imagined. He looked more like a boyish peasant in his rumpled shirt and smudged breeches. But his manners were courtly enough as he bent to kiss her hand. She smiled and nodded, but her eyes darted past him as they caught the movement of the other figure that had jumped down from the carriage and stood uncertainly, watching the little scene.

Could that possibly be Joseph? Could he have changed so much in a year and a half? She felt rooted to the spot, as she shielded her eyes against the light with her free hand to see him better. He was taller than she'd expected, and his hair, bleached copper by the sun, hung almost to his shoulders. He was dirty, awkward-looking, and barefoot. Suddenly all those changes melted away, and she could see only her son.

"Joseph!" she called, breaking away from Christophe and Julien and running toward him, hitching up her skirts as she ran.

Five-year-old Henri, who had missed his brother terribly, followed her gaze. He outran her and lunged affectionately at his brother. The two boys, so nearly the same size, were already tussling on the sand by the time Marguerite reached them.

"*Maman,*" Joseph said with a grin. She noticed a new front tooth, half grown-in, that gave him an impish look. Pushing his younger brother aside, he stood up, ready to leap into her outstretched arms.

"Oh, how I have missed you, my darling boy," she said, kissing his tangled hair as she held him close.

"I've missed you too, *Maman,*" he said, hugging her tightly. Then, catching sight of Christophe and Julien walking up the beach toward them, he wriggled out of his mother's arms and stood to meet his father.

Christophe greeted his son formally, with a handshake and a pat on the shoulder. Joseph blinked at the sun's glare as he looked up at his father. "Welcome back, Sir."

"You've grown, boy," his father said. "I hope you've not given Julien too much trouble in my absence."

"No sir," he replied, looking now at his mother.

"He's been a fine lad," said Julien. "And he's learned a lot of English since he's been here. It's about all they speak in Savannah. He's a smart boy, just soaks it up."

Marguerite smiled proudly. Christophe gave him a brief nod before he changed the subject.

"Is there room for all of us in the carriage?" he asked. "I can't wait to show Marguerite our new Bel Air house."

"There is room in the carriage, but I must tell you ..." Julien began.

"You can tell us on the way. Let's go," said Christophe.

MARGUERITE HAD RARELY SEEN CHRISTOPHE so angry. His face was red, and he seemed to sputter for words. Only two stone chimneys, one of them unfinished, stood where their new home should have been.

Julien had informed them during the carriage drive that there were some delays on the house, but they hadn't expected that there would be no house at all.

"*Eh bien*, where will my family live?" Christophe fumed to Julien. "Why has nothing been done?"

"I couldn't check on it very often since it's on the south end of the island. I didn't have anyone to leave in charge up at High Point. We were also concerned that the site was perhaps too near the water," Julien said by way of explanation, "and we didn't want to continue until you were here to advise us."

"Nonsense," sputtered Christophe. "We discussed all this before I left. You're making excuses." He looked around him. There was little evidence of any progress at all since his departure. "Do you have the remotest idea at all what you are doing here?"

Julien drew himself up to his full height and set his jaw like a petulant adolescent. "Are you questioning my judgment, *Monsieur*?"

"As a matter of fact, I am," Christophe responded.

Marguerite listened anxiously to the interplay between the two men, remembering the silly things that could cause a duel in France. She'd heard of good men dying when such quarrels got out of control and one cutting remark led to another, until someone proclaimed an insult to his honor. Then he would demand satisfaction in the form of drawn swords or, more likely of late, pistols at dawn. She saw little point in such recriminations. What was done was done. Julien was obviously unreliable and inexperienced, and that was that. To go on and on about it got them nowhere. It was already obvious, she thought wearily, that they would be sleeping aboard ship again tonight.

But Christophe wouldn't let it lie. His face grew redder and redder and his voice louder and louder as he continued to berate Julien de Chappedelaine.

The two little boys looked nervous as they watched the scene, uncertainty clouding their eyes, looking from one man to the other. When the shouting finally ended, Christophe turned to his two sons. "*Allons.* Let's go. We'll sleep on the ship until I can decide what to do." Henri immediately came forward and took his father's outstretched hand. But Joseph held back, looking from Christophe to Julien.

Julien took the boy's hand. "Villehuchet's gone back to his family in France, so there's room for Jason to have his own bed at High Point," he said, referring to the communal house that had been built as soon as the men had first arrived on the island.

"Jason? His name is Joseph," said Christophe. "Did Villehuchet go back home because he couldn't stand living with you any longer?" he asked with rancor in his voice.

Julien decided to ignore the last cutting remark and to respond only to the issue of the boy's name. "Jason is a nickname, his American name. He likes it, don't you, boy?" said Julien.

Joseph nodded faintly. He watched his father's face with caution, but Marguerite detected an air of defiance in his eyes.

"The ship will be cramped. Let him stay here. Henri can stay too if he likes," Julien said amiably. "Jason will share his bed, won't you, boy?"

Marguerite saw Christophe's jaw tighten.

"Please, *Papa,*" Henri begged.

Christophe looked at Marguerite. She could almost read his thoughts, as he considered the matter, clenching and unclenching his fists. A night alone with her in the captain's quarters with no children nearby clearly appealed to him, but leaving his sons with Julien, with whom he was still furious, rankled.

Christophe said nothing for a moment. Finally, he released his breath and pursed his lips.

"*Eh bien, d'accord*," he agreed finally. "Tonight we get some rest. Tomorrow we decide what to do."

Chapter 11

June 1, 1792

Aboard the *Sappello*, anchored off shore at Sapelo Island, Georgia

MARGUERITE AWOKE ONCE MORE in Christophe's arms, stiff from having lain so long in the same position. For a moment she wondered where she was. The light filtering in through the two small portholes seemed somehow different from the light of the mid-Atlantic. Then she remembered—everything. During the night she had dreamed again of Marie Clarice and little Paul, how her sweet-faced daughter had reached out to embrace the tiny shroud that floated on the surface of the sea. *I will not cry this morning. I will not cry*, Marguerite thought, keeping her eyes tightly closed to hold in the tears that threatened behind her eyelids. *I will think of something else.*

But all else she could think of hardly dispelled her gloom. Nothing was going as they had hoped. This island, Sapelo, was definitely not the Eden Christophe had first described. When she had walked there, sandspurs clung to the tail of her dress, and insects too small to see bit at her ankles. And there was no house, as he had promised.

It isn't Christophe's fault, she reminded herself. *He is only trying to protect us. I will make the best of it and not add to his problems. At least we are together.* She lay still as long as she could, so as not to disturb her sleeping husband, but her legs were cramping, and she tried slowly to rearrange her limbs. Her movements roused Christophe, and he pulled her closer.

"*Bonjour, Chérie,*" he whispered, lifting her hair. She felt his warm breath on the nape of her neck as his lips gently explored just below the hairline.

"Hmmmm," she murmured, turning her body to face him and putting her arms around his waist. She planted a soft kiss first on his shoulder. "*Bonjour,*" she whispered, as his lips found hers.

After a good night's sleep and the pleasures of her body, Christophe appeared to be in a somewhat better mood, or so she judged from the contented smile on his face. She hoped he was now ready to tackle the problem of his family's lodging with less rancor. They were both upset at the turn of events, but there was nothing to be done except to find a solution. She slipped out of the bunk and tiptoed across the cabin in her bare feet to find her clothes.

"Must you leave me?" he asked. He sounded like a little boy in his longing.

"You know we have things we must attend to. It's already late, well past seven," she said. "We should breakfast and go ashore."

A shadow crossed his face, but he nodded, threw back the sheet, and swung his legs over the side of the bunk. "You're right. Let's see what that bastard Julien has come up with overnight."

THE TWO MEN SAT ON OPPOSITES sides of a table on the shaded porch of High Point house, glaring at one another. They had brought the table outside to try to catch a breeze in the hot, still morning. Marguerite sat perched on the front steps, fanning away a fly as she watched them, listening with apprehension to their strained conversation. Joseph and Henri, seeming oblivious to the tension, romped barefoot together in the sandy yard.

"So … what do you suggest?" Christophe asked Julien, clenching his hands before him on the table in an effort at self-control.

"You could all move into High Point house until we could get your house built," Julien suggested, his clear, tan face looking hopeful. "There are three beds. That should do for you, your boys, and your servants."

"And where would you sleep?"

"Well, I will be there as well, Jason and I. A pallet perhaps for the servants?"

"Don't call him Jason," Christophe said sharply. "And Joseph will sleep with his brother, not with you. How long will the house take?"

"Two months. Maybe three or four. It depends on the workers and the weather and getting the materials. And what else has to be done."

"And what will we do when your uncle arrives with his family? Won't we be rather crowded then?" Christophe's voice was tight with irony.

Julien shrugged, his boyish face perplexed, "I suppose so."

"What the hell have you been doing all this time that neither my house nor his has been built?"

He shrugged again. "Well, there were other priorities. We had to build fences and pens to keep in the animals." He gestured vaguely toward the wooden fences that roped across the island and the smaller pens, where a few pigs rooted about. "We had to build sheds and a salting house to store meat and dry fish …" His voice trailed off. "Those were essential."

"And our house was not?" Christophe asked bitterly.

Julien said nothing for a long time, as he traced the outline of a knothole on the pine tabletop with his index finger. Finally, he lifted his clear hazel eyes and looked steadily at Christophe.

"There have been problems," he said. "You must have noticed from your earlier visit that the men do not get along well."

It was true. Dumoussay and Chappedelaine had brought a few indentured Frenchmen who came over with them on the *Silvain* to labor alongside the slaves they purchased in Savannah upon arrival. The Frenchmen had agreed to work for three years in exchange for passage and room and board. After that they would be free.

It was not a good mix. That was evident from the beginning. The French workers adopted an air of superiority that rankled the black slaves, who were doing the very same jobs. Some of the Frenchmen had taken to drink whenever they could get their hands on any kind of liquor, and several of them were unruly drunks, ready to fight at the slightest offense. Christophe had seen sailors like these, but obviously Julien had no idea how to deal with them.

Reared by his mother in better times in a household full of servants where a butler was in charge of the staff and a personal valet shielded him from any practical considerations, Julien had no experience whatever in coping with those of a lower class than himself. And he was not good at it. The French workers, most of whom were older than he, mocked him behind his back, and the slaves grew increasingly discontented. Julien's only solution was to have the offenders whipped, but the brutal punishment drove some of them to run away or at least to try. Usually they were caught and returned, but their bitterness only increased.

Christophe was not sympathetic. "Even so," he said, "you can't expect us to live under those conditions for that long." Marguerite could see his face beginning to redden again. "I have a wife and children here. Aren't there any other options?"

"Well," Julien said, "you could go to Savannah. Dumoussay is there most of the time and could arrange lodging for you, or else you could live in the company house with him."

Christophe wrinkled his nose with distaste. Marguerite remembered the complaints he'd written about Savannah during his earlier visit to Georgia, when he, Chappedelaine, and Dumoussay had stopped there to purchase supplies and labor needed for the cultivation of Sapelo. While it was a hub of activity and government, it was crowded, with unpaved streets where goats and chickens roamed untethered and unfenced. The streets were often muddy, and buzzards swooped about devouring whatever filth humans and animals left behind. It was not a good place for young children, she surmised, even though it was the primary city in Georgia. And it sounded like exactly what they had wanted to escape when they bought the rural manor of La Ville Hervé.

Observing Christophe's reaction, Julien went on, "But if you want to be closer than Savannah, there is a house on the north end of Jekyl Island where you could live until your place is built."

"A house?" Christophe asked. "What kind of house?"

"I've only seen it once, but it looked sturdy. It's made of tabby, and it's two stories. I think it was built when the English troops were in the area before the American Revolution. People call it the Horton House. I'm not sure why, but I've heard there was an English major by that name who built it."

"What is tabby?" Marguerite asked.

"It's a mixture of lime, sand, shells, and water all mixed together. When it dries and hardens it's a strong building material that's used a lot here on the coast," Julien responded.

Marguerite had heard her husband speak of Jekyl Island only once, after his return to France from his first visit to Georgia. The original purchase by Dumoussay consisted of the islands of Sapelo, Cabretta, Blackbeard, and another island whose name she had forgotten. The seller was said to be a rather colorful man with the odd name of Don Juan McQueen. Later, Christophe told her, the strong-willed and determined Dumoussay bought another island called Jekyl to increase their land holdings in timber and wild horses. At the time he'd said no more about it, but she got the distinct impression that he'd never actually visited the place. In fact, at one point, she recalled, he mentioned that the investors were already talking about selling it to raise money. Evidently, they had not done so.

"It's just a couple of islands south of here. You could sail from there up to Sapelo in that ship of yours in just a few hours, depending on tides and wind," Julien said. "That way you could supervise the work yourself, at least from time to time. It's not far by water."

Christophe pursed his lips before he turned to Marguerite. "Shall we take a look at that?"

She nodded, frowning slightly. "Does anyone else live there?" she asked.

"Not now," Julien said. "Until we bought it, the owner, a man named Richard Leake, kept an overseer there, but he moved him out when we took over."

"You mean, we'd be there all alone?" she asked. The prospect was daunting. She'd been promised the female companionship of other investors' wives. She had lived in a modest but gracious household of women when she was with her mother in Mauritius, and she missed the constant presence of Margot, whatever her shortcomings. Christophe had told Marguerite they would all live on Sapelo and make a new life in a completely French setting. That was the promise. It was what he too had been led to expect, but they both knew before they left France that there would be no other French women, except the servants, at Sapelo, at least not at first. What difference would it make if they were at Jekyl?

"Well, we'd have each other and the boys ... and Françoise and Marie will be there to keep you company," Christophe said. They had originally planned to bring Mustafa and Nanon with them to America, but Mustafa had vanished into the countryside two weeks before their departure. The black valet always prided himself on being a man of dignity, and, having heard about the enslavement of Africans in America, he preferred to take his chances in revolutionary France rather than risk becoming a field hand without pay. Nanon refused to come as well, fearing the sea voyage, and choosing instead to return to her impoverished family in Lorient.

They had chosen Françoise to replace her. She was a mature but uneducated woman, who had been hired in Lamballe to work as a chambermaid at La Ville Hervé. Marie was a sixteen-year-old village girl from Dahouët, who was eager for adventure and agreed to come along to help care for the baby, though Sophie Dechenaux had relieved her of much of her duty on the ship. Marie's parents were happy to have one less mouth to feed. Christophe decided not to try to replace Mustafa on such short notice. He could brush his own jackets if he had to.

Neither of the new servant women was very stimulating company, Marguerite thought. Françoise spoke only when she was obliged to, and Marie's idea of conversation was mindless chatter. But they were better than nothing, Marguerite supposed, if Christophe decided to take the lodgings at Jekyl. At least they could live as a family.

He sat quietly for several minutes, considering his options. Finally, he glanced at her and said, "It's only for a short while, Marguerite." He sounded apologetic. "I think we should sail down and have a look. If it's satisfactory, we'll stay." Then he narrowed his eyes and turned toward Julien, "If not, we'll be back by tomorrow, and the work on my house had better be started by then."

Julien nodded, looking relieved. "*Je comprends,*" he said. "I understand."

Marguerite wondered if he really did.

Chapter 12

Marguerite watched the Georgia coastline unfold in a series of small islands and rivulets that flowed gently into the sea. One wide-mouthed river that Christophe called the Altamaha, after consulting his map, looked inviting to explore. But for the moment, she had no real desire to explore anything. She just wanted to get off this vessel and find a place to live.

When Jekyl Island finally appeared on the horizon, it looked like a deserted isle of green. All she could see was a sandy shore and an expanse of trees. They dropped anchor in the wide sound that separated the north end of Jekyl from the south end of St. Simons Island, its currents flowing into the sea from the waterway that led to the nearby port of Brunswick. Christophe ordered the dinghy to be lowered at once so that he and his family could go ashore. Two of the sailors manned the oars to row them to the island. They reached the beach in only a few minutes, and while the sailors pulled the dinghy up onto the sand, Marguerite glanced about. She could see no house, no sign of life, past or present.

"Julien said the house was on the north end of the island," Christophe reminded everyone. He commanded the sailors and the boys to scout about to look for it. Then he himself walked into the woods, veering off in a different direction, leaving Marguerite alone on the beach beside the wooden boat.

She stood there, looking around at the stark fallen trees, their bare trunks and branches, smooth and dark against the gray water, seeming to underscore the lack of life on the island. But slowly she became aware of movement at her feet. Tiny, almost invisible crabs scuttled about, suddenly appearing or vanishing into tiny holes in the sand. At first they frightened her, until she realized that they were more afraid of her than she was of them. A large buck, his antlers branching majestically above his head, stood at the edge of the forest, watching her. A doe and two fawns grazed among the trees behind him. Then, she caught a movement from the corner of her eye—a fish, glinting silver in the sun, leapt from the water and splashed again into the sea. At almost the same moment, a gray seabird she had never seen before swept by her to land on one of the black branches of a fallen tree protruding upward from the sand. Perhaps there was more life here than she first thought. *But no people.*

She looked longingly toward St. Simons, which, according to Christophe, was home already to a number of families. Perhaps there she could find some compatible souls, some friends, but the waterway was wide and the separation great. And those who lived there, he'd told her, were, for the most part, English and Scottish, and she spoke almost no English. The distance might be greater than she thought.

At least it's peaceful here, she reminded herself. *And it's not much more isolated than we were at La Ville Hervé.* But there at least she could take a carriage to go into Lamballe or visit neighbors on other estates, which she did only occasionally. She had been pregnant so much of the time she lived there, and she'd had Margot and Nanon, who were both intelligent companions, for company. On the other hand, she had become so accustomed to solitude during Christophe's sea voyages and while Margot was away at school that she had learned to enjoy the sounds of birds, wind, and distant thunder almost, though still not quite as much, as the human voice. Here, there was also the gentle lapping of the sea against the shore.

Ten minutes passed. She was beginning to feel the sun burning hot on her back when she heard her son Joseph's voice.

"We found it, *Maman*, this way!" He stood just outside the line of trees, beckoning vigorously. She hurried across the beach toward her son, who stood waiting for her.

When she reached his side, he took her hand. "It's got a red roof, *Maman*," he said. "It's not big like our house in France, but it's got two stories. I peeked in a window, and there's some furniture. It's even got a garden ... sort of."

Marguerite almost tripped over the tangle of brambles and vines as she hurried through the forest in the direction her excited son was tugging her. Finally, in perhaps a quarter of a mile, she reached a wide clearing. There stood a rather plain two-storied house, overlooking a wide marsh that stretched toward the mainland. Weeds grew tall around the front door, and vines climbed up the outer walls. A large live oak tree stood at the right front corner. As she and Joseph walked toward the back of the house, where he wanted to show her the garden, she could see a rickety two-story wooden porch facing the woods. Christophe stood there, examining the shaky boards.

The walls of the house looked like sand-colored stucco, but seashells peeked out where the surface had chipped away. She had never seen anything quite like it before.

"Is this what they call tabby?" she asked.

"Yes, it's pretty common here. We're planning to use it at Sapelo to build Bel Air. The slaves know how to mix it."

"Can we go inside?" she asked.

"Of course."

They walked back to the front of the house, and Christophe, pulling from his pocket the large brass key that Julien had given him, inserted it into the lock. When he opened the door, Marguerite peered inside. Joseph was right. There was some furniture in the two rooms on the first floor, but not much. From the front door opening she could see large fireplaces at both ends of the house, a dusty sofa and a chair in what passed for a *salon*, as well as a wooden table with four unmatched chairs in the kitchen. Well, it was a start. If they stayed here for only a few months, it might be adequate.

For such a short time it was hardly worth bringing from the ship all the furniture they'd loaded in Dahouët. Christophe had not allowed her to bring very many of their possessions on the voyage in any case. He didn't want to slow the vessel down with too much weight. But she managed to pack her Limoges china and the silverware she had bought in Lorient, as well as her prized glassware with a teardrop bubble in each stem that she feared would be hard to replace in Georgia. She realized now how out of place it would be here.

Essentials like clothing, bed linens, blankets, and cooking pots were tucked away in trunks stashed in the ship's hold. She had insisted on packing a few rolled-up carpets and a single tapestry, a hunt scene from Beauvais, though her husband had made her leave behind many others she would like to have brought with her. They had transported none of the gilded furniture from the *salon* or the *salle à manger*. He'd thought the pieces too valuable to subject to the ocean voyage for a temporary move to America. He could only trust that they would be waiting when he and his family returned to France after all the upheaval ended. His two sisters, who were unwilling to leave France, had agreed to serve as tenant-caretakers in their absence. Marguerite had carefully packed small items, like their miniature portraits, snuffboxes, jewelry, and her precious books to bring along.

They didn't take up much room. But they were something to help her feel she could still make a home and enjoy a civilized life, even in this raw new country.

"The house could use a good cleaning and some fixing up," Christophe said. "We won't bother with many repairs, since we'll be here such a short time. But we'll set the servants to cleaning right away ... if the house suits you, Marguerite."

"It will do, I think," she said. He looked relieved. "I assume there are beds upstairs." She and Christophe, holding hands, mounted the wooden stairs together. There were two bedrooms, with one double bed each. They had brought bedsteads from France as well and could certainly make do.

"We can share one room and let the boys have the other. The maids can sleep on pallets in the boys' room," Christophe said. The sailors who had survived the voyage would stay on the ship for as long as he needed them and was willing to pay. That was understood. "At least it's better than one room for us all at Sapelo," he said. She nodded in agreement.

"For a short while, at least," she said.

"We'll have to patch the tile roof and the windows," he said, pointing out water spots on the upstairs ceiling and the broken panes of crude glass. "The crew can handle that."

THE FIRST NIGHT IN THE TABBY HOUSE was a restless one for Marguerite. Despite the soothing sounds of the wind soughing in the trees, the steady roar of breaking waves, and water lapping against the shore of the little creek, she lay awake, disturbed by the limbs of the live oak just outside their window scraping against the house as the wind blew. Occasional unfamiliar animal sounds from the forest pierced whatever sleep she tried to grasp. Toward morning, however, as the wind died down and the animal calls were replaced by morning birdsong, she drifted into a peaceful slumber beside her sleeping husband.

FRANÇOISE AND MARIE HAD SPENT the previous afternoon airing and beating mattresses and making beds. Now they set to work scrubbing floors and woodwork, dusting what little furniture was in the house, brushing away spider webs, and washing the grimy windows. Christophe determined what needed to be done, oversaw the work, and assigned tasks to everyone. The porch was in such disrepair that Marguerite considered it dangerous, so her husband brought the ship's carpenter ashore to prop up sagging beams and secure loose boards. Even the boys were put to work pulling weeds and vines away from the front door and ridding the house of nests where mice and even small birds had taken up residence. Françoise and Marie were too afraid to do it themselves, but Joseph and Henri, eager to show their courage, undertook the job with enthusiasm. Marguerite spent her time directing the placement of items the sailors brought in from the ship, things the family required for comfort and daily life—bed linens, cooking pans, chamber pots, oil lamps, and carpets. Her good china and crystal and anything else that wasn't absolutely essential remained packed away in the ship's hold. They would eat for a time off the ship's tin plates and pewter ware.

IT TOOK NEARLY A WEEK FOR EVERYTHING to be done to Christophe's satisfaction. Once it was finished, he kissed Marguerite with enthusiasm and set sail for Sapelo before dawn to check the progress on the Bel Air house. Marguerite remained behind with the children on Jekyl. As she surveyed the results of their cleaning, she thought, *it's still primitive, but it looks reasonably decent, all things considered.* She was cheered by Christophe's assurance that, before the end of the summer, they would surely move to their new house on Sapelo. She could live with the sparse furnishings until then. All it needed was a touch of beauty to make it livable. Perhaps she and the boys could find some wildflowers to decorate the table and the fireplace mantles.

She set out with the children after breakfast to explore the north end of the island, while Marie and Françoise rummaged through the food that still remained from the sea voyage to find something left to prepare for the day's meals. Soon the men would have to go hunting for meat and they would have to replenish their supplies.

Wildflowers Marguerite had never seen before grew in abundance on the edge of the marshes, in the fertile woods, and in the sunnier meadows, where, judging from the lack of trees, earlier residents had grazed livestock or perhaps planted a crop of some sort. Along the marshes they collected an armful of flowers she would later learn to call *swamp rose mallow* and *red cardinal flowers*, which they carried to Marie so that she could put them in a container of water.

Eager to explore farther, Marguerite and the boys followed a road, overgrown with weeds, which led from the house into the woods.

"This must be a road that Major Horton made," Marguerite said. "He was the man who built the house," she reminded the boys.

In a shady grove, penetrated only sporadically by sunlight, they came upon a bed of white lilies. Marguerite paused only briefly to admire them and breathe in their subtle scent. Perhaps they would gather a few as they returned. But for now they wanted to follow the road to wherever it led.

It opened onto a wide expanse of beach on the east side of the island. The strand, littered with shells of all sizes and shapes, was hard enough to serve as a road. Flocks of seabirds rose like a black cloud into the sky as she and the boys approached. The waves of the ocean broke with gentle rhythms on the shore. Marguerite stood entranced. As far as she could see to the south, the sandy beach spread before her. It was nothing like the small, rocky beaches she'd known in Brittany. She picked up a whelk shell and ran her finger across the polished surface of its rose-colored wall, which led with a graceful spiral to its inner chamber. It was magnificent, like a gift left by God upon the shore.

"Look at this, *Maman*," Henri said, holding up a round shell, bleached white in the sun. It had small perforations and a delicate design and looked like a small flat crêpe.

"How beautiful," she said. The beach was a treasure trove, and Joseph and Henri began to gather all sorts of shells, enough to fill the apron she was wearing. Before she knew it, nearly an hour had passed.

"Boys, that's enough." She laughed. "We still have to gather our flowers." Reluctantly, they all turned back toward the road that led through the woods. When they passed the shady grove once more, they gathered some of the lilies, which Joseph cradled gently in his arms, since his mother's apron was already full of shells. Henri ran on ahead to share the news of their discoveries with Françoise and Marie.

THE LILIES SPREAD THEIR DELICATE FRAGRANCE throughout the house. All the flowers and shells lined up on the mantle and windowsills gave it a cheerful look.

After their midday meal, Marguerite settled with her sons at the cleared table to begin their lessons. They were old enough now, at five and six, to begin to learn to read and cipher. She was determined that the boys would grow up with some learning, and since there was no school at either Jekyl or Sapelo, she would have to be their teacher— for now, at least—even though her own education was limited.

They had hardly begun when she heard a man's voice outside. He was speaking in English. "Hello ... Is anyone home?"

The voice was such a surprise that she nearly dropped the book she was holding before she gathered her wits about her and went to the front door.

A tall young man, who appeared to be about eighteen or nineteen, stood there. His dark hair hung loosely about his shoulders, and he peered at her expectantly with bright blue eyes shadowed by heavy eyebrows that gave his face a somber look. But he was smiling.

"*Bonjour, Monsieur,*" she greeted him.

"Ah ... French." His eyes grew serious. "*Bonjour, Madame.* I'm afraid I'm not very good at speaking French." Marguerite looked at him without comprehending. Oh, why hadn't she bothered to learn more English before coming to America? Suddenly Joseph was at her side.

"Hello, sir, my mother does not speak English. May I help you?" He sounded so grown-up, while she felt like a child.

"Hello there, young fellow. I'm Thomas Spalding from over on St. Simons Island. My father saw your boat arrive a few days ago and sent me over to pay our respects and invite you to visit us whenever you can. We live just across the sound at a plantation we call Orange Grove at the south end of the island. He gestured vaguely to the neighboring island to the north.

Four black men, evidently his oarsmen, sat outside under the trees to wait for their young master. Joseph translated as best he could for his mother, who could only smile and nod at her guest. She gestured for the man to come inside.

"Is your father at home?" young Spalding asked Joseph. The boy explained that he had gone to Sapelo Island.

"Oh, I'm so sorry I missed him. He must have left very early, for no one reported a ship passing by the island today."

"Oh, yes. He left before daylight," Joseph said.

"Perhaps I should come back another day ..." Thomas Spalding said, but Marguerite was already motioning him to come in and sit down and gave Françoise the order to prepare some tea. He obviously felt a bit awkward, but he smiled at her and did as she bid.

"Well, young lad," he said to Joseph, "you will have to serve as interpreter then. What is your name?"

"Joseph du Bignon, sir."

"And you are from France?"

"*Oui, monsieur.* From Bretagne ... Brittany."

"I hear there are troubles in your country just now."

"*Oui, monsieur.* It is why we come to America."

"And how is it that you speak English but your mother does not?"

"I have been in Georgia for one year already, *Monsieur.* She just arrived."

"Please ask your mother if there is anything my family can do to help her or your father since they are so new here."

Joseph did as he asked and waited for her reply.

"She says you are most kind, sir. She is curious about where one might purchase food and supplies."

"Well, now," said Thomas, his brow furrowed. "The closest place is a small store in Frederica on St. Simons Island. You might be able to find some things you need in Brunswick, the town on the mainland across the marshes from Jekyl and St. Simons. It really isn't much of a town, just a deepwater port. In fact, George Washington recognized it in 1789 as one of the five major ports of entry into the colonies. My father says we are fortunate to have it so close by, without having to live there." He gave a wry smile, but his overall look gave the impression of a serious young man.

Joseph told his mother what the man had said. Five-year-old Henri watched the entire exchange with silent interest and obvious admiration for his brother.

"*Ah, c'est bien,*" Marguerite said. "*Très bien. Merci beaucoup.*"

"She's glad to know all that," Joseph said. "She says thank you."

"My father was interested in knowing whether or not you intend to plant cotton here. If so, he would like to offer his assistance and perhaps some starter seed for the new Sea Island cotton."

Joseph translated for his mother, who expressed her thanks but replied they would not be here beyond the summer, but would be moving to Sapelo.

"Ah, Sapelo. We had all hoped you'd be staying here. This island used to belong to my father's friend, Richard Leake, who has a most delightful daughter named Sarah. We call her Sally." The young man blushed, as he said her name. Marguerite noticed the rising color in his face at the word "Sarah," and she smiled, wondering what he had said about the young lady.

"The two of them, my father and Mr. Leake, were the first gentlemen around here to grow Sea Island cotton. We think it's the highest quality and the best crop for the climate."

Joseph had to stop and think before he relayed the information to his mother, who asked whether Mr. Leake had once owned this house.

"Yes," said Thomas Spalding. "But he never actually lived here. This was the home of his father-in-law, a man named Clement Martin. As you probably know, it was built by an English officer named William Horton." He looked at Marguerite as he spoke slowly, accompanying his words with gestures, as though he could make her understand. Still, he paused frequently to let Joseph translate before continuing.

"He was the commander at Fort Frederica on St. Simons. At least that's what my father says. It was all so long ago—before I was born."

Marguerite could see that her son was having trouble remembering everything the man said and was struggling to explain it in French. His English vocabulary was still limited, and he was obviously doing the best he could. She felt embarrassed that her six-year-old son had to bear the burden. *I will learn to speak English*, she vowed to herself for the first time. Thus far, she had resisted, thinking that the whole world should speak French, which she considered the most important language in the world. Even Christophe knew more English than she did. He had learned a good bit during his seafaring days and his earlier trip to Sapelo, and he had made much more effort than she to learn the language, when he decided to move to America. She had wondered why she should bother, if she was going to be living in a French community. But now she could see that she would need it if she were to live in this country and have neighbors like the Spaldings.

She smiled and nodded, but she felt foolish and frustrated in her inability to communicate with this nice young man, who was obviously trying to be neighborly.

Françoise brought the tea, and Marguerite poured a cup for Thomas Spalding and herself. He took a sip of the warm liquid and turned to his hostess.

"*Le ... thé ... est ... bon,*" he said with a congenial smile. Marguerite beamed at his efforts to tell her the tea was good, which she suspected were remnants of the language studied long ago in a classroom or with a tutor. "I shall have to brush up on my French," he said soberly at his feeble attempt to communicate in *her* language.

"*Dis-lui que j'ai l'intention d'apprendre l'anglais,*" Marguerite said to Joseph. She had never seen such a serious-looking young man as Thomas Spalding.

"Maman says to tell you she plans to learn English," the boy said.

"Excellent!" said Spalding, and then added with a French pronunciation and almost a smile, "*Excellent!*"

He didn't stay long. Joseph was obviously growing weary in his role as translator, and Henri too was getting restless. As soon as the young man finished his tea, he rose and said, "I must get home and report the news to my father. Please tell Mr. du Bignon that I'm sorry I missed him. And whenever it's convenient, my parents would welcome a visit from your family. It's a short distance across the sound. We're the first plantation at the south end."

"I will tell him, *Monsieur*," the boy said.

The young man took Marguerite's hand and bowed slightly. "It was delightful to meet you, *Madame*, and I hope to have the pleasure of seeing you again soon and meeting your husband."

Marguerite sensed a genial farewell from his expression and tone, and without waiting for a translation, she replied, echoing his pleasure at meeting her and welcoming him back anytime. "*C'était un plaisir, monsieur. Donnez mes compliments à vos parents. J'espère vous revoir bientôt, et vous serez toujours bienvenu ici.*"

They both looked at Joseph for an affirmation that they were understanding each other. When the boy had expressed, as best he could, their mutual pleasure and offers of hospitality, as well as their greetings to those not present, Thomas Spalding smiled broadly and said, "Well then, I must go."

He offered a cordial bow to Madame du Bignon and shook hands with Joseph. He saluted Henri and then turned toward his waiting oarsmen, gesturing for them to ready the boat. Marguerite and Joseph watched from the porch as the men walked toward the creek that flowed toward the great Turtle River. Their narrow wooden boat, which looked as though it had been hollowed from a tree trunk and polished to perfection, was tied to the small landing Christophe had found the day they arrived. She smiled, remembering his words.

"We'll call this Marguerite's Landing," he had announced, as he tied up the dinghy they had brought around to the landing. It had made her feel like Eve in the Garden of Eden, with her Adam naming the things he encountered for the first time.

Thomas Spalding waved from the dock, and she and Joseph waved back. The oarsmen began to pull, chanting in unison, and the boat sliced through the water more rapidly than she would ever have expected.

Our first visitor, Marguerite thought, squeezing Joseph's hand. *And such a charming young man. Perhaps life here will be pleasant after all.* Clearly there were friends to discover on the other side of the sound. If Thomas Spalding was any indication of the quality of the people there, she looked forward to meeting them.

Chapter 13

WHEN SPALDING DEPARTED, Marguerite was relieved to return wholly to French. She hugged Joseph. "I'm so proud of you, son. What would I have done without you here today?" The boy smiled at her approval and stuck his tongue out at his brother, who returned the gesture.

"We will all learn English. Joseph, you will have to be our teacher for a little while so that Henri and I can catch up with you."

The boy took his role as teacher very seriously and went about for the rest of the day pointing at objects and telling his brother and mother their names in English.

"Table," he said, with great seriousness. "Chair … flower … door."

They would always repeat after him, but it soon became obvious to Marguerite that Henri could remember all the words better than she could, even though he was far less interested. Fortunately, among the books she and Christophe had brought was an English primer. She took it out that very night to begin to study the language she obviously needed to know.

CHRISTOPHE RETURNED THE NEXT DAY, somewhat mollified, to report that the slave workers, who were clearly more efficient and less quarrelsome than the Frenchmen hired to help them, were beginning to gather materials to lay the foundations of the house.

"They seem quite capable. I wish I could say the same for Julien, who is rather lax about overseeing the labor. I'll have to return at least once a week to make sure the work is being done properly," he told her.

"We had a visitor while you were gone," Marguerite told her husband.

"A visitor?"

"A man named Thomas Spalding from St. Simons Island," she said.

"*Ah, oui*, young Spalding. A Scotsman. Julien has mentioned his father—James Spalding. There are many Scotsmen in this area, especially up around Darien. What did he want?"

"Just to be neighborly. Joseph was our interpreter." She beamed with pride.

"Is that so? Well, perhaps the boy is good for something after all," Christophe said with indifference, gazing intently at the labels on several bottles of wine he had brought ashore.

"How can you say such a thing? He's a fine boy."

"He'll never make a seaman, that's certain," he told her, disdain in his voice, as he selected a bottle of red Bordeaux to open.

"There are other ways to make a living in the world," she said, annoyed at his judgmental dismissal of their son. Suddenly, she realized that Joseph had come up behind her and heard his father's words. Tears stood in the boy's eyes, and he turned away and rushed out the back door.

"Now see what you've done," she said to her husband as she turned to follow her son.

"He needs to grow a thicker skin and stop acting like a baby," she heard Christophe say as she trailed Joseph out the back door. The boy ran toward the shelter of the woods. He stopped just inside the tree line and was wiping his nose on the tail of his shirt when she caught up to him.

"Joseph, darling, don't cry. He didn't mean anything." She put her hand on his shoulder.

"Why doesn't he like me any more, *Maman*?" Joseph asked, choking out the words between sobs.

"He loves you very much, *chéri*. He just doesn't know how to express it. Sometimes men get like that when they have lived in a world of men for so long. Remember, he was on a ship for years at a time with only rough sailors for company. He doesn't mean to be gruff."

"Will I be like him when I grow up?"

"I don't think so, Joseph. You are a very sensitive boy. All people are different. Just try to understand your father. His life has been hard, and he was often forced to hide his feelings."

"He isn't like that with you, *Maman*," the boy said.

"It's different between men and women," his mother said. "But you're a boy. He's trying to toughen you up for what he sees as a hard world."

"I think he's just being mean. He doesn't like me any more."

"Joseph, that's not true. I don't want you to say such things about your father. Just try to understand him."

The boy looked doubtful, but he whispered, "I'll try, *Maman*."

Marguerite reached out and took him in her arms to give him a reassuring hug. She held her son tightly until his tears no longer fell.

When she and Joseph walked back into the house, hand in hand, Christophe was gone.

THAT NIGHT, AFTER THE BOYS WERE IN BED, the servants bustled about the kitchen cleaning the dinner dishes. Christophe asked that his evening brandy be served on the newly repaired porch to escape the heat inside and the servants' clatter from the kitchen. Marguerite joined him, and together they sat in the quiet darkness enjoying the cool night air. He had spoken little throughout dinner. Now, he said to Marguerite in a quiet but firm voice, "You mustn't coddle the boy."

"He's only six years old, Christophe. Sometimes children need a bit of coddling. You should try being kinder to him. I know you're upset, but you mustn't take out your anger with Julien on Joseph."

"I don't think that's what I'm doing, Marguerite. He has to learn to be a man."

"I agree, just not yet. Give him time to be a child first," she said.

"He must learn from early childhood what is expected of men."

"Perhaps so, Christophe, but he also needs to know his father loves him."

Christophe did not answer. He sat sipping his brandy and staring into the darkness as if he might find there the agreement he sought.

SHE WILL NEVER UNDERSTAND, HE THOUGHT. *She is soft, as women are.* But in his heart he felt a sting of truth. Almost everything the boy did seemed to irritate him now. He had been annoyed by the fact that Joseph seemed to prefer Julien to his father. He was angry that Julien had the audacity to give the boy a new name in his absence and that Joseph seemed pleased to be Jason, even to prefer it to his own name. Julien bragged that it was his American name and that the boy was half-American now.

Well, he will be Joseph in this household, Christophe thought with determination. The fact that Joseph now spoke English better than his father became an annoyance when the boy would sometimes correct him. His feelings of irritation with the boy had all begun, he knew, on their trip aboard the *Silvain*, when Joseph vomited on deck the first day out, and the sailors laughed not only at the boy, but at his father as well.

"Is this one a chip off *your* old block, Christophe?" they jeered, having the audacity to call him by his first name. He knew some of them from previous voyages, but the liberty they took in addressing him with such familiarity now that he wasn't their captain was infuriating. They seemed to see the weakness of the son as a reflection of the father.

Only Julien had shown any real sympathy to the boy. Christophe could hardly believe his son's inability to adjust to the motion of the waves. He was sick throughout the entire voyage, and his father was thoroughly disgusted by his weakness. By the time they reached Georgia, the boy could hardly walk, and Christophe, to his shame, had been compelled to carry him ashore—or leave him there, which he knew he could not do.

The sailors smirked as he passed by, the boy in one arm, his duffel in another. "I'll come back for the rest," he muttered as he walked past the ship's captain. The man nodded and turned back to the roster he had been studying.

Once ashore on Sapelo, Julien treated the boy with tenderness, encouraging him to rest a while each day and eat soup and bread until he felt better. Joseph responded to that mollycoddling with an all too obvious affection. Christophe openly mocked his son's reaction. He knew Julien to be the only son of a mother who had lost her husband when their child was very young. She had raised her son in a household of women. In France, he had shown impeccable manners and fine taste in clothing, but Christophe had had no earlier opportunity to observe him in a more natural environment, one without the formalities required by the French aristocracy to which Julien belonged. Now, at Sapelo, he could see the young man for the fop he truly was, even though on the island he was disheveled and careless in his dress. But the womanly tenderness he showed to Joseph, and which Christophe utterly despised, revealed his true nature. Joseph, on the other hand, grew fonder of Julien by the day.

When the time came for Christophe to return to France for the rest of his family, he was almost relieved when Julien offered to look after the boy. He didn't want another crossing like the last one. Nor did he want to show the boy off to any more of his seafaring friends. It would no doubt be worse than before. *Chappedelaine's turned my boy into a complete milksop like him,* Christophe thought. Thus, for reasons only he understood, he agreed to leave Joseph behind, but decided that, upon his return, he must toughen his son up, whatever it took.

But still, he felt a touch of jealousy at the thought that Joseph had let himself *become* Jason, that he liked being Jason, that he seemed to prefer Julien to his own father. *It is better,* he thought, *that we are here on Jekyl, away from his influence.*

Christophe gulped the last swallow of brandy, put his glass down hard on the table, rose and bid Marguerite good night with a curt *"Bonne nuit,"* and went abruptly up to bed, leaving her alone on the dark porch with her own thoughts.

WHEN SHE FINALLY WENT UP TO BED, Christophe was lying on his side away from the middle of the mattress. She suspected he was only pretending to be asleep and that he was hoping she might reach out to him so that they could mend their quarrel by making love as they so often did. But she did not reach out. Instead, she blew out the candle and went to sleep.

Chapter 14

AT FIRST CHRISTOPHE MADE NO EFFORT TO EXPLORE Jekyl Island since they would be there such a short time. His first priority was his trips to Sapelo to oversee the construction of Bel Air, which was progressing all too slowly in his view. He hardly wanted to bother about Jekyl, but the boys kept wandering about the island and reporting all sorts of interesting things they found—open fields that had once been cultivated, tabby outbuildings, wooden cabins near a small pond by the road Captain Horton had built. Finally, bored with the lackadaisical progress at Sapelo, Christophe's curiosity got the better of him, and he began to join Henri on long treks through the woods to let the boy show him the discoveries he and Joseph made.

Joseph usually stayed with Marguerite on such occasions, making the excuse that he needed to help his mother with her English or in her garden. The two of them worked together in back of the house to replant the small plot of earth that showed signs of having once been an herb garden. Christophe suggested it was a waste of effort since they would be here such a short time, but Marguerite felt the need to have her own garden.

"It's a pleasant task with Joseph here to help," she said. Back in France, a gardener had done the digging and planting, while she only supervised, but here, she and her son did all the work themselves. Christophe suggested they might buy a slave or two to help out.

"I don't like the idea of owning other people," she said. "And I rather enjoy working in my garden. It gives me a sense of satisfaction." In her own way, she was also trying to gain back all the time she had lost with her son when Christophe had taken him to America and left him there. She enjoyed these hours alone with Joseph now.

THE SAILORS ON THE *Sappello* were getting restless. Christophe had not paid them since their arrival. Although they had a place to sleep in their hammocks aboard ship and food to eat, much of which they had to hunt themselves, they were getting more and more disgruntled. Their weekly trips to Sapelo were hardly enough to keep them happy, and they were beginning to demand their wages.

"If I pay them," Christophe told Marguerite, "I suspect that some of them, maybe all, would jump ship and head for Brunswick or Savannah to look for other work. Right now I can't do without them."

She felt sympathy for the sailors, but she understood Christophe's hesitation. The only hold he had over them was their unpaid wages. On the island, the sailors were free to leave the ship, as long as they remained on the island to hunt or fish. There were plenty of deer, wild turkeys, and pigs, even a few stray cattle, and fish were abundant in the tidal streams. After one of them was viciously attacked by a boar, however, the sailors became afraid of the wild pigs. The sailor's leg was badly gashed. Marguerite bathed and bound the wound, changing the bandage every day until it healed. But the incident made the other men dubious about hunting wild hogs. Fortunately, there were plenty of less menacing deer, turkeys, and fish, so everyone ate reasonably well.

Some of the sailors caught the wild horses that roamed the island and tried to ride them. They were stubby and scruffy little beasts, but eventually several of them were tamed enough even for the children to ride, which helped them with their exploration of the island. They came home with arrowheads, broken pottery, English buttons, and once a tin cup on which were scratched the initials R.D.

Christophe had begun to take increasingly frequent treks through the woods with his younger son, and Marguerite was pleased that he seemed to enjoy them. He talked with enthusiasm about their excursions and occasionally even urged Joseph to come along. He had tried to be kinder to the boy in recent weeks, but Joseph, always politely, refused to go, which did not endear him with his father. Henri on the other hand led his father to several outbuildings the boys had discovered within a mile or so of the house and some wooden cabins with dirt floors that Christophe assumed once housed the slaves of previous owners. They all showed signs of needed repair, he told Marguerite, but the essential requirements for a working plantation seemed to be already in place.

"Perhaps I could set the sailors to doing some of the repairs. It would keep them busy and might increase the value of the island if the Sapelo group decided at some point to sell it." Marguerite listened to his suggestions and nodded at various points. She was delighted with his new enthusiasm for the island.

Christophe reported that fields were overgrown with weeds and decayed cotton stalks, but that they had been cleared of trees, and readying them for planting would not be too difficult.

"Maybe I could talk Julien into letting me bring some of the Sapelo slaves here to get the fields ready for cultivation. No need to let the land go to waste," he told her.

EACH TIME HE RETURNED FROM SAPELO, Christophe seemed more and more upset about the situation there. As the summer stretched on and the heat became more intense, the slaves and French workers alike began to move about like snails, he said. As a consequence, by the beginning of fall the Bel Air house, even under his supervision, was still barely begun, while Marguerite's herb garden on Jekyl, fenced now to keep out the deer and rabbits, was thriving. She listened sympathetically to Christophe's complaints—a lack of building materials, which the incompetent Julien frequently failed to order, sick workers, or workers needed somewhere else. There was always some excuse. Julien was also supposed to be building a house for his uncle, who was expected to arrive any day now with his family, but as yet, not even the foundation had been completed. Christophe grumbled constantly to Marguerite about the young man's ineptness at directing the workers and what he called his "womanly ways." He had taken to calling him, not Julien, but rather by his family name, to which he added a flavor of annoyance.

"Chappedelaine takes offense at the slightest criticism, then disappears into the High Point house and pouts for the rest of the afternoon. How can we expect ever to get anything done? I'm fed up with the entire thing."

Marguerite was sympathetic, but she was almost glad of the slow progress. She was beginning to like Jekyl more and more. Her herb garden, grown from seeds and cuttings she had brought from France, was doing splendidly, and she kept it carefully watered and weeded. The family was already beginning to enjoy the basil, chives, tarragon, mint, and parsley with which they could now flavor and garnish their meals. Now she was starting to transplant some of the blooming plants from the woods and marshes to see if she could grow a flower garden near the house. The more Christophe complained about the quarrelsome atmosphere at Sapelo, the less eager she was to move there. From his descriptions, it sounded as though Julien was also sick to death of the entire project and was growing increasingly angry that their partner Dumoussay, whom she had yet to meet, spent so much of his time in Savannah allegedly dealing with business matters. Chappedelaine, who had once worshipped his friend Dumoussay, seemed to think that the man was having a high time of it all in Savannah, while leaving him with the disagreeable task of dealing with the slaves and the disgruntled French workers at Sapelo. From Christophe's comments, Marguerite gathered that he put up an agreeable front whenever Dumoussay was present but took his annoyance out on others.

Christophe reported that Chappedelaine was also in a foul mood as he fretted over the imminent arrival of his uncle, Charles-César Picot de Boisfeuillet, who was bringing his entire family from Bergerac and should be arriving any day now. Boisfeuillet had written frequently and in vain the previous year to demand an accounting of the profits from the enterprise. Christophe himself had delivered one of the letters filled with complaints and demands on his return from France with his family. The letter infuriated Dumoussay, who made Julien his scapegoat for all the problems.

Christophe confided to Marguerite that he too was uneasy, not only about the lack of progress on his house, but also because Dumoussay kept making excuses for not providing an accounting or even legal titles to the partners' shares of Sapelo or the other lands they held in common. The man was bright, but he was also conniving, and Christophe was beginning to suspect his motives. The financial situation seemed to have become so confused that even the investors didn't know what was going on. At one point, Christophe had even sailed to Savannah to confront Dumoussay personally about the matter. He would never tell Marguerite exactly what happened there, but he came back to Jekyl in a rage. She had calmed him with kisses and a peaceful walk along the beach.

WHETHER IT WAS HIS EMOTIONAL DISTRESS over Sapelo or whether he fell victim to a malarial mosquito or some other ailment, Christophe became ill in the early fall and was bedridden for several weeks. Marguerite fretted over him and did everything she could to nurse him back to health. In her care, he soon grew better, though he was still too weak to undertake the frequent trips to Sapelo, even though he knew that the work on the Bel Air house would cease entirely in his absence.

In January, news reached Jekyl of the Boisfeuillet family's arrival in Savannah. By then Christophe had recovered his strength sufficiently to sail north to greet them and talk over their common problem of Dumoussay's handling of the legal titles and other business related to the investment. Before Christophe arrived, however, Boisfeuillet had already met with Dumoussay, who used his considerable charm to calm the newcomer and persuade him that all was well and that profits would come in due time.

Boisfeuillet seemed mollified. And he was relieved to be out of France, where the king was now in prison and undergoing trial. God knows what would become of him. It was not long before he learned, to his horror, that both the king and the queen had been executed. Before escaping from France Boisfeuillet had already observed the beheading of other noble prisoners and even priests, He shuddered to be reminded.

Thus, by the time Christophe reached Savannah, Boisfeuillet was predisposed to accept Dumoussay's interpretation of the facts, whatever they might be. In hopes that Boisfeuillet would understand the situation better when he reached Sapelo and could see the situation first hand, Christophe decided to accompany the newly-arrived family when they sailed for the first time to the island. By this time the two men, in an effort toward congeniality, were calling one another "Christophe" and "Charles."

Once on Sapelo Christophe stood back and watched with satisfaction Charles's reaction as he discovered the condition of the island and learned that no house had been built for him. He sputtered abuse and berated his nephew, who only made his usual excuses.

Unlike Christophe, however, Charles did not hesitate to move his family into the High Point house, making every effort to inconvenience Julien as much as possible in the process. For all he cared, his nephew could sleep in the yard.

"THEY LIVE LIKE PIGS ON SAPELO," Christophe told Marguerite when he returned to Jekyl. "Boisfeuillet was totally disgusted with what he found."

"What do you mean?" asked Marguerite.

"All they eat is boiled or roasted meat, whatever they can get, and they drink out of any old pot or pan. They've long since run out of wine and are drinking locally brewed beer. Half the time no one bathes. As I said, they live like pigs ... not just the workers, but Chappedelaine as well."

"Perhaps over time Madame de Boisfeuillet and her servants will civilize them a bit more."

"I doubt that she'll have much success in trying to civilize that savage bunch. They quarrel all the time. I'm so glad I brought you here instead, Marguerite. You're much too good for the lot of them."

From everything she heard, she too was glad they were not on Sapelo in the midst of all the bickering. She preferred the relative quiet and even solitude of Jekyl, especially when she listened to Christophe's constant complaints about Sapelo and his so-called partners. But she did miss having friends she could talk with. She did not think her

English yet adequate to visit the Spaldings on St. Simons, and most of the time she was happy to be alone with her family and her two servants, of whom she had grown rather fond.

The servant girl Marie was young and uneducated but reasonably intelligent. At the outset her language was limited mostly to Breton, but she spoke some French and had learned a great deal even on the voyage over. Now she was eavesdropping on the English lessons and was picking up quite a bit of that language as well. In some respects, however, Marie left much to be desired as a house servant. She chattered incessantly, giggled at the slightest whim, broke things in her clumsiness, and seemed always underfoot. Her dark unruly curls spilled from beneath the ruffle of her maid's cap, and she was constantly pushing them back beneath the narrow brim. Marguerite suspected that she was slipping out at night to meet one of the sailors, although she had not caught her at it yet.

On the other hand, the girl was cheerful and amused the children with her playful nature. She was learning to cook rather well, and Marguerite couldn't imagine the household without her. Marie did whatever Françoise told her. One might have taken the pair of them for mother and daughter.

Françoise, on the other hand, had spent her first twenty years near Tours and spoke excellent French for a woman of her class. She was at least a decade older and less outgoing than Marie, and she let nothing bother her, even when everyone else was upset about something. She was a source of tranquility in the household, obedient, thorough in her work, and good-natured, and she did her best to rein in Marie's effervescent nature. Although Marguerite had not wanted to leave Nanon behind, Françoise proved to be quite a good substitute. She learned quickly, and her presence was always unobtrusive.

Neither of the servants was very stimulating company, and at first Marguerite *had* been lonely with Christophe gone so much of the time to Sapelo. But she'd long ago learned to cope with solitude and found herself increasingly content with her family, her garden, her books, and her walks about the island.

The months went by uneventfully, except for Christophe's growing anger over all that was transpiring, or rather, not transpiring, at Sapelo. He still did not possess a legal deed to his share of the property, and he was finding Chappedelaine and now even Boisfeuillet, whom he once briefly considered an ally, so disagreeable that he seemed to have given up completely on the idea of ever finishing his Bel Air house. Marguerite sensed that he had lost all incentive to move to Sapelo. But it was she who first broached the question openly.

"Why don't we just stay here on Jekyl," she said, "and never move to Sapelo?"

He looked at her as though he were seeing her for the first time. "Do you mean it? Would you really like that?" He sounded incredulous.

"We could build our own little world here, Christophe, one suited to our tastes and needs, and not have to worry about all those quarrelsome people."

His face lit up with a wide smile and he reached out to pull her close. "You are an incredible woman, Marguerite. It's as though you've been reading my mind."

She smiled. *It wasn't that difficult to read,* she thought. But she said nothing.

"I've been thinking about the possibility for months, but I didn't dare suggest it. I thought you were lonely here."

"How could I be lonely? I have you, my sons, and everything I need. If only you weren't at Sapelo so much of the time." Suddenly she was truly excited at the prospect. "Just think, Christophe, our private island. It would be wonderful."

"I've been thinking about that, and I think I may be able to persuade the others either to sell—Lord knows, they need the money—or even better, trade my share of Sapelo for their shares of Jekyl." It was as though the noonday sun were beginning to shine again in their lives.

The very next morning a cheerful Christophe ordered the *Sappello* crew to unload the rest of their furniture and personal belongings from the ship. When Christophe told them that they would all receive their back pay before Easter, the men grinned and worked at a lively pace. The tabby house at Jekyl Island was beginning to feel more and more like home.

Chapter 15

February 1793

Jekyl Island

I T WAS A CHILLY BUT SUNNY DAY that held already the bright promise of spring. Christophe was poring over a map of the island, spread open on one of the tables recently unloaded from the *Sappello*. So much had changed since he and Marguerite had made their decision to stay on Jekyl. He had sold the ship, which he no longer needed, and paid off the sailors from the profits.

When the sailors departed, the du Bignons' serving girl, Marie, also left with the tawny, brown-eyed second mate, who had promised to marry her. Françoise did not remain long afterwards. She found the island too lonely without Marie, she said, and in her view there was too much work for one woman. Two months later, she'd found another position on the mainland and gave her notice. Marguerite was distraught. What on earth would she do now, with no French women at all on the island and no one to do the work?

Christophe made an effort to solve the problem for her, at least in part. When he sold the *Sappello* for a very good price in Savannah, he was able to pay off his sailors and buy a smaller vessel named the *Anubis*, a forty-foot *chaloupe*, or what the Americans called a sloop, which could be navigated in the shallow waters along the coast. For shorter trips he bought a sleek log-hewn vessel called a *piragua*. With the remainder of the money he purchased a few slaves, including two destined to be house servants to replace Marie and Françoise.

Caroline, a dark-skinned woman in her late forties, had worked as a house servant before, spoke passable French, and was well enough trained to suit Marguerite. Rosetta, the younger one, was another matter. Rosetta's previous owner had passed her off in the sale as an apprentice cook. However, as the du Bignons would soon discover, her qualifications had been considerably exaggerated. Her first meals were disasters, and she confessed she had been a field hand and only an occasional kitchen scullery maid as the need arose on her former plantation. Nevertheless, Rosetta proved to be bright and willing. After Marguerite had read and explained to her a few recipes, she learned quickly and seemed relieved to have become, for the first time in her life, a real house servant. Soon her cooking was at least better than average, and she seemed eager to learn and willing to experiment.

"I don't like the idea of owning slaves," Marguerite told Christophe when he first brought the two women home. "I don't know how to treat them."

"Well, you don't have much choice here if you want servants," her husband answered, "unless you want to do all the work yourself. They'll be fine. You'll see."

Even as widows she and her mother had not lived without at least one servant. And for people of any means whatsoever in this coastal society, it simply wasn't done. Either one was dirt poor and bred many children to help with the work or one had slaves.

"I'd prefer to think of Caroline and Rosetta as servants rather than slaves. I just can't consider them property the way some people around here do."

"Suit yourself," Christophe said. "But the advantage is that they can't give you notice and quit or just walk away, like Françoise and Marie did. Believe me, that's an advantage."

Marguerite was happy to have the help, he noticed, but after a short time she began to fret that things just weren't the same.

"Caroline and Rosetta seem almost afraid of me," she said. "I'm not accustomed to that. And they're so quiet. I even miss Marie's constant chatter."

"You'll get used to it, *chérie*," he said.

The two women did not live in the big house as the white servants had done. Instead they lived together, an arrangement they seemed to prefer, in a cabin closer to the big house than most of the other slave quarters so that they could be summoned day or night, when needed.

Only a few of the other slaves were women. Christophe had bought several females for breeding purposes, but mostly he had sought male field workers, whom he had already set to clearing lands for spring planting. He didn't want to try to cultivate too much just yet, since he still did not own the entire island and there were many knots to untangle before he could detach himself completely from the Sapelo Company.

He didn't have the same qualms about slave ownership that Marguerite had, even though he too was unaccustomed to it. Still, a sailor in mid-ocean wasn't that different. He was pretty much at the mercy of the captain. For Christophe, the relationship of master and slave was not unlike that of sailor and captain. Mutiny was the only option for either, and so far he had not had such trouble with either.

Christophe's finger traced on the map the limits of the property he already owned, as he considered where he might put more slave cabins when the time came. His pondering was interrupted by the sound of a bell signaling a boat's arrival at Marguerite's Landing. He was expecting a delivery of supplies ordered from Brunswick several days earlier. In anticipation, he folded his map, laid it on the table, and walked out briskly toward the dock to greet the vessel, signaling for a couple of his newly acquired slaves to follow him. The boat crew was already unloading barrels, which, Christophe knew, contained sugar, molasses, flour, and gunpowder.

"Morning, sir, I brought your mail." The captain handed him a single letter.

"Much obliged," said Christophe. It was an English expression he often heard on the docks in Brunswick instead of "thank you."

The letter was from France. He opened it and glanced at the signature. It was from Grandclos Meslé. Christophe read it, still standing at the landing. The morning sun glinted off the marshes, and a damp chilly wind blew from the northeast. He read it again, his anxious frown gradually turning into a wide smile. He could hardly believe his eyes.

"I have informed Dumoussay that Villehuchet and I, who share one-fifth of the Sapelo Company's assets, are withdrawing permanently from this partnership," the letter said. *Even from France, he can see it's a losing proposition*, Christophe thought, delighted. His friend in Saint-Malo was as fed up as he was with Dumoussay's delays in providing legal deeds and his mishandling of virtually every aspect of their partnership.

"I have demanded that the property be divided, as promised, and that our share be excluded from any future joint efforts," the letter said. "I plan to have nothing more to do with this unfortunate enterprise. I hope this will not inconvenience you in any way."

On the contrary, Christophe was elated. Here at last was his chance to bring Dumoussay to his knees and secure deeds to his own share of the property, which he could sell or trade. He knew it would be unpleasant, but he was determined that he would not be cheated out of his investment. Best of all, it was Grandclos who would be forcing the issue, not him, at least not entirely, but it provided a golden opportunity to shed himself entirely of the Sapelo Company and all its quarrelsome associations.

HE WAS RIGHT. IT WAS UNPLEASANT. Dumoussay fumed and fretted, accusing Grandclos and Christophe both of treachery for wanting to withdraw from the Sapelo Company and demanding their deeds and their share of the property or else the return of their assets. But Christophe stood his ground. He would not concede or be silent any longer, certainly not now that he had Grandclos on his side. The two of them had probably brought more assets to the partnership than anyone else. Now they both wanted out once and for all. Dumoussay had played fast and loose with their money and they had little to show for it, no income certainly and not even the promised deeds to their land. There appeared to be no solution other than letting the courts decide how to settle the matter.

Finally, in early May, and only after Christophe had finally threatened to expose Dumoussay's underhanded dealings and his untrustworthiness to his hoity-toity friends in Savannah, they agreed to take the matter to court. A date for the hearing was set for May 7. Dumoussay arrived, prepared to prevail. He was dressed in his finest clothes, a ruffled shirt, a gray silk waistcoat under a royal blue cutaway coat, and dark velvet breeches with silk stockings. He even wore his powdered wig and silver buckles on his shoes. Christophe, who had long ago abandoned wigs or powdering his hair in the Georgia heat, arched his eyebrows at the fancy dress, as he watched his erstwhile partner strut about the courtroom as though he were at high tea in the royal court. He thought it was ludicrous and requested unbiased arbitration of the matter.

Regardless of Dumoussay's effort to appear entitled and in control, no one was impressed. His account of what had happened to the money and who owned what was so garbled that even the judge couldn't figure it out. In the end, Dumoussay had no choice but to accept the requested arbitration in a division of the land, slaves, livestock, and payment of debts.

Although Christophe knew that nothing would be final for several months, he did not trust Dumoussay and wanted it known publicly that the partnership was being dissolved. He took out an ad in the *Georgia Gazette* on the day of the hearing to announce the coming dissolution of the Sapelo Company and noting that he would not be responsible for his partners' debts.

"THANK GOD THIS IS SOON GOING TO BE OVER," he said to Marguerite, when he returned from Sunbury, the seat of Liberty County where the court session was held. He knew she was well aware of the tension he had suffered in recent months and of his disgust not only with Dumoussay and Chappedelaine, but with the entire Sapelo debacle. He was a man who always wanted to chart his own path, and he was never patient being at someone else's mercy. It was difficult for him to admit to her that he had been wrong about the Sapelo investment, particularly after making so many brave promises. But Marguerite made it easy for him, as she always did, by reminding him that he may have saved their lives by bringing his family to America. Even now he could hardly believe his good luck in finding such a wife.

She always listened with a sympathetic ear whenever he ranted and raved about Julien's ineptness and Dumoussay's untrustworthy ways, and it was she who had first opened the door for a way out of the Sapelo Company by suggesting that they remain at Jekyl. They both knew, when he'd sold his ship, that there was no turning back. She supported him and encouraged him in ways he never dreamed possible for a woman. He realized now that, all along, she had understood far more than he thought. They were both apprehensive about the outcome of the court case but relieved that the situation was finally coming to a head. He had greater trust in the Liberty County court system than he did in either Dumoussay or Chappedelaine. And he loved his wife more than ever.

"ARE YOU SURE WE'LL BE ABLE TO STAY on at Jekyl once all this is settled?" she asked, as they lay side by side in their bed the night he had returned from court, holding each other and talking softly so as not to wake the boys.

"I'll do everything in my power to make it happen. We have to stay. It isn't safe yet to return to France." He reached out and took her in his arms.

"Perhaps once it's all final," she said, nestling her head in the hollow place on his shoulder, "we can begin to meet some of the people on St. Simons." He hoped so as well. But for now he was just enjoying this moment of closeness and common purpose.

WHEN THE ARBITERS FINALLY DECIDED on the matter in November, Christophe was at last able to obtain legal deeds to his share of Jekyl and his 500 acres of Sapelo. It was all he had been waiting for to begin putting his ultimate plan into action. Boisfeuillet, who was still living at High Point House with his family and who always needed money, was only too happy to sell to Christophe his share of Jekyl, which had little value to him. Christophe also began negotiations with Dumoussay and Chappedelaine to trade his one-fifth share of Sapelo, which they considered far more valuable, for their shares of the much smaller island—Jekyl—the total of which they believed had only 500 acres of arable land.

By the following summer, he would own all of the island, except that part which still belonged to Grandclos Meslé and his old partner Villehuchet, both of whom were still in France.

"They'll sell, I'm sure," Christophe told Marguerite. "I don't think Grandclos ever had any intention of coming to Georgia, and it's unlikely that Villehuchet will ever come back, now that he's returned to his family. It will probably be a relief to them to get rid of their share of Jekyl. I doubt they've ever seen it."

"I hope, so, my dearest. It will be nice to have it all settled."

"There's no real hurry, since they're not here. I think I'll wait until final matters are decided before I write them with an offer," Christophe said.

Marguerite nodded. If he was happy, she was happy.

"I wish you could have seen the faces of Dumoussay and Chappedelaine," he said with a laugh, "when I proposed an exchange of my land at Sapelo for theirs at Jekyl. You could see their delight in thinking I was cheating myself by giving them twice as much land as I would receive in the exchange. Neither of them hesitated for even a second to agree."

She smiled at his self-satisfaction. Both of them knew that, for Christophe, the amount of land was never the most important issue. For him it was full control and economic independence.

BUT IT WAS NOT ALL OVER YET. Only the land division had been decided. There was still the matter of all other common property. To Christophe's dismay, the court named Dumoussay as the responsible partner in all the legal papers and charged him with settling the company's debts and dividing its remaining assets. In his usual desultory fashion, Dumoussay showed no inclination to act with any haste, if at all, and it would take another lawsuit, finally filed by Christophe in January

1794, to get it done. The two men finally agreed in May, a full year after the original request for arbitration, to hold a public auction at Sapelo and divide the proceeds equally.

Only Boisfeuillet balked at that decision.

"This is absurd," he argued. "An auction will never bring full value." As always, he needed money, and he was already furious at everyone for the way things were going. The fullest extent of his wrath and his accusations of betrayal fell, as usual, on his nephew Julien, whom he had once trusted, but who was an increasing annoyance to him while they all lived together in tight quarters at High Point house. Boisfeuillet was planning, as soon as he could scrape together the money, to build his own house at a place he called Bourbon Field in honor of the fallen king and to spit in the eye of the new revolutionary government in France.

Although neither Christophe nor Boisfeuillet had managed to get their houses built on Sapelo, Dumoussay had somehow used his influence to obtain sufficient building supplies to build one for himself. It was particularly infuriating to Boisfeuillet, considering that Dumoussay was rarely on the island. However, it was also a relief in that it gave his nephew, Julien, another place to live. It was significant, considering that the feud between uncle and nephew had grown increasingly more tense. Without hesitation, Julien moved out of High Point House and in with Dumoussay, whom he considered his best friend, the man to whom he too had entrusted a great deal of money, money drawn in advance from his future inheritance, and the man who had promised to make him rich. He felt a far greater kinship with Dumoussay than he did with his stingy uncle.

NONE OF THE SAPELO QUARRELS TROUBLED THE LIFE of Christophe and Marguerite, who were increasingly content with their situation at Jekyl.

"We're getting the best of the bargain, Marguerite," Christophe pointed out once more over breakfast one morning. "We'll be more productive here, even on fewer acres, than they will ever be, given all the squabbles."

She smiled in agreement. "You made a wonderful decision," she said. "And we've avoided the squabbles at Sapelo as well as the troubles in France."

Christophe accepted her accolade with a cheerful nod. Even he congratulated himself on having eliminated both problems. They were both aware that the situation in France grew worse with each passing day.

"We only need to acquire the Jekyl land that still belongs to Grandclos and Villehuchet. That shouldn't be a problem. Once those papers are signed, Jekyl will be all ours. And I will *never* have partners again, no matter what," he announced, determination in his voice. In spite of his earlier decision to wait until everything was settled before writing to Grandclos Meslé and Villehuchet, Christophe was growing impatient. Thus, even before the auction was complete and the profits divided, he sent Grandclos Meslé a letter containing a good offer for his Jekyl land.

No reply arrived until late April. When the mail packet delivered it, he was surprised to see that the letter's postmark was not from Saint-Malo, but from London. The return address was 120 Bishopsgate. Still standing on the landing, he read the letter with growing shock. Then he rushed toward the tabby house, eager to share the news with Marguerite. He found her on her knees, cutting herbs in the garden. When he touched her shoulder, she rose quickly and turned toward him with a smile. It faded when she saw the gravity in his eyes.

"What's wrong?" she asked.

"If you ever had doubts about the wisdom of our leaving France when we did, this letter will confirm that we did the right thing," he said. "Let me read it to you."

"Who is it from?"

"Pierre Grandclos Meslé. You remember—the investor from Saint-Malo?"

"Ah, yes. I remember. The man who bought the property at La Vigne," she said.

"That's right, and he was a partner in the Sapelo Company."

"Yes, I know—the other one who wanted out. Read me the letter." She sat down in a wooden chair on the porch. He stood in the sunlight, his back to the garden, as he read the letter.

February 23, 1794

Mon cher ami,

Be happy that you and your family are safe in America, as I am happy, by the grace of God, to be safe in England.

I was put under house arrest on December 9 of last year while Jacobin agents invaded my home in Saint-Malo, accusing me of all sorts of revolutionary crimes. They claimed they were there to inventory my property, which took well into the night. They locked me in my third-floor bedroom with armed guards at the door while they ransacked my house and went through everything I own.

Fortunately, I had the forethought to be prepared. I always kept a rope ladder under my bed that would reach the ground in case of fire or some other emergency. I managed to stuff my pockets with all the money I could find in my room, which was very little, I assure you. Most of it was downstairs in my safe at the mercy of those hoodlums. I secured the rope to my bedpost, climbed down, and made my escape. I had to scale the town wall and swim to the mainland because I could not find a boat outfitted with oars or a sail, quite a long swim for a man my age, but it was either swim or die, I suspected.

Needless to say, I have probably lost most of my fortune, but I still have my life. I managed to get a ship to the island of Guernsey. From there I was able to make it to London, where my brother lives and where, as a precaution, my children, at my urging, had already resettled. Thus, I am finally safe from the current insanity that is going on in France. It is a blessing that my wife did not live to see what our country has come to.

As you have no doubt heard, they are sending people to the guillotine right and left. Being of the nobility or having a great deal of property seems to be enough to convict anyone of crimes against the Republic.

You have perhaps already heard that my friend and our partner Villehuchet was arrested in December—that old problem of having killed one of the men who invaded his house a couple of years ago. He was totally justified in my view, but now he is to stand trial again, this time before the Revolutionary Tribunal in Paris. I have little hope that he will be spared the guillotine, but we can only pray for his life or for his soul.

Your offer to purchase my share of Jekyl Island is a generous one, but at the moment, I would prefer to wait until this madness is over and I can gather my wits about me to make such decisions. There is another factor: My brother-in-law, Louis Harrington, is coming to Savannah. I am encouraging him to buy Villehuchet's shares of our properties in Georgia, and for the foreseeable future, he will also control mine. I want to see what use he intends to make of them. In the meantime, you may utilize my Jekyl land in any way you see fit. And may God grant that we meet again one day in this life and in happier times.

I hope that you and your family are well and content in a land of freedom. I'm sure you are happy, as I am, that such lands still exist.

I assure you, dear friend, of my most sincere homage.

Pierre Grandclos Meslé

Marguerite's face was drained of all color when he finished reading the letter. She sat, unable to speak, trying to force herself to breathe.

"It only confirms the fact that we made the right decision, doesn't it?" Christophe said.

She nodded in agreement, then shook her head in dismay. "I can't believe all this is happening in France, even in Brittany. Have people gone insane?"

"Yes. Quite simply, yes. They have. Give power to a peasant, and you see what happens. They are nothing more than barbarians. They have no mercy and no fear of God. Remember what they did to the churches and monasteries in France? The revolutionaries claim to worship Reason, but I don't see much reason in anything they are doing now.

"I will surely pray that they spare the life of Monsieur de Villehuchet."

"I suppose that's all we can do."

CHRISTOPHE'S GOAL TO BUY THE LAST quarter of the Island from Grandclos Meslé no longer seemed so important. He felt blessed to have deeds to the majority of Jekyl in hand. The rest belonged to absentee landlords who, for the time being at least, would give him no trouble if he planted their share.

He finally felt he was in a position to begin serious preparations for his own plantation. The first order of business was to buy more slaves. In such purchases, particularly in choosing the men, Christophe always searched their eyes for visible hatred. When he saw it there, he passed on to the next offering, looking instead for eyes filled with fear. Those were the slaves who worked hardest and were never much trouble.

He preferred not to buy the ones brought directly from Africa, since they knew neither English nor French, but sometimes he had no choice, for they were less expensive. The ones he liked best came from Caribbean islands like Saint-Domingue and spoke at least a dialect of French. They were of no particular value to the English or Scottish buyers, but to him, they were choice purchases, for they could understand his orders. By the end of the summer he had purchased or acquired in the division of the Sapelo property a total of sixteen prime field hands, enough to consider himself a true plantation owner.

He congratulated himself on his ingenuity. *La fortune sourit aux audacieux*, he thought to himself. *Fortune smiles on the bold*. By God, he thought, he had done well for himself.

He was never more convinced of his good fortune than when, the second week in September, news reached the Georgia coast that Villehuchet was dead. Guillotined. The entire French émigré community was shocked, not so much by the outcome of the trial, but at hearing of the beheading of someone they knew. They were well aware of the massacres taking place in the name of revolution and thanked God they had all had the wisdom to flee to Georgia and stay there. They couldn't believe the man had been foolish enough to return to France. Christophe and Marguerite had prayed for Villehuchet, but when he was tried a second time, they realized that there was never much chance of his survival. Such a brutal death.

Another letter arrived from Grandclos Meslé giving all the details. Villehuchet had been publicly guillotined in Paris on July 19 with two elderly cousins in their eighties. *How could such men be a danger to the revolution?* Christophe wondered. But it was no longer just a revolution. It had become a bloodbath. People seemed to have gone crazy, killing for the sake of watching other people die. They were calling these massacres the Terror.

When Christophe shared the news about Villehuchet with Marguerite, her eyes widened with horror. She flung her arms around his neck, and he could feel her damp tears on his cheek.

"Thank you, my dearest," she said, her warm breath grazing his ear. "Thank you for keeping us safe." He had never loved her more than at that moment.

Chapter 16

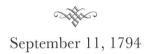

September 11, 1794

WE SHOULD GO TO SAPELO to tell the others of Villehuchet's death," Marguerite said to her husband. He nodded with resignation. Even though she and Christophe were no longer part of the Sapelo Company and had no wish to plunge their family into its contentious atmosphere, they wanted to maintain civil relations insofar as possible with their fellow *émigrés*. Since Grandclos Meslé's letter had arrived more quickly than usual, it was quite possible they had not yet heard the news of the execution of their former partner. It would not be an unwelcome visit, Marguerite thought, for they received frequent invitations from Madame de Boisfeuillet, who seemed desperate for female company. In fact, one had arrived by mail packet just two days before the letter from Grandclos Meslé. Marguerite had not yet responded, but she felt they should set sail soon, while the weather was still good and the news was fresh.

Such a visit would also give their boys a rare opportunity to play with other children. Although Boisfeuillet was already in his fifties, his wife, Marie, was younger by more than fifteen years. It was his second marriage, and they still had young children.

The du Bignons sent word by the next mail packet from Brunswick that they would arrive on September 14. It was not much notice, but Marguerite felt that Marie de Boisfeuillet, who often begged them to come, must be so starved for civilized company that she wouldn't mind.

FORTUNATELY THE DAY WAS MAGNIFICENT and the waters were calm. The small sloop traveled well, though poor Joseph leaned against the bulkhead, white as a ghost, sick the entire way.

Charles de Boisfeuillet met them at the dock. He was not exactly smiling, but there was a look of relief about him that puzzled Marguerite.

"We're glad you've come," he said. "Otherwise we should have had to bring the news to you." He reached out his hand to help Marguerite from the vessel.

"Oh, then you know about Villehuchet?" Christophe turned to shake Boisfeuillet's hand, as soon as he had made sure his slaves had properly secured the boat to the dock.

"Yes, we've just heard about that. Terrible. Terrible. But that's not the news I mean."

"You mean there's more?"

"Dumoussay is dead as well," Charles announced.

"What? When? How?" Marguerite was dumbfounded by the fact that two of the Sapelo investors had died so close together.

"Some kind of fever. He'd just come back from Savannah, and we didn't see him for a couple of days. Then Julien came to the house and told us he was ill. Marie did what she could to help, but he died last Thursday."

As the du Bignons made their way to High Point house, Charles filled them in on the details. They had carried out only the most required formalities, providing a coffin and a prayer, to bury him on the edge of the marsh.

"I wish I could say I was sorry," Charles said, "but to be frank, my feelings are good riddance. He was nothing but trouble to any of us. But Julien's pretty upset about the matter."

"I suppose he was closer to Dumoussay than we were," Christophe said.

"That's not the problem. He's not so upset about the death as about the will. He feels betrayed and angry. It's been hard to live with him since he found it."

As Charles talked on, Marguerite was able to form a clearer picture of the situation. Julien had found the will only the day before. He had come to High Point house in a rage, waving the document in his hand. It had been drawn up and filed recently, yet it did not acknowledge any of the money Dumoussay had borrowed from him, money that really belonged to Julien's mother but which he hoped to inherit someday. Nor did it make mention of the slaves and land they had purchased jointly, all of which Dumoussay had registered in his name alone.

When they reached High Point house, Julien was pacing back and forth in the yard, muttering curses. His face was a thundercloud, his hair uncombed, and his eyes wild. When he greeted them, Marguerite could smell liquor on his breath. And she could feel tension throughout the entire household.

"He's been like this all day yesterday and today," Marie de Boisfeuillet said by way of apology, as she greeted them. She had big, sad-looking brown eyes and a long, pointed nose that seemed to emphasize the skin beginning to sag beneath her eyes. Though she was two years younger than Marguerite, she looked much older.

"Perhaps it would be better if we came another time," Marguerite said.

"Oh, no, please don't leave," said Marie. "I can't imagine what Julien might do if you weren't here. His mother is my sister-in-law, and I know she didn't raise him to behave in such an uncontrolled way. But then, he's been behaving badly ever since we arrived. But now it's much worse. Please stay. You must at least spend the night. I have had the whole house rearranged to make you more comfortable."

Marguerite was sympathetic, but she felt ill at ease in the strained ambience at Sapelo. She had expected tension, but nothing like this. The du Bignons had come prepared perhaps to stay for several days, but while Marguerite had no desire to have her family on a small boat in the Atlantic after dark, she didn't want her children exposed to such a venomous atmosphere.

IN FACT, THE CHILDREN SEEMED OBLIVIOUS to the tensions. Joseph and Henri were chasing the Boisfeuillets' three children around the yard. Their son, Michel, who was a bit younger than Marguerite's two boys, seemed delighted to have bigger boys to look up to. His two older sisters, Jeanne-Marie and Servanne, were trying to entertain the boys as they had been instructed to do by their mother. Servanne was about the same age as Joseph, while Jeanne-Marie was well aware of her status as the oldest of the group. She took charge of directing the other children, while the adults talked. When she tired of the chasing game, she ordered the younger children to go inside, where she and Servanne would take turns reading from the fairy tales of Charles Perrault. Jeanne-Marie selected the first story, "*La Belle au Bois Dormant*," and handed the book to Servanne to read. It was a tale about a princess who, cursed by a wicked fairy, pricks her finger on a spindle and falls asleep for a hundred years, to be awakened only by a handsome prince.

"Ewww ..." Henri interrupted, his face scowling in disgust, when the prince and princess fall in love and start having babies. The other boys agreed and made gestures of throwing up.

"I think it's romantic," Servanne said with a haughty lift of her chin.

"Aren't there any stories that don't have love in them?" asked Joseph. He couldn't imagine why a prince, who could do whatever he wanted, would choose to spend time with a girl.

"It gets better," young Michel said, trying to defend his sisters. "The wicked queen tries to eat the babies." But the other two boys looked skeptical, and Michel finally suggested another story he thought the boys might like.

"Read the one about Bluebeard," Michel said. He had heard them all before.

"I don't like it much. It's too bloody," Servanne said. "Bluebeard kills his wives instead of loving them."

"That sounds good. Read that one," Joseph said. Henri and Michel nodded with enthusiasm.

Servanne and Jeanne-Marie laughed at the eager boys.

"Your turn," said Servanne, and her older sister began to read the cruel story of Bluebeard and his wives, wrinkling her nose in distaste when the last wife discovers the bloody bodies of all the man's former wives. "I can't see why anyone would like this story," she said. But she read it nonetheless, enjoying the limelight. The boys listened with rapt attention, their eyes sparkling at the gory details.

THE ADULTS TALKED LONG INTO THE NIGHT about the revolution with its own gory details of the beheadings in France, their relief at not being there, and the irony of Dumoussay's death so soon after Villehuchet's.

Julien was not present. After supper, during which he had hardly said a word or eaten a bite, he'd risen abruptly from the table and, without excusing himself in any way, announced that he was going to bed.

"How long has he been like this?" asked Marguerite.

"Since yesterday morning when he found the will," Marie answered. "I'm really worried about him."

"Is he still living in Dumoussay's house?"

"Not at the moment. He's refused to sleep there since Dumoussay died," Marie answered. "He's made up a pallet in the larder."

"Maybe he's afraid of ghosts," Charles said wryly.

JOSEPH AND HENRI WERE BOTH sound asleep in the children's room by the time their parents went to bed. They had started out with their heads at the foot of the bed, while Michel de Boisfeuillet slept in the other direction. But by the time Marguerite looked in on them to say goodnight, they were all in a hopeless tangle, their limbs akimbo. She smiled but didn't wake them, for they all appeared to be sleeping peacefully. *If only adults could relax so completely,* she thought, closing the door softly behind her.

MARGUERITE WAS AWAKENED BEFORE DAWN by the slamming of a door. She peered out the window and saw Julien striding across the dark porch. He took the steps two at a time and walked rapidly in the general direction of Dumoussay's cottage. His eyes looked bloodshot, and his hair was in a tangle.

I wonder where he's going, she thought, but she said nothing, not wanting to rouse her sleeping husband. The sour rage on Julien's face haunted her as she tried to go back to sleep.

When Marguerite and Christophe were both finally awake and preparing for the day, she told her husband what she had seen.

"He looked out of his mind," she said. "It frightened me. Let's pack up and start home as soon as the tide turns. It's just too upsetting around here." He nodded in agreement.

"I'll find the children," she said. If she knew little boys, they were already up and looking for breakfast.

Marguerite dressed hurriedly and went to the dining room where Marie de Boisfeuillet was inspecting the table her house servant had set. She straightened a fork, then looked up to see Marguerite.

"If you're looking for your sons, they've already had their breakfast and all the boys have gone down to the beach. Don't worry. I sent Servanne and Jeanne-Marie to keep an eye on them and make sure they stay out of trouble," her hostess said with a laugh, reversing the position of a knife and a spoon.

"These servants know nothing about setting a proper table. But it's not surprising. The way the men lived before I arrived was disgraceful," Marie said. "They taught the servants nothing. And these Africans have no notion of French gentility."

"I'm sure your influence will be a good one, Marie." Marguerite smiled. "But you needn't have gone to so much trouble for us."

"The house servants need the training, and goodness knows, it's nice to have someone around who appreciates a properly set table. I can assure you that neither Charles nor Julien cares a whit, much less the children. I have seen the men drink beer out of a cooking pot."

Marguerite laughed, picturing it in her mind. She wasn't surprised because she had heard Christophe comment on the same thing. "I saw Julien leave the house quite early. He looked … well, … upset. And where is Charles?"

"He went to find Julien for breakfast."

Christophe cleared his throat as he entered the room. "Good morning, ladies. I trust I'm not interrupting."

"Not at all. The other men should be here shortly."

Their hostess picked up a bell from the end of the table and jangled it vigorously. A dark face appeared at the door leading out to the kitchen, which was set apart in a separate structure from the main house. "*Oui, Madame?*"

"Bring us some coffee, Yvette." Marie de Boisfeuillet turned to her guests. "It's such a blessing that the planters from Saint-Domingue have brought so many of their slaves to Georgia. Of course, I'm sorry about the slave uprising there, but at least we can find slaves who speak French, more or less ..." she said. "You know, among themselves they have their own language, a kind of Creole, a mixture of African, French, English, who knows? I can't understand it."

Marguerite nodded, watching Marie fuss over the arrangement of another place setting, but she thought it quite amazing that people from so many parts of the world had managed to create a language they could all understand.

"Shall we wait on the porch?" Marie asked.

As the three of them were settling in their porch chairs, they saw Charles stumbling toward the house. He looked confused, and his face was ashen.

"Where is Julien? Late as always ..." Marie said with annoyance. But the dazed look in her husband's eyes suddenly caught her attention and interrupted whatever she was about to say. She stood up to greet him. Christophe stood as well and stepped forward with concern.

But Charles did not mount the wooden steps, nor did he look at either of them. Instead, he sat down heavily on the edge of the porch, his back bent, as though he could stand no longer. Tears tracked the lines in his face, and his shoulders were heaving.

"Charles ... Charles-César, what is it?" his wife asked, alarmed. Then her voice was suddenly quiet and grave. "Where is Julien?"

He dropped his face to his hands, drew in a deep breath, and began to sob. Marguerite and Christophe exchanged worried glances.

"Get hold of yourself, *mon vieux*. Where is Julien?" Christophe asked.

Silence weighed on the hot morning air, until finally Charles spoke.

"*Il est mort*, dead …. I … My sister's son … I killed him." It was a whisper. He broke down again.

"What?" his wife recoiled and fell back. Christophe steadied her and eased her into a chair before turning to Charles again.

Christophe echoed her question. "What? Why? Tell us, what happened?"

"I went to call him to breakfast …. I found him going through Dumoussay's papers. He was in a mindless fury …. He turned … and came at me. He was out of control. I think he wanted to kill me." Charles hesitated, as if trying to remember how it happened.

"Then what?" Christophe asked.

"He grabbed my shoulders and started shaking me. He … he even called me François, like I was the ghost of Dumoussay. He was out of his head. He wouldn't let go. He tried to choke me …. I had my pistol …. I … I always carry one in case I run into rattlesnakes." He dropped his head into his hands. "He wouldn't let go. He was going to strangle me. I … I had no choice."

"And you shot him?" Christophe asked. Marguerite was holding the arm of Madame de Boisfeuillet, who appeared about to faint.

"Yes. I'm sure he's … dead." Despair ravaged his face, and he was beginning to sob.

"Perhaps not. I'll go see," Christophe said, as he bolted down the steps and began to trot toward Dumoussay's house. The others sat still, unspeaking. Marie was quietly crying, and Marguerite held her hand.

They all waited in silence until Christophe returned a short while later.

"*Pas de question*," he said, shaking his head. "No doubt about it. *Il est mort*. He's dead." His face was dark.

"What shall we do?" asked Marie, her voice shaking.

181

"We'll have to send someone for Sheriff Middleton," Christophe said evenly.

"But they'll hang me," Charles whimpered.

"You can plead self-defense. I'm sure they won't hang you." Christophe tried to reassure him.

"Can't we just bury him?" Marie asked.

"This is a land of laws," Christophe said. "We can't do that. I'm sure Charles will get a fair trial."

Marie was crying again, more softly now.

"Is there a trusted man we could send for the sheriff?" Christophe asked. "One who won't run away or make up stories that aren't true."

It was decided they would send Allain Cabaret, one of the French workers who had been brought to work on Sapelo.

"He's a good man when he isn't drinking," Christophe said. "I think we can trust him."

Everyone had forgotten about breakfast, and the Boisfeuillets went back to their bedroom to lie down. Christophe and Marguerite gave up all thought of sailing with the tide. Once Cabaret had his orders and departed on his errand to the McIntosh County mainland, all they could do was wait. The du Bignons sat together on the porch, holding hands in silent apprehension as the hours began to creep by.

IT WAS LATE AFTERNOON WHEN SHERIFF MIDDLETON finally arrived. Marguerite squeezed Marie de Boisfeuillet's hand as the man led her husband away. The woman was hysterical. Her three children, taking their cue from their distraught mother, clung to her skirts and wept loudly.

"What will I do? How will I manage?" she sobbed, her legs collapsing beneath her. Servanne and Jeanne-Marie struggled to keep their mother on her feet and, with Marguerite's help, tried to ease her toward a porch chair.

"I'll go with Charles to the county judge and try to arrange bail," Christophe told them. "Marguerite, you stay here with Marie until I return." Marguerite could tell he was eager to get away.

Allain Cabaret stepped forward. "Don't worry, *Madame*, I am here to help." He seemed pleased to have been the one chosen to go for the sheriff, and he responded well to the trust Christophe and Charles had placed in him. "I will look after you, *Madame*," Allain assured her.

"And I will be checking in from time to time," Christophe said. "You'll be all right. And it won't be long until Charles is back. You'll see."

CHRISTOPHE DID NOT RETURN UNTIL THE NEXT DAY. Charles was with him.

"The bail was stiff," Christophe said. "Ten thousand dollars. I signed as guarantor. He'll be free on bail until his trial."

"Thank you, Christophe," Marie said, tears of relief in her eyes, as she clung to her husband. She held his arm as they walked back into the house. They seemed to have forgotten the du Bignons, whose bags Marguerite had already packed and who, eager to leave Sapelo, were trying to say their goodbyes.

NO ONE TALKED MUCH ON THE RETURN SAIL HOME. Marguerite kept a comforting hand on Joseph's back as he leaned over the rail to vomit every now and then, while his brother Henri tried to help the slaves Christophe had trained as sailors. Although most of the time Henri was more in the way than anything else, the men seemed to like the boy and gave him little tasks to do. He trotted eagerly back and forth, coiling ropes or swabbing puddles of water from the deck.

Marguerite could hardly believe all that had happened so quickly. Villehuchet guillotined, Dumoussay dead of fever, and Chappedelaine shot to death by his uncle—half of the Sapelo investors gone in such a short time. Only three remained: one indicted for murder and all in exile from France. How could this miserable revolution have happened to her country? How could any of this have happened? *We are blessed to be alive and free*, she thought. *Surely we have seen enough misfortunes to last a lifetime.* But just in case, she squeezed her husband's arm in gratitude and made the sign of the cross.

THE TRANQUIL BEACH AND THE CANOPY of trees on Jekyl looked almost like Heaven, a place of sanctuary, serene and beautiful as they made their way toward Marguerite's Landing. How could she ever have dreaded coming here? How could she be so lucky? The tabby house looked warm and welcoming as they walked from the dock. When they entered the house, small fires the servants had just lit crackled in both the *salon* and the kitchen. Marguerite felt a great sense of relief, as she smelled the burning pine logs and saw the flicker of bright reflections around the room. The weather was still quite warm during the day, but the evenings were beginning to cool just enough to make an occasional evening fire welcome.

The boys raced up to their room with the book of fairy tales Servanne had let them bring home. Once on land after such a short voyage, Joseph was fine again. He was the better reader of the two and enjoyed reading to his brother whenever he got the chance. *I will need to buy them some books in English so that Henri can learn as much as Joseph*, Marguerite thought. When the boys were born, she dreaded having them so close together, but now she was glad. They were best friends as well as brothers. They had to be. The island afforded them no other playmates, and there were no slave children their age. Despite all the turmoil at Sapelo, the boys had enjoyed interacting with other children even for a little while.

Once the boys were upstairs, Marguerite turned to Christophe. "Do you really think Charles will be found innocent of murder?"

"Only if they take his word for what happened. After all, no one else was present. It will also depend on how determined the prosecutor is to convict him. It does look rather bad. Julien was unarmed, and Charles sought him out with a gun in his hand. He'll have to convince a jury it was only for killing rattlesnakes. It could be difficult. Many people knew that the two were often at each other's throats."

"Oh, Christophe, I'm so glad we're settled here at Jekyl, away from all that upheaval at Sapelo. It was a wonderful decision on your part. Just like leaving France."

She'd said it before, but he always smiled at her praise. He gave her a gentle kiss on the forehead before he sought her lips.

Chapter 17

February 1795

THE DU BIGNONS VISITED SAPELO ONLY RARELY NOW. Nearly five months had passed since the shooting, but it was still a Damocles sword hanging over the island. The atmosphere, while less contentious, was even gloomier than before.

"You know," Marguerite said one afternoon in late February, as she and Christophe sat on the banks of the marsh watching the sunset, "I was thinking it would be nice, now that we're here to stay, to make some friends on St. Simons. It's so much closer than Sapelo."

"Are you so confident of your English now?"

She pondered the question. She felt she had learned enough English to communicate on a relatively simple level, but she wasn't sure how far it would go.

"Not really, but there's only one way to test it. And making new friends would give me an incentive to work harder at it. Besides, the boys will be growing up before we know it, and they'll want some social life with other young people. We mustn't wait too long."

"You're right, *ma chère*. We must visit very soon."

"I think we should call on Mrs. Spalding," she suggested. She had never forgotten the gracious, standing invitation from the Spaldings more than two years ago now. Marguerite had written to thank them for their kind invitation and assure them that they would visit very soon. But time had crept by, and they had been so absorbed in the problems at Sapelo that she had thought little more about it. So much had happened. And then, the preceding November, just two months after the shooting of Chappedelaine, they heard about the sudden death in Savannah of James Spalding. He had been on his way to a legislative meeting in Augusta when he took ill. They had sent condolences to Mrs. Spalding, of course, but still had not called on her. It was high time, Marguerite thought.

She shuddered to think what she would do here without her own husband. Mrs. Spalding was a relatively young widow, she knew, only a few years older than herself. Of course she had her unmarried son, who was a man now, but he was reading law in Savannah much of the time. She had McIntosh relatives on the mainland in Darien who would look after her no doubt, but Marguerite knew from experience how hard it was to be a widow, even with such support.

And so it was decided. Christophe sent word by Apollo, his most timid and trusted slave, to the Spaldings' plantation on the southern tip of St. Simons Island, with a message that he and Madame du Bignon would like to call on the first Sunday in March, weather permitting. Everyone on the islands fully understood that all plans depended on the weather, which could be uncertain.

Apollo returned three hours later, bearing a written note from Margery Spalding, expressing pleasure at their impending visit and urging them to come early. The message indicated that she would expect them for Sunday dinner, which was served at two o'clock and that they were welcome to stay the night. Christophe made Marguerite read it aloud to him twice.

"Very good, *ma chère*," he commented. "Your English is progressing quite well."

She felt herself blushing at his compliment. "But I don't think we should plan to stay overnight," she said, "at least not this first time. If we leave by five or five-thirty, we could make it home before dark." With even two men rowing the small piragua they used for short trips, they could reach St. Simons in less than an hour.

THE FIRST SUNDAY IN MARCH WAS SUNNY and warm, with virtually no wind to propel or impede the progress of their piragua. Hollowed out of a single cypress log, well sanded and varnished, the small boat, smoothed at each end to pointed perfection, could cut through the water like a knife. Every planter on the coast had at least one of them, for they were surely the swiftest and most efficient way to go short distances from plantation to plantation. Some of the planters even competed in races with these small vessels. Christophe's piragua was more than twenty feet long and could carry six people easily. He had even been talking of entering the boat races in the spring. He'd heard that they always provided a festive occasion for the planters and their slaves to socialize. The men who rowed the boats, all slaves selected for their strength and endurance, seemed to take great satisfaction in outrowing workers from other plantations.

"I think you and the boys would enjoy such an event, *chérie*," he said. She agreed that it sounded like a wonderful outing.

Marguerite seldom traveled in the piragua, but she always enjoyed it when she did. The men sang to the rhythm of the oars as they rowed. She loved to hear the deep chants of the rowers echoing off the waterways that wound through the marshes and across the sound. As she listened, she thought of how her life had changed and how much delight she took in things she would never have known back in Brittany—the long expanse of marsh that stretched between Jekyl

and the mainland, the magnificent live oaks that graced the island, the gray moss that hung from the limbs and gave the atmosphere such a mysterious look, even the shell mounds left from some long ago Indian feast. She loved the privacy of the island, where visitors were always unexpected and brought such pleasure when they did arrive with the latest news from the mainland or adjacent islands. She loved the orderly look of the fields of corn and cotton and especially her small garden, which still thrived with herbs and now also with sweet potatoes, strawberries, melons, and beans native to the region. From a grove not far from the house, she could savor the scent of orange blossoms in the spring that would yield the sweet taste of oranges in the summer.

What surprised Marguerite most was the realization that she found real glory in the coastal wilderness. She marveled at the brilliant-colored wildflowers that grew in such profusion, at the tangle of grape vines that knotted the forests, and trees, always green, that grew just as God intended—sheltering the soft-eyed deer and the skittish raccoons and rabbits that were so difficult to keep out of the cornfields and the garden. The woods offered nesting places for the multitudes of birds that came and went throughout the year—painted buntings, plovers, wood storks, herons, cranes ... there seemed no end to their variety. It was all so different from the carefully sculpted gardens in France, and it appealed to a wildness inside her that she hadn't known existed before she came here. Even the occasional alligator spotted in the island ponds, looking like a dragon from prehistoric days, gave her a shiver of pleasure. She recalled how she had felt like Eve in the Garden of Eden when they first arrived on the island. It still remained her Eden in many ways. Who could want more?

As she considered her blessings, she also felt a sharp pang of regret that her other children were not here to enjoy it all with her. Little Paul and Marie Clarice—they had never known one another in life, even though they were brother and sister, but surely God had brought them together in Heaven. She knew that she would never stop grieving for them.

As for her children back in France, she had thought of them often since the family's arrival in Georgia. Once she had even raised the question of their coming to live here, but Christophe had made it clear that they would not be welcome at Jekyl. Marguerite doubted that Margot would take much pleasure in the island anyhow, for she enjoyed parties and frivolities, which were not often any part of their life here. And Louis would probably be restless for the sea and the taverns. *Perhaps it's best this way,* she thought. They are free to make their own lives without interference from us. It was her way of trying to make their absence palatable. Still, she missed them and worried for their safety. And she longed to know her grandchildren.

These brief rides across the sound always put her in a contemplative mood, one she knew she should shake off before they arrived on St. Simons. She and Christophe had not brought Henri and Joseph on this first visit with Mrs. Spalding and her son. The boys had been only too happy to stay behind with Caroline and Rosetta, and they whooped with joy when their mother told them they didn't have to go. A formal dinner with strangers was never something they looked forward to. And Marguerite was nervous enough about her English, without having to worry whether her children were behaving themselves or not. Her English was far from perfect, she knew, but she was eager to try it out on someone besides Joseph and Christophe.

As the sun glinted off the open water, Marguerite was glad she had worn a wide-brimmed bonnet to keep her face shaded. She pulled her shawl tighter around her shoulders and leaned back, closing her eyes to listen to the oars plashing in the water and the rich voices of the men as they rowed in rhythm with their chant.

When they reached the Spalding plantation on the south end of St. Simons, Thomas Spalding, who had seen them coming, was at the dock, waiting with another well-dressed gentleman. While the slaves tied up the piragua, Christophe helped Marguerite from the boat. Thomas reached down to give her another hand up.

"It's so good to see you again, Madame du Bignon," he said. She was reminded once again what a handsome young man he was. His eyebrows were heavy and his cheeks ruddy. He had a full head of dark hair. But despite his welcoming smile, his eyes held the same somber cast she had noticed the first day they met. She suspected that his sobriety was constant and not directed at any particular person or event.

"Let me present you both to Mr. John Couper," the young man said, gesturing toward the florid-faced man with a broad smile standing next to him, "one of our neighbors on St. Simons. You may already know that he and his wife came here as newlyweds, not long after you moved to Jekyl. Mr. Couper's plantation, Cannon's Point, is at the island's north end."

"Now you can say that your friends on St. Simons stretch from one end of the island to the other," John Couper said as he greeted them, chuckling at his own joke. "And, by the way, my friends call me Jock."

"Mother took the liberty of inviting him and his lovely wife to dine with us today so that you could make their acquaintance," Thomas said.

Marguerite judged Mr. Couper to be about Christophe's age. He was a Scotsman, she could tell from his accent, which she found charming though difficult to understand at times. His eyes seemed to dance with delight at making new friends, and his voice was jovial. The two gentlemen who greeted them could not have been more different.

Marguerite felt a bit flustered, even overwhelmed, as the men spoke too rapidly for her to comprehend all they said. She smiled a great deal but said little, as a waiting carriage drove them back to Orange Grove, the Spalding plantation house.

Christophe also did more listening than speaking, she noticed, but he seemed to understand the men's talk, which was all about the year's crop of cotton, rice, and indigo. Marguerite was impressed with how much Thomas Spalding seemed to know. He was clearly a very intelligent and serious young man. She understood only snatches of the conversation, but nonetheless, she enjoyed the ride past the well-plowed fields, the orange and lemon groves, and the fig trees heavy with fruit. She would plant figs at Jekyl, she decided, as she looked at the wide lush bushes. They would make delicious preserves.

Finally, the wooden plantation house, built high off the ground with a tabby foundation, came into view, and standing on the front porch was an attractive woman, not tall, but stately and dignified nonetheless. Her dark hair, just beginning to show sprinkles of gray, was wound into an abundant chignon at the back of her neck. She did not appear to be much older than Marguerite, though Marguerite thought her much more dignified. There was a sadness about her eyes, and her black dress emphasized her mourning.

"This is my mother, Margery Spalding, Madame du Bignon. She has been looking forward to meeting you," Thomas said by way of introduction.

Mrs. Spalding held out her hand. "How do you do, *Madame*," she said.

"Please, call me Marguerite."

"And I am Margery," she replied. Mrs. Spalding's smile warmed the afternoon. Marguerite liked her at once.

As the men trailed into the parlor, Margery took Marguerite by the elbow and guided her to a small, sunny room lined with books, where they could speak privately. They sat in two chairs facing one another beside a window that extended all the way to the floor and overlooked a small garden filled with early spring flowers. Marguerite wondered where Mrs. Couper was, but she did not ask.

As though she had heard the question aloud, Margery said, "I sent Mrs. Couper upstairs to rest for a moment. She has a young baby, you know, and she had a bit of a headache. Besides, I wanted to have you all to myself for a while. I hope you don't mind. She'll be down shortly, I expect."

"I hope it is not serious," Marguerite said.

"No, just a small headache, but I am glad to have this chance to talk with you alone. My son was so pleased to meet you when you first came to Jekyl Island," Margery said, speaking slowly and very clearly.

"He ... tell you I not speak good English," Marguerite replied.

Margery laughed. "Well, I can understand you, and I have looked forward to meeting you."

"I look forward too," said Marguerite. Her face grew serious. "I want to tell you how sorry I am of your husband's death."

Sudden tears sprang to Margery Spalding's eyes, but she quickly blinked them away, dabbing at the corner of her eye to dry the one that almost escaped.

"That's very kind of you. He was a good man," she said.

"I heard that. I regret not to meet him," Marguerite said. She paused for a moment, mentally assembling her words. She wanted to say them right. "I too was a *veuve* ... a widow ... before I marry Christophe. I understand your pain."

Margery took both of Marguerite's hands into hers for a moment. "You must have been very young, my dear. I'm so sorry, but I'm glad to see that you have found happiness again. And I hear you have two young sons."

"*Oui*, Joseph and Henri." Marguerite's face brightened as she mentioned her sons. Although she sensed the sadness in her hostess, she did not know what more to say. She wanted to tell her that she had other children back in France, as well as two that she had lost, but the effort of forming all those words, given the heavy sorrow of both women, seemed too difficult. Instead, they sat in silence, gazing first into each other's sympathetic eyes and then, thoughtfully, at the garden.

Finally Margery turned to her and asked, "How do you like our coastal area so far?"

"It is very beautiful, very different from *La France*."

"No doubt, and especially now," Mrs. Spalding said sadly. "I am so sorry to hear of the upheaval in your country."

"It is why we come to America. *La France* is very dangerous now."

"Do you still have family there?"

Marguerite nodded, "*Oui*, I have a grown son and daughter still *en France*."

"I'm sure you must worry about them," her hostess said. "But I am so glad that you and your husband are safe. I have heard that you and Monsieur du Bignon have decided to remain on Jekyl Island. Is that true?"

"*Oui*, at least until it is safe to return to our home *en France*."

"I for one wish you would stay on Jekyl for good. We're so pleased to have you for a neighbor and delighted that you finally landed closer by instead of on Sapelo. I've heard about the Sapelo Company, all the sad events. I was so sorry to hear about them."

Marguerite nodded, not sure what she should say.

As though she were trying to brighten the conversation, Margery said, "But all those long French names. How did you keep them all straight?"

"*Eh bien*," she said, "they were not as unfamiliar to me, perhaps, as to you, but I too had some difficulty. I divided them in twos ... how do you say? ... in pairs. There were two young, unmarried ones who started the colony—Boisfeuillet and Dumoussay. They are both dead now." She crossed herself. "There were two more who were in France, Grandclos and Villehuchet. Monsieur de Villehuchet—he is the one who was, how do you say, *guillotiné*?

194

"Beheaded," Margery said quietly. "He should have stayed here, I think."

Marguerite ignored her comment as she tried to complete her pairings. "And finally the two with families who are still here, Boisfeuillet and du Bignon, us. There are only three names to remember now," Marguerite said sadly. "But I know that for English ears even three can be very confusing."

"We were so sorry to hear how things worked out," Margery said.

"*Merci.* Thank you. We were lucky to be at Jekyl instead," Marguerite replied. But she did not want to dwell on the deaths and misfortunes of Sapelo. In an effort to steer the conversation in a new direction, she said, "Your house is charming."

"It's rather small, I'm afraid. My husband and I always intended to build something larger. When we first came to Georgia, we lived in the old house built by General Oglethorpe, who founded the colony. It was called Orange Hall. That's why we call our cottage Orange Grove, and of course, we've planted many orange trees to justify the name."

Marguerite listened intently, trying to understand every word, but she was growing weary of the effort to speak only English. Margery had just offered to take her on a tour of the garden, when a lovely young woman suddenly appeared at the parlor door. Her pale blond hair was pinned into stylish, but casual rolls, with two large curls dangling just behind her left ear.

"Am I interrupting?" she asked cheerfully.

"Of course not, Rebecca, my dear, I do hope you are feeling better," Margery said.

"Much better, thank you." Rebecca smiled.

"Do let me present you to Marguerite du Bignon, our neighbor on Jekyl Island. Marguerite, this is Rebecca Couper," Margery said.

Rebecca held out her hand, "*Enchantée, Madame,*" she said with a warm smile.

"*Enchantée*," Marguerite replied, instantly responding to Rebecca's graceful demeanor. She did not appear to be more than twenty years old at most, which surprised Marguerite, for her husband seemed much older.

"I thank you for allowing me to lie down for a short time," Rebecca said to Margery. Then she turned to Marguerite, "And I do apologize for not being here to greet you when you arrived."

"It is not a problem," Marguerite replied. "Madame Spalding will give me a tour of the garden." She was eager to learn the names of all the flowers in bloom.

"How wonderful," Rebecca said. "May I join you?"

"Of course," Margery said cheerfully and led the two women outside.

Marguerite tried to settle into the background to listen to the women chatter on about the flowers and shrubs, which gave her an opportunity to listen and build her vocabulary, but relieved her from having to talk much herself. Their walk and conversation filled the time until dinner was called.

THE MEAL WAS SUMPTUOUS AND ELEGANTLY served by two well-dressed male servants who stood unobtrusively at either end of the sideboard waiting for the next course to be brought in. One by one, they offered the guests various dishes of she-crab soup, grilled sea bass, roasted quail, and braised beef, along with mounds of English peas, scalloped potatoes, and a dish of corn pudding. Marguerite was struck by the contrast to the meals they had shared with the Boisfeuillets on Sapelo.

As though he were reading her mind, Christophe commented, "Your servants are so well trained. I almost feel I am back in France."

"Hardly so elegant as that, my friend," said Thomas. "I have heard about those aristocratic households. As a nobleman you must have had one yourself."

"*Hélas*," said Christophe, "only briefly. I was a sea captain, and when I took my *retraite* ... my retirement ... from the sea and bought my manor house, we had only a few years before the revolution."

"Ah, what a shame," said John, "but it's lucky we are that you came to Georgia and became our neighbor. I've only recently moved to St. Simons myself, as you know, but I would be honored to have you visit my plantation, Cannon's Point. Our house isn't much at the moment, but we're preparing to build a new home there very soon."

"We'd be delighted to have you," his wife added with a warm smile.

"We thank you for the invitation, and we should like very much to visit, I'm sure." Christophe said. Marguerite nodded with enthusiasm.

When dessert came, there was an orange cream cake and a lemon soufflé served with a side of chocolate almonds. Christophe commented on how delicious the dinner was. "You must have a very good cook."

Margery laughed softly. "Wait until you have a dinner at the Coupers' house. Their new chef, Sans Foix, is without equal. In fact, he's been giving our cook some pointers."

"That's true," said her son. "Sans Foix is already becoming a legend on the island."

"How do you happen to have such a fine slave?" Christophe asked.

"Oh, Sans Foix is not a slave," John said quickly. "He's a free man and well worth his salary. I'm lucky to have him."

"You are indeed," Margery said, arching her eyebrows. "There are, as I'm sure you know, those who have tried to steal him away.

But he seems loyal to you and your family."

"I'm glad to hear that," said John.

"We do not yet have such a fine chef, though our cook Rosetta is learning. Perhaps we should send her to Cannon's Point for a few lessons. In any case, we would be pleased to invite all of you to visit us at Jekyl Island." Christophe said. "We live in the old tabby house that was built many years ago by the Englishman, Major Horton, we are told. It is rather small, but we plan to add to it as our children grow."

His statement surprised Marguerite. He had never mentioned enlarging the house before, but she knew he enjoyed gracious living. And hearing the Coupers talk of building a new home may have spurred his thinking.

"I'm sure we would all enjoy such a visit," Rebecca said.

Margery nodded. "Indeed we would."

The rest of the afternoon passed with great congeniality, as the men settled in the larger parlor with brandy and cigars, while the ladies had cream sherry served on the porch, where they could still feel the warmth of the afternoon sun. It was in all ways a lovely day, and Marguerite felt reluctant to leave when Christophe emerged from the house and pointed out that it was already well past five o'clock and that they must head back to Jekyl to arrive before dark.

"I do wish you could stay," said Margery, "but I know your boys are expecting you back." Marguerite nodded and took her hand to say goodbye.

All farewells said, the men accompanied the du Bignons to the dock to see them off. They stood waving, as the piragua began to cut its way back across the sound. Marguerite listened once more to the chanting of the rowing men as she drank in the ever-changing colors of the sunset. She had never seen it so rich and exquisite. The sky, reflected in the waters of the sound, was a constant flux of flame at first, burning hues of orange, red, and gold, surrounding a sun that seemed to grow larger as it approached the horizon. The closer they got to Jekyl and the lower the sun sank in the sky, the softer the colors became—like burnt sienna and coppery rose fading slowly. Once the sun dropped completely below the land, it left behind clouds glowing pink, interspersed with purple, violet, and a gentle shade of blue.

Marguerite was almost sorry when they reached the Jekyl landing, but she was home again, where she knew she could look forward to such sunsets almost daily across the marshes. She was where God in his grace intended for her to be and where she felt at the end of this glorious day that nothing more could go wrong. *Perhaps we are lucky*, she thought, *that we cannot see the future.*

Chapter 18

late August 1796

Jekyl Island

TWO YEARS HAD PASSED SINCE THE SHOOTING of Chappedelaine, and the murder case still had not come to trial. Every week after scouring the *Georgia Gazette* from cover to cover in vain for possible news about the trial, Christophe would pace back and forth in front of the *salon* fireplace, his fists clenched tight as he ranted to Marguerite.

"Will the bail money I pledged never be freed from obligation? There is always some new delay."

Joseph Clay, Charles's lawyer, had persuaded the judge to hear the case only after all the complicated property issues involving Dumoussay and Chappedelaine could be sorted out at Sapelo. The prosecution agreed, believing that disputes over money and property could make Boisfeuillet's motive all the clearer and would perhaps even guarantee his conviction. The judge, who was not much interested in the case of squabbling Frenchmen, was happy to agree since both sides were in concurrence.

Only Christophe was annoyed by the postponement. On many evenings, by bedtime, he would still be pacing around the bedroom wringing his hands. "I knew at the beginning it would take a few months to get it all sorted out," he grumbled. "If I'd known it would take years, I'd never have tied up my money for so long."

"Of course you would, *chéri*. He's your friend," his wife said. "He needed help."

"Hmph. *On récolte ce qu'on sème.* You reap what you sow. I should have let him stew in his own juice," he muttered.

When he was in such a mood, there was little Marguerite could do but commiserate with him and try to soothe him in the best way she knew how.

"Why don't you come to bed, *chéri*. We can talk about all this tomorrow." Her caresses were the only thing that seemed to calm him, even for a little while.

HIS TEMPER ERUPTED EVEN MORE FORCEFULLY the day he learned from the men on the mail boat that Charles's lawyer had convinced his client to sue the estates of both his nephew and Dumoussay. He strode from the dock toward the house virtually shouting. "*Je ne peux pas le croire.* I can't believe it. I just can't believe it." Once inside the door, he slammed it behind him and informed Marguerite of what he had heard.

"It will only delay things more and puts Charles in the absurd position of suing the estate of the man he killed," he said. "Can you think of anything more ridiculous?" Marguerite shook her head in dismay.

As time dragged on, Christophe grew increasingly pessimistic. "I think by now they've forgotten all about the murder charge in this tangled mess of legal issues." Then, suddenly, late in the year, he read in the *Georgia Gazette* that Charles had finally been ordered to appear in court to stand trial. The date was set for the following January in Louisville, Georgia, which had just been named as the new state capital.

"Hallelujah," Christophe shouted, but only a few days later, he learned of yet another complication. Charles's lawyer, by now a family friend whose son was courting the Boisfeuillets' oldest daughter, was suddenly appointed by President Washington as judge to the United States District Court of Georgia. Thus, he was compelled to turn the case over to another attorney, an up-and-coming Savannah lawyer named Charles Harris. The young man, educated in France during his youth, spoke fluent French and was able to establish an immediate rapport with the Boisfeuillet family. But Christophe wondered, *did this portend another delay?*

Rather than argue the case, as it turned out, the new lawyer, who, Christophe suspected, doubted his client's innocence, contended that the delay had taken too long, that Charles de Boisfeuillet had been denied his constitutional right of a speedy trial under the sixth amendment, which had become law in 1791.

At first, the tactic did not seem to succeed. Then, suddenly, the charges were dropped altogether, and Christophe's ten thousand dollars were, to his joy, finally freed from obligation.

"I wouldn't be surprised at a little behind-the-scenes finagling going on," he confided to Marguerite. "Probably at the hand of Judge Clay. His son is engaged now to the Boisfeuillet girl, you know, and he wouldn't want his heir married to the daughter of a convicted murderer. Who knows? All I can say is, good for him. I don't care a whit who was responsible. I'm just glad it's over." He needed the money. Cotton prices had reached a new low.

MARGUERITE WATCHED HER HUSBAND'S REACTION to the settlement without surprise. For such a man, who could be so loving and tender with her, he could be so heartless where others were concerned. Surely he must be pleased that Charles no longer stood under the murder charge, but the only delight he openly expressed was for the money, which was now free to invest in more slaves or land.

She could understand his reaction to some extent. Christophe's family, despite their noble rank, had been relatively poor when he was a child, which is why he had been compelled to go to sea at the age of ten. Maybe that was the reason he always seemed more concerned about making and holding onto money than about people's lives or happiness. *I think it's different with women,* she thought. She couldn't imagine caring more for money than for family, love, or friendship, which seemed to be his way. But in her heart, she knew all women weren't like that, any more than all men were like her husband. In fact, their new friend, John Couper, had a reputation for valuing friendships and hospitality above all. She and Christophe had often talked about it, though they had somewhat different viewpoints.

"He'll bankrupt himself one day with all his open-handedness," Christophe would say. He made it sound foolhardy, though she knew he liked the man.

As for herself, Marguerite admired him very much. She liked his open face with its high forehead and the frankness in his eyes. He never seemed to worry about the future, as Christophe constantly did, always making it sound as if they were at the door to the poorhouse whenever cotton prices dropped, but her husband knew perfectly well he still had resources in France to fall back on. She wished, for Christophe's sake, that he could live more in the present—not dwell on unpleasant things in the past or worry constantly about what was to come. But then, she would remember, it was her husband's foresight that got his family out of France before the onset of the Terror. Perhaps his concern about the future was justified. *If only he could let go of the past,* she thought. *Perhaps that would be enough.*

WHILE CHRISTOPHE FRETTED ABOUT the past and the future, Marguerite's greatest concern was for her children back in France— Margot and Louis. Although neither of them was rich enough to be a revolutionary target, she could not help but wonder how they were faring. She heard from them so seldom. As far as she knew, they were carrying on with their lives and families, both of them married now, without apparent harm. Still, one could never be sure. It seemed strange that her son had a wife she had never met and who had recently given birth to their first child, a daughter named Marie Mélanie. Most of Marguerite's information came from Margot, for Louis almost never wrote unless he needed something.

"Do you think we'll ever return to France?" Marguerite asked Christophe one evening after supper, as they were sharing an after-dinner *digestif* on the back porch of the tabby house.

"Would you like to?" he asked.

She thought about her answer for a moment before she spoke. The Terror had finally ended just weeks after Villehuchet's beheading, when the man she could only describe as a tyrant, Robespierre, was himself guillotined. The greatest danger seemed to be over. But Marguerite could only wonder about the stability of the new political system under the rule of a five-man group called the Directory. Margot's letters led her to believe that life in France had returned to some semblance of order, but the country must be much changed by all the recent violence and political upheavals it had experienced. While Marguerite wanted desperately to see her children again and get to know her grandchildren, she would prefer to have them come to America, which she doubted they would ever do, knowing that they would not be welcome by her husband at Jekyl.

"Would you like to go back?" Christophe asked again.

"Not for good," she answered slowly, but feeling a tinge of nostalgia for their manor house and the rose garden she might never see again. "To visit perhaps, but not for good. I'm sure it must be very different now. Besides," she said, tenderness in her voice, "I like it here." Crickets, frogs, and owls, along with other night creatures she couldn't identify, filled the darkness around them with soothing sounds. She could hear water lapping at the banks of the creek that ran along the leeward side of the island.

"Do you think France will ever be like it was?" she asked, looking at Christophe's face, sculpted by shadows cast by the flickering light of the oil lantern on the table.

"Never. America set the example of a country without a king. Now France has overthrown the monarchy. I don't think this thirst for what people are calling liberty will ever end, now that they've had a taste of it. People in France will want to choose their own leaders, as they do here. I'm just not sure they know how." They sat in silence, listening to the night, letting their thoughts go where they would.

Finally Christophe leaned toward her, took a sip of his cognac, and asked, "Do you really like it here?"

"I do," she answered, closing her eyes for a moment and letting the peace of the island seep into her very bones. She meant it, though she would never forget the magic of those few years at La Ville Hervé, when they were both younger, when Joseph and Henri were just toddlers, and when all her children were welcome—those fleeting years when life stretched before them with such promise. But in the end, even that had been spoiled not only by the revolution, but also by the rift between Christophe and her Boisquenay children.

Jekyl had become a place to start over, a new land of grace—a different kind of grace perhaps, but one that was equally, if not even more, perfect. Jekyl Island with its clear air and its surrounding marshes displayed God's splendor in such natural and extraordinary ways, like creation still in its original form. *Yes*, she thought, *it's true. I really do like it here.*

"I'm glad to hear that." Christophe paused for a moment and then added, "Because I've been thinking of selling La Ville Hervé."

Her eyes opened wide in surprise. "But aren't your sisters living there?"

"They are, but I think they're growing tired of looking after the place, and we could surely use the money."

Marguerite knew that cotton prices had dropped sharply since 1796, but she really had only the vaguest idea of Christophe's present finances. Although she knew he worried constantly about money, he rarely shared details of his economic situation with her. She did know, however, that he still received some income from Monsieur Peltier in France.

"I wish we had brought more of our things with us," she said.

"We can have more of them shipped if we do sell." He hesitated for a moment before adding, "I've had a letter from Peltier. There is someone who may be interested in buying the manor. Of course, we'll never get what we paid for it, but it would be one less expense to worry about."

Marguerite thought of their furniture in France and how ridiculous the gilded pieces of the dining room and *salon* would look here, but more of the items she had bought for the bedrooms would be quite nice. They had brought only the bedsteads with them, but she thought how splendid the carved armoires and the fine blanket chests would look. She would like to have more of the tapestries and carpets and perhaps a few small tables and chairs. She thought longingly of the dressing table in her bedchamber at the manor house. Surely Christophe's sisters would see to the packing, if they could manage to get the items out of France.

So there was little question about it any more. It seemed they were here to stay. It was nothing like what they had once planned. It was different, but it afforded them all the peace and privacy they could ever need, and it was theirs. The few carpets she'd insisted on bringing now lay on the floors of the tabby house. Her one tapestry hung over the *salon* fireplace, and several small pieces of furniture, like the writing desk she had refused to leave behind, were neatly arranged inside the house. Christophe had even ordered a chair rail added to the walls of the *salon* to dress it up a bit. And he was talking of adding a detached kitchen, like the one at Orange Grove, to give them a real dining room in the house.

Whatever funds Peltier managed to wrest from Christophe's creditors in France had been a godsend during these recent years. Getting started on a cotton plantation had not been easy. It took a great deal of money, and there seemed to be many ups and downs. *Even so,* she thought, *we are both grateful to have this peaceful island as a refuge. Our family is safe in this young country, and we live a good life.* She was determined to rear her growing sons to be gentlemen, even here.

February 1799

EVER SINCE JANUARY CHRISTOPHE had been in higher spirits than usual. Marguerite was not surprised for she knew that a heavy load had been lifted from his shoulders. His financial situation had greatly improved. Not only had his bail money been freed of obligation, but the sale of La Ville Hervé had been finalized the previous October when Peltier sold it to a man named Amateur Lerestif de Molan. It brought only 18,000 *francs*, the French currency that had in 1795 replaced the old *livres tournois* at roughly the same value. It was considerably less than they had paid originally for the property, but at least it was no longer a drain on the family coffers.

She thought of the day in January when Christophe, waving a letter from Peltier in his hand, had burst into the house to tell her about the sale. She was sitting at her small writing table in the *salon* with a quill in her hand, writing a letter to her sister.

"It's done, Marguerite. The manor has been sold." Christophe sounded delighted. She looked up, her quill poised in mid-air.

"*Vraiment*, really?" was all she said. She was not terribly surprised by his jubilance, for he was not a sentimental man, but she was astounded by the tears that sprang to her own eyes. As much as she had come to love Jekyl, she had mixed reactions to the sale. Although she was pleased to think of the money it brought in, she also felt an unexpected pang of regret. It was as though they were cutting their final ties to France. Owning the graceful manor house and all that went with it had been the dream of their early married life. It was the umbilical cord that still attached them to their native land. It was the promise, albeit a vague one, of a chance to return. Now it was gone. Although she had given her consent to the sale, which she knew was for the best, she still felt a tug at her heart to see it go. It was a door of her life that was now closed forever. This island, this peaceful island would be her home for the rest of her life.

Chapter 19

THE NEW CENTURY—1800—dawned on Jekyl Island with little fanfare, but on January 10 a rare snow began to fall and looked as though it would never stop. It fell in big flakes like soft feathers all that day and into the next, until the island was covered with nearly a foot of snow. Marguerite had never seen such a beautiful snowfall in her life. In fact, it was the first one she had ever seen at Jekyl. She sat by the *salon* window most of the morning, watching it slowly blanket the island with quiet whiteness, marred only by occasional deer or rabbit tracks, which were soon buried beneath new drifting flakes. For the most part, however, even the wild creatures burrowed down to keep warm.

The boys, although now in their early teens, loved it and spent much of the day outside, wearing layers and layers of clothing, building snow forts and having snowball fights. Neither of them had ever experienced such an event before, and their mother smiled to watch their virtual reversion to childhood. Even Joseph, usually so taciturn, was red-cheeked and enthusiastic, pelting his brother with snowballs and laughing like a little boy. They stayed outside until they were cold and wet and their mother called them in to eat some of the hot soup Rosetta kept on the stove and to dry themselves by the *salon* fire.

They were growing up so rapidly. Joseph, at fourteen, was taller than both his parents. He was a handsome boy with a wide forehead and hair that had long since darkened from its original light brown to the same chestnut color as his mother's. He had become increasingly reticent as he passed into adolescence, spending more of his time alone in the woods, collecting artifacts—Indian pottery, arrowheads, an occasional pipe or a button from a British uniform. These he kept in a wooden box in his bedroom, a box no one was permitted to open without his specific consent. Marguerite was pleased to see him relaxing and playing outside with his brother.

Henri, on the other hand, was always more outgoing and less tense than Joseph. He bore a greater physical resemblance to their father, with his raven hair and deep blue eyes. He was taller than his mother, but had not quite reached his father's height, though he was fond of standing back-to-back with Christophe to see how much progress he was making. That he would outgrow his father, Marguerite had no doubt. He was only thirteen and could already make himself taller if he stood on tiptoe. Henri would reach his growth spurt soon, and she suspected he would tease his father unmercifully once he outgrew him. But he loved and admired his father keenly. That she knew. They often rode together around the island to check on the workers and inspect the fields. Henri took pride in the fact that he was the son of a plantation owner with so many slaves and so much land, and he was learning all he could about growing Sea Island cotton, corn, and sweet potatoes.

Unlike the boys, Christophe sat by the blaze in the *salon* grate most of the day, grumbling that such weather was a harbinger of a bad year for crops. In the afternoon, Marguerite joined him by the fire and snuggled against him. He pulled her close and kissed her first on the ear and then on the lips.

"You have to admit, *mon chéri*," she said, "that, whatever all this snow portends, it's beautiful."

"Yes, but beauty can be treacherous," he said. She laughed at the glum expression on his face and snuggled closer until he finally smiled.

BY MID-MONTH, CHRISTOPHE WAS IN A BETTER MOOD. The snow was gone, and he had just received a most welcome letter from Louis Harrington in Savannah, indicating that he and Grandclos Meslé were now, finally, willing to sell him their one-fourth of Jekyl Island. The most important factor in their decision was the settlement, at long last, of the estates of Dumoussay and Chappedelaine. It brought not only an absolute end to this entire ill-fated venture, but also the change of heart for Harrington and Grandclos Meslé, who, as partners themselves, wanted to buy Chappedelaine's portion of Sapelo Island. Proceeds from the sale of their Jekyl land would help them pay for the property at Sapelo.

On the last weekend in January, Christophe travelled to Savannah to be present the following Tuesday to sign the papers for the sale. His purchase of the last quarter of Jekyl, he grumbled to himself, would cost him twelve thousand *livres*, for he still thought in the old currency, but it was well worth it for his peace of mind. He had waited for it much too long to quibble over the cost.

Louis Harrington was, as he expected, the only seller present for the signing.

"Have you heard from your brother-in-law lately?" Christophe asked.

"As a matter of fact, I received a letter last week. Grandclos is still in London. He is, I fear, a much poorer man now that all his property at Saint-Malo has been confiscated. But he's not lost his spirit. He plans to start over again."

"That's good to hear. How does he like England?"

"I get the impression he's quite happy and will most probably stay in London for good. His brother and children are there, as you perhaps know. And he sees many opportunities."

Christophe nodded. He had always felt a greater kinship with Grandclos Meslé than with any of the other Sapelo investors, and he was glad to know that his friend, as usual, had landed on his feet. The two of them were alike in many ways. Both were survivors and always looking for the grand scheme. During their days in France, Grandclos had been much the wealthier of the two, but now they were more or less on the same level financially. In fact, Christophe thought with pride, with this last piece of Jekyl in his possession, he was probably better off than his old friend.

He congratulated himself on how cleverly he had made things work out in Georgia. He was independent now. The island, every inch of it, was his to do with as he pleased. He and his family lived in relative comfort and, above all, in freedom.

What's more, unlike Grandclos, he still owned some assets in France. They all had less value now than before the revolution, but they were still his. His lawyer Peltier continued to represent him well, just as he had when he had obtained the necessary documents to convince officials, eager to confiscate all his property in the name of the revolution, that the du Bignons were not *émigrés*, but rather American citizens who had important reasons to leave the country. For as long as he was in France, Peltier had looked after Christophe's interests as though they were his own, and Christophe felt lucky to have such a friend.

Even before he left Savannah after the sale, he wrote to Peltier of his good fortune. "I am now the sole owner of Jekyl Island, living in a land of liberty. What more can a man ask? Should you encounter misfortunes, you will always find in Georgia a sincere friend who will receive you and welcome you."

In fact, Peltier *had* fled France for a while, but now that things were calmer he had returned to Brittany and was working once again on behalf of Christophe, trying to collect debts and rents that had not been paid during all the years of trouble. The Directory had been replaced by a Consulate, and a young Corsican general by the name of Napoleon Bonaparte had taken firm control of the country and been given the title of First Consul. There was even talk of his being named emperor, which could be even worse than a king, Christophe thought. He was glad they had decided not to return to France. Who knew what was to come?

Although he had come to Georgia as a French royalist, Christophe had begun to be a firm supporter of this American democracy. He liked the fact that landowners could vote to elect capable leaders and vote out those who were incapable. He did not always agree with the American president, but he admired Mr. Washington for having refused to accept the title of king and for refusing to run for a third term in office, which proved he was not power-hungry. Although Christophe had supported the French monarchy and the privileges the nobility enjoyed, he had begun to see the benefits of a republic. He had no desire to return to France.

Marguerite, on the other hand, occasionally suggested the possibility of a visit back to Brittany. She would fix her eyes on her husband and remind him that "the boys are growing older and will soon be looking for wives. There are not so many Catholic, French girls in Georgia. Here they have few choices. A visit to France would give them an opportunity to meet some young ladies." On one occasion when she felt especially emboldened she added softly, looking down at her embroidery, "I would like to see my children again—those still in France—and meet my grandchildren. Margot says that Louis now has a son and two daughters. Just imagine."

His brow furrowed, as it always did, at the mention of her Boisquenay family, though he carefully ignored that part of her argument.

"I'm sure we can help our sons find suitable brides here," he would point out. "There are the Boisfeuillet girls at Sapelo—well, the younger one at least. What was her name?"

"Servanne," she replied.

"And don't forget," he reminded her, "there are a good many French families in Savannah with the influx of sugar planters that fled Saint-Domingue during the slave uprising there."

She sat silent for a moment, saying nothing. But he wasn't fooled. He knew very well that her real reason for wanting to visit France again was to see her Boisquenay brats.

"You know I love the island," she said, after a while. "But I miss the company of French women. I know we can go to Savannah or Sapelo for visits, but there is no one close by." It was a new argument, but one for which he was well prepared.

"*Ma chère,*" he said. "I promise you now that we own all of Jekyl Island, I will see to it that you have French women nearby. I've been thinking about it, and if we leased some portions of the island, we would have neighbors, but we would still be in control of the land. We could pick and choose our neighbors. What do you think of that?"

Marguerite smiled, but he could see it took an effort for her to look enthusiastic. He knew very well it would still not address her real concern about her children in France, but at least it would distract her to have French friends on Jekyl. As far as he was concerned, the matter was closed. She would simply have to settle for the occasional letter she received from Margot.

Christophe never wanted to lay eyes on any of them again, or their offspring for that matter, as long as he lived. He remembered bitterly their distrustful and insulting accusations against their mother. They were nothing but *salauds ingrats*, ungrateful wretches, to him. They disgusted him. Had their scheming been directed at him alone, perhaps he could have gotten over it. But their attack was directed at their mother as well, the woman he would give his life to protect. That treachery and ingratitude he could never forgive. And neither should she.

As a result of such conversations, after closing the deal with Louis Harrington, Christophe made an impulsive decision to buy a modest house in Savannah so the family could spend more time there. *That should give Marguerite ample opportunity to scour the French Catholic community for potential daughters-in-law*, he thought. It would also give him a place to stay while he conducted business there and considered possible tenants for Jekyl Island.

Perhaps Thomas Dechenaux could recommend possible tenants. He had been Christophe's best friend in Savannah ever since their arrival together aboard the *Sappello*. Christophe knew that Thomas would never move to Jekyl, for he was doing quite well in Savannah, partnering in several enterprises with Bernard Lefils, whom Christophe also knew from their earlier voyage together on the *Silvain*. In fact, they represented him as his cotton factors, who arranged for the sale and shipment of his Sea Island cotton from Savannah to other parts of the world. They might know some potential planters who would be interested. Perhaps, with the help of the pair of them, he could take home to Marguerite even more good news.

Chapter 20

January 29, 1800

Jekyl Island

WHEN THE *ANUBIS* DOCKED, upon Christophe's return from Savannah, Marguerite was waiting at the landing, eager to hear all about his trip. She always missed her husband when he was away, and she was delighted to see that he was returning home in a euphoric mood.

"What a beautiful sight!" he called from the sloop. "Marguerite at Marguerite's Landing." She laughed, never tiring of hearing her name on his lips and always happy for the memory of that long-ago arrival and his sweet gesture of naming for her this special spot of welcome on Jekyl Island. She was touched that he never seemed to forget.

As soon as the vessel was secured, he bounded off the boat and lifted her in his arms, swinging her around. It reminded her of that day he returned from Saint-Malo after signing the papers to become part of the Sapelo Company. She could feel that same exuberance now.

"It's all ours, Marguerite. We are now as much landed gentry in America as we ever were in France. Even more so. We own an entire island, where no one can ever bother us. And," he announced grandly, "we also now own a house in Savannah, where you can search to your heart's content for brides for our sons."

"Really?" She tried to share his obvious delight. She knew these were marks of distinction to him in this land where, as he often pointed out, social class was based more on money and property than on birth. But she also knew it probably closed the door to ever returning to France, even for a visit.

"I am now one of the largest landowners in Glynn County," he boasted, taking her right hand and tucking it into the crook of his arm, as he started to walk her toward the house. She was determined to embrace his enthusiasm and accept with grace the reality of her permanent separation from her children in France.

"I met with several married men in Savannah about coming here to live and bringing their wives, just as I promised," he told her as they walked. Marguerite smiled to convey her gratitude.

"With some fellow Frenchmen as tenant planters, we can earn back some of the money I had to spend to buy the land. They can cultivate their own crops here until they can afford to buy their own plantation. Not on Jekyl, of course," he added hastily. "I'll never sell a single acre. It's all ours forever." He raised her hand to his lips and gave it a series of enthusiastic kisses. "And best of all," he said, "if they don't fit in, we can always make them leave. It's our land after all."

His loquacious mood continued even after they had reached the house, as he poured out all his news.

"I met with a man named Jean-Baptiste Goupy, who's coming to visit the island in early spring with his wife, Marguerite Vidal. I've done some business with Goupy before. Remember? We bought some of our slaves from him."

"I remember," she said. "Alexis and Ben once belonged to him." Christophe nodded absently. He could never remember the names of all the slaves, except for Caroline and Rosetta who, he often complained, were constantly underfoot.

"When word got out that I was thinking of leasing land on Jekyl, I had a very interesting visit from another young man—a boy really, not quite seventeen—who expressed an interest. He's not married, of course, but he would bring his mother. You've met her, my dear," he said.

"And who might that be?" she asked.

"Marguerite Bernardey." She recognized the name at once. Marguerite had met her briefly in Savannah when they docked to let the Dechenaux family go ashore. Her husband was a doctor who had planned to serve as physician to the Sapelo Company. The Bernardeys had only one son, a boy named Pierre, she recalled. The one time she had met Madame Bernardey, she had liked her very much.

"I'm sad to say that the boy's father died recently, leaving only a very small estate. The lad is eager to have his own plantation, but he can't afford it yet. Still, he'll have to support his mother, so naturally, he's looking for opportunities."

"I'm sorry to hear of his father's death," she said.

"Yes, it's a shame. He was a fine fellow. But his son talked with me about leasing a hundred acres on Jekyl and learning from me how to cultivate cotton. His plan, when he could save enough money, would be to buy his own land."

"Did you agree?" she asked.

"I said I'd think about it. He told me that he learned many of his father's doctoring skills and thought he might be of use to us here. But the boy can't sign a legal agreement since he's not of age, and his mother would have to sign on his behalf. What do you think? Would she make a good neighbor?"

"Oh, yes, I think she would be a delightful neighbor," said Marguerite.

"Good. I liked him very much. He seems to be an eager and responsible young man, but I wanted to make sure you found his mother agreeable before I said yes. I will write him tomorrow."

Marguerite was especially pleased at the possibility of having Madame Bernardey as a neighbor on Jekyl. The two women were almost the same age and would, no doubt, be good company whenever they could get together.

"Good heavens! Three Marguerites on one island. You named the landing well, it seems." She laughed. "I only hope it won't cause too much confusion."

"I assure you it will not confuse me." Christophe laughed as well. "Everyone else will refer to the three of you as Madame du Bignon, Madame Bernardey, and Madame Goupy. To me you will always be *ma chérie*."

MARGUERITE WAS DELIGHTED when the Goupys and the Bernardeys settled on Jekyl. Madame Goupy, as it turned out, was pregnant, and the other two Marguerites, with the assistance of Sophie, an older female slave who also sometimes served as midwife, helped deliver her little girl on October 22.

"What will you name her?" asked Marguerite Bernardey.

The new mother laughed. "Anything but Marguerite. There are already enough of us here." She settled on the name Anne Georgienne, and the following year, all three families were present for her baptism when the priest from Savannah came to the island in mid-July. The baby gurgled and smiled throughout the ceremony. Marguerite thought of the child as emblematic of everyone's happiness, certainly hers, for she found that she thrived on the company of women.

August 1800

DESPITE CHRISTOPHE'S DIRE PREDICTIONS during the January snowfall, the cotton crop was doing well. A few of the bolls were already bursting with what he liked to call their "white gold." Although the final harvest would not take place until fall, he was convinced that it was going to be a banner year. Marguerite always seemed most contented when her husband was relaxed and happy with his lot. It was almost like their early days together, when they talked of their dreams and when he would take her in his arms and tell her he loved her.

In their meandering conversations, they often spoke of how fortunate they were to have abandoned the Sapelo experiment so early, for nothing good at all had come of it. Even while they were enjoying their prosperity and good fortune, they never forgot what they had escaped.

CHRISTOPHE WAS LULLED BY THEIR MUTUAL contentment and actually smiling when he ambled to the landing to meet the mail packet that late August morning. Nothing much. A newspaper and a letter from Marie de Boisfeuillet, addressed to both him and Marguerite. No doubt another invitation to visit. He would wait until he was back at the house and let his wife open it, as he often did when the letters came from Marie or another of her female correspondents. He listened to the mocking bird trilling through the still summer heat. For August, the day was not particularly hot, but with the humidity, he was sweating before he made it back to the house.

When he stepped into the *salon* and handed the letter to Marguerite, she sat down at her little desk and opened it carefully with her brass letter opener. She unfolded the single page and began to read. He paid little attention until he heard her gasp.

"*Mon Dieu!*"

"What is it?" he asked.

"Boisfeuillet is dead."

"Dead? How? What on earth?" He could hardly believe it. Dead now, after all he and Marie had been through following the shooting of Chappedelaine. After all *he* had been through, with his money tied up for so long. Now, less than a year after the man had been cleared … well not cleared, but no longer charged … how could he be dead?

"Fever … just like Dumoussay," she told him, handing him the letter. "Such a shame. They had just finished their new house."

It was true. The Boisfeuillets had finally completed their long-desired dwelling on the northern part of Sapelo Island in the grassy meadow they called Bourbon Field. They had finally abandoned to workers the common house that held so many unpleasant memories. Christophe, squinting, scanned the letter, shaking his head. Marie's handwriting was almost illegible. She had clearly been upset when she wrote it, and he thought he even detected a tearstain that blurred some of the letters.

"Things seemed to be going so well for them," Marguerite said.

Except for being constantly in debt, Christophe thought, but he said nothing. It did not seem the time to bring up such matters, even though he was thinking it. He knew that Marguerite was probably worrying instead about their new baby. Although Charles was fifty-six years old, his wife Marie was only in her late thirties and had recently given birth to another son. Their world looked so much more promising than it had in the past. Then, suddenly, Charles was gone.

"We must go to Marie. She'll need us," Marguerite said.

He could not say no.

WITHIN THE WEEK, THE FAMILY SAILED TO SAPELO to pay their respects to Boisfeuillet's widow. They found her haggard and devastated by her husband's death. Dark circles sagged beneath her eyes, and her skin was sallow. She held a whimpering infant in her arms.

Handing the baby over to a nearby slave, she fell into Marguerite's arms and began to sob uncontrollably the minute her friend stepped off the sloop.

"What will I do?" she wailed. "How can I live? *Je suis perdue.* I am lost." She had just learned about the mountain of debt her husband had left, and she was overwhelmed by having to deal with such obligations when she still had three children to support. At least her oldest daughter was married.

"I'm sure things will work out," Marguerite said lamely, feeling helpless to console the widow, who clearly needed more than kind words and embraces. She doubted that Christophe would be willing to offer much in the way of aid, for she recalled several recent occasions when Charles de Boisfeuillet had approached her husband asking for loans. Each time Christophe reminded him that, in guaranteeing Charles's bail, he had already tied up a sizeable amount of money without interest for several years, and he refused to lend any more. Christophe always considered Boisfeuillet a poor risk with little, if any, collateral to secure his obligations. Yet somehow the man had managed to acquire enough loans to leave his wife, Marie, buried in debt. Marguerite knew that Christophe would consider a penniless widow an even greater risk.

Marie had never been a strong woman. Now she was deeply depressed and clearly needed someone to lean on. The two women talked deep into the night after the children, who had played quietly all afternoon, were in bed and after even Christophe had said good night. Marie was disconsolate.

But Christophe was eager to get back to Jekyl Island.

"So much can go wrong in my absence. We can't stay long," he said, urging Marguerite to say her goodbyes just one day after their arrival.

Marguerite hated to leave Marie in such a state and persuaded him to remain a while longer, but he was increasingly insistent. After only a few days, when they finally departed, she invited the grieving widow to come and stay a while with them at Jekyl. Marie just looked at her helplessly and shook her head, her eyes wet with tears and sunken with worry. She stood alone, unmoving, on the dock, watching as they set sail.

MARGUERITE WAS SHOCKED BUT SOMEHOW not surprised when word reached Jekyl Island the following February, less than six months after Charles's death, that Marie de Boisfeuillet was also dead. She was not yet forty years old. They did not know how she had died.

"Do you think she took her own life?" Christophe, taking a sip of wine, asked Marguerite as they sat as they sat on a bench they had placed at the edge of the marsh to watch the sunset.

Marguerite quickly crossed herself. "Of course not," she said without hesitation. The day was chilly, and she pulled her cloak more tightly around her. "She was a good Catholic." She did not look at him.

"I wonder." Christophe said nothing more, as he gazed out over the greening expanse of spartina grass. They often sat there in the late afternoon to share a glass of wine and chat about the news in the latest copy of the *Columbian Museum and Savannah Advertiser*, delivered weekly by the mail packet. Christophe took another large swallow of the dry Bordeaux, while Marguerite focused her attention on the needlepoint butterfly she was embroidering on a pillowcase.

"I wonder what will become of the Boisfeuillet children?" Marguerite said finally, lifting her eyes to follow Christophe's gaze across the winter marsh.

"I hear Marie left a will and named a guardian—a cousin by the name of Joseph Emile de Charon and his wife," Christophe said. "The oldest girl, Jeanne, is already married, and Servanne is practically grown, but I guess the boys will need looking after, especially the baby."

Considering the Boisfeuillets' misfortunes, Marguerite thanked God once again for her own situation, feeling almost guilty that she fretted so over being separated from her children in France. Overall, she was happy, and she was lucky to have a living husband who, at least for the moment, seemed content with his lot.

Only the day before, Christophe had read to her with pride in his voice another letter he was sending to Peltier, boasting yet again of owning all of Jekyl Island, which he described as "a very large estate." He predicted to Peltier that he expected a profit for the year of more than forty thousand *livres*, almost $7,500, a very great sum, considering that the average farm in Georgia brought in less than $500 a year. It was more than he'd ever expected to make on his cotton crop. Marguerite could tell that he was quite satisfied with himself, and she was pleased. Having him for such a long, uninterrupted time in a positive frame of mind certainly made her life better. *If only*, she thought, *it could last.*

Unfortunately, it did not. Good seasons were followed by bad seasons. A summer drought in 1802 ravaged the yearly crop, and the following February there was another snowstorm—not the soft, lovely blanket of two years earlier—but a bitter, swirling storm that left several inches of wet, slushy snow, which soon melted and refroze as unfriendly ice. Then, by summer, when the ice was long gone, the island suffered once more under the burning summer sun.

"*Mordieu*," Christophe muttered to his groom, Ben, as the two men rode home from the fields late one afternoon. "This is the worst heat wave I've ever seen. If only it would rain." But when the rains finally did come, they brought the devastating cotton worm. Christophe complained daily that it was one calamity after another.

He was growing discouraged. One day he shuffled toward the house, his shoulders slumped, dust dried on his cheeks and under his eyes. He was carrying a ruined cotton stalk in one hand and in the other a caterpillar, one of the many he had found munching on what was left of the cotton crop. He encountered Marguerite, waiting just inside the *salon*.

"Now this—this is what I have to deal with. Will it never end?" He threw the caterpillar to the floor and smashed it under his heel. "*Foutre!*"

He rarely used such language except when he was completely out of control. Then he took his bad temper out on everyone—his slaves, his sons, especially Joseph—everyone but Marguerite, the only person who could soothe him even a little in such times. Everyone dreaded the darkening of his brow and his bitter moods as summer took its toll.

"We'll make little profit this year. We'll have to live off whatever income Peltier can wring from my investments in France.'

"But we are so much better off than those who have to depend entirely on the cotton crop," she reminded him. "We should consider ourselves lucky."

"Lucky indeed," he scoffed. His face wore a determined scowl, as he clung to his darkness and brooded over the swarm of black and yellow striped caterpillars, whose hungry mouths were attacking his crop. He had ordered the slaves to pick them off one by one, but it was a losing battle.

"They're eating every single leaf and boll," he complained. "They can strip a whole field in a week's time." His only comfort seemed to lie in the fact that every other cotton planter on the coast was suffering the same misfortune.

MARGUERITE TRIED NOT TO LET HIS MOODS ruin her days, choosing instead to enjoy the presence of the other families on the island. Opportunities to visit back and forth with Marguerite Bernardey and Marguerite Goupy brightened her winter and spring. Even when she spent her days at home, she was thankful that there were neighbors nearby, not close enough to disturb the wondrous peace she found among the moss-draped live oaks, but close enough to know there was company when she needed it.

Although she too hoped for financial stability, she no longer cared so much about material things, as long as they had peace and love, a place to live, and enough to eat. And they always had a trickle of income from France to rely on. While she had secretly longed in her youth to belong to the landed gentry, life had taught her that wealth was no guarantee of happiness. She felt sick when she thought about what it had done for the wealthiest families in France, many of whom had known the savagery of the guillotine—even Marie Antoinette and King Louis. In spite of all their wealth and elegant living, *even they weren't immune to bad fortune,* she thought. It was their extravagance and self-indulgence in living the wealthy life, regardless of anyone else's hard times, that had cost them their lives.

Marguerite had learned to appreciate what she had, rather than bemoaning what she had lost. She found joy now in simple things, visits with friends, teaching her sons, and working in her garden, where she took pleasure both in the work and in what it produced. They gave her a sense of profound satisfaction.

She felt sad for Christophe though, who seemed to see life as a continuing battle to beat fate, accumulate wealth, and to hold it tight in his fist. She thought it was becoming almost all he cared about. She knew he had tried, tried so hard, and felt certain twice that he had attained his dream, only to have it slip through his fingers. While she understood and appreciated his efforts, she would much have preferred him to leave it all in God's hands so that she might have her kinder and gentler husband with her at all times no matter what. But something inside him seemed to shrink a bit more with every passing misfortune.

He cursed his fate, ranting in her presence. Would nothing ever go right? Would he never be able to end this struggle not only to become a wealthy man, but to remain one? Was his entire life to be a catastrophe, a downfall, a battle against one thing and another? Marguerite watched helplessly as he sank more and more deeply into his dark moods, which only a good cotton-growing season could dispel. *Perhaps next year's crop will be better,* she thought hopefully.

Chapter 21

October 1803

Jekyl Island

F OR CHRISTOPHE, ALL HIS SLAVES WERE pretty much alike. Only a handful of them had made any real impression on him as individuals. He knew he could always count on his dark, heavy-set driver Big Peter, whom he judged "a good man," to have the slaves in the field and well at work by dawn. And the quiet stable hand, Ben, was also in Christophe's view "a fine fellow," always subservient, always concerned about his master's well-being, always wearing a cheerful smile. He'd grown rather fond of Ben, he had to admit.

One other slave he could always distinguish, aside from the house servants and his sailors, whom he saw most frequently, was Tom, an "ornery young buck," who constantly sought ways to be insolent and run away any time he saw the slightest opportunity. He had regretted his purchase of Tom from the day he bought him. He would sell him if he could, but the scars on Tom's back told the story of his disobedient nature and would make any buyer wary.

Christophe was sitting astride his gray horse, enjoying the cool October day and watching with satisfaction as his slaves bent over their work in the cotton rows, dragging their heavy bags alongside them as they picked the white balls from the prickly bolls. He was thinking how fine a cool drink of water would be about now, when suddenly he heard a shout.

He turned and instantly recognized the dark shape of Ben running across the cotton field, waving his arms, his bare feet leaving deep footprints in the soil.

"Massa, Massa," he hollered. It was what Christophe instructed the slaves to call him, even when speaking French, because it was the term used by slaves on the other plantations in the area. "There's a gentleman at the landing who wants to see you," Ben hollered in the best French he could muster.

Christophe nodded once, turned his horse around, and trotted north toward the dock. He hated to leave the fields on such a fine morning in cotton-picking time, but a visitor was always a novelty and usually brought news. He wasn't worried about the work. Big Peter would keep his eye on things. Christophe dismounted as he saw a well-dressed gentleman standing near Marguerite's Landing, his three servants busy tying up the small boat in which the man had arrived.

"*Bonjour, Monsieur*, welcome to Jekyl Island," Christophe greeted him. "What can I do for you?"

The man held out his hand, "Good morning, Sir. Captain du Bignon, I presume? I'm Alexander Wylly." From his speech, Christophe could tell he was English. The tall man, his ruddy face sober and earnest, had a firm handshake—always a good sign.

"I heard you might be leasing some land on Jekyl Island," Wylly said.

"That's true," Christophe replied, "but so far only to fellow French *émigrés*."

"Well, I'm not French, as you can obviously tell, but I'm willing to pay well for a homestead here, for a few years at least."

It's worth considering an offer, Christophe thought. Nevertheless, he pointed out, "You might like St. Simons better. There are more English and Scottish people there."

"Yes, I know, but I don't seem terribly welcome there at the moment."

Christophe was puzzled. "Why not?"

"In the interest of complete candor, I should tell you my whole story. The folks on St. Simons are still upset with me because during the American Revolution I was a Tory. You may have heard about me—Alexander Campbell Wylly—from some of your friends over there. I was a captain in the King's Rangers and fought against the Loyalists."

Christophe listened with interest, nodding from time to time. He had never heard of the King's Rangers and knew nothing of their role in the Revolution, but he was curious.

Wylly went on, "Although I was born in the colony of Georgia, I was educated in England and remained loyal to the Crown. I was banished from Georgia after the war, and since then, I've been in exile in the Bahamas. It wasn't a bad thing, as it turned out, because that's where I was fortunate enough to meet the woman who would become my wife—Margaret Armstrong," he said with a smile. "But I've been away for more than twenty years now, and I want to return to Georgia, which I still consider my home. Unfortunately, some of the people on St. Simons have not forgiven me my role in the war."

"*Vraiment?* Really?" Christophe almost laughed. It was a silly reason, he thought. As a privateer he, like those on St. Simons, had been on the side of the Americans and an enemy to the English. But he could hardly hold it against the man that he had fought on the other side. That was a quarter of a century ago. Besides, the cause had meant nothing to Christophe except for the booty he'd been able to capture. If Wylly was willing to pay sufficiently, why not have an Englishman on the island? Christophe could certainly use the money. There was still unused land and no other Frenchmen were currently interested, as far as he knew.

Christophe ordered Ben to saddle another horse, and the two men rode about Jekyl for several hours, looking for a suitable site for Captain Wylly to build a house. They found a spot about mid-point on the island and settled on a price that Christophe considered quite sufficient to justify the acceptance of at least one British family on the island. *Surely Marguerite won't object to a non-French family on Jekyl. Now,* he thought, *she can practice her English whenever she wants.*

WHEN WYLLY LEFT TO MAKE ARRANGEMENTS for the construction of a new house, a road to get to it, and a move to Jekyl, Christophe told his wife of his agreement to lease a hundred acres to the gentleman.

"An Englishman?" Marguerite said. "But I thought you wanted to make the island entirely French." She was not upset about the decision, just surprised.

"He has the money, and he needs a place." Christophe had no motive, other than wanting to rent more land. "Apparently he is not welcome on St. Simons."

"Why not?" Marguerite asked. Christophe briefly outlined Wylly's story, concluding with, "He's having trouble getting those who fought against the British to lease or sell him land."

"Does he have a family?" she asked.

"Seven children and a wife, he says." He hesitated and smiled sheepishly. "Her name is Margaret."

"The English version of Marguerite. Wouldn't you know?" Marguerite laughed. "Not another one. You have named our landing well, since it seems that no other women but Marguerites or Margarets can ever land there. How old are their children?"

"All ages, I gather. He tells me that the oldest is a fifteen-year-old girl named Susannah for her grandmother, but they call her Susan. She has a sister Ann, two years younger. I don't know about the rest."

"We'll have to keep an eye on our sons," Marguerite said, half-teasing. She was only a bit apprehensive that the Wylly girls would be so close as her sons were becoming young men. She had spoken to them so often about the need to marry a Catholic girl that she was pretty sure they would respect her wishes and keep their distance.

THE WYLLYS WERE EAGER TO GET settled, for Margaret Wylly was pregnant again. She gave birth to another daughter in their hastily constructed house on Jekyl Island on February 19, 1804. Marguerite could only laugh in amazement to learn that there would be yet another Margaret on the island, for the Wyllys named their new daughter Margaret Mathilda.

MARGUERITE HAD NOT COUNTED ON SUSAN WYLLY being such a pretty girl. Her hair was dark, and her wide-spaced eyes even darker. There was no question that both the boys found her attractive and took any opportunity to be in her presence.

It was a relief to Marguerite when, in mid-July 1804, John Couper, well aware of Madame du Bignon's concern for her sons' future, sent word to Jekyl that he had several young French ladies as his guests at Cannon's Point, and he thought their sons might want to meet them. Couper's note explained the situation:

The visitors all lost their fathers in the slave uprising in Saint-Domingue. One of the three, Anne Amélie Nicolau, is an orphan who has come to Georgia to join her older brothers. They have recently settled in the area, but their futures are uncertain, as we will explain when we are together. Her friends, Mimi and Elisabeth Grand Dutreuilh, have joined her briefly on St. Simons. Rebecca and I would be honored to have you and your sons come for a visit on Saturday, August 18, and stay the night or even for several days, if you can.

Marguerite was delighted. She had been watching her sons grow up all too fast, and she was increasingly concerned that one of them might fall in love with a Protestant girl from St. Simons or Savannah, where non-Catholics were definitely in the majority. She was concerned that, when they came of marriageable age, and they were almost there, no suitable Catholic girls would be available for them to choose from. She had once considered Servanne de Boisfeuillet as a possible daughter-in-law, for she suspected that Joseph had been briefly smitten with her, but the girl had shown little interest in him during their few times together. Then, after the death of her mother, when Servanne was only fifteen, news reached Jekyl Island that she had married a French widower by the name Jean Bérard de Moquet, best known in Savannah as the Marquis de Montalet. Rumor had it that he was a good many years older than she and that he had his eyes on the Sapelo property as much as on the girl herself. The news dashed any hope Marguerite might have had for the girl's betrothal to her son. Then, only a few years later, she heard that Servanne was dead in childbirth. She was stunned. *Such a shame*, Marguerite thought, *dead at only eighteen.*

Now, with new prospects in view, Marguerite insisted that both her sons, seventeen and eighteen, have their hair trimmed by the slave Apollo, who shaved their father and trimmed his beard every day. She sent them into Brunswick to buy new clothes, for they had outgrown all the decent clothes they had for their occasional visits to Savannah. She wanted them both to look their best.

Although Joseph did as his mother bid in terms of hair and clothing, he was not particularly interested in meeting Mademoiselle

Nicolau and her friends. He talked very little and usually seemed uncomfortable in society. Girls his own age intimidated him—all but Susan Wylly, with whom he seemed relaxed and able to speak freely. But Marguerite sensed that they were only friends, that there was no romantic attraction between the two of them. Still, she would keep her eye on the situation. He would always be the taller and the more handsome of her sons. His hair was darkening, but still had an auburn cast like his mother's when he stood in the sunlight.

Henri, on the other hand, had grown more attractive as he grew older, and his amiable nature was better suited to most social settings than that of his brother. As his mother had predicted, Henri was now a head taller than his father, though despite his height, he still bore an uncanny resemblance to him. Unlike his older brother, he was delighted with the opportunity to meet French women his own age. He would soon be eighteen, and he had begun to notice the slave girls who occasionally came to the house bringing gifts of berries or jam to his mother. He teased them and made them giggle, but as yet, he had not touched one of them, at least as far as his mother knew. Still, she was growing concerned that it was time for both her boys to begin thinking of marriage to keep themselves out of trouble.

Chapter 22

O<small>N THE SECOND WEEKEND IN</small> A<small>UGUST</small>, just eight days after
Henri's eighteenth birthday, the family set sail on the *Anubis*
to reach Cannon's Point at the north end of St. Simons. The
sloop, one of the fastest vessels of its type in the coastal waters, was a
smaller version of vessels often used by corsairs for their speed and
maneuverability. It reminded Christophe of his days as a privateer,
chasing British ships in the Indian Ocean. It was especially useful in
the shallow and sometimes unpredictable waters around the islands
and in St. Simons Sound. In a pinch, he could sail it with only Henri
and Joseph as crew, but this time he had brought along Big Cain,
Germain, and Apollo to handle the vessel.

From the Jekyl landing to the Coupers' Cannon's Point plantation
on the north end of St. Simons was a trip of more than fifteen miles
and could take several hours, depending on wind and tides. Dinner
at the Couper House was served at half past four, and the meal and

proper social amenities would last until at least seven or seven-thirty. They would, of course, accept the Coupers' hospitality to stay the night to avoid making the trip home after dark. It was common practice to spend the night or even several days when one had to travel such distances.

With or without the opportunity to meet the young ladies, Marguerite looked forward to the trip. It would be their first time to visit the Coupers in their recently completed new house, and she was eager to see it. Both she and Christophe always anticipated with pleasure any meal prepared by Sans Foix, whose repasts were by now renowned on the Georgia coast. The Marquis de Montalet was reputed to have a chef at Sapelo named Cupidon, whose cuisine was said to surpass even that of Sans Foix. She found that hard to believe, but she would have welcomed the opportunity to compare the two.

THEY REACHED THE MOUTH OF THE HAMPTON RIVER in just under three hours, then sailed upriver, dropping anchor near the Couper dock at Cannon's Point. The crew lowered the wooden yawl and rowed the du Bignon family through the shallower water to the dock. As they approached, even from a great distance Marguerite could see the new house not far from the riverbank, built up almost five feet on a tabby foundation in case of floods. Dormer windows rose above the second floor, and a large brick chimney stood out against the sky. John Couper had spied their sails from a distance and was waiting on the dock to greet them.

As he helped Marguerite from the boat and shook her husband's hand in warm reception, he said in his hearty Scottish brogue, "How marvelous that you've brought your sons. Mademoiselle Nicolau and the Grand Dutreuilh sisters will be delighted to meet some Frenchmen nearer their own age. My French, I am sorry to say, is quite inadequate."

Marguerite smiled and accepted when he offered his arm to walk her to the house.

"Your new home is lovely," she said, "but I will wait and pay my compliments when Mrs. Couper is present, for no doubt she also had much influence on its design."

"Indeed she did, *Madame*. That marvelous wide verandah, for one thing. And she will be delighted to hear that influence appreciated."

Rebecca Couper was standing at the top of the porch steps, her arms outstretched to welcome them.

"How wonderful to see you again," she said to them all with a wide, friendly smile.

"It's wonderful to be here. How lovely your new home is." Marguerite was much more confident of her English now than she had been the first time the two women met. She was practicing frequently with Margaret Wylly, as Christophe had suggested.

"Thank you for gracing us with a visit. May I show you around?" She was clearly eager to escort them through the house that she and John had planned with such loving care.

"Oh, yes, please do." Marguerite nodded. She was interested in seeing new building ideas, for Christophe was still talking of adding wings to the old Horton house on Jekyl when the children married. Her hostess led them through the large front door.

It was gracious inside, but not at all pretentious. The first floor consisted of a spacious dining room for entertaining, and a smaller one just for the family, two parlors, and a library, filled with Mr. Couper's books. Through the large windows, Marguerite could see the wide verandah that stretched around the first floor, the one Rebecca had designed herself. The views of the marshes were spectacular, and the adjacent island called Little St. Simons sparkled in the distance. The Coupers had planted palms and a variety of other trees that would one day be tall enough to shade the verandah.

"Where are Mademoiselle Nicolau and the other young ladies?" Marguerite asked.

"They are in their room upstairs writing letters, I believe. They should be down soon. Your rooms are upstairs as well," Rebecca said. "Let's not disturb them just yet. I'd like to have you all to myself for a while. But I'll have the servants take your things up and leave them in your rooms."

After a tour of the first floor of the house, the men, including Joseph and Henri, settled on the verandah to talk, leaving the women alone together.

"Would it be possible to see your kitchen?" Marguerite asked. "Christophe and I have been thinking of adding a detached kitchen to the old Horton house. That way we could turn our present kitchen into a dining room, which we badly need."

Rebecca looked surprised at the request, but she smiled and acquiesced. The Couper plantation had a large kitchen built apart from the main house to minimize the danger of fires and to eliminate heat and cooking odors. It was the way most plantation homes were built in the South, and Marguerite knew that if she and Christophe could separate the cooking area from the house completely, they would have a much more pleasant situation.

When Rebecca led her out to the kitchen, Marguerite studied the outbuilding carefully. A brick fireplace large enough to stand in dominated one end. Cauldrons and pots hung from hooks over the fire, and long-handled toasters were lined up on either side. An enormous beef roast and a turkey were on spits, both being turned by a young boy, his dark face glistening in the heat. There were cupboards and cabinets that held the cooking utensils and a large preparation area for Sans Foix and his helpers.

"This is so well done, Rebecca," Marguerite said, admiration in her voice. When they left the kitchen, Rebecca led Marguerite through the orchards.

"As you know, John is interested in agricultural experiments and discovering what he can grow on his plantation." She pointed out orange and lemon trees, as well as plum and peach trees and fig bushes. "He's even interested in seeing whether he can grow olive trees in this climate. There seems to be nothing he's unwilling to try in terms of horticulture," Rebecca said with a laugh.

As they headed back toward the house, Marguerite caught sight of a child's face, peeking around one corner of the verandah, spying on the adults. Rebecca saw him too.

"That little scamp," she said with a laugh. "He's always curious." The Coupers had three children now. Their oldest, James Hamilton, named for one of John Couper's dearest friends, was already ten years old. His sister, Ann Sarah, was three years younger. The child on the porch was the youngest of the three, John Jr., who had turned five in April. Just then, his nursemaid found him, took him by the hand, and led him back to the family dining room, where the children were sitting down for an early meal.

WHEN THE ADULTS' DINNER WAS READY, one of the servants, a tall black man called "Old Tom," blew on a large conch shell to summon the guests from wherever they might be scattered. It was in the dining room that Marguerite and her family finally met the French visitors.

Young Henri du Bignon looked thunderstruck when he saw Mademoiselle Nicolau. She wore her dark hair pulled back and secured loosely at the nape of her neck, but cut shorter around her face to form ringlets, which called attention to her wide-spaced, brown eyes and fair complexion. Her nose was a trifle long but balanced well with her full lips. She was pretty in an unconventional, but nonetheless stylish, way. Her white voile dress was gathered beneath her small breasts and hung loosely in a neo-classical style popular in Napoleonic France. Her arms were bare, but she wore a shawl of deep rose that lifted the color in her cheeks.

"I am so delighted to meet you," she said to the du Bignons in general. "It is good to know there are other French families here on the Georgia coast." Her smile took them all in.

"We are so happy you are here," Marguerite said.

"Indeed," Christophe added. Henri nodded with enthusiasm, while Joseph gave a single nod of acknowledgment.

The Grand Dutreuilh sisters stood behind her and gave small curtsies when they were introduced. Both were dark haired, modestly dressed, and appeared to be several years older than Mademoiselle Nicolau.

"You are all so fortunate to be guests of the Coupers," Marguerite told them all. "Their hospitality is legendary." The young women all smiled with appreciation, but Marguerite could tell from the puzzlement in their eyes that the Grand Dutreuilh sisters felt uncomfortable with the conversation in English. She remembered her own early days in Georgia when she was the one who could understand so little, and her heart went out to them. *They will soon learn*, she thought.

Once the introductions were made, everyone took their places in anticipation. Almost at once, the serving girls started bringing in the food. The meal was sumptuous but not pretentious. It was not their wealth or elegance that made guests flock to the Couper home, but rather the quality of their hospitality. Their genuine warmth and the feasts Sans Foix routinely prepared for the guests, always served with the finest of wines from John Couper's ample wine cellar, were sufficient to make anyone covet an invitation.

The Coupers rarely dined alone, and one never knew how many people might be at their table on any given day. Rebecca could never inform the kitchen staff how many to expect until shortly before the meal, and ample food had to be available at a moment's notice.

Dinner that afternoon began with crab bisque. Crabs were abundant on the islands, and the Coupers took full advantage of the local fare. The bisque was followed by a magnificent sautéed sea bass. Then came courses of wild turkey and roast beef, served with mountains of potatoes au gratin and an array of side dishes—sautéed mushrooms stuffed with crabmeat, spinach dressed with cream and served with puff pastries, baked tomatoes, stewed cucumbers with sweet onions, and corn pudding.

"Are you aware," Christophe said to the young ladies, "that your host is a very important man on the Georgia coast?"

John Couper gave a hearty laugh. "I hardly think so," he said.

"*Mais oui*," Christophe said with enthusiasm. "I think he knows everyone in the entire state of Georgia. He has served in the state legislature and even helped write the state constitution. And he is one of the most respected horticulturalists in the entire United States."

"You exaggerate, my friend," John said. "To clarify, dear ladies, I served only one term in the legislature, and I am but a humble experimenter willing to try any plant that might consider growing in this climate."

"You are all so fortunate to experience the Couper hospitality, which, as my husband has already mentioned, is without equal on the Georgia coast," Marguerite said.

"That, *Madame*, is due only to the gracious efforts of my wife, I assure you." He smiled down the table to Rebecca who sat at the other end. Marguerite always enjoyed watching the interplay between the two of them. They were so obviously still in love. She recognized the symptoms well.

"Not to mention Sans Foix," Rebecca added with a laugh.

The Grand Dutreuilh sisters ate quietly, trying to follow the discussion, to which they contributed only friendly smiles. If something particularly important was said, Joseph would lean over to whisper a translation to Mimi Grand Dutreuilh, who was seated beside him. She would, in turn, share it with her sister, whom everyone called Treyette.

Anne Amélie Nicolau, on the other hand, proved to be a most gracious young woman. Her English was far from perfect, but it seemed not to bother her in the least. She made every effort to participate in the conversation, whenever it seemed appropriate. Marguerite judged her to be about seventeen or eighteen, near the age of Joseph and Henri. She gathered from the conversation that the families of the young women had known each other in Saint-Domingue before the uprising.

The lilt of her French accent suggested her origin from the Bordeaux region. Most of the dinner conversation, however, was in English out of respect for the host and hostess, though every now and then, Henri would address something to the young ladies, mostly to Mademoiselle Nicolau, in French. Her cheeks would sometimes flush whenever he spoke directly to her, and she always replied with her eyes lowered toward her dinner plate. Marguerite watched the interaction between the two of them with concealed amusement, remembering her own youthful efforts toward a modest demeanor. She had never seen Henri so obviously smitten. From the first moment he laid eyes on Amélie Nicolau, he was clearly her servant.

The girl responded with grace, but Marguerite also noticed that her eyes strayed now and then across the table to Joseph, who was blatantly, almost rudely, ignoring her. Except for his occasional whispers of interpretation, he had eaten in a silence almost as complete as that of Mimi and Treyette.

Christophe, noticing his younger son's attraction to Mademoiselle Nicolau, made an effort to engage her in conversation.

"What brings you to Georgia?" he asked.

"Two of my brothers are here, and both my parents are dead. *Papa* was killed during the slave revolt in Saint-Domingue, as you may know," she said sadly. The other two young women both nodded

gravely, no doubt remembering their own slain father. "We all fled back to France, but *Maman* died there quite recently." Tears sprang to her eyes.

"I'm so very sorry," Christophe said. "And where are your brothers now?"

"They will come. My oldest brother, Joseph ..." she glanced at Joseph du Bignon when she said the name, "sent for me to join him here after the death of our mother. He's on a brief voyage to Savannah just now. My middle brother, Bernard, is working on their plantation, which they call Marengo. He will come when he can, I'm sure. My youngest brother, Pascal, is still in Bordeaux, helping to settle *Maman*'s estate, but he too will come soon. All my brothers are older, but none of them are married yet. We will make a life here together." It was a brave statement and her longest one throughout the entire evening.

Marguerite caught a glimpse of John Couper's suddenly somber face as she spoke. He exchanged a knowing look with Rebecca, who tried to replace the expression of concern that wrinkled her brow with a smile. What was this all about? Where were Amélie's brothers? There was something the young woman wasn't saying or else something she didn't know.

Everyone's attention was suddenly diverted by the arrival of dessert—chocolate mousse with whipped cream. Mr. Couper lightened the mood by raising his glass to toast his guests. They too lifted their goblets, which had just been filled with Rebecca Couper's famous Orange Shrub, her own blend of sweetened brandy steeped with Seville oranges.

After the meal ended, the young people went out to stroll in the garden, while the two men enjoyed a glass of Madeira in the library. Rebecca Couper asked the serving girl to bring another cup of Orange Shrub to her and Madame du Bignon on the verandah. Once they were settled in their chairs, Rebecca leaned toward Marguerite.

"We should have told you when you first arrived, I suppose, but we just learned this morning that Mademoiselle Nicolau's brother Joseph was drowned in a boating accident during a sudden storm near Savannah. We haven't told her yet, for we didn't want to upset her, especially since her other brother Bernard, who is at Marengo, has come down with yellow fever and may not survive."

She lifted her glass to her lips and took a quick sip before she continued. "We didn't want to worry her unnecessarily, and so we haven't told her about that either. We just pray that he is improving, but Jock and I thought it best to wait until he is fully recovered and can be of comfort to his sister before we tell her about Joseph. The poor girl has been through so much, losing both her parents so young. And now a brother. For such a short life, hers has been tragic indeed."

"Oh my," Marguerite said. "How dreadful."

"All three of the young ladies have suffered great losses. The father of Mimi and Treyette was also a victim of the uprising in Saint-Domingue."

Marguerite nodded. "So I gathered. It must have been awful."

"There's more," Rebecca said. "There is another sister and a brother, who are both with their mother in Trenton, New Jersey. After the worst of the uprising, their brother went back to Saint-Domingue to see if he could find out what happened to their father. At the time they still didn't know whether he was dead or alive. He discovered a rather gruesome story. Apparently their father was taken to a riverbank along with five other captives and stabbed to death with bayonets."

"How horrible," Marguerite said.

"Amelia tells me that her brother Bernard has offered to go back to Saint-Domingue and try to find how their father died, but after hearing the story of Monsieur Grand Dutreuilh, I don't think she really wants to know. She doesn't want to deal with such realities, which is one reason we haven't told her about her brother Joseph.

Do you think we are wrong to keep it from her?" asked Rebecca.

"I'm sure you are doing what you think is best. I will add my prayers for her other brother's recovery."

"She seems such a delicate child. We hope to keep her here until Bernard is well again. The other two young ladies are leaving on Monday to meet their other sister and visit friends in Savannah. John thinks if we told her about Bernard, she would insist on going to Marengo to nurse him. I wouldn't want her to expose herself to such danger. Do you think it's terrible of us to keep it all from her?" she asked again.

"Not at all. I know you just want to spare her. But who is looking after her brother?"

"He has servants, who seem to be almost immune to the disease. I'm told that he is being carefully watched and cared for." The two women sat on the porch and chatted as darkness fell. Evening sounds of crickets and frogs began to gather around the house, and one by one, stars appeared in the night sky.

Marguerite said a silent prayer for Bernard Nicolau's recovery. She had already come to like Anne Amélie, who was so innocently enjoying the Coupers' hospitality, without knowing that her world could be crumbling around her. Marguerite made a special place for the girl in her heart.

WHEN THE DU BIGNONS WERE AGAIN ABOARD the *Anubis* the next day, Christophe began to quiz his sons about their reactions to Mademoiselle Nicolau. Joseph, who, as he grew older, had finally overcome his tendency to be seasick or at least to succumb to it, said very little. When he learned of Amélie's ignorance of her brothers' misfortunes, however, a small frown crossed his brow. He made no comment, but Marguerite could see sympathy in his eyes. Henri, on the other hand, sang the girl's praises almost the whole way home. She was, he said, the most beautiful, charming, sweet, bright girl he'd ever met—adding whatever complimentary adjective crossed his mind—as they sailed through the morning light.

"What did you think of her, Marguerite?" her husband asked.

"I found her most pleasant, attractive, and quite congenial," she said.

"What would you say to her as a daughter-in-law?" he asked.

"I think you may be getting a little ahead of the situation, Christophe," she said. "Our sons barely know her or she them. And there is so much happening in her life right now that I think she needs time to cope with it all, once she finds out."

"On the other hand," he suggested, "perhaps she needs something else to look forward to. I thought she would make quite a suitable match for either of our sons. What about it, boys?" he asked, looking at Henri. "Is anyone interested?"

Before either of their sons could react, Marguerite said, "I think the young woman should make up her own mind. She may not want either of them."

"Be that as it may," her husband said, "we should make an offer before someone in Savannah beats us to it."

"If you're thinking of us as husbands, perhaps you should stop calling us *boys*," Joseph said curtly. "You sound as though you're talking to one of the slaves."

Christophe clamped his lips together, and Marguerite could see that he was grinding his teeth. Then he said, "I'll call you a *man* when you start acting like one." Father and son glared at each other for a moment, and then both turned away to stare at the dark waters ahead, their jaws fixed. They sailed the rest of the way home almost entirely in silence. Marguerite watched the interchange, thinking sadly, *in some ways, they are too much alike.*

CHRISTOPHE WAS IMPATIENT. He found the girl extremely desirable. He envied his sons' youth and their upcoming opportunities to enjoy such sweet young flesh. What he wouldn't give to be young again. He was convinced that he had many rival fathers, some from France, some from Saint-Domingue, waiting in Savannah to offer to this charming and marriageable girl a proposal on behalf of their sons. Look what had happened with Servanne de Boisfeuillet—snatched up and married at fifteen. Christophe knew that Marguerite wanted him to wait to make a marriage proposal until all the uncertainties of Mademoiselle Nicolau's life were resolved and she had sufficient time to recover from her brother's death. His wife also thought it appropriate that he broach such an offer to the girl's guardian, presumably her sick brother, Bernard, rather than to the girl herself. He saw the logic in that, but by the end of the month, he had heard nothing further about the condition of young Bernard Nicolau, and he was growing increasingly impatient that he might miss the moment.

Chapter 23

September 2, 1804

Jekyl Island

WHEN WORD ARRIVED ON JEKYL that the vice president of the United States, Aaron Burr, had arrived in Georgia and was staying on St. Simons at the plantation of Pierce Butler, which adjoined the Couper plantation at the north end of the island, Christophe was delighted. Here was his chance—a good excuse to visit the neighboring island. He would like nothing more, he told Marguerite, than to make Burr's acquaintance.

"But why is he here?" she asked.

"Because of the duel," he said.

"What duel?"

Christophe thought he had already told her about it. Nonetheless, he related once again how Mr. Burr had killed the secretary of the treasury, Alexander Hamilton, in a duel the preceding July. There was such an uproar that Burr fled New York, where he had been running for governor and where Hamilton had been doing everything he could to undermine him. The two men hated each other.

"I suppose Burr is now taking refuge outside the city until the matter dies down. I'm not sure what all the brouhaha is about," Christophe said. "Duels happen all the time in France, and from what I've heard they're not that uncommon in Georgia either. In my view, Mr. Burr had ample reason to challenge Hamilton to a duel. And he beat him fair and square. ... In any case," he said, "I would like to meet the vice president. He would be a good man to know—a man of influence."

He planned to call on Burr the very next day, and while he was on the north end of St. Simons, although he didn't mention it to Marguerite, he would stop by the Couper plantation to visit Mademoiselle Nicolau as well. This time he would not take Marguerite or the boys. He would go alone except for his slaves, Big Cain, Germain, and Apollo, who had accompanied him to Cannon's Point during their last visit.

THE NEXT DAY DAWNED BRIGHT AND CLEAR, with a steady breeze—a great day for sailing. The first stop of the *Anubis* was at Cannon's Point, where he planned to carry out the real purpose of his visit. Christophe arrived before eleven a.m. He had not sent word in advance that he was coming, but he knew that the hospitality of the Coupers was always available to any passer-by, and he didn't want to let another day pass without speaking with Amélie Nicolau.

Rebecca Couper greeted him warmly on the porch and offered him tea and ham biscuits, which he accepted, since he had eaten breakfast before six. As he ate, he confided to her the nature of his call and asked if there were any news about Bernard Nicolau.

"He is much better, we hear, but still too weak to travel. As yet, we have not informed Mademoiselle Nicolau of her brother Joseph's death. We thought it best to let Bernard tell her when he's on his feet again," Rebecca replied. "It's such a sad situation, but we're happy to have her as long as she will stay."

"Where is she now?" he asked.

"In the library talking with Mr. Burr, I believe."

"The vice president? He's here?"

"Just for a few days. Mr. Butler had to make an unexpected trip to Philadelphia, and we invited Mr. Burr to spend those days with us. Would you like to meet him?"

"Yes, I would like very much to meet him," Christophe said.

Rebecca rose and signaled to the maid to take away the empty cup and plate. Then she led Christophe toward the library, where the pocket doors stood open, and where Amélie sat, chatting with a small, elegant man with long sideburns and a receding hairline.

"Excuse us," Rebecca said. "I do hope we're not disturbing you, but I wanted to introduce Mr. Burr to another guest—Monsieur Christophe Poulain du Bignon. And this is Mr. Aaron Burr." Burr stood and stretched out his hand to Christophe, who shook it heartily.

"It's an honor to meet you, sir," Christophe said.

"Likewise," Burr said amiably.

"And you already know Mademoiselle Nicolau," Rebecca said.

Christophe bowed slightly in her direction. "*C'est un plaisir de vous revoir, Mademoiselle*. It's a pleasure to see you again."

She smiled and nodded. "*Et vous aussi, monsieur*. How is your family?"

"Quite well, thank you. Please don't let us disturb your conversation," Christophe said to Mr. Burr.

"Not at all. I'm afraid my French was getting a bit rusty. Mademoiselle Nicolau has been indulging me with an opportunity to brush it up a bit."

"*Au contraire, monsieur, vous parlez bien*. You speak well."

"*Merci, Mademoiselle*," he said with a slight bow. "I studied French at Princeton and have, of course, been to France. But with two native speakers, I'd best stick with English," he said with a chuckle. "The fact is, I was just about to go for a walk by the river. You're welcome to join me," he said to Christophe.

"Thank you, but I can only stay a short time. As much as I would like to join you, I must take this opportunity to speak with Mademoiselle Nicolau on an important matter."

"Of course. I'm sure your conversation will be a welcome respite for her. I've been boring her for the last half hour trying to explain our electoral process."

She gave him a charming smile. "It was fascinating, Mister Burr," she said.

"You are too kind, *Mademoiselle.* It's a pleasure to have met you, Monsieur du Bignon."

"The pleasure is mine," Christophe responded, with another slight bow.

As Burr left the room, Rebecca Couper said, "Well, I'll leave you two to your chat. If you need anything, please let me know." She pulled the doors partially together as she left to give them more privacy.

Alone for the first time with Amélie Nicolau, whom the Coupers called Amelia, Christophe felt awkward and unsure of himself. She was as pretty and desirable as he remembered, which only increased his discomfort. For a moment, he wished he had listened to his wife and waited to speak with Mademoiselle Nicolau's brother instead. The girl would no doubt think him a fool for coming to her with such an offer. But he was here now, and he had no choice but to go through with it. A diplomatic man would most likely begin the conversation in an oblique way, but Christophe was straightforward and not given to diplomacy.

"I hope you will pardon this unexpected intrusion in your day, Mademoiselle Nicolau, but I've come to speak with you about a very private and personal matter," he said, feeling stiff and uncomfortable, even in French.

"*Oui, Monsieur?*" She stood by the fireplace of the library, her hands gripping each other, her knuckles white. Her eyes looked at him almost fearfully, as though she were expecting bad news. He wanted to put her at ease.

"Please, *Mademoiselle*, let's sit down." She nodded and sank into a blue damask chair in front of the fireplace. He sat down in the matching armchair opposite her and placed his hands firmly on his knees as he leaned forward.

"I will, of course, expect you to discuss all this with your brothers and take time to think about a response. That I understand." He was careful to use the plural "brothers," for he did not want to cause an eruption of grief by hinting at her oldest brother's death. And, after all, she did have another brother in France, in addition to Bernard, who, despite all reports, might still be fighting for his life.

"*Oui, Monsieur?*" she repeated, leaning forward.

"And I will speak to whichever brother is your guardian as soon as I have the chance, should the prospect interest you."

Her brown eyes widened at the unspoken question.

"Mademoiselle Nicolau," he said, "I have come to offer you a marriage proposal on behalf of either one of my sons you choose." There. He had said it. Now he held his breath, waiting for her reply.

Her mouth dropped open in surprise, and she emitted a nervous sound that was almost, but not quite, a laugh. When he said nothing else, she filled the silence with the words, "I am flattered, *Monsieur*."

"I know this comes as a rather sudden offer. But my wife and I both took a great liking to you, as did our two sons."

"I don't know them very well, *Monsieur*."

"Well, let me tell you a bit more about them. Joseph, the older of the two, is almost nineteen. He is probably the more clever of the two, but I want to be candid and tell you their bad points as well as their good. Some also find him more handsome than his brother, but quite frankly, I can't always count on him when there are tasks to perform. He's a quiet boy … still waters, you know. But I'm sure he has his good points."

"And Henri?" she asked.

"Well, in my view, Henri is the more reliable of the two, and he would probably be the better choice. He doesn't have the quick mind of Joseph, but he is not without learning. My wife has seen to the education of both young men. Henri turned eighteen in July. He is a responsible fellow, who has been a great deal of help to me, and he knows all the ins and outs of cotton cultivation. He will be a fine plantation owner someday. In fact," he went on, "whichever of the two you choose, should one of them be to your liking, I will certainly provide him with land and slaves on Jekyl, so that he can begin married life as an independent planter." Surely that would sweeten the offer for her.

Amélie listened quietly, a smile playing on her lips. Her hands now appeared relaxed, though they were still carefully folded in her lap. She thought for a moment before she replied.

"It is indeed a fine offer, *Monsieur*, but as you suggest, I will need to think it over and discuss it with my brothers and perhaps with Mr. Couper as well, if you have no objection."

"Absolutely none. However, until the decision is final, would you be willing to have my sons come to call, while you are visiting with the Coupers? That way you could get to know them better."

"I would be most happy to receive them," she said, with a careful nod.

He had said what he had come to say, and he was not one to make small talk. She didn't say no, and he had not really expected an immediate answer to such an unexpected proposal. Now it would be up to Joseph and Henri to help her decide, if she liked either one of them. Perhaps it would be a good thing for her, in the event that

Bernard had a relapse, to know that she still had an option for a secure life here on the Georgia coast.

"You are most gracious, *Mademoiselle*," he said, taking the hand she offered and bringing it to his lips in a gesture of respect and courtesy. Her fingers smelled of lavender. "Now I must go. My men are waiting for me at the dock."

"You are not staying for dinner?"

"I'm afraid not. But it was a pleasure to have the opportunity to speak with you and to meet Mr. Burr."

"He is a most interesting man," she said.

"Indeed, he is." He stood and, with a slight bow, said, "Now, *Mademoiselle*, I must bid you *au revoir*," and left her alone with her thoughts in the library.

JOHN COUPER AND AARON BURR were sitting on the shady verandah, deep in conversation, when Christophe emerged from the hallway.

"Ah, Mr. du Bignon, Mr. Couper here has been telling me about your narrow escape from the French Revolution and that you now own all of Jekyl Island just south of here. What good fortune. I'm certainly glad you decided to come to America," said Burr.

"So am I, Mr. Burr. We have, for the most part, been quite happy here," Christophe said, as John motioned for him to sit down and join them.

"We all suffer the ups and downs of weather here on the coast," said John, "and this year, I was just telling Mr. Burr, we have a plague of caterpillars we call cotton worms to contend with. Are they as bad on Jekyl as they are here?" he asked.

"Probably worse," Christophe answered. "There's not a leaf left on the cotton stalks." Changing the subject, he turned to Burr, "But let's talk of better things. It's a pleasure to have you here in Georgia, Mr. Burr. How long will you be with us?"

"Ah, a very good question. As you may know, I left New York under certain ... shall we say, somewhat imperative circumstances. I will return only when I feel the time is right." Burr chuckled. "I am at the moment not the most popular man in the North."

"Well," said John, "you're always welcome in the South. We are enjoying your visit immensely."

"As you can see, Mr. Burr, as I have informed Mademoiselle Nicolau, you have the pleasure of visiting the most hospitable man on the Georgia coast, perhaps in all America," Christophe said.

Burr smiled. "So I've been told. His reputation is well known, even in my home state of New York."

"You are both too kind," Couper said with a smile. Then in an effort to shift the subject, he said to Christophe, "I trust your conversation with Mademoiselle Nicolau went well."

"Well enough," Christophe replied. "I expect you will be seeing more of my sons on St. Simons." He smiled back, having no doubt that Couper suspected the real purpose of his visit.

"We shall welcome them with open arms," he replied.

The men talked on for nearly an hour, with Christophe relishing his *tête-à-tête* with the vice president, which he considered a rare opportunity. They talked of politics, of President Jefferson and his purchase of Louisiana from the French, of the Lewis and Clark expedition, and of the Napoleonic wars in Europe. It was an exhilarating conversation. Only with reluctance did Christophe finally stand and announce that he must be on his way back to Jekyl.

"It's an honor to have met you, Mr. Burr. I hope you will enjoy your visit."

"I do wish you'd stay for a while, at least for dinner," said John. They were all standing now.

"I wish I could, but as you know there are many duties on a plantation, and Marguerite is expecting me back this afternoon."

"Then I will have Sans Foix pack some food for you and your

men to enjoy on the trip home."

"You're very kind," Christophe said. "But that won't be necessary. I believe your lovely wife saw to it that my men were fed, as I was, upon arrival." He smiled broadly and shook hands with them both, adding, "Well, gentlemen, I have interrupted your morning quite long enough. I must be off."

"It's been a pleasure," Burr said with a smile. The men shook hands.

Couper made a move to walk to the dock with Christophe, who said, "Please, don't let me take you away from your conversation. I can find my way back to the landing, but I thank you for your most gracious hospitality, especially when I had given you absolutely no notice of my coming."

"You're always welcome," Couper said.

Christophe made a final quick bow and started for the dock as both men watched his departure.

It was late afternoon by the time Christophe and his small crew made it back to Marguerite's Landing. They had been compelled to sail against a stiff wind that was beginning to blow from the southeast. As the men lashed the boat securely to the dock, Christophe strode toward the house, congratulating himself on a day well spent—but he could only wait to see whether his errand would bear fruit.

Chapter 24

September 4, 1804

Jekyl Island

BY MORNING, THE WIND WAS A VERITABLE GALE and rain was blowing hard, pelting the windows of their bedroom, awakening Marguerite and Christophe before daylight. It was obvious there would be no work in the fields today. Christophe had feared as much. The rain had begun late the night before, but conditions grew increasingly worse as the day wore on. The most severe wind and rain came between noon and three when the storm was at its peak. The family and servants crouched in the house. The wind tore at the trees, and they could hear limbs cracking all around. The rain was falling like blades against the windows.

They had seen storms before, but nothing like this one. It went on and on and seemed determined to destroy the entire island. As the hours passed, bringing high tide, water began to rise on the island. It trickled in under the doors of the tabby house until, little by little, it flooded the entire downstairs. *Why didn't Major Horton have the good sense to build his house on a high foundation like almost everyone else in the area?* Christophe wondered. The family and house servants had no choice but to move upstairs and pray that the roof would hold. The tabby walls were thick, built to withstand such winds, but the roof was another matter.

As the wind blew more fiercely and the rain fell harder and harder, Christophe fretted over what was left of the cotton crop, already so devastated by the caterpillars. The fields were now flooded, and no doubt anything that remained was being completely ruined.

MARGUERITE WORRIED LESS ABOUT THE CROPS and more about the slaves, who did not have a strong tabby house to protect them. Their cabins were made of wood, with floors built low to the ground, at least those that had floors. They would all be flooded as well, even if they stood against the wind. There were tabby outbuildings, of course, but except for the storage barn near the river, most of them were only one-story high, and if the floods got worse, their people had no place to go, except into the trees, where she feared the winds would blow them again into the water. How many would survive?

Marguerite sent her house servant Caroline out into the storm to summon Ben from the stable. From the window she watched the girl's difficult progress as she bent against the wind and waded in the knee-high water toward the stables. She worried until Ben and Caroline returned together, soaking wet, pushed this time by the wind against their backs.

"Ben," Marguerite told him once they had reached the house, "find anyone you can and tell them to come to the big house. They'll be safer here. We're all upstairs." The slave cabins, she was increasingly sure, would not withstand this storm. They were in danger of being washed away or blown off their flimsy foundations.

Ben was not gone long, evidently unwilling to risk the crashing limbs and rising water for a great distance. When he hurried back down the plantation road as fast as the deepening water would allow, only a few men, women and children, his own family among them, buffeted by the wind and shielding their heads as best they could against the flying debris, trailed behind him as they made their way toward the big house.

They all waded into the house, as they were instructed.

"They was all I could find, Miz Marguerite," Ben called out.

"Well, then, all of you had best come upstairs," Marguerite called back. The wet, shivering people climbed gratefully to the second floor, where they huddled together at one end of the hallway. The children whimpered, as their mothers tried to shush them. There was little talking among them as they all waited in terrified silence, listening to the storm outside. Like the du Bignons, all they could do was wait and pray.

THE STORM CONTINUED INTO THE NIGHT. Finally, about midnight, when everyone was so exhausted that most had fallen asleep despite the howling winds, it began to die down. They slept fitfully through the damp night and waited for the waters to abate.

THE NEXT MORNING THE SUN PEEKED in through broken windows. The house smelled damp and marshy. Downstairs all sorts of things floated in the brown water. The family and servants had carried everything they could upstairs when the first rivulets appeared under the doors, but now pans from the kitchen floated beside drowned mice and spiders. Outside, snakes slithered through the still water, littered with broken tree limbs and the occasional body of a dead rabbit or chicken. It looked as though it would be days before the floodwater would subside sufficiently to restore order.

At Christophe's command, Ben would be the first to wade outside, in water up to his waist, to explore the damage. When his master gave him a warning to "beware of alligators," Ben paled noticeably. Nevertheless, he had his orders and he had no choice but to venture into the dark waters that flooded the island.

When he returned, he reported that, *grâce à Dieu*, the tabby stable had withstood the storm, and the horses, though up to their hindquarters in floodwater, were all still alive. In the following days, when the water had sufficiently subsided, Christophe and his sons rode through the mud-slick plantation to inspect the devastation.

The fields, even those on the highest ground, had flooded, as Christophe expected, and what little cotton remained from the caterpillar infestation was beaten down, mud-soaked, and ruined. Many of the slave cabins had washed off their foundations and lay in rubble. Worst of all, seven slaves were missing and presumed dead. A search turned up the bodies of one man, three women, and two children. The last body, a little boy named Claude, was never found. Marguerite was amazed that more of the workers had not been killed. A few had taken refuge in the tabby structures, but many had to climb trees, as she had feared, to escape the floodwaters. Some had crawled into the lofts of their cabins, but when the cabins were swept away, one of the women and her two children, all huddled together, were crushed. The others had apparently drowned, perhaps blown from the trees they had climbed.

As the bodies were found, the entire plantation began to mourn. The slaves arranged to bury their dead in the small plot of useless hardscrabble land that Christophe designated for their cemetery. The funerals took place at night, which Marguerite found odd, but

it pleased Christophe because it did not interfere with their working hours. The du Bignons dutifully attended the first part of the burial service, driving their carriage along the dark road while the slaves, some of them carrying lighted torches, all walked behind the six crude wooden coffins piled on the back of a wagon pulled by two mules.

Well before they reached the site, Marguerite could hear what sounded like drums, but she knew they were really only sticks being beaten against hollow logs, for drums were forbidden on the plantation. Distant voices were singing low, mournful tunes, while those walking along the road joined in. Once they arrived, Christophe and Marguerite stood to one side and watched as the coffins were lowered one by one into the still-damp earth of the six empty graves. They were shallow by necessity, for to dig deeper after such a flood, water would certainly rise in them. The slaves filed by, tossing handfuls of sandy soil onto each wooden box. The graves were covered, and several dark shapes stepped forward one by one into the light of the torches now planted at the head of each grave and laid small, everyday objects on top of the mounds—a broken cup, a straw doll, a sea shell, every one different.

Marguerite watched their movements with quiet interest, but feeling somehow as though she and Christophe were intruding on the privacy of these people they saw every day but did not really know. They did not stay long, but soon said their goodbyes and started home. They could hear the keening sounds of the mourners as they drove, but before they arrived at the big house, the doleful songs gave way to rejoicing. Marguerite had heard about that from Rosetta—how the slaves didn't just grieve. In the end, she said, they always celebrated with joyous song the heavenly homecoming of the deceased and their liberation from earthly woes and toil.

When they reached the tabby house, climbed the stairs, and dressed for bed, Christophe crawled in and fell asleep almost instantly. Marguerite lay awake beside him and listened to the strange harmonies of jubilation that echoed through the woods long into the night.

ONE BIT OF GOOD NEWS REACHED the islands while coastal planters were still clearing away the hurricane's devastation. Bernard Nicolau, Amélie's brother, though still weak, was finally on his feet again. The first thing he did as soon as he was able to ride was rush to the Couper plantation to greet his sister and tell her the sorrowful news of the death of their older brother, Joseph, in an earlier storm. Both brother and sister remained for several more weeks, mourning together at Cannon's Point, while John and Rebecca saw to their every need, even as they presided over the rebuilding of portions of their house, damaged by the September hurricane, and tried to comfort the families of the nineteen enslaved workers they had lost.

During that time, young Henri du Bignon took full advantage of Amélie's permission to visit. He was quite smitten with the young woman and wanted to meet her brother while he paid court. Joseph, who had the same permission to visit, took little interest in the prospect and responsibility of a wife. He had scoffed at his father's suggestion that they put their best foot forward. However, when his mother also urged him to call on Mademoiselle Nicolau, out of deference to her he joined Henri just once in visiting Amélie and her brother. When he saw Henri's obvious affection for the young woman and his annoyance at any attentions she paid to Joseph, however, he decided it best not to accompany his brother again on such visits.

It was not long before Bernard Nicolau and Christophe du Bignon began to discuss a marriage contract for Amélie and Henri.

It was certainly no disappointment to Joseph. In fact, he was happy for his brother, for he himself took little interest in romance and the company of women, aside from his mother, of course, to whom he was deeply devoted.

That would change, all too suddenly, on the day his father took him and his brother to their first slave auction.

Chapter 25

January 1806

A farm outside Darien, Georgia

J OSEPH HAD NOT REALLY WANTED TO GO the slave auction, but his father insisted, frowning at his son's disinterest.

"You have to learn how to select the darkies you buy, Joseph, whether you want to own a plantation or not. You'll still have to have servants. It's time you and your brother both learned what that means."

They had come to Darien on the sloop and rented a wagon when they arrived. It would carry them all as well as the two new field hands their father intended to buy. The sale was on a large estate a few miles from town, and there were fewer hands to choose from than they had hoped. When Christophe looked over the younger men, he shook his head.

"These are the kind of slaves you never want to buy—the defiant ones. Look at their eyes," he told his sons. "They're nothing but trouble." Joseph looked into the eyes of the men in the holding pens.

He could see the pent-up anger his father was talking about, but under such circumstances, he thought that he too would be defiant.

"I learned my lesson when I bought that young buck, Tom," Christophe said. "How many times now has he run away? How many whippings has he endured rather than obey my orders?"

His sons, now nineteen and twenty, nodded, remembering the dark, whip-scarred man on the plantation who still stood tall and straight, his teeth clenched as he waited for an opportunity to run away again. Joseph admired the man's courage and secretly hoped he would make it to freedom someday.

"Let's take a look at the women," Christophe said. "Maybe we'll find some good field workers there." He walked past the slave pens where the women were being held. Most of them looked tired and listless. As the young men followed their father, feeling awkward and not sure what they were looking for, Christophe stopped abruptly in front of one of the pens. A pretty, light-skinned girl, who appeared to be in her late teens, and a darker, older woman sat on the ground holding each other and weeping quietly. Joseph wondered whether they were mother and daughter. His father made a sudden gesture toward the pair.

Joseph was shocked to see an ugly curl on his father's lips and naked lust in his eyes as he eyed the women. When Christophe saw his son staring at him, his demeanor became more neutral, and he said in a business-like voice, "The younger one looks healthy enough." He sent Henri to find one of the auctioneers.

"When is that one to be sold?" he asked when the man arrived.

"Comin' up next, Mr. du Bignon," the auctioneer said, "if that's one you wanna bid on. The young one, I assume." Christophe nodded curtly, ignoring his two sons who were exchanging glances, their eyebrows raised.

The girl whimpered and clung to the older woman, as the auctioneer tried to pull her away. He pried her hands loose and jerked her to her feet, leaving her mother still sitting in the dirt of the holding pen, her face in her hands as she sobbed and called "Maria" repeatedly until they were out of hearing distance. The girl stretched her arms back toward the woman and tried to dig in her feet as the man dragged her toward the auction block. She was crying over and over again "Mama, Mama," until her voice was drowned out by the sound of the other auctioneer touting his wares and the mumbling of the buyers, all men, milling about the sales area.

When the bid for the teenage boy they were currently selling closed at three hundred and fifty dollars, the gruff auctioneer shoved the girl onto the block. "This one is lot four, number two," he said to the man wearing a pencil behind his ear, apparently keeping the records. "We're puttin' her up out of order." The bookkeeper nodded and wrote something in his black leather book.

The girl stood there, trying with her arms and hands to cover the strategically located rips in her rag of a dress. The torn garment was a technique some owners would use to show off young women to what they considered their "best advantage." This girl's owner had also oiled her skin, Joseph noticed, to make her look healthier.

The auctioneer said, "Now we have here a fine-looking filly by the name of ...," he looked at a card in his hand, "Maria Theresa." Holding the end of his whip, he poked at her a few times to make her turn around so that the men in the crowd could see her from all angles. Catcalls and whistles erupted from the men. The girl's eyes filled with tears.

Christophe opened the bidding at once. "One hundred dollars."

The auctioneer scoffed. "A hundred dollars? Now gentlemen, you know a desirable commodity when you see one. Let's have a serious bid." Joseph saw his father's face redden at the man's words.

"Two hundred dollars," a gruff voice yelled from the crowd. The man waggled his index finger as he bid.

"Two hundred and fifty," another man called.

The bidding grew spirited, as the auctioneer played the bidders one against the other. Although it was the first time Joseph had ever been to a slave auction, he had seen cattle sales, which were not much different. It was as though the girl were a cow being sold for slaughter, he thought. It sickened him to see her humiliation and fear.

The bids went higher and higher by twenty-five or fifty dollars each time. Finally, the man with the waggly finger jumped the bid to four hundred and fifty dollars. The crowd gasped. It was a lot for any slave, Joseph knew. A prime field hand might bring that much, but women usually came cheaper.

Joseph watched the girl's reaction. If anything, she looked more terrified than ever. He wondered if she had ever been away from her mother. And what would become of her in the hands of the bidder? Where was her mother now? Still in the pen, he supposed.

There was silence among the crowd, with only the voice of the auctioneer rising above their heads, taunting and tempting the bidders, and trying to eke out a little more money from the buyers. "Do I hear four seventy-five?" he shouted.

Suddenly, Joseph heard his father's voice beside him, loud and clear. "Five hundred dollars," he yelled.

A stir went through the crowd. The men smirked and murmured among themselves, some pointing toward Christophe as they all strained to gape one more time at the girl. Joseph and Henri exchanged glances, their eyes wide with disbelief.

The auctioneer turned once more to the previous bidder, "Do I hear five-twenty-five?" he called out. The other bidder's fingers twitched nervously around his lips as he looked the girl over once more, hesitated, and then shook his head.

"One black bitch is just like another," he said loudly and spat on the ground.

A few minutes later, when no one else upped the bid, the auctioneer yelled, "Sold to Captain du Bignon for five hundred dollars." Tears slid down the girl's cheeks now, and she wiped her nose with her forearm.

Christophe stepped forward to claim his property and settle his account.

"I can't believe you did that," Joseph muttered. "Anybody can see why you wanted her."

Christophe glared at his son with contempt. "You think you're so smart, but you're nothing but a fool," he said. Joseph's jaw tightened and his nostrils flared, but he said no more.

Christophe held the girl's arm as he bound her wrists with a rough rope and then motioned to Henri, "Here, boy, put her in the wagon."

"Maybe we should buy the mother too," Joseph suggested.

"She's too old to work in the fields. She'd be nothing but a burden," his father answered gruffly. "You've got to learn, boy."

Joseph said nothing in reply. He knew better, but he hated to see a family divided.

As the rented wagon rattled down the road, Henri sat beside his father on the driver's seat, while Joseph rode in back with the girl. In addition to the rope that bound her hands, her foot was shackled to the rail by a chain. She strained to look back toward the slave pens, as though she hoped for one last look at her mother. But the older woman was nowhere to be seen. Tears still trickled down her cheeks.

The wagon jolted along the rutted road that led to the dock, where the *Anubis* and its crew were waiting. As his father returned the horse and wagon to the nearby livery stable, Joseph unlocked the shackle and lifted the girl from the wagon to help her on to the boat, mouthing the words "I'm sorry" so that no one else could hear. The girl glanced at him for a moment with vacant eyes and then stared down at her hands, finally freed from the ropes that bound them. The three members of the slave crew stared at the girl with obvious curiosity, but remained silent as they cast off.

WHEN THE CREWMEN FINALLY TIED UP THE SLOOP at the Jekyl landing, Marguerite was waiting.

"Where are the new field hands?" she asked.

"Nobody else looked suitable," said Christophe.

She stood on the dock, her hands gripping her elbows, looking at the girl. Joseph watched his mother's face. She was in her fifties now, not as pretty or physically appealing as she had been when she was younger. Her face was often taut with worry, especially when his father was in one of his ill-tempered moods, as he was so often these days. Sometimes, when she walked the woodland paths or strolled the beach or she worked in her garden, she seemed to relax and look more like her old self again. But, around her husband, her face showed worry more often than not.

"She doesn't look as though she's worked in the fields a day in her life," Marguerite said. It was true. The young woman was small. Her bones appeared frail, even delicate. Her raven hair and her oiled skin reflected the late afternoon sunlight. It suddenly occurred to Joseph that she was the most beautiful woman he had ever seen.

A spark of anger flashed in his mother's eyes. "Did you buy her for yourself, Christophe?" she asked. Her husband looked annoyed at being questioned. He stammered a bit. "I ... I thought you might like to have her for a lady's maid," he said. "And she's a fine seamstress, or so the auctioneer said."

Joseph's mouth fell open at his father's lie.

Their mother would not likely want her as a lady's maid, hanging around the house day and night. She was no fool. *It would be like placing a bone in front of a hungry dog and expecting him to ignore it,* Joseph thought. But now that Marguerite was openly questioning her husband's intent, Joseph suspected that his father would not have the nerve to make the beautiful slave his mistress, at least not right away.

To his humiliation he suddenly realized, when he caught an unexpected glimpse of Maria Theresa's dark nipple through one of the holes of her dress, that his own thoughts were not so different from his father's. He was ashamed to find himself thinking that it would be a pity for her to go to waste. She was young, about his age, Joseph guessed, and tempting. Her skin was the color of caramel. *And probably just as sweet*, he thought. While Joseph was not interested in a wife, his sexual instincts were fully awakened by Maria Theresa's beauty and availability. Suddenly unable to control his own body, he held his jacket in front of himself and walked quickly toward the house before anyone noticed.

GIVEN HIS WIFE'S REACTION and to hide his true intentions, or so Joseph suspected, Christophe put Maria Theresa to work in the cotton house, where cloth was woven and garments made for the slave population. It kept her out of the summer sun, which might ruin her flawless skin and seemed to justify his purchase of a "seamstress." Then, in an effort to get back into his wife's good graces, he began construction of the new detached kitchen thirty yards in back of their house. And when it was done, he had the old kitchen converted into a rather pleasant dining room.

Joseph knew it was not unusual in the slave-owning society in which they lived for a planter or his son to have a special woman in the quarters. He watched his father's whereabouts with curiosity for a while, but saw no signs that Christophe was visiting Maria Theresa. He did notice, however, that he put her in one side of a cabin by herself, while a family of four lived on the other side.

Joseph often lay awake at night thinking about the girl and feeling temptation gnaw at his body. She had such beautiful mahogany eyes and such fine, high breasts, evident even in the faded cotton dresses she now wore to replace the rags she had arrived in.

Joseph took to dropping by the cotton house in the afternoons to see how the work was progressing. Sometimes he would wait until sunset and walk Maria Theresa back to her cabin. Then he started pretending to take a walk after supper, but returning instead to her cabin, bringing her tidbits from their meal in the big house. She especially liked sugar cakes and lemon tarts. So far he had only talked with her. Then came the night when finally he reached out his hand to touch her breast.

She flinched, but only for an instant, as though she had been expecting it. He was immediately aroused. She was the first woman whose body he had ever touched that way. Now that he had begun, he felt free to explore it in any way he wanted. It was a miracle— her body—soft and warm and musk-smelling. She trembled when he laid her down on the cot and touched her between the legs, but she was moist and inviting, or so it seemed to him. It was his first time, and he was awkward and unsure of himself, but his body seemed to know what to do. He felt he would burst the moment he entered her. She moaned at first and then lay there, not reacting when he was done, just staring at the ceiling.

He wanted to believe she desired him as he desired her, but all he found in her response was a lack of resistance, an acceptance. If it had been his father instead of him who came so quietly to her dark cabin after the moon rose, he wondered whether she would have reacted differently. She would let him hold her as long as he wanted and then, when he slipped away, she gave no sign of regret.

Each night he would lie in his own bed until he heard his father's snoring. Then he would tiptoe down the dark staircase and make his way in the moonlight to her cabin in the quarters.

He always hoped she would be waiting for him, but he sometimes found her already asleep. He liked to pretend she cared for him and waited eagerly, but deep inside himself, he knew she let him do what he came to do because she had no other choice.

Chapter 26

MARIA THERESA HAD BEEN ON THE PLANTATION only eight months when Marguerite noticed the unmistakable swelling of her belly. She eyed her husband with suspicion. "How could you?" she said. "I knew that was why you bought her. I knew it!"

"I am not the father," he said, raising both his hands, palms up in denial, as though to keep her from striking him. "I swear it. I haven't touched her." She was almost convinced by his avid protests of innocence, but not quite. When Maria Theresa gave birth to a daughter with skin considerably lighter than her mother's and a headful of hair that was straight and light brown, she blamed him again. Joseph would have taken some delight in his father's being falsely accused on his account, if only it didn't upset his mother so.

He found her on the porch alone late one afternoon, her mouth tense, stabbing at her needlework.

"*Maman,* will you take a walk with me? There's something I need to tell you."

"Of course, Joseph." She laid down her embroidery hoop and bright-colored thread and took his proffered arm. "I could use a pleasant walk this afternoon."

Once they were beyond hearing distance of the tabby house and her frown had relaxed into pleasure at enjoying the walk along the sandy road with her son, he turned to her, feeling the color rise in his face as he spoke.

"I'm not so sure how pleasant this walk will be, *Maman.* But I have to tell you something important."

She lifted her face toward his, her curiosity aroused.

"I don't know how to say this, except to just to come right out and say it," he began. "I'm the father of Maria Theresa's baby." He watched her face register the shock of his words. He studied her expression trying to understand its complexity as she absorbed his words. Finally, he saw her taut mouth relax and a smile begin to play around her lips. He could almost read her thoughts. *Then it's not your father.*

"I should have guessed. You're over twenty-one now ... a man. And men ..." she laughed. "Well, I know the ways of men—even if I don't always approve." Despite her words, she was smiling as she gripped his hand tightly. She pulled his face toward hers and gave him kisses on each cheek.

"I can certainly understand, Joseph. She is young and pretty, and it's only natural that ..." her voice trailed off. Then she added with a harsher tone, "But you should be ashamed of yourself." Then her face lit up with a new idea. "We must have the baby baptized as a free mulatto. I will not have a granddaughter who is a slave."

"I'm sorry, *Maman.* I know you're disappointed in me," Joseph said, feeling the blush fade from his face, as he too began to relax. "But I have no fiancée like Henri, and I too have needs ... not that they … I mean … well, you know what I mean. At least I assume so."

"I do understand, but don't plan to make a habit of such behavior," she said, as sternly as she could manage under the circumstances. But he knew his confession had made her happy.

BY THE TIME MARGUERITE AND JOSEPH returned to the tabby house and settled on the veranda, the sun was setting. Shortly after their return, Christophe and Henri rode into the yard. They had been inspecting the cotton field just north of the quarters near what they called Horton Pond.

Marguerite's face lit up when she saw her husband. She rose from her chair and threw herself into his arms. He looked surprised, for she was rarely so demonstrative in front of others with her affections, but he seemed to welcome her embrace.

"Christophe," she said, "I have just had the most interesting news. Joseph tells me he is the baby's father." Henri looked at his brother with sly admiration in his eyes.

"What baby?" Christophe asked, casting an annoyed look at his oldest son.

"Maria Theresa's baby, of course. What other baby is there?"

Christophe pressed his lips together, and his eyes narrowed as he continued to stare at Joseph.

"You?" he said.

"Yes, *Papa. I* am the father. " Joseph stressed the word "I" and returned Christophe's glare with a satisfied smirk. He could see how much it annoyed his father to realize that he, Joseph, his oldest son, had taken what he had bought for himself.

AFTER THREE DAYS, THE CHILD STILL HAD NO NAME. Marguerite toyed with the idea of Josephine, but Christophe firmly rejected it.

Still fretting over the unnamed child, Marguerite asked Joseph to drive her to the Wylly house for tea. As she and Margaret Wylly sat gossiping in the parlor, Joseph perched on the edge of a porch chair just outside a window, sharing a cup of tea with Susan Wylly, half-listening as the two women chatted inside.

"A new baby girl has been born on our plantation," Marguerite announced. Joseph's ears perked up. He noticed that she made no mention of the father, though he supposed the Wyllys, like everyone on the island, already knew about the baby and probably suspected whose it was. News traveled quickly among the slave population. Susan Wylly was looking at him, curiosity in her eyes as they eavesdropped on their mothers' conversation.

"What do you plan to call her?" Margaret Wylly asked, pouring another cup of warm tea in Marguerite's cup.

"We haven't decided yet," Marguerite answered.

"I've always favored the name Harriot," Margaret suggested. "If I have another daughter, that will be her name." Margaret was accustomed to naming babies. She had named all the slave children, as well as her own eight offspring, one of whom had died in infancy before coming to Jekyl, where she had given birth to two more, Margaret Matilda and John Armstrong.

"What a lovely name. It's unusual. Would you object to our calling the new slave child Harriot?"

"Certainly not. It's a charming name."

"Well, then, Harriot it will be."

MARGUERITE, SOMETIMES ALONG WITH JOSEPH, visited her new granddaughter during the mornings while Maria Theresa worked and while the baby, along with other slave children, was being tended by an old woman named Maum Sophy. The child was a beauty. With olive skin, big brown eyes, and pale brown hair a shade darker than her father had as a baby, she looked unlike any other child in the quarters.

As Harriot grew, Joseph knew that his mother continued to be concerned about the child's future. She often broached the topic with her husband. With so little privacy in the household, Joseph, upstairs in his bedroom, could often hear them talking downstairs. The conversation varied from time to time, but the gist of it was always the same.

"Christophe, the baby Harriot, we both know she's Joseph's child. That makes her our granddaughter."

"Humph," muttered Christophe. "So?"

"I think we should have her baptized as a free mulatto."

"Against the law. Her mother is a slave. By law, the child is a slave."

"But who would know that in Savannah? And those who might know here on the island would never mention it. Why would anyone care?"

"Would you have me free the mother too?" he asked.

"Certainly not," she said. "Just the child."

"Just Joseph's bastard."

"She's our granddaughter, Christophe. Our own flesh and blood."

In spite of her husband's resistance, Marguerite persisted, bringing it up again and again until she finally wore him down. Joseph suspected that his father, after thinking it over, may also have seen it as a way to please Maria Theresa, *whose body he no doubt still covets,* he thought with disgust, *but hasn't dared to enjoy under Maman's watchful eye.* Joseph himself, in deference to his mother, had reluctantly ceased his nightly visits to the quarters.

Thus, finally, after Marguerite refused to give up, Joseph watched, as Christophe stood, rigid and sullen, beside his wife as grudging godparent to the child at her baptism. Marguerite made certain that young Harriot's baptism was listed as that of a "free born mulatto" in the records of the Catholic diocese in Savannah. At her request, the priest, understanding the delicacy of the situation, agreed to baptize the child without recording the names of her parents.

ANY GOSSIP ABOUT JOSEPH'S FATHERING a daughter by one of his father's slaves never left the island. It was, after all, nothing particularly unusual and hardly noteworthy on a Georgia plantation. And attention was diverted from this relationship by what some in the community considered the carryings-on of his younger brother and the woman he was courting and calling his fiancée. While gossipy matrons in Glynn County clucked their tongues over Henri's all-too-frequent, and sometimes unchaperoned, visits to his beloved Amelia, now living at her brother's Marengo plantation, some of them dismissed it with disdainful remarks.

"They are French, after all," they smirked.

By now, almost everyone, including Henri, was calling Mademoiselle Nicolau by the Anglicized version of her name, "Amelia," which she seemed to prefer. By the same token, Henri had begun to pronounce his own name in the American way whenever he was with English-speaking people, and he started writing it "Henry." That the couple intended to marry, there was no doubt. In fact, Christophe and Amelia's brother, Bernard, were already negotiating the marriage contract, which they finalized and signed at the end of April 1807, when Amelia and Henry began to live as man and wife.

When all the gossip about the young couple's relationship finally reached their ears, Christophe and Bernard wondered what all the fuss was about since it was nobody else's business. But they finally recorded the agreement in the county registry on June 20, 1808, four months after the birth of the couple's first daughter, Louisa.

Amelia seemed especially anxious that it be recorded. It might quiet some of the talk, for even though she and Henry had taken part

in a civil ceremony at the time the marriage contract was signed, the religious celebration of their wedding was not performed under Catholic rite until January 18, 1808, just thirty-seven days before their daughter's birth on February 23.

Christophe kept his word and the terms of his agreement with Amelia's brother, Bernard, granting Amelia and Henry, as everyone called them from then on, the use of ten slaves and forty acres of land. Although Amelia brought no dowry to speak of to the marriage, she was of noble French blood and she was Catholic. It was enough for Christophe. He wanted to keep Henry, whom he considered his *good* son, nearby. Thus, even though by now Christophe owned acreage on the mainland as well, the land he granted the young couple was on Jekyl Island. He had already begun to build wooden wings onto the tabby house, as he had suggested years earlier he would do, to make room for his son and daughter-in-law and give the new *ménage* some privacy.

The additions also provided more room for guests, and as soon as Amelia had recovered from the birth, she invited the Grand Dutreuilh sisters once more for a visit. Her brother Bernard had taken a special liking to Treyette, and the couple planned to be married on December 6.

The bride's brother, Louis Grand Dutreuilh, also stayed on Jekyl Island to visit with Amelia and Henry when he came to Georgia for Treyette's wedding. Amelia's third brother, Pascal, had also recently arrived in Georgia. He was sharing a bedroom in the main part of the tabby house with Joseph and Louis, until he could build his own small house on Jekyl, where he planned to settle, at least for a time, to be near his sister and new brother-in-law. The big house was crowded.

All the du Bignons took a great liking to Louis Grand Dutreuilh during his stay. He was affable, charming, and got along well with everyone, and Christophe seemed to see in him another son-like figure. The young man rode out in the mornings with Christophe and

Henry to inspect the plantation. Finally, one day when Joseph decided to ride with them, Christophe, in an unusual surge of generosity, said to Louis, "Why don't you consider staying in Georgia, where you can be near your sisters? I could offer you a good lease on a plot of land on Jekyl Island and help you get started as a planter."

"I thank you for the kind offer, sir, but I'm not sure I'm cut out to be a planter. I was thinking of becoming a merchant."

"Well, in that case, I think we could use a store on Jekyl Island," said Christophe. "There are a number of families living here now, and I'm sure that some of the people on the south end of St. Simons would come here to shop as well, now that the store at Frederica has closed. I could also offer you as many acres as you would like to cultivate."

Louis Grand Dutreuilh took some time to think over the idea, especially after Christophe sweetened the offer by agreeing to put up half the capital to get the store started. In the end, however, he decided to return to his mother's home in Trenton, New Jersey. He felt his mother needed him, especially since his sisters had now decided to stay in Georgia.

JOSEPH HAD WATCHED HIS FATHER FAWN over Louis Grand Dutreuilh with no little annoyance and feigned disinterest. He liked the young man well enough, yet at the same time he resented him. To his own surprise he had to admit that he felt a current of jealousy. In spite of his outward indifference, to his surprise, he still wanted his father's approval. As it turned out, Joseph was the only member of the family who was pleased when Louis decided to return to New Jersey.

Even with the young man's departure, Joseph's resentment did not wane. As the months passed, he found new fodder for anger almost daily as he watched his father act the fool over his new granddaughter, little Louisa. Joseph could not deny that she was a sweet child whom everyone loved—even him. But he couldn't stifle his feelings on the days that his mother would go to the quarters and bring back his daughter Harriot to play with Louisa. Both little girls, so near to each other in age, were walking now and just beginning to say a few words. Christophe would ignore Harriot as though she didn't even exist, while he doted on Henry's baby girl.

Joseph watched as his father dandled Louisa on his knee, playing horsey until the child giggled with delight, while little Harriot jumped up and down beside his chair with excitement saying, "Me. Me. Me," begging her turn. Christophe never even acknowledged her presence. What hurt Joseph most was to observe how much his mother, although she tried to make both little girls feel welcome with hugs and cookies, seemed to completely ignore Christophe's attitude towards his illegitimate granddaughter. Marguerite only smiled with obvious pleasure as she watched him play with little Louisa, never insisting that Harriot have her turn as well.

"He ignores Harriot only because she's my daughter," Joseph complained to his mother, picking up the little girl, who was beginning to cry, to cuddle and comfort her. "Don't you even notice how he treats her?"

A shadow crossed his mother's face, but she merely touched his arm and smiled sadly at the child in his arms. "It's not that I don't notice, son. But you can see that Louisa brings out the best in him, the natural affection of a grandfather. I can't deny him that. Perhaps it will help him develop a more loving nature toward others." Joseph merely rolled his eyes.

She was aware, of course. *How could she not be?* he wondered, for Christophe also made no pretense of loving his sons equally. He had heard his mother, when she thought he was not listening, chide his father for his all-too-obvious favoritism toward Henry. Joseph, as he grew into a young man, had tried to harden his heart against it, but his father no longer made any attempt to hide his feelings, often responding to his wife's disapproval in a loud voice that Joseph thought was intended for him to overhear. One such conversation took place not long after little Harriot's baptism.

"What has Joseph ever done to show his love for me?" Christophe asked when Marguerite pointed out his obvious favoritism.

"He's your son. That should be enough," she replied.

"Well, it isn't. Love must be earned."

She was shocked. "Love is a gift. It should be like God's grace, freely given—not something you have to earn."

"Well, I think that, like a father's love, grace has to be earned through good works."

"Christophe, we are talking about our son, not some heretic. One should always love one's children, one's family, whether they deserve it or not."

"And again, *ma chère*, there we disagree."

Marguerite said no more. Joseph knew that she would try, as she always had, to love him all the more, as she did with Harriot, to make up for his father's indifference. But he had had enough. The next day he departed for Savannah. He had taken such trips occasionally, just to get away for a while when he could abide his father's ill will no longer. He would spend a few days in his family's house in Savannah, where he would not encounter his father's indifference on a daily basis. This time he did not plan to return.

Chapter 27

J OSEPH HAD NOT BEEN GONE A MONTH, when Marguerite received an unexpected letter from her Boisquenay son, Louis. It had been written two months earlier and bore the date November 12, 1810.

Chère Maman,

By the time you receive this letter, three of my children will be on their way to America, headed for the port of Savannah, Georgia. I hope you can forgive me for not giving earlier notice and asking permission, but I have only recently come to the realization that I can no longer care for them. It breaks my heart to part with them, but it is in their interest that I must do so.

Eight years ago I was laid off once more by the navy with only a very small pension. Although I have had occasional work since then, jobs are

*hard to find in France, and I do not have the resources to support my family.
I have held on as long as I can, but I cannot allow my children to starve.*

*I know you have never met my children, and this will perhaps give you an
opportunity to get to know them. I am sending two of my daughters, Marie
Mélanie and Clémence, as well as my dear son, Louis Alexandre, into your
care. I know that you and your husband are doing well there in Georgia, and
I beg you to look after my three children. Their mother and I will miss them.*

*They should arrive on a French ship called the Méduse sometime in
January. I know your loving nature, and I am trusting you with my most
precious possessions.*

Your faithful son,
Louis

Christophe did not ask about the contents of the letter, and
Marguerite did not mention the children. Without his knowledge,
she consulted a Savannah newspaper and discovered that the *Méduse*
was expected to arrive sometime the following week. Only then did
she show the letter to Christophe and announce that she was going to
stay with Joseph for a few days. As Christophe read the letter, his jaw
tightened, and his face grew red.

"How could Louis presume to take such liberties?" he fumed.

"Christophe, he is my son. He is family. What's past is past. You
must learn to forgive. He needs my help."

"Don't you dare bring them here. Those brats are no doubt little
money-grubbers just like their father."

"You have no right to speak in such a manner." Her voice was
angry, and this time she was determined. She loved her husband,
but she also loved her children and grandchildren, even those she
had never met. In this matter, she would not be deterred. She would
have liked for them all to live as one family, but she could see that the
children could never be happy in this household. She would take care
of them, no matter what.

"I am going to Savannah to meet them. I'll do what's in their best interest," she announced firmly. His eyes widened at her defiance. It was something he had never seen before. But she was determined. She packed her bag and took passage two days later on the weekly packet boat from Brunswick to Savannah.

SHE FOUND JOSEPH LIVING IN THEIR PLAIN, frame house near the corner of Liberty and Montgomery Streets. He had only one servant named Pauline, an old, dark-skinned woman who cleaned and cooked for him whenever he ate at home, which he rarely did. At least his father continued to pay his bills, even if he made no effort to see his son or even inquire about him.

When Marguerite arrived, she brought with her only Caroline, who, at her orders, began to clean and freshen the house. Rosetta remained behind to cook for the family. Pauline seemed happy to have the help and the company of another servant.

"We will soon have guests here," Marguerite announced to Joseph. "Your nieces and nephew are arriving from France."

"Really? Are they going back to Jekyl with you?"

"No, your father won't allow it. But I've talked with Rebecca Couper about boarding schools. Her daughter Ann attends Mademoiselle Julie Datty's school in Charleston. I'm looking into placing them there—the girls at least.

"Will *Papa* pay for it?"

"Yes, he will pay for it, not because he cares for the children, but because I hope he cares for me." She hesitated, then added, "But as his wife, I have some rights as well. He will have no other choice."

Joseph was impressed with his mother's determination. He had never before seen her assert herself in such a manner. He hoped she was right. It would be an interesting situation.

JOSEPH WENT WITH HIS MOTHER TO THE DOCKS to meet the *Méduse* and greet his nieces and nephew. He had almost forgotten the face of Louis, having seen him so seldom and only when he was very young. But when the children walked down the gangway, Joseph's memory was suddenly restored. The oldest girl, who chose to be called simply Mélanie, and the boy resembled their father so much, with their plain, open faces, that suddenly Joseph recalled him vividly. The middle one, Clémence, bore no resemblance to the Boisquenays. *She must look like her mother*, he thought. She was only nine years old, but she promised to be a beauty, with her wispy, honey-colored hair and hazel eyes.

Joseph had not seen his mother so happy in a long time. She gathered all three children in her arms and wept with joy.

"What should we call you?" thirteen-year-old Mélanie, asked.

"How about *Mamie*?" Marguerite suggested. It was a common grandmother's nickname in France. So *Mamie* it was.

THE WEEKS THAT FOLLOWED WERE A DELIGHT, as Marguerite got to know her Boisquenay grandchildren. Joseph gave them plenty of time alone, but he enjoyed seeing his mother so happy. He found the children agreeable enough and decided to take the boy, whom everyone called Alex for short, under his wing to show him about Savannah, while Marguerite spent time with the girls, buying them new frocks and introducing them to the *émigré* community. When Marguerite saw Joseph and eleven-year-old Alex together, she was reminded of her husband and Louis, when they first met. She smiled sadly, wishing they were still so amicable.

Savannah was a bustling town now, with more than five thousand residents. The little girls were wide-eyed to see America and all its wonders. They had heard about the black people there, so many more than in France where only a tiny fraction of the population had dark skin, but here the black people were treated differently from white people, and all of them seemed to be servants or worse, which surprised the girls. It was nothing like that in France. The black people there were citizens just like everyone else. The children were curious.

"Why are the black people treated like slaves, *Mamie*?" Clémence asked her grandmother one afternoon as the five of them were sharing tea in the parlor.

"Why, because they *are* slaves, darling."

"But I thought the slaves had won their freedom in the war in Saint-Domingue," the girl persisted.

She was surprised that her nine-year-old granddaughter knew so much about what went on that far away, but she supposed that she had heard her parents talk about it. It had caused quite an upheaval, after all, with so many French planters there being killed and so many others escaping without their fortunes either to America or back to France.

"That is true in Saint-Domingue, *ma chérie*, but not here in America," Marguerite said. "The Negroes are still slaves here."

"Are they all slaves?" the girl asked, incredulous.

"Well, not all. There are some free Negroes in Georgia. For example, one of our neighbors on St. Simons has a chef who is a free man, but he is unusual. Most of them must buy their freedom, and few have the means to do so."

Clémence looked thoughtfully out the window before she turned back to her grandmother and asked, "Do you have slaves, *Mamie*?"

"Well … yes. The women who clean and cook here are slaves. Your grandfather …" she hesitated and then changed her word to "my husband … he bought slaves mostly to plant and tend the crops. One can't do it without them here."

"Why not?" the girl asked. "They don't have slaves in France, and the crops get planted."

"Too many questions, little girl," her half-uncle Joseph said with a laugh, seeing that the questions made his mother uncomfortable. "Why don't we just enjoy our tea? We can talk about all that some other time."

She smiled at Joseph. If anyone could distract her from her questions, it was he. He liked all the children, but even though he spent more time with Alex than with the girls, Marguerite could tell that Clémence was his favorite. He liked her spunky ways and her inquisitiveness. She was intelligent and lively, while her sister and brother tended to be more docile.

There had been a few slaves in France before the revolution, Marguerite recalled, but even then, they were mostly household servants or coachmen dressed in fine livery, never in the kind of rags so many of them wore in Georgia. And for the entire lifetime of Clémence, slavery had been outlawed in France, so the girl knew nothing else. *If one has never known slavery*, Marguerite thought, *it must be very hard to understand how one person could ever have the legal right to own another.*

MARGUERITE'S FIRST EFFORT WAS TO FIND appropriate schools for her grandchildren. She knew better than to take them back to Jekyl with her. She enrolled Alex in a Catholic school for boys in Savannah run by Abbé Antoine Carles, the rector of St. John the Baptist. The girls, however, were another matter. She had written to Rebecca Couper to inquire about the school her daughter, Ann, attended in Charleston.

With Mrs. Couper's praise of the school in hand, Marguerite and Joseph set out for Charleston to enroll the girls at Mademoiselle Datty's school for young ladies, where Ann was a student. It was expensive, Marguerite knew, but she was adamant that they would have the best, since she could not take them to her home. And Mademoiselle Datty's school seemed perfect. The headmistress spoke French, of course, and taught all the girls in both French and English at her school.

Ann Couper, who was almost the same age as Mélanie, was delighted to welcome her neighbor's granddaughters. She was there to greet them when they arrived and took both the girls by the hand.

"I'll look after them, *Madame*," she promised Marguerite "and make sure they meet all the pupils." Ann was sure that the Boisquenay girls would feel quite at home.

Joseph seemed pleased to see Ann Couper again. Although he was more than a decade older than she, he always seemed more at ease with younger girls before the world turned them into coquettes. Ann, like Susan Wylly, had always been natural and friendly with him and his brother when they had visited the Couper family, and she did not seem much changed by her years in Charleston. Marguerite liked her too and trusted her to steer her granddaughters in the right direction.

HER DUTIES DONE, IT WAS TIME FOR MARGUERITE to go home. She felt that she had done right by her grandchildren, without making them a burden, other than financial, to Christophe, who, she thought, could well afford it, in spite of occasional financial setbacks. It was the best she could do and still take everyone's needs and feelings into consideration. Joseph accompanied her to the dock in Savannah to catch the boat back to Brunswick.

"What will *Papa* say?" he asked his mother.

"He'll be furious, I'm sure. But he will calm down after a while and pay the bills. He always does, but it will be unpleasant for a while."

"Why don't you stay here with me, *Maman*? Why even go back? Stay here for good."

"Joseph, you know I can't do that. I need to be with your father."

"But why? He can be so awful sometimes, even to you."

She touched his cheek. "But my dear son, I love him. You don't love someone because they're perfect. Love must overlook the flaws. Your father will be angry, but he will eventually forgive me for obligating him to pay for their tuition because he loves me as well. At least I hope so. In turn, I must forgive him for being occasionally disagreeable. Just remember, none of us is ever all good or all bad."

"But *Maman*—" he began.

She interrupted him, placing a finger over his lips. "Joseph, I made a vow before God to love your father for better or worse. I intend to honor that promise. Besides, we depend on each other. We need each other. And if you were honest with yourself, you depend on him too. Now ... no more of this. The packet is about to sail. I must board."

Joseph looked at her, shaking his head slowly as though he couldn't believe her. He would learn, she thought, if he ever fell in love, really in love. Married life was never the blissful dream unmarried people thought it should be. It was a constant negotiation and effort, a constant lesson in self-control and learning to live for the other. Christophe could be trying at times, but he would always be her husband, and she would always love him. She hoped Joseph would one day find someone to love. Then he would understand.

The boat whistle blew. Joseph handed her bags to the porter and gave her a kiss on the cheek. "I'll miss you, *Maman*."

"I'll miss you too. Now behave yourself, son, and come home soon."

He only smiled. "*Je t'aime, Maman,* I love you. I'll always be here for you."

"And I for you, Joseph. *Sois sage.* Be good." It was what she used to say when he was a little boy, when life was simpler.

The vessel pulled away from the dock, water slapping at the boat's hull, as she stood by the railing, waving goodbye. She lingered there for as long as she could make out the faces on the dock. Then, with one last wave, she went to her cabin to think about how she would tell Christophe what she had done.

Chapter 28

CHRISTOPHE DID NOT TAKE THE NEWS WELL, but it assuaged any guilt he might have felt about his actions during the weeks while Marguerite was away. He had been infuriated and fed up with her catering to the presumptuousness and greed of the Boisquenays. In her absence and with Joseph out of the way, he had taken it upon himself to claim what was rightfully his. He might be old, but he was still a man. *A man has his needs*, he thought, and his wife wasn't here to fulfill them.

Still in an angry mood the night following his wife's departure, he had marched resolutely through the woods to Maria Theresa's cabin, with dark thoughts in his mind. He'd flung open the door without knocking. The young woman was sitting there in the lamplight, a needle in her hand mending a tear in a garment. Her child slept on a nearby pallet on the floor. She looked up, her eyes wide with surprise and fear.

"Put down that needle," he ordered, between clenched teeth.

Without looking at him, she nervously anchored the needle in the garment and laid it down on the hearth.

"Now get up," he said in a rough voice.

She stood, her movements apprehensive as she edged her way between him and her sleeping child. He strode across the floor and grabbed her wrists. She struggled against his firm grip, terror in her eyes. He might be smaller and weaker than his two sons now, but he found satisfaction in the fact that, even at his age, he was stronger than a woman. Her fear excited him all the more. Despite her efforts to resist, he forced her backward toward the narrow cot. Pinning her to the bed, he held both her arms over her head with one of his hands, while with his other he jerked up her skirt, tore away her ragged undergarment, and pulled down his already unbuttoned pants.

She cried and struggled to free her hands, but it only made him feel more powerful to take her by force, brutally, however he wanted. What better way to punish her for cavorting with Joseph, he thought, and it was long overdue. She had to learn who her owner was. He had bought her, and by damn he would have her whenever he wanted. And it served Marguerite right, too. If she was not in his bed, if she preferred to be away with those Boisquenay brats, that was no reason for him to be deprived of a woman's body. *She's not the only woman on the plantation*, he thought, *and it's time she learned it*. He thrust angrily at the body beneath him until he found some relief—not with the force of the old days, but it was better than nothing.

When he was done, he got up, wiped himself with his handkerchief, and rebuttoned his trousers. Maria Theresa sat on the edge of the cot, crying and disheveled.

"I'll be back," he said as he left, slamming the door behind him, paying no mind that the noise might wake her sleeping child. As he walked home through the woods, he wondered whether she cried when Joseph took her. *Did he have to do it against her will? Maybe she liked it with Joseph. The bitch.* Well, it didn't matter. Forcing her was part of Christophe's pleasure.

It was the first of many times, and each time she would struggle and weep. Sometimes a sense of shame would come over him as he walked back along the dark road to the tabby house, but he would quickly shake it off.

Even after Marguerite came home, Christophe continued his nocturnal visits to the quarters. When his wife told him of all the new expenses the Boisquenays were forcing on him, it made him even more determined. *That infernal brood. It serves her right,* he thought, thinking of his evenings with Maria Theresa. *It serves all of them right.*

AFTER A FEW MONTHS, IT WAS OBVIOUS that Maria Theresa was pregnant again. And, when the baby came, it was another girl. When Marguerite went to the quarters to see the child, Maria Theresa was sitting up, though she was still weak from the birth. She looked down at the floor when her mistress came into the cabin. Marguerite said nothing. She merely gazed for a long time at the baby's light almond skin, dark straight hair, and blue eyes. The air was heavy with silence as Marguerite turned around and left the cabin, softly closing the door behind her.

"Well, Christophe," Marguerite said dryly when she returned from the quarters, "This time Joseph isn't here to take the blame." Christophe made no effort to deny it. "What shall we name this one—Christine?"

Christophe gritted his teeth. "No, I've decided to name her Marguerite in your honor." His voice was sarcastic.

She stared at him as though he were insane. But he was serious. He named the child Marguerite. Both of them knew that this was the nadir of their marriage, though they would carry on before others as though nothing had changed.

MARGUERITE SPENT MORE TIME WORKING in her garden, reading, and sitting at her desk, writing letters to her sisters, children, and grandchildren. Christophe went less often to the quarters, absorbing himself instead in plantation duties. He took special comfort in the unconditional love of his granddaughter, Louisa, who came to have breakfast with him every morning and put her arms around his neck to kiss him hello with a cheerful *"Bonjour, Papi."*

Little by little, as time passed, tensions began to ease. Slowly and involuntarily, in what passed for forgiveness, the two began to grow accustomed once more to their daily life together, letting the reasons for their fury fade into the fabric of every day. Whatever anger they had felt dissipated—leaving behind only a lingering kernel of sorrow and discontent. They both assumed that things could get no worse.

Chapter 29

Saturday, November 26, 1814

A SHARP POUNDING ON THE DOOR AWAKENED the entire household. Christophe peered into the crisp morning air out the window of their upstairs bedroom, where he and Marguerite had been sleeping. A group of English sailors were gathered outside the house. With his spyglass, he could see their ship, barely making out its name, the H.M.S. *Lacademonian,* anchored in the sound.

A chill pierced his heart. He had no fondness for English sailors.

"What do you want?" he yelled from his window. They looked mean, and he could see the thirst for plunder in their eyes.

"We want in, old man," called the officer in charge. Without any further wait, the men lunged and broke open the front door of the tabby house.

"What is it, Christophe?" Marguerite was sitting up in bed and holding the coverlet up to her chin. "What's happening?"

"The damned British navy has just invaded Jekyl Island," he

shouted, reaching for his trousers and his musket. *How the hell could this be happening?* Jekyl Island overrun by the cursed English navy he had fought so hard against in his youth? Was there no place on earth he could escape them?

Yet it was not entirely a surprise. Two years earlier, in 1812, the American Congress had declared a new war against the British, who were interfering with American trade and impressing American seamen into service in their navy.

"Just like France, getting into another unnecessary war against England." Christophe had grumbled more than once to his son Henry. "The Americans were lucky to have won their revolution against the greatest navy in the world. But another war so soon. It's foolish."

"Maybe they thought that since the British and their allies were so busy fighting Napoleon in Europe they might win an easy victory," Henry pointed out. But after the emperor's defeat at the Battle of Leipzig in the fall of 1813, Napoleon was forced to abdicate his throne and go into exile on the Mediterranean island of Elba. Britain was free once again to focus its forces westward against its former colonies.

Christophe had heard about the American defeat by the British at the battle of Bladensburg in August, followed by the invasion of Washington and the burning of the capitol and various other federal buildings. Since that time he and other planters along the Georgia coast had become alarmed at seeing British warships ominously patrolling their shores and blockading their ports. They had begged for help from the government, but President Madison and the military seemed to have their hands full elsewhere, and no help came. Up to now there had been no invasion in Georgia, but coastal residents feared it was only a matter of time.

Now here they were at his front door, already pouring into his home. Christophe swore under his breath. He thought he'd seen the last of the British navy when he gave up his career at sea, but here they were again, attacking his place of refuge from the French Revolution. Was he never to find peace in this world?

For the past twenty years, Jekyl Island had been the one place Christophe thought he was safe, a place where he could enjoy his life, Henry's growing family, and the release he still occasionally found in the bed of Maria Theresa, now that Marguerite had grown old and, he thought, indifferent to the pleasures of the body.

His musket in his hand, he crept down the stairs. As he reached the bottom step, one of the sailors leapt toward him, knocked him down, and grabbed his gun with a laugh.

"What did you plan to do with that, old man?" Henry rushed in just in time to see the man strike his father. He hurried over to help Christophe to his feet, shaking his fist at the English sailor, who hit him in the jaw with the butt of his rifle, causing both men to tumble back against the staircase.

"Well, well," said one of the officers pointing a finger at Christophe. "If it isn't Captain du Bignon. I heard you had a plantation here. I've been looking forward to seeing you again." He smirked.

Christophe was puzzled. He had never seen the man before in his life.

"Oh, you don't remember me, I expect. I was just a cabin boy on the *Merchant of Bombay*, the treasure ship you plundered during the American Revolution." The man laughed as Christophe's eyes widened. "I must say I've been anticipating this moment and the opportunity to reward you in kind for what you did that day."

The officer touched a deep scar on the left side of his face, and Christophe had a sudden memory of one of his men swinging his saber wildly as he boarded the vessel, accidently striking a child on the cheek. The ship's doctor had stitched it up as best he could, and his face was bandaged when the men were all taken back to Port Louis to be ransomed. Christophe was horrified to realize that this man was that child grown up. He shrank back, expecting a sword blow at any moment.

"Don't worry, old man." The officer laughed at him. "I'm not a barbarian. Unlike you pirates, we don't kill old men and children. We'll take our retribution in other forms. Have at it, men," he shouted to the sailors who were already ransacking the house.

The English seaman made fun of Christophe and Henry, who could only watch as the sailors rummaged through their possessions and wrecked the house. Christophe stood helpless as they stuffed his personal belongings into their bottomless pockets—his wife's rings and bracelets, silver spoons, his pocket watch, whatever money they could find, anything of value, even the miniatures of Marguerite and himself, painted back in Saint-Brieuc when they were young.

Some of the sailors went upstairs, where Marguerite and Amelia had gathered the children in their arms and were trying to hide in one of the bedrooms. There the men made lewd remarks to the women as they jerked open dresser drawers and armoire doors, scattering their contents. Whatever seemed of value they took. Whatever they could not use or sell, they destroyed, ripping apart the women's garments and even the children's clothes Marguerite had been mending.

By now the slaves had gathered around the house to watch. Two of the men, the field hand Tom and the sail maker Alexis, both of whom had escaped at various times and been captured and returned, only to be lashed brutally at their master's orders, stood laughing and cheering on the English sailors, while others wrung their hands in confusion. The sailors began to talk with the slaves.

"You can come with us and be free," they promised.

"Sho' nuff?" asked Alexis. "What I gotta do?"

"Nothing, just come aboard our ship, and we'll take you to freedom."

Christophe watched in horror as his slaves began to talk over the offer among themselves, encouraging each other to take this chance. Tom and Alexis were the first to step forward. The older ones hung back, as did a lot of the women, who feared what might happen to them on a ship full of lusty sailors. Many of them knew from experience that there were even worse places to be enslaved than Jekyl Island. But the younger ones lined up eagerly to march to the beach.

"What are we waitin' for?" hollered Tom, as he motioned for the people to follow.

Even Big Peter, Christophe's trusted plantation driver, took his wife's hand and, grinning all the way, led his family away without a backward glance. Many of those who went were important to the running of the plantation, especially the blacksmith and the carpenter. They all went off singing about the day of Jubilee.

"You'll be sorry," Christophe yelled behind them. "They'll throw you into the sea or sell you into Mississippi territory."

A look of worry crossed several of the faces, and they glanced back, but they did not stop their march toward the shore, where small boats waited to row them to the British frigate anchored in the sound. At least half of them were young males, mostly men like Tom and Alexis, but a few women and Big Peter's two children were among those who climbed into the boats and left the island.

WHEN IT WAS OVER AND THE ENGLISH had set sail again, everyone just stood there, family and slaves alike, waiting for Christophe to collect himself and tell them what to do. He looked around the house with dismay, touching the few things the English had left behind. They had not taken his quadrant or his spyglass, thank God. And they had left the cotton alone. Much of it had already been picked, and it was time for the ginning to start. At least they would have that income for the season, he thought with relief. Although the losses were great and many of them were personal, the family would survive. But Christophe couldn't allow his wife and grandchildren to stay here until the war ended. It was too dangerous. He tried to restore his dignity and assess the situation before he made any serious decisions. The departure of almost thirty of his best slaves, all valuable property, was the most serious blow. He felt a flood of affection for those who had chosen to remain. But the war was still going on, and things could get worse.

Finally he turned to Marguerite. "We can't stay here. It's not safe. They could come back at any time. We must all move into Brunswick for the duration of the war."

"What about the slaves, *Papa*?" asked Henry. "What should we do with them?"

"We'll hire an overseer. I think I know a man who might be willing. That way we can finish the cotton picking and get it ginned and baled. But I won't let my family risk their lives by staying here."

And so it was decided. All the family members gathered up what they could carry of their remaining belongings and sailed into Brunswick.

BY LATE DECEMBER, PEACE TALKS WERE UNDER WAY. But it was not until mid-February that the du Bignons learned that the Treaty of Ghent, which specified terms to end the war, had been signed on Christmas Eve. They breathed a sigh of relief. Cotton picking was over now, and the ginning and baling were well under way. In fact, a large number of the finished bales were ready for shipment to the factors in Savannah. The process had taken longer this year, with mostly older and very young hands to help, but the overseer, a man named Daniel Parrot, had done a good job of organizing the remaining slaves to accomplish the task at hand. Christophe was relatively pleased. The war was over, and they were all safe.

He instructed his family to get ready to return to Jekyl.

Before they finished packing, however, word arrived in Brunswick that the *Lacademonian* had returned and was once again anchored off Jekyl Island. *Mon Dieu*, Christophe thought, *what do they want this time? Surely they know the war is over?* He and Henry hurried to the Brunswick dock to make their way back to Jekyl and find out what was happening there.

By the time they reached the island, it was too late. The British sailors were gone already, but the house had once again been ransacked. This time even the spyglass and quadrant from Christophe's corsair days were gone. He cursed himself for not taking them with him when he left for Brunswick.

Even worse, the entire plantation lay in ruins. Both baled and unbaled cotton were now only piles of ashes, and the burned embers of the cotton house still smoldered. Dead cattle lay in the fields, their bloating carcasses already being picked apart by eager buzzards. The storehouse, which had been full of salted meat put away for the winter, was empty. What the British couldn't take with them, they destroyed.

"I'm sorry, *Papa*," Henry said quietly. "What will we do now?"

"Damn them," said Christophe. "Damn the English. They have been nothing but a curse throughout my life. I'll sue. I'll make them pay. They had no right. The war was over."

The treaty that had been signed on Christmas Eve, but still not ratified, required the British to return any property they had taken, but it did Christophe little good. Although he intended to file a claim with the British government for a reimbursement of almost eighty thousand dollars, he suspected he would never live to see a penny of it.

He had nowhere to turn for financial help, except to his tenant farmers and his faithful French lawyer, Peltier, who could still provide some needed income from Christophe's holdings in France. But getting those funds would take months. What would they do in the meantime?

Things had been bad enough after the first British raid. But now they were critical. He wrote Peltier at once, but had to make other arrangements in the meantime. He had already sold his house in Savannah in 1813 to try to make ends meet during these already bad economic times. His good friend, Thomas Dechenaux, had been kind enough to purchase it and allow Joseph to rent it for the pittance his mother managed to send him each month. Fortunately, some of the funds from that sale remained in the bank to tide them over for a while, but they would simply have to scrimp and hunt their own food. Surely the British couldn't have shot *all* his cattle. Perhaps they could find a few stray cows somewhere. And the island was filled with game like rabbits and even raccoons. The slaves ate them. Why not his family? They would do what they had to do to survive, and if worse came to worst, he would have to borrow money.

His thoughts turned again to his old friend, his closest friend in America, Thomas Dechenaux, and tears welled up in his eyes. Thomas had always been willing to help when he needed it, but he had died the summer of 1814, at only forty-seven years of age. Instead, it was his wife Sophie, godmother to the du Bignons' granddaughter, Louisa, who needed *his* help now. As soon as sufficient funds arrived from France, he intended to repurchase the house in Savannah, which was now only a financial burden to his friend's widow. He wanted to repay the favor Thomas had done him. He thanked God for such good friends and cursed Him for taking them all too young from this earth. If the money didn't come soon, where would he turn?

MARGUERITE'S HEART ACHED FOR HER HUSBAND in his first real financial crisis since they had come to America, and she felt a new surge of love and admiration for his determination to face adversity once again with such courage. If any good could come from so much bad, all the troubles brought Christophe and Marguerite closer together again, and he ended his visits to the quarters altogether.

Sympathetic to his new financial dilemma and without being prompted, Marguerite decided to take her Boisquenay granddaughters out of Mademoiselle Datty's school in Charleston and enroll them instead at a less expensive school in Savannah. It was run by Madame Luce Cottineau de Kerloguen, the widow of a hero of the American Revolution and the sister of the man who had called himself the Marquis de Montalet—the man who had married Servanne de Boisfeuillet. Even with such distinguished connections, Madame Cottineau needed to earn her own living. Although her school was somewhat less prestigious than Julie Datty's Charleston school, she had a good reputation and certainly spoke French as well as Mademoiselle Datty. Above all, it allowed Marguerite to help Christophe in his financial difficulties.

In addition Marguerite cut back as far as she could on household expenses until, finally, the needed funds arrived from France. They all breathed a sigh of relief. They could now buy seeds to plant for the coming year and try to recoup at least some of their losses.

BY SEPTEMBER 1816, WITH FAMILY FINANCES now on a somewhat firmer footing, Marguerite and Christophe sailed to Savannah for a fall visit and to finalize the repurchase of the house on Liberty Street. As soon as they arrived, Marguerite received a brief note from her granddaughter, Mélanie, asking if she could come to call.

"Of course," her grandmother responded, suggesting a time when she knew Christophe would be gone for the afternoon. Marguerite was sitting in the parlor of the Liberty Street house, reading Chateaubriand's novel *René,* when she heard a knock at the door. She laid the book on a table, patted her hair, and collected herself before she rose to answer the door.

"I'll get it, Caroline," she said, waving away the maid who had just hurried out of the kitchen. She knew it would be her granddaughter even before she opened the door.

"Mélanie, how good to see you." She held out her arms to the girl, a young woman now. She had grown taller, and Marguerite realized for the first time that she had to look up to meet the girl's eyes. "Am I shrinking or are you just growing taller every day?"

"Maybe a little of both, *Mamie.* Thank you for letting me come on such short notice."

"It's always a pleasure to see you, my dear." She gestured for Mélanie to sit down, while she rang the little bell on the table beside her own chair.

It was obvious to Marguerite almost from the first moment she saw the sparkle in her granddaughter's eyes that the girl was bursting to tell her something. Mélanie said nothing, however, until Caroline had brought in the tray with a pot of tea, two cups, and a small plate of cucumber sandwiches. Then she could hold it back no longer, and a bright smile of anticipation crossed her face.

"*Mamie,* I am going to be married."

"Married? My word, when? Shouldn't the young man ask our permission first?"

"He wrote *Papa,* and *Papa* said that it was all right. I thought that was enough."

"Well then, I suppose it is. When is the event to take place?" asked Marguerite.

"On November 22 at St. John the Baptist."

"And who is the lucky man?"

"His name is Stanislaus. Pierre Stanislaus Laffiteau. His family came here after the Saint-Domingue uprisings." Marguerite wrinkled her brow thoughtfully. Anticipating her concern, Mélanie said, "Madame de Cottineau has always seen to it that we are chaperoned," Mélanie said, to put her grandmother's mind at rest. "It's all been quite proper."

"Well, tell me about the young man."

"He is young—in fact, three years younger than I."

Marguerite could not stop her sudden intake of breath. Her granddaughter was only eighteen. That meant the groom could not be older than fifteen.

"He's very mature for his age and quite well situated financially," the girl added with a quick and reassuring smile.

"I would like to meet the young man before the wedding," Marguerite said.

"I was hoping you might give us an engagement party," Mélanie said.

Marguerite was silent for a moment, considering the complications and expense such an event could entail. If it could be arranged when Christophe was not in Savannah, it would be best, but she was not sure how it could be worked out. She knew he would object, but she didn't want to say no. The girls asked for so little.

"Perhaps we could hold it somewhere besides this simple house we own in Savannah. A public hall somewhere? Or someone else's home?"

"Your husband would not approve, I gather," Mélanie said without expression.

"No, he would not approve." Marguerite's voice was quiet.

"Why does he dislike us so much, *Mamie*? We've never even met him."

"It's not you he doesn't like, my dear. It's your father and your aunt he doesn't like, for reasons that happened a long time ago and have nothing to do with you."

"What reasons, *Mamie*?" Mélanie asked.

"They're of no concern to you, my dear, nothing for you to worry about. Perhaps you can discuss it with your father some day. In the meantime, let me talk with Christophe to see what I can do."

MARGUERITE APPROACHED HER HUSBAND that very evening, with the only argument she thought might convince him to foot the bill willingly, especially now that the worst of the crisis was over. It was after supper, and only she and Christophe had dined at home. Joseph, though he slept in the house even when his father was there, never took his meals with them, and made every effort to avoid crossing paths with him. Marguerite had grown accustomed to their estrangement and rarely spoke of it any more. She and Christophe were still sitting at the table sharing glasses of port wine when she decided to broach the subject.

"Christophe," she said, leaning forward in the candlelight so that her husband could see her earnest face more clearly. "Mélanie came to see me this afternoon. She is getting married."

"Who would want to marry her?" he asked, leaning back in his chair. His voice was peevish.

"A young man named Stanislaus Laffiteau."

"He's just a boy. I know his family."

"She would like us to hold an engagement party for her," Marguerite said, as she watched Christophe's face darken. Before he could say anything, however, she added hastily, "If we encourage this marriage, then we will no longer be responsible for any of her expenses. If she is a burden, she will be a burden to the Laffiteau boy and his family, not to us. I think we should sponsor this party to show our approval."

He said nothing for a long time, and she could see him thinking through his answer. "Give her a party then, nothing too lavish, and not here," he said.

She smiled. "Thank you, Christophe. I'll make the arrangements."

MARGUERITE WORKED WITH LUCE COTTINEAU, the girl's tutor, to plan the event. Until recently Madame Cottineau had been in mourning for her brother, the Marquis de Montalet, who had died quite suddenly in June of the preceding year. The Marquis had despised Napoleon, and when news reached Savannah of the emperor's defeat and the signing of the Treaty of Fontainebleau in mid-April, followed by Napoleon's exile to the Tuscan island of Elba, the Marquis was exuberant. His excessive celebrations were said to have caused the stroke from which he died the following June 3. Madame Cottineau's year of mourning was now over, and she had begun to attend social events once more. She was delighted to help with the engagement party of Stanislaus and Mélanie.

"It's too bad my brother's plantation house at the Hermitage has been sold, or else we could hold the event there," Luce Cottineau said. Marguerite knew, as did everyone else in Savannah, that all of the Marquis's Georgia properties were being sold to pay his many debts.

"Instead," Luce continued, "I would be happy to hold the party at my home on Warren Square." Marguerite admired Luce's strength. She had also lost her only son, Achille, only three years earlier. Yet she somehow found the fortitude to carry on. Her pupils had become, in many ways, her surrogate family. The girls were her protégées. She protected them all like daughters, and her enthusiasm about helping with the party was genuine. Of that Marguerite had no doubt.

"Thank you so much, Luce. You don't know how much this

means to me. Thank you for understanding the situation. I will, of course, take care of all expenses," Marguerite said. Luce nodded.

IN THE PREDICTABLE ABSENCE OF HIS FATHER, Joseph attended and made the necessary toasts, and the event came off without a hitch. Abbé Carles, Alex's teacher and a close relative of Luce Cottineau, blessed the young couple and clearly enjoyed the party, laughing and drinking with the guests. Mélanie and Stanislaus, who still looked to Marguerite like children, seemed happy as they smiled and danced and chatted with the guests. Toward the end of the evening, they announced that after their November marriage, they planned to make their home in Charleston.

The bride's siblings, Alexandre, now almost seventeen, and fourteen-year-old Clémence joined in the celebration. They both seemed so much more mature than they had when they first arrived in Georgia. In fact, Clémence was only a year younger than the groom. She had grown even more lovely as she turned into a young lady. Already she seemed quite poised in the company of the guests, and she expressed to her grandmother her pleasure at being back in Savannah near her brother and her uncle Joseph.

How wonderful it would be, thought Marguerite, *if all the people I love could love one another. It would make my life complete.* Now she was in a position where she had to parcel out her love, spending time only with her husband, her son Henry, and his family at Jekyl, or with the rest of those she loved—her Boisquenay grandchildren and her son Joseph—in Savannah. She longed for a day when they could all be together, united, as one family. *Would that day ever come?*

Chapter 30

late January 1817

Savannah Harbor

MARGUERITE, JOSEPH, ALEX, AND CLÉMENCE waited impatiently at the dock as the crewmembers of the two-masted square-rigger, the *James*, struggled to get the gangway in place. Standing boatside, they could see passengers lining up to debark, but they couldn't spot, among the taller travelers, the eleven-year-old girl they had come to meet.

"I'm not sure I'll even recognize her," said Clémence. "She was only four the last time I saw her."

"There won't be many eleven-year-olds traveling alone," Marguerite replied. "We shouldn't have any difficulty finding her."

"She'll be like a stranger," said Alex.

"Not for long," his grandmother answered with a smile.

Then, suddenly, the gangway secured, they spotted her. It wasn't hard to recognize her. She looked so much like Clémence at that age. But she seemed frightened, almost in tears, as her eyes darted through the crowd waiting at the dock.

"Eléonore," called Clémence. "Eléonore de Boisquenay."

The girl's eyes followed the voice, as the four of them rushed toward her to gather her in their arms.

"Clémence? Alexandre? I was afraid you wouldn't be here," the girl said, relief in her voice. "*Papa* made my reservation only two months ago and wrote to you just before we sailed. I was afraid you wouldn't receive his letter in time. Then what would I have done?"

"But we *are* here, *chérie,* and we are so glad to see you safe and sound," Marguerite said, brushing back the wisps of windblown hair that had crept out from under the girl's blue bonnet. "I'm your grandmother. Call me *Mamie.*"

Christophe had been furious to learn of the arrival of what he called "yet another Boisquenay brat." He complained bitterly, especially when Marguerite took it upon herself to ask his French attorney Peltier to pay for the girl's passage. But he had finally resigned himself to paying the bills. Fortunately, cotton prices were up, and he was no longer feeling like the pauper he thought he was after the British invasion of his island. He would still have nothing to do with the Boisquenay grandchildren, but he grumbled less about Marguerite's frequent visits to Savannah to spend time with them. If it made her happy, it made no difference to him, one way or the other.

Luce Cottineau, on the other hand, was delighted to hear of the arrival of a new pupil and another girl to mother. Clémence was almost seventeen now and would not be at the school much longer, but her little sister would fill the gap once she was gone.

THE GROUP OF FIVE LEFT THE DOCK in a jovial mood and took a carriage ride through the streets of Savannah to show Eléonore the sights before they made their way back to the house on Liberty Street. Marguerite smiled to watch the little girl's eyes widen with excitement as Clémence and Alexandre pointed out all the things they had first noticed when they came to Georgia—the teeming market place, people of various skin colors roaming the streets, some with baskets on their heads, and the grassy squares with houses built all around.

As usual, when Marguerite's visits to Savannah focused on her grandchildren, Christophe, remained on Jekyl Island. She no longer asked his permission to make her frequent trips to Savannah. She did what she wanted now, assuming that he could find satisfaction in the quarters for any needs she would not be there to meet. She had attended the wedding of Mélanie and Stanislaus on the arm of her grandson Alexandre, as she would attend many more such family functions with either him or Joseph. The Boisquenay children no longer even invited Christophe to join them, for they knew he would never attend.

Jekyl Island, July 1817

Christophe seemed content, at seventy-eight, to stay at Jekyl most of the time now and play the role of doting grandfather to Henry and Amelia's children. His favorite was still their first-born, Louisa, on whom he lavished most of his attention. She had grown into a sweet-tempered and lovely girl who resembled her grandmother when she was younger. There were five children now, with the youngest, Joseph, already five years old. Christophe had argued against the name at the time the boy was born and could not seem to let it go.

"You already had a boy named Charles Joseph. Why did you want to name another one Joseph?" he asked Henry one evening after supper.

"*Papa*, I love my brother. I know you and he have your differences, but he is still my brother. This Joseph, however, is named for Amelia's brother—the one who drowned."

Christophe could not argue against that choice and pushed back from the table, muttering to himself.

MARGUERITE TOO HAD WONDERED about the name. Although her husband would never openly say so, she knew that he had wanted the boy named for himself. Three boys now and none named for their grandfather. It would have been an honor, she thought, and a courtesy for them to name at least one of their three sons for Christophe. After all, Henry had always been his favorite, and her husband seemed to have trouble understanding why he and Amelia were willing to name two sons for Joseph and one for John Couper, the man who introduced them, but none for himself. *But,* she thought, *who am I to criticize? I didn't name one of our sons for him either.* She'd often regretted that decision.

After Christophe had left the table, she turned to Henry, "Did you ever consider naming him for your father?"

"I brought it up, but Amelia wouldn't hear of it. She argued that Charles Joseph was named for *my* brother and that everyone calls him "Charles." She wanted to honor the memory of her own brother and have a son called "Joseph." I respect her wishes. Perhaps we can name the next son for *Papa*." But five years had already passed, and there had been no new son.

CHRISTOPHE, PREOCCUPIED WITH THE HARVEST and the uncertain prices, seemed hardly to notice his wife's increasingly frequent absences. She spent much of the fall in Savannah trying to reassure Mélanie, who had returned from Charleston to be with her grandmother and sisters for the birth of her first child. Mélanie was terrified of the ordeal, and her young husband had no idea what to do to quell her fears.

Fortunately, the baby arrived without mishap, and, once it was over, with autumn sunlight pouring through the window of the house on Liberty Street, Mélanie basked in her motherhood, surrounded by her family and adored by her husband. The couple chose to name the baby Stanislaus Marc, for his father and for the father of his mother's Charleston tutor, who had helped the young couple settle into their new house and who was to stand as the baby's godfather. The little family was already beginning to plan their return to South Carolina.

"Must you leave so soon?" Marguerite asked. "You're welcome to stay on through Christmas."

"Oh no, *merci, Mamie*. But we want our son to spend his first Christmas in his own home. Besides, you know you will be needed at Jekyl Island." Mélanie was rocking little Marc gently in her arms, her eyes fixed on his.

It was true. Marguerite would be both needed and expected at Jekyl by Christophe and her du Bignon family, but she felt so torn. "Oh, I wish we could all be together," she said wistfully.

"So do I, *Mamie*," Clémence whispered, reaching out to hug her grandmother. "Perhaps one day ..."

Marguerite smiled and patted her arm, "Perhaps."

WHEN MÉLANIE, STANISLAUS, AND THEIR NEW BABY returned to Charleston in mid-November and with Clémence and Eléonore both focused once again on their lessons with Luce Cottineau, Marguerite began preparations to go back to Jekyl. The Savannah house seemed so empty now without all of them there.

"Let's have one more family dinner before I leave," she said to Joseph. "You, me, Clémence, Eléonore, and Alexandre. I haven't seen him for what seems like weeks." Alex had put in only one brief appearance after his nephew's birth. Now that he had completed his studies and found himself a job, he had rented his own rooms on Bryan Street and was spending more time with his friends. Marguerite could see that he was proud of his new independence.

"Go and find him, Joseph, and tell him that he must come and say goodbye to his grandmother. And let Mélanie and Eléonore know as well. We'll plan a lovely dinner on Sunday after mass."

JOSEPH WAS GONE FOR NEARLY AN HOUR before he came rushing back. Clémence was with him, wringing her hands, her face damp with tears.

"*Maman*, Alex is ill with fever," she said. "We must get a doctor to him immediately."

"Take me to him, Joseph, and then go and fetch Dr. Waring and send him over at once," his mother said, as she began to assemble the few medical supplies she had on hand.

They all hurried out to the waiting carriage, and Joseph drove as quickly as the cobblestone streets would allow to transport his mother and Clémence to Bryan Street. Then, off to find the doctor, he left them there, changing the linen on the putrid bed that Alexandre had soiled, cleaning him up, and putting cool cloths on his burning forehead to try and bring down the fever. When the boy moaned, opened his eyes, and tried to talk with them, his words were incoherent. Marguerite noticed that the whites of his eyes had taken on a yellowish tint like that of his jaundiced skin.

WHEN JOSEPH RETURNED, a stranger was with him. "*Maman*, Dr. Waring was not available, but I brought his new associate ..."

Marguerite did not wait for introductions. She knew that Alex's health was critical. "Thank you for coming, Doctor. Please, do whatever you can for him," she pleaded, wringing her hands.

Clémence, Joseph, and Marguerite waited as quietly as they could, while the young doctor examined the patient, pulling back his eyelids, taking his pulse, putting his ear against Alex's chest to listen to his heart. Blood trickled from the patient's nose, and Marguerite reached down to wipe it away with her handkerchief. Then the doctor stood up and faced her.

"I'm afraid there's nothing I can do at this stage," he said sadly. "Had I been called earlier, I could have bled him and purged him, but the illness is too far advanced now for that to do any good."

"What's wrong with him, Doctor?" Marguerite asked, her voice wavering.

"It's yellow fever ... a bit late in the season, but not unheard of." At that moment Alex's chest began to heave. The doctor reached down to help him sit up so he would not choke, and Clémence rushed for a basin to catch the vomit he expelled, which was almost black.

"I think the best we can do is try to keep him comfortable," the doctor said once the spasms had ended. "He doesn't have long to live, I'm afraid. I'm going to leave you with some laudanum to ease his pain."

"Can't you do *something?*" Clémence begged, tears standing in her eyes.

"Nothing that will help, I'm afraid, Miss." The doctor opened his medical bag and took out a bottle, handing it to Marguerite. "Give him forty to sixty drops of this, whatever it takes, whenever he needs it to help him sleep." He picked up his bag and moved toward the door. "I assume you will drive me back to my office," he said to Joseph.

"But he's only eighteen," Marguerite insisted, putting her hand on the doctor's arm as though to detain him. "Are you sure there's nothing else you can do?"

"Quite sure, Ma'am. Bleeding would be superfluous at this point." He patted her hand before removing it. "Just try to keep him clean and comfortable. He's in God's hands now."

ALEX DIED TWENTY-SIX HOURS LATER, the ravages of his illness etched on his face. He had barely completed his studies and begun his life. The few months he'd spent in his rented rooms on Bryan Street had been his only real moments of bourgeoning manhood. Neither Marguerite nor Clémence left his bedside throughout the ordeal.

Now his grandmother was exhausted and distraught, grieving not only for young Alex, but also for her own son back in France. How could she write to tell him both that he had become a grandfather and lost his only son in just a matter of weeks? She remembered the letters she had received telling her of Marie Clarice's death and the months of anguish that followed. She knew the parental pain he would likely suffer.

She hurt also for Clémence, who wept openly and uncontrollably at her brother's bedside as he breathed his last ravaged breath. Joseph took her in his arms, smoothed back her silken hair, and held her until her sobbing ceased. Marguerite was especially concerned for the girl, for, despite her lively nature, she'd always seemed delicate beside her sturdier sister. Joseph's tenderness toward his niece was a sweet gesture, she thought. *He's a good man, in spite of what his father thinks.*

FEW PEOPLE ATTENDED ALEX'S BURIAL. His grandmother, his two younger sisters, and his uncle Joseph were the only mourners, except for Luce Cottineau, Alexandre's tutor, and three of his former classmates.

WHEN MARGUERITE FINALLY RETURNED to Jekyl Island just before the beginning of December, she found Christophe to be of little comfort. His reaction to her news of the baby's birth as well as Alex's death was the same—a brief nod accompanied by a noncommittal grunt. As a consequence, she kept her grief to herself as she and Christophe continued to live their parallel lives, civil and courteous to each other, but going their own ways much of the time, even when they were both at home on Jekyl.

Marguerite missed the old days when they used to snuggle before the fire and when she could always soothe his ill tempers with her caresses. They still slept together, but rarely touched. *Perhaps it's normal at this time in our lives*, she thought. *We are after all getting on in years.* She could hardly believe she was already over seventy. But truth be told, she missed her lover, and at night she ached to have him hold her in his arms. He seemed indifferent most of the time, sleeping on his side of the bed, leaving only a telltale hollow each morning in the mattress.

IN SPITE OF HIS APPARENT INDIFFERENCE, Christophe too regretted their estrangement, but he refused to dwell on it and was too stubborn to reach out to her in the night. As much as he missed their closeness and the comforts of their early days together, he felt he had more serious things to think about. He was just beginning to feel fully recovered from his financial losses of 1814, when an early spring drought and a killing frost in 1818 once again devastated his cotton harvest. What little he was able to salvage, he could fortunately sell at a higher price.

By the beginning of 1819, however, England had grown weary of paying such high prices and turned instead to India for a new market. To Christophe's horror, the price of Southern cotton dropped dramatically—twenty-five percent in a single day. By autumn, prices had fallen by fifty percent, and he was experiencing the same panic that seemed to be spreading throughout the entire country.

Whenever he talked with Marguerite, it was mostly to complain.

"I thought this was supposed to be the Era of Good Feelings," Christophe said. It was a term he had read in the Savannah newspapers to describe the administration of President Monroe. "Well, I don't have very good feelings about it," he muttered.

It wasn't just the cotton prices. There were other factors as well—inflation, unregulated banking, and paper money being printed without gold or silver to back it up. It was upsetting the entire economy. Much of the situation resulted from the fact that the United States had borrowed heavily to finance its most recent war against England.

Christophe was fed up. *Will there never be financial stability in my lifetime? Can the damned government never be trusted to control its finances?*

"It's just what France did," he told his wife. "Borrowing to finance a war we shouldn't have fought in the first place."

He was growing increasingly depressed, feeling that stupid economic upheavals and wars had plagued him all his life. He was sick of it. No matter what he did, it seemed, he could never truly attain financial stability. All his adult life he had sought to establish himself and his fortune well beyond the reach of outside forces. Twice he thought he had accomplished it—when he settled his family at La Ville Hervé, only to have the French Revolution destroy that dream, and then again when he finally obtained all of Jekyl Island in 1800. This time his efforts were undone by economic chaos, low cotton prices, droughts, wars and *those damned English sailors*. As hard as he had worked throughout his life, he seemed unable to attain his goal.

"Sometimes, Marguerite, I think I am cursed."

SHE WOULD LISTEN SYMPATHETICALLY to his rants and try to remind him that he still had income from France he could count on. Fortunately, there seemed to be less upheaval in their home country now. The situation was uncertain for a while when, in March 1815, Napoleon had escaped from his exile on the Tuscan island of Elba and proclaimed himself emperor and military leader once more. But he had been finally and definitively defeated at Waterloo the following June and was now safely tucked away under guard on the island of St. Helena in the South Atlantic, where he could never escape. The French Revolution was over. The Napoleonic Wars were over. And the monarchy, albeit a constitutional monarchy, had been restored, with Louis XVI's brother, known as Louis XVIII, on the throne. The new king didn't have the power his older brother had, but for the time being, at least, things seemed calmer in France.

"You are so much better off than many others who don't have resources outside the country," Marguerite would suggest to her husband when he seemed most sunken in despair, but she could see that his worries were aging him. Despite her efforts, he grew increasingly morose.

Chapter 31

October 30, 1819

Jekyl Island

THE MORNING SUN OF LATE OCTOBER spilled through the muted green of trees and splayed out over the gilded marshes. A mockingbird called from somewhere deep in the forest. Christophe sat brooding on the front porch of his house. His right hip was bothering him, and he had not ridden out this morning. It was getting harder and harder for him to climb on his horse, and he had to use a mounting block now like an old woman. He found it humiliating.

There was also less incentive for horseback riding now that Henry had built his own house a mile or so farther south on the island. They didn't ride together each morning to survey the fields as they once did. Worst of all, little Louisa wasn't at breakfast every morning to give him a kiss and whisper, *"Bonjour, Papi,"* as she once had. He missed her most of all.

An unfamiliar piragua suddenly rounded the last turn in the marsh creek and pulled up to his dock. While Christophe didn't recognize the vessel, he did recognize one of its occupants, but just barely, for the young man looked quite different from the last time he had laid eyes on him. It was his son Joseph, who had not set foot on Jekyl Island for almost seven years now. They saw one another from time to time in Savannah, but Christophe was well aware that Joseph made efforts to avoid such encounters. Now here he was, dressed like a dandy and with a pretty blond woman in tow. The black oarsmen tied up the boat and sat on the dock, waiting.

Offering his arm to the woman, Joseph walked toward the house where his father was now standing to better see the new arrivals.

"Hello, *Papa*," Joseph said, as he approached. "It's been a long time." He let go of the woman's arm and stretched out his hand.

Christophe stood, looking at the two of them with suspicion. "*Bonjour*, Joseph," he said. It dawned on him that Joseph had just had a birthday. *He's thirty-four now*, he thought after a quick calculation. *Maybe he's finally grown up.* With that thought, he stretched out his hand toward his son for a quick shake.

"You've changed," he said, gesturing to his own chin to indicate the beard his son was now wearing. He hoped it was an indication of new manhood.

"I have indeed, *Papa*."

"And who is this lovely lady?" Christophe asked, and not completely forgetting his more courtly days, he gave her a nod and a slight bow.

Joseph did not answer at once. "Is *Maman* here?" he asked.

"Marguerite," Christophe called. "We have visitors."

After a moment the front door opened, and Marguerite stepped out onto the porch, straightening her skirt in anticipation. Christophe saw her look of shock when she glanced up and saw Joseph and the smiling young lady, who was untying her bonnet.

"Joseph, Clémence … what on earth?" She appeared dumbfounded.

"*Maman, Papa*, I want you to meet my wife. We were married just a few days ago—on the 27th—the day after my birthday."

"You were ... married?" Marguerite's mouth fell open.

"Your wife ... Clémence ..." Christophe looked at his son in disbelief. "Is this who I think it is?"

"It's my wife, *Papa*, Clémence du Bignon."

Christophe turned to his own wife. "Marguerite? Is this girl ... one of the Boisquenays?" He thought of saying "Boisquenay brats," but decided, just in case it wasn't, to restrain himself.

Marguerite was standing there, her hand over her gaping mouth, as though she could not speak. She nodded just once.

Christophe looked about to explode. His face reddened, and a vein pulsed in his head as though it would burst. He turned on his heel, walked into the house, and slammed the door. Joseph took Clémence's hand and gave it a squeeze.

The blood drained from Marguerite's face as she stood before her son and granddaughter. "I don't understand," she said finally.

"*Maman*, Clémence and I are married. It's as simple as that," Joseph said. Clémence, her hair, now loose, the bonnet in her hand, was blowing in the wind. She stood in silence, a frown of worry wrinkling her forehead, as she held tightly onto Joseph's hand.

Marguerite looked from one to the other. Finally she whispered, "How could you?"

Joseph took his mother's hand and led her to the chair in which Christophe had been sitting when they first arrived.

"*Maman*, I thought you'd be happy. We love each other."

"Joseph, she's your niece. She's just a child. And you know how your father feels."

"My half-niece, *Maman*. She's eighteen now, hardly a child. And I thought perhaps when Clémence and I were married that *Papa* would ..." Joseph's voice trailed off. Even he knew it was a lie. Marguerite could tell from his eyes.

"We love each other, *Mamie*," Clémence said softly.

Marguerite sat silent for a long moment. Finally she took a deep breath and said, "Then we shall have to make the best of it." She rose slowly, feeling heavier than usual, and embraced her son and granddaughter. "May you find happiness," she whispered.

She ushered the couple into the house, where Christophe was nowhere to be seen. She supposed he had gone upstairs or perhaps to walk off his anger in the woods, though she doubted it, knowing that his hip was hurting so. She motioned for Joseph and Clémence to sit in the *salon*, while she went out to the kitchen to ask the cook to prepare dinner for two extra people, though she felt certain Christophe would not join them.

AFTER A SIMPLE MEAL OF ROASTED CHICKEN, sweet potatoes, and green beans from the garden, Joseph and Clémence borrowed a carriage and paid a short visit to Henry's family at their new home farther south, then headed back for the mainland, hoping to make it before dark. After the couple left, Marguerite went upstairs, carrying a tray of food for her husband. He was lying on their bed, his eyes closed, but she could tell he was not asleep.

"Please eat something, *chéri*," she said, setting the tray on a table beside the bed.

"You know it's incest, don't you?" he said, his eyes still closed. "As if things weren't already bad enough."

"But that isn't your real objection, is it?"

"It's enough. He did this just to irritate me."

"They say they love each other."

"Love? What do they know about love?"

"What do *you* know about love, Christophe?" she asked, her voice quiet.

He opened his eyes to slits and looked at her. "I used to know a lot, but I don't seem to have much experience with it any more." His voice was accusing.

"I have always loved you, Christophe."

"You don't always show it," he answered.

"You push people away. And sometimes you find what passes for love elsewhere."

"Only where I can," he said, closing his eyes again and rolling over, his back now facing Marguerite.

The conversation was over.

JUST OVER TWO WEEKS LATER, on November 16, an ad appeared in the *Savannah Daily Georgian*:

> For sale: the island of Jekyl. It is undisputedly the finest property on the sea coast of the Carolinas or Georgia for the cultivation of Cotton, or the enjoyment or preservation of health—near ten miles long, about three and a half wide; venison and other game abundant; well timbered with live oaks, pitch Pine, etc; and has excellent water. Apply to Poulain DuBignon, Esq. at his residence on the island, or in Savannah to Richard Leake.

When Marguerite saw the ad, she gasped in shock. She found Christophe sitting on the sofa, staring into the dying flames of the afternoon fire.

"Christophe, what on earth are you doing?" she asked, holding out the newspaper, her hand shaking, and pointing to the ad.

"Selling out. Moving back to France. Finishing my life anywhere but here. Giving up on what is obviously a failed effort. It was you who reminded me that things were better in France now."

"We have no place to go back to. You sold La Ville Hervé, remember?"

"We'll find another property," he said.

"Have you considered the fact that all of Jekyl Island does not belong to you? What about the portion you gave to Henry and Amelia when they married?"

"I didn't give it to them. I gave them a lifetime use of it as long as the marriage was intact."

"What's the difference? Clearly their marriage is 'intact,' as you put it. It's still theirs to use as they see fit. You can't sell it out from under them."

"I'll find them something else."

"Christophe, this is insane. We've been here too long. We've put our life into this island. You can't run away from your troubles. There will still be troubles wherever you go. There will be economic problems. I will still have the children I had before I married you. I will still love my grandchildren—all of them—and Joseph, whatever faults you think he has, will still be your son."

He did not reply. A log dropped in the fireplace, sending up a spew of sparks and breaking into a small hot flame.

"I know you did this in a fit of anger," she continued, holding out the newspaper. "Now please undo it, and let's get on with our lives."

HE DID NOT REPLY, BUT THE AD NEVER REAPPEARED, and any offers he may have received remained unanswered. Nevertheless, for Christophe his life as a planter was over. He was too old now to do all he had done in his younger years. It was Henry and a new slave driver who oversaw the plantation. Some of the tenants were leaving. Pierre Bernardey had bought his own plantation, Plum Orchard, on Cumberland Island, and he, his mother, and their slaves took up residence there in 1820. The Wyllys, including three more children born at Jekyl, had long since moved their household to St. Simons, their old Tory loyalties finally forgiven by the island's occupants.

Christophe realized that he was no longer the true master of Jekyl Island. It was his son Henry who was recognized in the coastal community as an up-and-coming young plantation owner and valued citizen. He was already a commissioner of the public school system in Brunswick and treasurer since 1818 of Glynn Academy, one of the first public schools in Georgia, where he was educating his older children and where they were about to construct their first building.

Christophe was proud of his younger son's fine reputation. He wished he could be proud of both his sons, but that was impossible. Joseph he considered a wastrel. He had always wanted to love his son Joseph as he did Henry, but the boy, now a man, seemed to have done everything in his power to drive him away. The father's heart, already hardened against his son, had turned to stone with the young man's marriage. Joseph's only reason for such an act, he was sure, was to mock him, to taunt him, to wound him. *I can endure no more from him,* he thought. He had reached a time in his life when he felt he was only marking time, waiting for death.

The old man looked out the window of the tabby house toward the marshes, all too aware of his dimmed vision, both in terms of eyesight and foresight. Looking back, even his hindsight was not all that clear. He had made mistakes, no doubt, but he was not sure what he could or should have done differently.

Chapter 32

December 4, 1823

Jekyl Island

THE PANIC OF 1819 AND THE FINANCIAL DOWNTURN of the two following years had finally ended. Marguerite, ever hopeful that her husband might become a bit more optimistic about life than he had been earlier, made one more effort to try to get Christophe to embrace all their children and join her on a trip to Charleston for the baptism of two new great-grandchildren.

"Why don't you come with me, Christophe? Why don't you just bury all this rancor and come to see the babies," she urged. "One of them is your grandson—your own blood."

"You can't be serious," he scoffed, walking onto the rear porch and slamming the door behind him.

His reaction came as no surprise. She felt foolish for even daring to consider the possibility of such a reconciliation, but she knew in her heart she would never lose hope. Although she, like Christophe, was feeling her age, she thrived on the joys of being a great-grandmother and only regretted that he was depriving himself of these same joys.

WITHOUT HIM, SHE MADE THE TRIP TO CHARLESTON with Joseph and Clémence, for the baptism of their son. The baby, born in October, was named Joseph Alexander du Bignon for his father and Clémence's late brother. The christening, to be held at St. Mary's Church, was to be a joint one, with Mélanie and Stanislaus's second child, Marie Emilia, born just three weeks before the du Bignon baby. It would be a joyous event, and Marguerite would not miss it for anything.

THE TWO BABIES, THEIR EYES OPEN WIDE, looked around in wonder at all the strangers—godparents, priest, and acolytes—surrounding them. Little Marie startled and cried, but only for a moment, when the priest poured the baptismal water over her tiny head. By this time, baby Alex, as they had decided to call him, had fallen asleep and slept through the rest of the ceremony. Marguerite had brought two silver cups, carved with the babies' initials, one for each of them.

She thought babies were God's promise to the world that there could always be fresh beginnings, that the world was not necessarily the dismal place her husband seemed to find it these days. It was what one made of it.

The baptism put her in a joyous and celebratory mood. On the ship back to Savannah the following day, however, she found herself in a more pensive state as she gazed out at the sea, reflecting on her marriage to Christophe. She wanted nothing more than contentment and harmony at this stage in life, a loving husband and all her children, grandchildren, and great-grandchildren surrounding her. But one could never have everything one wanted, she supposed.

Still, she was unwilling to hold grudges, even against her husband for his indifference toward her and his indiscretions with Maria Theresa, which, she was almost sure, had ended by now. Certainly she did not blame Maria Theresa, who, she knew, was a victim in the matter. Marguerite would have put a stop to it if it had been in her power, for everyone's sake, including that of the enslaved woman. But she refused to dwell on what she could not do. Life was too short, too precious, too precarious, not to enjoy every moment of happiness that God made available. She no longer allowed her initial shock at the marriage of Clémence and Joseph to affect her. She refused to let herself wonder to what extent the marriage was a deliberate attempt on Joseph's part to antagonize his father. All such worries she tried to banish from her mind. It was what it was, and she could not change it.

In fact, she was happy for the couple. They seemed to truly love one another, although they were obviously struggling financially. Joseph spurned the plantation life but was trained for nothing else. He drifted from job to job, trying his hand as a shopkeeper's assistant for the moment. But it paid little and promised no future advancement.

Christophe, who seemed bitter inside and out, was making himself older than his years by carrying inside all the weight of past disagreements. If only she could make him realize what he was missing by confronting life with a scowl rather than a smile, with a closed fist rather than an open mind.

"I'm so sorry your father wasn't at the ceremony," she said to Joseph, as they stood beside the rail, watching the vessel dock. "If he could only see the babies ..."

"I don't think it would make any difference to him, *Maman*. He's a determined man. Determined always to hate me and everything I do." Joseph tightened his jaw and leaned forward on the rail where she could not see his eyes.

"Now don't you go feeling sorry for yourself like him. I'm sure he doesn't hate you, Joseph," she said, trying to reassure both her son and herself. "You must admit you haven't always tried to please him, and he has difficulty with forgiveness, especially forgiving defiance, whether in his slaves or his family."

"You're wrong, *Maman*, he does hate me, with all his heart. Thank God for you, *Maman*." He turned to face her. "At least little Alex will have a loving grandmother."

"And great-grandmother," she said wryly.

He laughed. "And a great-grandmother with a sense of humor." He kissed her wrinkled cheek. "Did I ever tell you I love you, *Maman*?"

"Oh, a time or two," she smiled. "But I never tire of hearing it."

She embraced Joseph, Clémence, and the baby as they left the ship at Savannah. She would continue on to Brunswick, where she hoped her son Henry would be waiting for her. She knew that Joseph and Clémence would soon be coming to Brunswick as well, as soon as they could find a suitable place to live. Christophe had forbidden them to stay any longer in his house in Savannah. He had found a renter instead. The young couple thought they could perhaps get cheaper lodging in Brunswick, where Joseph would look for another job, rather than stay in Savannah. He had won a tract of 490 acres in Appling County in a land lottery in 1820, but neither he nor Clémence wanted to leave the coastal area. He was hoping to sell the land for enough to give them a new start.

Brunswick Harbor, December 6, 1823

HENRY WAS WAITING AT THE DOCK AT THE END of Gloucester Street when the packet, two hours late, finally arrived. He smiled broadly when he caught sight of his mother waving from the gangway. He hadn't really minded the delay, for he took almost any opportunity to come into Brunswick these days. He'd begun to develop a keen interest in the town and its business opportunities. While he was by no means bored with plantation life, his interests had begun to spread in many directions, and he saw Brunswick as a growing community where a smart man could make a fortune. He had the same drive for financial security as his father, and he listened when people talked of opportunities in banking or in building a canal to connect the Altamaha with the Turtle River, like the one New Yorkers were building between Lake Erie and the Hudson. It was mostly talk at the moment, but talk sometimes led to action. He liked rubbing elbows with the Glynn County elite—people like John Couper's son, James Hamilton, who was also waiting at the dock and with whom he had chatted much of the afternoon.

Henry had watched his father's problems with the cotton crops and knew how much he had to depend on his other investments in France from time to time. He was determined that he too would diversify his financial interests, but rather than having them thousands of miles away on the other side of the Atlantic where they were out of immediate reach, he planned to have them here in Georgia.

James Hamilton Couper tipped his hat to Marguerite as she came down the gangway. She smiled at both young men.

"Welcome back, *Maman*," Henry said once they stood together on the dock. "I hope the christening went well."

"Very well, indeed," she said. "How is your father?"

"Well enough, I think. He'll be glad to have you home."

"I doubt he'll even notice."

"*Maman*, you have no idea how he mopes about the plantation when you're away. He loves you, you know, despite his crankiness. Just to have you safely home will perk him up. You'll see."

"I hope you're right, Henry. I missed him," she said wistfully. "How are the children?"

"Louisa is getting over another cold, but the others are hale and hearty as always. And baby Catherine is getting a new tooth. They'll all be happy to see you."

She smiled thoughtfully. "Wouldn't it have been wonderful to have baptized all three babies at the same time? Just imagine, Catherine, Alex, and Marie together, my three grandchildren and great-grandchildren all born in a single year. What a blessing."

"I'm sure it would have been very nice, *Maman*. But sometimes things aren't that easy."

"Sometimes when things aren't easy, one must make a greater effort."

"You're strong and determined, *Maman*. But you know *Papa* would have apoplexy if we had tried to have a joint baptism with Clémence and Mélanie. Besides Amelia and I hardly know them."

"I thought Joseph and Clémence visited your home the day they came to tell us of their marriage."

"They did, but it was a rather awkward visit. I was glad to see Joseph of course, but I really didn't know what to say about their marriage. It was … strange."

"They seem happy together."

"I hope so. I hope it was worth it."

"Worth what?"

"*Maman*, you know *Papa* will never forgive Joseph for this. He told me he was sure the only reason Joseph married her was to defy him. He's very angry with my brother."

"I know that. It's why the rest of us must make some effort to make your brother's wife feel like part of the du Bignon family, which she is now. What's done is done, Henry. We must all make the best of it. I was as surprised as anyone else, but she is a lovely young woman. She is my granddaughter, and now she is your brother's wife. I will never turn my back on them."

"I know, *Maman*. I wish I could make things better."

"Perhaps you can, Henry."

BUT THINGS DID NOT GET BETTER. In January, even though the economy had begun to recover, Christophe felt compelled once again to request that Peltier send money from his French holdings to make ends meet at Jekyl Island. His eyesight, which had always been keen, had begun to fail, and he felt old and broken. The only joy in his life was the youth and vigor of the grandchildren Henry and Amelia had produced—especially Louisa, their firstborn, on whom he lavished his love and who adored him in return. Otherwise Christophe felt like a dried-up lemon. He was no longer capable of taking any physical pleasure with Marguerite or Maria Theresa, even if he wanted to. And Maria Theresa, though she was still young, had begun to display symptoms of an old woman, professing great pain in her joints. Despite her complaints, she went to the cotton house every day and tried to stitch garments, but she was getting to be of little use. Her two daughters took more care of her now than she did of them.

Only Marguerite was still there for Christophe. She tried to make him comfortable. She read to him, once his eyes were so dim he could no longer make out the words. She wrote both his letters and her own. But there was hardly anyone for him to write to any more, except Peltier. Christophe's brother, Ange, who'd managed to preserve his limited fortune in Mauritius by embracing the revolution, had died in 1806. Four years earlier their sister Angélique had rejoined her convent and become mother superior to the few remaining nuns before her death in late May 1808. Their sister Jeanne, too, was dead, having died the April before her sister. Christophe was the only one left now. He had invited his sisters to join him in America at various times, but they had refused, choosing to live out their lives in their native land, in spite of all the calamities.

He was the one who had taken all the risks, he told himself, the one who had succeeded over and over, only to have all he had strived for ripped away again and again. *Was there no justice? Was there no God?* Why had all these misfortunes befallen him when he had worked so hard?

The days passed slowly for him, one just like another, all plagued with pain and a thousand what-ifs. What if he had never come to America? What if he had stayed in France and agreed to wear the stupid tri-colored cockade of the revolution? Perhaps the new authorities would have left him alone, and he would still be living now at La Ville Hervé, where there were no British sailors or hurricanes or cotton worms. What if he had embraced the revolution to preserve his skin? It was what Ange had done, and he had died in comfort in his own chosen home. What good was loyalty to a crown that had been trampled into the dust? Even the king had finally donned the revolutionary cockade in an effort to save his crown, though it had done him little good. They had still beheaded him. Sometimes Christophe felt he had been a fool all his life—holding on to principles and making fruitless efforts to preserve the things he valued, not just material things, but dignity and pride. And loyalty, when it was deserved. Had the king deserved it?

HENRY INFORMED HIS FATHER IN LATE SUMMER that the cotton crop looked good for the year. Christophe listened and nodded, but said nothing. He had grown wary of senseless optimism. He hoped, of course, that Henry was right, but he would simply wait and see.

Sometimes he couldn't remember any more what day it was. The days and months all ran together, repeating themselves over and over. The seasons changed so little on the island that he had to stop and remember whether it was autumn or spring or just a warm winter day. He remembered bathing, but was it today or yesterday? It wasn't that he was senile, he was sure. He could remember anything he focused on. It was just that his present life was hardly worth bothering with. One day after another—waking in the morning, eating meals, watching the light brighten and dim on the marshes, listening to Marguerite read from some book or other, going to bed, and blotting out the world with his dreamless sleep.

ONE AFTERNOON IN MID-SEPTEMBER, Christophe, dozing in his large chair in front of the fire, was startled by the quickened pace of the household as servants hurried to close the shutters against the blackening sky, and the room grew dark inside. Marguerite lit the oil lamps. The winds picked up, and rain began to hammer against the house's tile roof. He heard the sound of a rushing wagon stopping in front of the door. Horses stamped outside and mingled with the sound of many voices—Henry, Amelia, and the children. Suddenly the door flung open, and they dashed inside, dripping wet. Two of the slaves worked against the whipping wind to put their horse and wagon in the barn, while the young family joined Marguerite and Christophe to wait out the storm.

The hurricane of 1804 and all the deaths it had caused when he was still a boy had left an indelible impression on Henry, and he always wanted his family to be in the safest place on the island—the tabby big house—when the wind threatened like this. There had been another bad storm two years later and still another in the grim year of 1813, and he worried whether his clapboard house would stand in a hurricane, after so many similar structures had been washed or blown away in the earlier storms. The roaring winds, already bending the trees and snapping off limbs, promised a big storm. One could never tell, but he and Amelia always took the precaution of finding refuge in the big house during the autumn gales, which were always the worst.

Christophe and Marguerite were both delighted that they came. It helped to know that all their family members on the island were safe. With all the children in the house, there was always noise and laughter and a flurry of greetings. Louisa, now sixteen and conscious of her responsibility as the oldest of the seven children, gave her grandmother a hug and then sat down beside her grandfather in his oversized chair, put her arms around him, and leaned her head on his shoulder, as she did so often when they were all together.

"You are soaked, my girl," he said with a smile. "Here, let me dry you off." He took the afghan that was covering his legs and wrapped her in it. She laughed.

"*Bonjour, Papi.* You look very handsome today." She kissed his cheek.

An unaccustomed smile played across his lips. She looked so much like her grandmother when she was young. It made him love her all the more. She was the only person who could lighten his mood at will. He was a different man when she was around.

"And even more handsome when you smile," she teased. "Look, I've brought you something." From her pocket, she drew a small white packet.

Her grandfather took it, untied the ribbon that held it together, and unfolded what proved to be three white handkerchiefs.

"I made them myself, from cotton grown here on Jekyl Island. And see, I've embroidered your initials on the corner of each one." Sure enough, elegant initials, *CPdeB*, were there, the ecru threads a subtle contrast to the white cotton.

"Well, look at this," he held them up for Marguerite to see.

"You do such fine needlework, my dear," Marguerite said, bouncing chubby baby Catherine on her knee.

"I wish they were of linen, but I thought you might like them made of our very own Sea Island cotton from the finest of our looms. Eliza helped to weave the material," Louisa said.

"Well, this is just about the best gift I've ever had." Christophe was beaming now. "Come here, my rare girl, and give me a hug."

She obliged him willingly. Louisa's sea-blue eyes reflected the gleam of the lamp and sparkled in the firelight just like her grandmother's the first time he had seen her.

"Think of them as an early Christmas present," Louisa said. "With the weather changing, I thought you might need them sooner." They all laughed. The weather was indeed changing. A limb crashed outside, punctuating her words.

WHEN CHRISTMAS CAME, CHRISTOPHE WOULD RECALL this scene many times, as he sat alone in his chair beside the fireplace, the mantle of which, in spite of everything, Marguerite had decorated with holly leaves and berries from the forest. It was what he remembered most about that stormy day and night, when they finally all slept, Henry and Amelia in the spare bedroom upstairs and the children here and there on pallets on the floor, as the storm raged outside, once again flattening and flooding the promising cotton crop.

Now it was after midnight. The Christ child had come. The evening had finally ended, and Henry and his family had gone home. As they did every year, they had held the traditional late-night meal called a *réveillon*, with oyster stew and a roasted turkey that fifteen-year-old Charles Joseph himself had shot on a hunting excursion with his father, and which the cook had prepared with pecan stuffing. The servants had passed around what seemed like dozens of dishes, including their usual *haricots verts, flan aux morilles, pommes de terre au gratin*, and their annual dessert—*bûche de Noël à la bretonne*, which Marguerite made herself every year. The family had tried to go on with the occasion as they always did, but even with the many glasses of spiced wine they had consumed, it had not been festive.

Everyone was too conscious of the empty place that Christophe had insisted on setting beside himself at the table. It was the chair where Louisa should have been, but where she would never be again.

A sob caught in Christophe's throat as he remembered.

Perhaps he had not dried her well enough that day. She had caught another cold shortly after the storm, or what they thought was a cold. She coughed, ran a fever, and felt constantly tired. Her mother put her to bed and fed her chicken broth, but it did not go away. Louisa grew weaker and weaker and began to have difficulty breathing. As soon as her parents realized how serious the situation was, they knew they had to send for a doctor. Unfortunately Pierre Bernardey, who had served as Jekyl Island's doctor for so many years, had moved his household to Cumberland four years earlier. There was no other physician closer than Brunswick. Henry sent Charles Joseph to fetch him. The boy returned with the news that the doctor was out delivering a baby and would come as soon as possible. It was almost thirty hours before he arrived.

In the meantime Marguerite and Amelia continued to do all they could, dosing the girl with garlic, lemon, and honey and keeping a pot of water boiling steaming on a hook in the bedroom fireplace to help clear her lungs. But the fever and chills grew worse. Louisa coughed and struggled to breathe. All Christophe could do was sit by her bed, hold her hand, and whisper encouraging comments. He had thought there could never be worse days than some of those he had already lived, but he was wrong.

By the time the doctor finally reached Jekyl, there was nothing he could do. Louisa was struggling to take her final breaths. It was the worst day of Christophe's life. He wept as he had never done before. It was as though all the losses of the past, his son, his sisters, his brother, his friends, and now Louisa were all rolled into one upheaval of grief, as though all the hurt and pain he had refused to acknowledge earlier in his life now bore down relentlessly. Although the whole family suffered from Louisa's death, no one took it harder than Christophe.

Louisa had represented to him the only positive thing he felt he still had to live for. She was his firstborn grandchild, his "rare girl," as he often called her. She was all that remained of the daylight of his life, the embodiment of everything worth living for, his only promise for the future. He had poured all the love he had left on the child, adoring her innocence, her beauty, her sweetness.

As the days passed, he thought of the will he had written several years earlier, and he remembered that she was the only grandchild he had chosen to mention. There were many others, but he had wanted her to know that he loved her best, that one of his dying thoughts was of her. He had thought of that will many times since her death. There were no doubt things in it he needed to change. But the effort seemed too great. Why bother? What did it matter? What had it ever mattered?

Chapter 33

September 14, 1825

Jekyl Island

ONE YEAR HAD PASSED SINCE THE LAST HURRICANE. Eleven months since Louisa's death. And the caterpillars called cotton worms had once again invaded the crop. Christophe wondered why God still kept him here, only to weigh him down with more and more misfortune.

The only good thing he'd noticed in these recent months was that, at night, when they lay together, Marguerite now moved her body close enough to touch his thin arms and legs, a habit she had begun after Louisa's death in an effort to comfort him. They went to bed each night now not long after dark, the weariness of the day heavy in his heart. She would kiss him goodnight and sometimes even reach out to hold him, warming his cold body with her own, as best she could. Had she forgiven him? He had no idea. All he knew was that her touch also warmed something inside him, something he had thought frozen forever.

One evening he turned his face toward her and whispered in her ear. "I have not always been good, Marguerite."

"I know," she whispered back. "No one is ever always good. We do the best we can."

He reached out and touched her breast. She did not flinch or pull away. It was still soft, not as firm and round as it had once been, but even now it responded to his touch. And it was a comfort to him. His weak body was capable of little more, but this tiny moment of intimacy drew her even closer to him, and she nestled herself in the bony contours of his arms.

"I have always loved you," he said, kissing her gently.

"I know. And I have loved you. I love you still."

Her words brought tears to his eyes. How could she love him after all he had done to make her unhappy? He had done nothing to help her see her children in France again. He had betrayed her with Maria Theresa, and he had behaved badly toward her grandchildren. And Joseph. *They deserved it,* he thought. *But she didn't.* He could have put aside his desires and resentment to bring her happiness, but he had not. Had she forgiven him? He didn't know. He only knew that, along with everything else, his heart felt the burden of guilt.

"Can you ever forgive me, Marguerite?" His words were almost soundless, and at first he thought she had not heard them.

Finally she spoke in the darkness. "What's done is done. I will always love you."

"Does that mean you can forgive me?"

"Can one truly love without forgiving?"

"But I have not earned your love," he insisted.

"I believe love is a gift, freely given, like God's grace. Remember?" she said softly, her lips brushing his ear.

He did not answer, but he felt a tear escape from one eye and roll down his cheek toward the pillow. *Love was one thing,* he thought, *forgiveness another.* He only knew that she had tried to be the peacemaker between him and her children. She'd tried to weave them all into one family. He too had tried—at least at first. But once he'd felt betrayed by her children and by Joseph, there was no going back. He thought again about the will he had drawn up after Joseph's marriage. Was it a mistake? He pressed his lips together and, removing his hand from Marguerite's breast, he repositioned his body to relieve his aching bones. *No*, he thought, *they all got what they deserved.*

WHEN MARGUERITE AWAKENED the next morning, Christophe's arm felt slightly cool as it lay across her body on top of the coverlet. She removed it and covered him up, deciding not to wake him up but to let him sleep until he awoke on his own. *Let him rest*, she thought. He had been so tired the night before. She dressed and went downstairs, where Caroline had already laid the table for their breakfast. When the dark-faced woman inquired about Monsieur du Bignon, Marguerite told her that he was still asleep and that she was not to wake him up. The bed linens could be changed later in the day if necessary.

When he had not arisen by the time the sun was high in the sky, Marguerite went upstairs again, one step at a time, clutching the handrail to keep from falling. It was getting more and more difficult for both of them to climb these stairs. She already used a cane now when she went walking alone.

The covers had not moved. She touched his hand. It was cold, and it was clear he was not breathing. She sat down beside him, reached out to hold his hand, and gazed at his still face for a long time. His mouth was slightly open, but his eyes were closed, his forehead fixed in the all-too-familiar frown he wore most of the time. She touched his face again, trying to smooth away the angry lines in death, as she always wanted to do in life. But it was too late. They were fixed there.

She felt no sense of his presence, of his spirit, as she had felt after the deaths of Louisa and Alexandre. Only emptiness in the room. He had already slipped away. He was gone. She sensed only his absence. She felt that she should cry, but there were no tears left in her, only numbness. Life without Christophe was unimaginable. He had been a far-from-perfect man, she knew, but he was hers. And she would miss him, for as long as she lived.

When she went downstairs again, she told the servants what had happened, but asked that they leave him alone for now. She sent Apollo to find Henry and notify Amelia.

Soon the house was bustling with activity. Amelia, sweet Amelia, seemed to be everywhere at once, trying to console her mother-in-law, helping her bathe and dress Christophe's body, making sure everyone was fed and that the appropriate people were notified, while Henry went to the quarters to order the construction of a coffin. He sent his father's most trusted slaves, Apollo and Big Cain, first to Brunswick, where they were to find Joseph and tell him of his father's death. They were then to go to the Wylly plantation, known as The Village, located on the southeastern side of St. Simons, to give the Wyllys the news of Christophe's passing. Marguerite was sure that they would want to know and would inform John and Rebecca Couper and any of their other friends on St. Simons.

Even though it was mid-September, the weather was still hot and it was important to bury the body as soon as possible. There would be no time to bring a priest from Savannah, and there was no closer Catholic church. Christophe had expressed a desire to be buried beside Louisa under the largest live oak tree near the marsh.

JOSEPH AND CLÉMENCE ARRIVED WITH LITTLE ALEX just before dusk. Marguerite and Amelia walked arm-in-arm to meet them. Henry was already waiting at the dock. Joseph stepped out of the boat and took his mother in his arms.

"I'm so sorry, *Maman*, I know this must be hard for you."

"Thank you for coming, son, and for coming so soon." She wanted her children and grandchildren around her. They were the remnants of her life with Christophe.

After greeting his brother and Amelia, Joseph turned back to his mother, "Where is he?"

"We have him laid out in the *salon* at the house," she said.

"I'd like to see him. It's been a long time."

"I hate that you can see him only like this."

He took her arm in his, and all together the little group walked back to the house, where the servants were lighting the lamps.

Joseph went at once to the coffin to gaze at his father's face. He stood there in silence for several minutes. Then he reached down and touched his father's hand. Marguerite watched her son as his back slumped and he began to weep. "I'm sorry, *Papa. Rescuiescat in pace.* May you rest in peace." Marguerite suspected that her son's tears expressed grief for what had never been, more than for the death of his father. She touched Joseph's shoulder. He turned around and held her close.

That night, after the children were put to bed, Marguerite and the two couples, Joseph and Clémence, Henry and Amelia all sat in a semi-circle around the coffin in a nightlong vigil. The servants were also compelled to stay awake to make black coffee for the mourners throughout the night. At dawn, they blew out the lamps.

IT WAS TEN O'CLOCK AND THE SUN WAS HIGH before everything was ready. Henry selected six of the strongest and most dependable slaves—Toussaint, Charles, Germain, César, William, and Robert— to carry the simple, wooden coffin. The family and the other slaves trailed along behind in a brief procession from the house to the grave.

Maria Theresa was there, with her two daughters, one on each side of their mother, supporting her, for she no longer walked with ease. The mourners formed a circle around the newly dug grave beneath the live oak tree not far from the river, In the absence of a priest, Marguerite entrusted her prayer book to Joseph to read the service, but neither he nor Henry could read Latin well enough to say the ritualistic words properly. Instead, they all recited the *pater noster* together, and each of Christophe's sons said what was in his heart.

Marguerite was especially moved by Joseph's words.

"As most of you know, my father and I had some difficult times. I was never his favorite son." Henry stared down at the sandy soil as his brother spoke. "I probably didn't deserve to be, but, in spite of everything, I loved my father. And I'm grateful that he brought us to America, where my life has now taken a happy turn." He reached for Clémence's hand and smiled at little Alex, who was quiet in his mother's arms. "I harbor no anger toward my father. I only wish he could have forgiven my trespasses and accepted my wife and son before he passed away. He will live on in all our hearts." Clémence pressed her lips tightly together and looked away as she listened to her husband's voice.

Even as a tear slid down her cheek, Marguerite smiled, warmed by the tone of forgiveness she heard in his words. Christophe could hurt him no more, she thought, and Joseph seemed willing to help commemorate his life.

The slaves, who stood on the other side of the grave, murmured among themselves in affirmation. One of them began to hum a mournful melody that Marguerite remembered hearing at the burials after the 1804 hurricane and again at Louisa's funeral. Soon other voices joined in, humming softly so as not to interfere with the words being spoken. Their backs were to the marshes, where the light glinted off the high tide waters and created a bright aura around their bodies. They looked like dark angels.

Henry's words were almost as brief as Joseph's, but they reinforced the hope in his mother's heart that all would be well and the family strengthened. "I loved my father and honor his memory. I want to say to my brother that he and his family will always be welcome at Jekyl, and I'm glad he is here today. My father could be a harsh man." A few of the slaves nodded almost imperceptibly. "But he was a good man. He meant well, and he suffered many misfortunes in his life. One of those was the death of my daughter Louisa. I hope they are together now in God's hands. He would have been happy to be buried beside her as he is here. May you find rest in Heaven, *Papa*."

There were no more words. Marguerite was not able to speak. Instead, she took the small bouquet of wildflowers the children had gathered for her and laid it on top of the coffin, touching the wood briefly with her fingertips. As she stepped back and looked around the circle of mourners surrounding the grave, it occurred to Marguerite that, for the first time in her grandchildren's lives, members of her whole family were together, gathered in one spot, and feeling a sense of common purpose. Fullness flooded her heart, as she considered that, in the end, it was Christophe and this final event of his life that united them.

Henry nodded toward the six men who had carried the body to the graveside, and they moved nearer to lower the coffin by ropes into the grave. Their task completed, Marguerite stepped forward once more and stooped down with Joseph holding one of her arms to keep her from falling, picked up a handful of sandy soil in her wrinkled hand, and sprinkled it onto her husband's coffin, symbolically giving his body back to the earth.

"Ashes to ashes and dust to dust. Amen," she said. She added "*Adieu, mon amour*," almost under her breath. It was her last act of love. The rest of the family followed her example, each dropping a handful of soil onto the coffin.

When their little ritual ended, Marguerite's two sons flanked their mother to lead her back to the house and let the coffin-bearers fill in the grave.

THE FAMILY SHARED A QUIET SUPPER, then sat, not speaking, in a circle around the *salon*. It was growing dark outside and the lanterns flickered, as shadows danced around the room. Finally Marguerite broke the silence.

"I suppose we should read his will while we are all together," she said, hoping against hope that Christophe's will would contain the forgiveness in death he had not expressed in life, the largesse of soul that Joseph had shown at his graveside. Her husband had not shared its contents with her, and she could only pray that he had done the right thing. Both of her sons nodded without speaking.

She rose and went to the desk, opened a bottom drawer, and pulled out the tin box where Christophe kept all his important papers, including his will and deeds.

"Who would like to read it?" she asked. No one spoke. She turned to Joseph. "You are the oldest son. Suppose you read it to the rest of us."

Wordlessly he reached out for the document, broke the seal, took it out of its envelope, and began to read. "In the name of God. Amen."

It had been drawn up on April 2, 1823, more than two years earlier, and contained, before any bequests, all the usual statements of being of sound mind and body and a request that his "just debts and funeral expenses" be paid.

The first bequest was to his "beloved wife," to whom he left what he proclaimed to be almost one-third of his annual income in the form of a six hundred dollar annuity, payable quarterly, as well as what the will called his "Mansion house," along with its furnishings, outbuildings, and "House servants," all for her lifetime use. If she chose to live with Henry and his family, the annuity would be reduced to four hundred dollars. It was no more and no less than custom and the law provided.

Marguerite nodded. It was a good sign. Perhaps the rest of the will would involve a similar traditional division of assets between his two sons. To Marguerite, it mattered little where she lived, as long as her family was happy and could live peacefully together, preferably here on the island.

But the will went on in unexpected ways. Christophe mentioned only one grandchild—his favorite, Louisa. He had drawn up the will before her death and had not changed it. To her he left a slave, Susannah, who had been her friend and playmate as a child. Such bequests were not extraordinary.

The third bequest, however, brought a sharp intake of breath from various adults around the room, especially Marguerite's two daughters-in-law. It involved his slave mistress—Maria Theresa. He ordered that she and "her" daughter, Marguerite, be freed and allowed to leave the state. He also left her an annuity of eighty dollars per year and her own slave, Nelly. In addition, the will ordered his executors to aid and support her from his estate whenever she was in need. Such a bequest would, in fact, raise eyebrows. It was not only illegal in the state of Georgia to free a slave in one's will, it was as much an acknowledgment of their sexual liaison and his paternity for her daughter as anything could be. And it would have to be probated, registered at the courthouse, for all to see.

Both of Marguerite's sons looked at her to see if she was upset by this clause in the will, but she was determined not to react. It *did* surprise her, but she considered it perhaps retribution for her insisting that Joseph's child, Harriot, be declared free so many years ago. And considering the way her husband had used Maria Theresa all these years, it seemed only fair that he should support her in her later life. She felt no animosity toward Maria Theresa—only sadness that her husband had made such a public bequest necessary by his actions.

She was even more surprised, though pleased, by the statement that followed, a request that "my old Negroes be treated with all the humanity & kindness necessary to their comfort." In light of the fact that he had never been so concerned with humanity and kindness in their treatment during his lifetime, it was a welcome provision to Marguerite, as it would be no doubt to his aging slaves. It boded well, she thought, that he was trying to make amends after death that he had been unwilling to make during his lifetime. She nodded and looked at Henry for affirmation. She caught his eye, and he nodded back.

So far the will had made no bequest to either of his sons. Joseph's voice quivered as he came to his own name: "I give and bequeath to my son Joseph du Bignon ..." His eyes darted over the rest of the will. He drew in his breath, laid the document on the table beside him, stood up, his face an unreadable mask, and walked out the front door into the early evening light. He seemed overcome with emotion, but even his mother couldn't discern whether it was grief or something else.

What has Christophe done? she wondered. *Oh God, what has he done?*

Clémence followed her husband outside, but quickly returned. "He says he wants to be alone," she told them.

"Henry," Marguerite said, her voice uneasy, "you read the rest. Let's get this over with."

Henry walked across the room to where Joseph had been sitting and picked up the will. He fumbled with the pages for a moment before finding the right place. Then he sat down and read in a quiet voice, "I give and bequeath to my son Joseph du Bignon the sum of Eighty Dollars per year during the term of his natural life, this sum to be paid quarterly from and after the day of my death."

There was absolute silence in the room.

Henry took a deep breath and continued, "As to all the rest & residue of my Estate Real & personal here and elsewhere out of the United States I give and bequeath unto my son Henry Charles du Bignon now living on my Island of Jekyl, to his heirs, Executors, administrators and assigns forever."

Clémence was crying softly. Amelia put her arm around her sister-in-law, and Marguerite rose, with the help of her son Henry, and moved toward the two women to embrace them both together.

"It was cruel of Christophe," she said. "I'm sure he must have done it in an angry moment. He couldn't really have meant it as it sounded." In fact, she wasn't so sure. It was drawn up not too long after Clémence and Joseph let her know they were expecting a baby, *when he was still in a rage over the marriage*, she thought.

"It isn't the property," Clémence said, dabbing at her eyes. "It's just such an insult to Joseph. *Papi* du Bignon left his son less than he left a slave woman."

"I know, my dear. And I'll do whatever I can to make it right," Marguerite said. But she didn't know what she could do. After all, Christophe had left her nothing outright either, only the use of the house and income for her lifetime. She would have nothing of her own to bequeath to her older son. She could only help them from her income as long as she lived.

"I'll help too, Clémence," Henry said. "I don't feel right about this."

"Don't you see? That isn't the point. Joseph's father could not have hurt him more if he had completely disowned him. This was intended only to humiliate him. And me. And our son. Even the eighty dollars is only for the duration of Joseph's life. It leaves nothing to our son, while your bequest continues on to your heirs forever. He knew exactly what he was doing."

Marguerite knew that Clémence was right. The will had been drawn quite consciously as a deliberate insult to their oldest son, as well as to her Boisquenay children and grandchildren. Christophe had left an airtight clause that allowed her, even upon her death, to leave nothing to them, for the will stated the bequest was for her lifetime only and that it stood "in lieu & full of all claim of Dower or otherwise on my Estate." In short, if she accepted his bequest to her, and she had no choice but to do so, she renounced all claims to any property she had brought into the marriage, which wasn't very much, granted. She was sure the wording must have been that of his lawyer, but the ideas were Christophe's.

It probably wouldn't have mattered in any case, for in the state of Georgia, as a woman, she did not have the right to make a legal will. But how could Christophe do this? How could he hurt his son more after his death than he had in life? It was a deliberately cruel gesture that had been carefully thought out and drafted.

To make the will's impact even greater, he had arranged for it to be witnessed by two very prominent gentlemen from nearby McIntosh County. One of them, Armand Lefils, was the son of Bernard Lefils, who, with his family, had come as Christophe's fellow passenger aboard the *Silvain* when he made his first trip to Sapelo. Armand, then only a child, now lived in Darien, where he served in several key posts, among them city treasurer. The other McIntosh County witness was William Carnochan, a well-known and wealthy owner of a plantation called The Thicket.

As executors, the will appointed Christophe's younger son Henry, along with Charles Harris, once Boisfeuillet's lawyer and by now a former mayor of Savannah, along with Petit de Villers, Christophe's current Savannah cotton factor. There was no way Joseph's humiliation at his father's hand would be overlooked. Christophe had involved enough influential people to make certain that it would be known and no doubt the subject of much gossip throughout the entire coastal community, from Glynn County, where the will would be probated, to McIntosh County, where it had been drawn up and witnessed. And certainly in Savannah, Chatham County, where two of the executors lived. Yes, Christophe had thought it out very carefully to make certain his decision to disgrace his oldest son would be made public.

Marguerite could only grieve for Joseph and his family. Christophe's will seemed designed to make Joseph *persona non grata* in the business community of the entire coastal area. She wondered once again how he could have been so cruel, and what she could do to make things better. Joseph still did not have a steady job and had already been compelled to sell the land he had drawn in the 1820 lottery just to support his family. He took whatever work he could get and was trying to ingratiate himself in the Brunswick community. His only close contact with the men in town was his service, alongside that of his brother, in the local militia. They had elected him captain before his marriage, but nothing had come of it in the way of job offers. It worried Marguerite that Joseph seemed unable to get his life together in any promising way. He *had* been irresponsible in many ways, she knew. And despite Clémence's protestations, Marguerite suspected that Joseph *had* underestimated his father's fury and, as the eldest son, had counted on a significant inheritance.

As the others sat in the parlor discussing the situation, Marguerite took her cane and headed outside in the darkness to find her oldest son. He was standing on the bank of the marsh creek, outlined against the barest strip of sunset that still clung to the western horizon, his back toward his father's grave.

"Joseph," she said, when she had hobbled close enough to call out. He turned toward her and rushed to offer her his arm.

She took it, and they walked slowly back toward the edge of the creek.

"I know you're angry now," she said. "But don't let that anger eat away at you, as it did your father."

"Why did he hate me so, *Maman*?"

"I don't know what was in his heart when he drew up that will, Joseph. Anger, disappointment, hurt ... who can say? But I remember so well his joy at your birth, how he rushed out of the house to tell anyone he could find that he had a son, a fine son. He was so proud."

"He thought I married Clémence just to spite him, didn't he?"

"Probably so. You know how he felt about my Boisquenay children and grandchildren. Your father could hold a grudge for all eternity, I fear. In other ways, he could be a good and wonderful man, and I loved him. I kept hoping that as he grew older he would learn to forgive, but he never did. He didn't talk about it as much, but I gather that he let resentment grow inside him until it became an ugly, dark disease that ate him up inside." She turned toward him and took his face in her hands.

"Don't let that happen to you, Joseph. You know I'll help you as long as I live. I want you and Clémence and little Alex to come and live with me, if you will. It will help me enormously."

Joseph did not reply. She took his arm again.

"And I think Henry is willing to share the inheritance with you," she went on. "He feels terrible about what's happened, but I should let him speak for himself."

"I won't take it, *Maman*. I won't touch a penny of *Papa*'s estate—including the eighty dollars. I won't give him the satisfaction."

"Joseph, don't be foolish. Eighty dollars a year won't let you live lavishly, but it will keep your family from starving, and you know you can always live with me on the island. You'll get by, and I know you'll be able to find suitable employment sooner or later."

"Not if *Papa* has anything to do with it. When people learn about that will …" His voice trailed off. He spoke of his father as though he were still alive.

"There are always things in life we must somehow overcome, Joseph. Tell me that you and Clémence and little Alex will come here to live with me. Promise me."

"I promise, *Maman*. As long as you are here, we will stay."

"That may not be a very long time, son. I am old and tired. But having you here will give me a greater will to live. I want you brothers to be close. You can help Henry on the plantation."

"*Maman*, you know how I hate plantation work. I'd like to help Henry, but I simply can't order slaves around and do the things he does. I won't."

"I love you both, Joseph. It would be my greatest pleasure to spend my final days with both my sons and their families nearby."

Joseph lifted her hand to his lips and kissed it. "I love you too, *Maman*. We'll work it out."

Chapter 34

THE DAY AFTER CHRISTOPHE'S BURIAL was a Saturday. Although it was normally a workday on the island, Henry declared it a day of mourning for the plantation, and the slaves were freed from work both Saturday and Sunday—two back-to-back days of leisure—a rare occurrence on Jekyl.

Late in the morning, the two brothers walked the old plantation road just to get out of the house, where the women fluttered about Marguerite, who seemed to have grown even weaker after her husband's burial. There was much to be done and much to discuss in the wake of Christophe's death, and everyone was eager to get it over with.

"What are you going to do about Maria Theresa and her daughters?" Joseph asked his brother, as he watched a rabbit hop across the road in front of them.

"I don't know. For one thing, *Maman* doesn't want them listed in the slave inventory I have to file with the estate," Henry said. "She thought that should make things easier. And who outside the plantation knows who our slaves are?"

"*Your* slaves, Henry, not *ours*," Joseph said.

"*Mon frère*," Henry said, "I have told you that I'm willing to share the inheritance. Please don't be angry with me for what *Papa* did."

"I'm not angry with you, Henry. But I won't accept his cursed money. I'd rather starve."

"Don't be a fool, Joseph. We can run the plantation together."

"I'm not cut out for plantation life," Joseph said. "I think I've made that pretty clear over the years."

"What are you cut out for, Joseph?" his brother asked.

The question stung. Joseph did not think Henry asked it with ill intent, but still, it stung. And just for a moment, Henry reminded him of their father. As Joseph was well aware, he himself had accomplished little in his life, except to infuriate his father at every turn. He had failed to follow in his footsteps as either a sea captain or a planter. Both professions sickened him. The thought of being at sea for endless weeks was unbearable, and the idea of owning people and ordering them around was unthinkable. They were human beings like himself, and he would have no part of it. He'd considered trying the life of a merchant, but he had no head for running his own business, and he didn't like being subservient to another.

When Joseph married Clémence, he had promised her a life of relative ease, and she'd believed him. But so far he had not succeeded at anything he tried. Until this moment, he hadn't realized the extent to which he had counted on a sizeable inheritance—an inheritance he would never have. It was not his brother's fault. And he was determined to make his way without his younger brother's help. That would be too humiliating. He would find some way to support his family, in spite of his father's efforts to poison his chances.

When Joseph made no answer to his brother's question, Henry kicked at an oyster shell that lay in the roadway and returned to the previous topic.

"I don't know what to do about Maria Theresa and Marguerite. You know the whole thing is illegal. I refuse to be involved, and I'm pretty sure the other executors will feel the same way. I just don't want any trouble." Henry had never been one to defy authority.

It was a touchy issue in the state of Georgia. A law had been passed in 1801 banning the freeing of slaves and forbidding any last wills and testaments that included manumission of slaves to be probated. But the legislature had softened the law in 1815, allowing such wills to be recorded and probated, but only with the stipulation that any parts that involved the freeing of slaves be disregarded. There was now even talk of new legislation to prohibit the removal of any slaves from the state of Georgia. It hadn't been passed yet, but port authorities were already on the alert for efforts to sneak slaves out of the state for the purpose of freeing them. One could still travel with servants, but it was getting more and more difficult every day.

"Surely there's some way to work it out in spite of the laws," Joseph said. He had no qualms about defying authority and, in fact, welcomed the challenge. "But they'll need help in getting started over somewhere else, if you have any idea where they might go. I'm willing to do what I can." It seemed only right, considering that the situation also involved his own daughter, Harriot.

THE FAMILY DEBATED THE TOPIC ALL TOGETHER later in the evening.

"I'm willing to give it a try to get them out, but we'll need assistance from somebody up North," Joseph pointed out.

In the end, it was Amelia who finally came up with what they all agreed was a workable solution or at least a couple of good possibilities.

"Why don't we ask James Hamilton Couper for advice," she said, referring to the oldest son of John Couper, her first benefactor in Georgia. "He graduated from Yale College, and he might know somebody in a Northern state who would be willing to help. He's also in contact with his namesake, James Hamilton, who lives in Philadelphia now. Maybe he's a possibility."

"I think the fewer people with Georgia connections who know about this, the better," Henry said, his brow furrowed, obviously nervous about the whole thing.

"Hamilton still owns a plantation and has a lot of business connections here." Joseph reminded him.

"Too many, I think. A total stranger might be better," Henry agreed.

"Let's go over to St. Simons tomorrow and see if young Couper is willing to help," Joseph suggested.

"Do you think we can trust him?" Henry asked, tugging at his lips.

"Of course. He's John Couper's son, remember?" Amelia added. She had absolute confidence in the Couper family and never forgot their kindness toward her when she had first come to Georgia. It was at her insistence that she and Henry had named one of their sons, now thirteen years old, John Couper du Bignon.

AND SO IT WAS DECIDED. They would confide only in the Coupers' eldest son.

Marguerite sat quietly throughout the animated discussion. Now, she raised her voice. "Even if we do find help up North, they can't make the trip alone," she said. "They have no experience with travel, and I don't think they could do it without getting caught. Someone will have to go with them, to make sure they get safely out of Georgia and make their contact in the North."

"Not me," Henry said. "I don't plan to be involved in anything illegal. I'm already sticking my neck out enough by not listing them in the slave inventory I'll have to submit when the will is probated."

Joseph laughed. He didn't give a fig about the laws of Georgia, and he had less to lose. "I'll go," he said. "We'll both go. Right, Clémence?"

She nodded without speaking. He knew she didn't like to be reminded that Harriot was his daughter, but he felt responsible for the girl and her mother. If Christophe's child, Marguerite, was part of the package, well, then, so be it. None of this was her fault. It was the one good thing his father had done in his will—to free Maria Theresa and Marguerite. At least there was that. As his mother always pointed out, no one was ever all good or all bad. Not even his father. Although this latest slight by his father was a final insult and more cruel than the others had always been, what did it matter? He had been long dead to Joseph. He was no more dead now, just out of the way.

"And what about Nelly?" Amelia asked. It would be complicated to give a bill of sale to Maria Theresa. It was a detail that still needed to be worked out.

As it turned out, Nelly would be no problem at all. When Henry told Maria Theresa that his father had freed her and her second daughter in his will, she shouted "Hallelujah." But when he told her that Christophe had left her a slave of her own, she shook her head.

"I ain't gone be no slave owner, Mister Henry," she vowed, lapsing in the fervor of her freedom into her Geechee dialect. And she would no longer call him "Massa." She chose quite deliberately to speak the language her people used among themselves rather than the French of her former master, now that she was free. "And if I leaves here, I sho ain't gone take Nelly away from Jekyl. Her daughter Phyllis be here, and two of her grandbabies. No sir. I ain't gone own no slave. And I ain't gone break up no fam'bly. No sir."

He understood her words. When he passed the news on to his brother, Joseph nodded without surprise. Henry would keep Nelly then, listing her in the slave inventory at a value of fifty dollars.

Chapter 35

November 1, 1825

Savannah, Georgia

THE SMALL GROUP OF TRAVELERS SHUFFLED ABOUT NERVOUSLY as they stood on the dock, waiting to board the sailing ship *Louisa Matilda*, which would take them as far as New York. Joseph, forgetting he had a pair of gloves in his pocket, rubbed his hands together against the chill. A cane was curved over his left wrist, and he wore a borrowed top hat and spectacles he did not need, in the hope that no one he encountered would recognize him. Clémence doubted that anyone would know her in any case, but as a precaution, she had braided her blond curls and stuffed them under a dark, large-brimmed hat. Harriot, who needed no disguise, for she had not left Jekyl Island since she was brought to Savannah as a child to be baptized, held little Alex, who fidgeted in her arms. Given her light skin and strong resemblance to Joseph, the general consensus had been that he should claim her as his niece. Clémence had balked at the original idea that he should list her as his daughter.

They were traveling under the name of Proctor. Their final destination was Long Island Sound and the port of New Haven, Connecticut, where they would be met by a Rev. David Ogden, pastor at a Congregational Church in Southington, about twenty miles or so north of New Haven. He had been a Yale classmate of James Hamilton Couper and, at Couper's request, had agreed to help Maria Theresa and her daughters find jobs and resettle in the area.

Slavery was still legal in Connecticut, but it was gradually being phased out, and fewer than one hundred slaves remained in the entire state. The Rev. Ogden agreed with Joseph that the emancipation of Maria Theresa and her daughters would be honored there.

Posing as family servants, Maria Theresa and Marguerite carried their "master's" and "mistress's" light luggage, while most of the things the travelers expected to need had already been loaded by porters into the ship's hold.

MARIA THERESA STRUGGLED TO CONTAIN her excitement as she waited for the boarding of the ship's passengers. She had not been away from Jekyl since the day Christophe had bought her at the slave auction and brought her there. This morning when they had all set out from the island before dawn aboard the sloop *Anubis*, Henry had accompanied them as far as Brunswick, where they boarded the packet boat that took them to Savannah. As the sun rose and flooded the marsh grasses with its early glow, Maria Theresa had taken a deep breath and tried to focus on her new free world. The spartina grass caught the sun's rays and displayed its glorious fall colors, grayish green at the bottom, where the roots sank into the rich black silt that bordered the creek, and rust at its tips. She was amazed at all the different shades of the morning—green and brown and copper and gold—that she had never noticed before. *Things don't look the same in freedom as they looked in slav'ry*, she thought.

She wore a dark-blue cotton dress that Amelia had given her just the day before. It was a bit too large and worn at the hem and cuffs, but for her, it was a magnificent gown, one like she had never worn before. And she had a black wool shawl draped around her shoulders to stave off the cool November air.

She looked at her two daughters, their olive skin bathed by the light of the rising sun. *They bof so beautiful*, she thought, *and now they bof free*—if they could just make it out of Georgia without being stopped. As soon as they reached Brunswick, she would try hard to look like a slave again if that's what it took, a slave about to accompany her master on a trip. But for the moment, she could not stop herself from smiling.

Harriot and her sister Marguerite were as excited as their mother. The younger daughter wore a simple brown cotton dress and an ill-fitting brown sweater. Harriot was better garbed in a green light-wool gown with a matching jacket and bonnet that had belonged to Miz Marguerite. She needed to look like a white girl in her role as her father's niece brought along to help with the baby. She could grin and laugh all she wanted, though she was told to speak as little as possible and only in French. But as Mr. Henry had instructed them before they left the island, Maria Theresa and Marguerite were to keep their eyes on the ground, do what they were told, and never show any emotion until they were well out of Georgia, even out of Southern waters.

They were to behave like the slaves they no longer were. That was the hardest part of all because Maria Theresa could hardly keep herself from shouting and dancing and letting her face shine with joy. Harriot was luckier, her mother thought. *At least she can smile all she wants. She can laugh out loud fo' her mama and sister.* It made a mother's heart glad.

Once they arrived in Savannah to catch the ship that would take them north, the wait on the dock seemed forever, but finally passengers began to board the vessel. It was an old sailing ship. The new steamers didn't run all the way from Savannah to New York yet. There was one steamer that stopped occasionally in Charleston on its voyage from New Orleans to New York, but neither Henry nor Joseph saw any advantage in an even longer wait at another Southern port, which could only increase their chance of getting caught. As long as they were on the water, sailing north, Maria Theresa didn't much care.

Harriot, with Alex still in her arms, followed Joseph and Clémence up the gangway. Her mother and sister, toting various small valises, trailed along behind. Once on board they did not lift their eyes or speak until the anchor was lifted and they were in open water. Then Harriot leaned over to whisper to her mother, "Mama, you looks really spry today," she said. "I ain't seen you lookin' so good in a long time."

"Freedom do that to a woman," Maria Theresa said softly so that no one else would hear. She hid her quiet laugh behind her hand.

"I reckon so." The girl smiled. She had suspected for a long time that her mother's infirmities came more from sorrow and discouragement than from real physical ailments. And maybe, just maybe, she put on a little bit to make the old man feel sorry for her and leave her alone. She wasn't yet forty years old, but she could walk bent over like she was eighty. Harriot reckoned she'd have done the same thing in her place. Her mama's back seemed a lot straighter now.

At every port, Maria Theresa and young Marguerite stayed below, while Harriot stood on deck with the white folks, holding her breath. She was not worried about herself because of her light skin and her freedom papers from childhood. Her baptism as a free mulatto would save her, she thought. But she was concerned for her mother and sister. They had papers too, she knew, drawn up at Joseph's urging by Henry du Bignon, but if the authorities investigated, they would likely not hold good in law, and they could be turned back. She'd also heard stories about freed slaves being kidnapped by patrollers, who then sold them for profit to some plantation owner who paid no attention to their claims of freedom. She would rest easy only when they were out of Southern waters.

By the fifth day, after brief stops in Charleston, Wilmington, and Norfolk, when they were well past any Southern port where they could be apprehended, only then could they finally relax. They all stood on deck now, Joseph and his family, Marie Theresa and her two daughters, jubilant as the vessel cut decisively through the waters.

"We's safe, Mama, We's all free!" Harriot whispered to her mother, "and we's together."

Her mama smiled for the first time that big, broad smile everyone knew she had been holding back.

"Well, I reckon we'll just have to pray for Mister Christophe's soul. Seems like there must've been some good in that old man after all. I 'speck I might have to try and forgive his trespasses."

Joseph, standing not far away, heard her words. *I wish I could do the same*, he thought, wondering if he were too much like his father ever to find forgiveness in his heart.

Jekyl Island, November 4, 1825

MARGUERITE LEANED ON HER CANE AS SHE STOOD on the verge of the landing Christophe had named for her so many years ago. How life had changed since that day, how many arrivals and departures from this very dock had altered her life. She gazed out over the vast expanse of salt marsh, which had taken on the amber tint of fall. She thought about that last departure and wondered where the little group of travelers was by now and whether they were safe. Clouds blocked the sun and cast a gray shadow over the swaying spartina grass, so neatly sliced by the silvery tidal creeks that led toward the mainland.

It was lonely on the island now. Christophe, her husband, lover, and companion for so many years, was gone. She missed him. In spite of his misdeeds and dark moods, she missed him. It was like a part of her was missing. There would be no one to turn to on dark nights when she needed to be held, no warm body beside hers when the terrifying storms came, no ear in which to whisper those words of love that welled up inside her. Never again. The big house was empty without him, empty and silent. Rosetta spent most of her time out in the kitchen, and both she and Caroline went to their own cabins at night. Even when they were in the big house, they rarely spoke, except to each other. Henry, Amelia, and the children were back in their own home now, tending to their daily duties as the plantation returned to normal. And Joseph and his family were en route to Connecticut on their errand of liberation.

Marguerite was more aware than ever of the rapidly increasing weakness in her body and the effort it took for her to walk even this far, just over three hundred paces from the house to the landing, without assistance. But she planned to walk those steps as long as she could, though she knew it would not be long.

Her thoughts turned toward her son Joseph. With the activity of preparing for departure and all his efforts to help the three women escape their bondage, he seemed, for a time at least, to forget his own bitterness towards his father. Marguerite would never understand Christophe's rejection of his oldest son, his determination to punish him and push him away—even from the grave. How could he let his anger with Margot and Louis taint his relationship with his own flesh, his own blood? It had poisoned his last years, and she could only pray that finally, in death, he could find the blessings of peace and pardon he never found in life. After Joseph's marriage, his father had never again seemed like the man she'd met in that ballroom in Mauritius so long ago—more than fifty years now. *Could it have been so long?* Closing her eyes for a moment, she seemed to hear the music of their undanced waltz as she prayed for her husband's soul and for Joseph—that he not let his own time on earth be destroyed by harboring a lifelong grudge against his father.

As though God were answering her prayer, the last gray cloud that blocked the sun drifted westward, unleashing a dazzling morning light that bathed the broad expanse of marsh in autumn gold. A sudden movement in a nearby stand of the tall spartina grass caught Marguerite's eye. A great egret she hadn't noticed before, for it had stood so still, suddenly unfolded its large, white wings against the black bank of the creek. Flapping noisily, it rose upward, upward until it began to soar in splendor against the brightened sky. The unexpected flight broke the stillness of the morning, and Marguerite felt a sudden surge of relief, almost joy.

"It's a sign," she whispered, even as other, unbidden words drifted into her thoughts. *All manner of things will be well.* Where had she heard that before? Somewhere a long time ago. Its message seemed to have taken root in her heart. *We can never know the future,* she thought. *We can only trust that love and forgiveness will ultimately prevail.* It was just a sprig of hope, but it was enough, just enough to bring a faint smile to her lips, as she turned slowly and hobbled back toward the tabby house at the north end of Jekyl Island.

Author's Afterword

MARGUERITE OUTLIVED HER HUSBAND by only three months. After her death on December 29, 1825, she was presumably buried on the island near the same live oak tree that sheltered the graves of Christophe and Louisa. None of those graves are marked today, but one may suppose that they were located in the general vicinity of the small cemetery on the north end of Jekyll Island, where only the rotting stump of an oak is found today and where, in 1898, the Jekyll Island Club built a tabby wall around the carved stone slabs that mark the graves of later family members.

The names *Marguerite's Landing* and *du Bignon Creek* no longer appear on contemporary maps, though both are preserved on historic maps of the area. Over time *Marguerite* became Americanized in oral tradition and is recorded rather as *Margaret's Landing*. Certainly a fair number of Marguerites and Margarets have landed on Jekyll Island, but only Marguerite du Bignon has ever lived at the site, located today in the Horton House historic district.

Marguerite's story and the research from which it derives has taken many unforeseen directions and has entailed some extraordinary adventures, as I explored the details of her life and tried to present them in convincing historical fiction. I have previously written brief nonfiction accounts of the du Bignons' story, most notably in *Jekyll Island's Early Years* (University of Georgia Press, 2005; paperback, 2014). In the notes and bibliography of that book, I clarify many of the historical sources used in writing this fictional account. Copies of many of them are now available in the DuBignon Collection at the Georgia Historical Society in Savannah.

In writing *Marguerite's Landing*, I have not set out to change the facts or dramatize the events, which are already dramatic enough, but rather to have them make sense to a modern reader. I have sought to fill the gaps left in the historical record, to provide motivations for my characters' behavior, and to show their logical reactions to various situations and the deeds of others. In the case of the Sapelo Company, I have made some effort to simplify the tangle of legal issues and economic complexities. For that, I beg the indulgence of my historian friends and colleagues.

However, readers who want to examine further the complex details of the *Société de Sapelo* can consult the groundbreaking 1989 article by Kenneth H. Thomas, "The Sapelo Company: Five Frenchmen on the Georgia Coast, 1789-1794," contained in the *Proceedings and Papers of the Georgia Association of Historians*, 10, as well as Martha Keber's meticulous biography, *Seas of Gold, Seas of Cotton: Christophe Poulain DuBignon of Jekyll Island* (University of Georgia Press, 2002). Her book is, as one reviewer described it, "a triumph of research." This novel owes much to Dr. Keber's work, particularly concerning Christophe's life before coming to Jekyll Island. Readers interested in his seafaring career will find much fascinating detail about this aspect of his life in her book. My work would not be complete without recognizing these scholars who have been so influential in its creation.

In my novel, however, I have chosen to focus primarily on Christophe's wife, Marguerite, who must have been a courageous woman to face all she had to face. She was a woman with two families and a desire to weave them into one—a situation that many women in second marriages face today—and a woman whose life had to be refocused, virtually recreated, on several occasions because of politics and other forces over which she had no control.

The simple facts of the du Bignon story are remarkable in their own right, but one writes historical fiction not just to tell what happened, but also to suggest why it may have happened and how those involved may have responded. As a novelist, one is freer than the traditional historian to explore the motivations of characters and to seek ways to make events believable to the modern reader. Although certain scenes in the book are fictional, such as the description of the freed slaves' departure from Georgia in the final pages, the essential structure of the story is based on fact.

The following comments and observations may be of interest to the reader:

• Concerning the death of Marguerite's third son by her husband Christophe, I have found only one unreliable record, an online family genealogy that lists the year of his death as 1792, but it does not specify a date. We know he set sail that year with his family, but if he arrived in America, he played no significant role in their lives here. Thus, I have chosen to have him die aboard ship on their way to Georgia. The name I have given him is purely fictional, as I am unaware of any official document that has recorded his name. He is referred to in the ship's manifest simply as "*fils anonyme*" (unnamed or anonymous son).

• The daughter of Marguerite, whom I call Margot, was legally named Marguerite Anne Étiennette. I have chosen to call her Margot, a typical nickname for Marguerite in French, in order to distinguish her from her mother. I chose not to use Étiennette, which is a name less familiar and more cumbersome for readers of English.

- The friends I give to Marguerite and Christophe while they live at La Ville Hervé are fictional. Although I have borrowed the names of families who lived in the area at the time, I cannot be sure that the du Bignons ever entertained them in their manor house.

- The misspelling of *Sappello* as the name of Christophe's ship is recorded but not explained by the historical record; I describe it in my narrative as an error made by the painter of the ship's new name. Surely Christophe, who had signed various documents concerning the island, must have known the correct spelling, though legal records of the period were less concerned with such matters than they are today.

- It may surprise readers to learn that Louisville, the seat of Jefferson County, a city with only about 2500 inhabitants today, was for a time the capital of Georgia. In fact, the state has had five different capital cities over the years: Savannah, Augusta, Louisville, Milledgeville, and Atlanta, which became its capital only after the Civil War in 1868.

- The appearance of Vice President Aaron Burr at John Couper's house is a historical fact. Burr took refuge for a time on the Georgia coast after his deadly duel with Alexander Hamilton. He was at the Couper house at the time the 1804 hurricane raged. It is, in fact, thanks to a letter Aaron Burr wrote to his daughter Theodosia that we are aware of Amélie Nicolau's presence as a guest at the Couper home and her lack of knowledge of her brother Joseph's death and Bernard's illness.

- Amélie Nicolau's name, as carved on her tombstone, still visible today on Jekyll Island, is Ann Amelia, an Anglicized version of her French name. Both she and Henry seemed to have preferred these spellings as they began increasingly to identify themselves as Americans. Thus, I have shifted the spelling as the novel progresses.

- Historical records contain the names of neither the father nor the mother of the mulatto child named Harriot; however, historians agree that she is most likely the daughter of one of Christophe and Marguerite's sons. For two reasons, I have chosen to make Joseph and Maria Theresa her parents. First, she was born the same year that Maria Theresa was purchased and brought to the island, and second, Henri was busy with his own courtship of Amélie at the time. Given the growing animosity between Joseph and his father, such a relationship could only serve to widen the wedge between them.

• I am aware that the British invasion of Jekyll Island in November 1814 actually took place in the late afternoon. I chose to set it in the morning in order to heighten the impact of surprise for the du Bignon family. The man who claims to have been cabin boy on the *Merchant of Bombay* is purely fictional, though these British sailors do seem to have had some special grievance against Christophe, to have returned a second time to ransack his property.

• One will search in vain today for the streets in Vannes, Brittany, that Marguerite wandered with her daughter in seeking a place for her marriage to Christophe. The parish of Saint-Salomon was suppressed in 1791 and combined with the parish of Saint-Pierre. The church of Saint-Salomon itself was demolished during the French Revolution. The street names in the book, which are accurate for the pre-Revolutionary era, have been changed, sometimes several times. For example, the rue de la Vieille Boucherie now bears the name rue de la Loi.

• The reader can, however, still find La Grande Ville Hervé near the village of Planguenuoal in Brittany. The manor house of Christophe and Marguerite, with all its appurtenances, stands today as fine as ever. It is listed on contemporary maps only as La Ville Hervé, as distinguished from the nearby Petite Ville Hervé. My one visit to the manor was unforgettable and a rather surreal adventure, which I will be happy to share in my talks about the book with readers' groups.

- Slave names in the book are taken from the property inventory and appraisements recorded in Glynn County Probate Court after Christophe's death or borrowed from other historical records.

- The terms of Christophe's will are quoted from the original document and are recorded in the form given in the text.

- The Richard Leake whose name appears in the advertisement for the sale of Jekyl Island is not the same Richard Leake who originally sold the island to the Société de Sapelo, and who died March 11, 1802. Nor is he his son, for Leake had only one daughter, Sarah, who became the wife of Thomas Spalding. He may well be a nephew, though the relationship is uncertain.

- I am well aware that some of the French names may seem rather daunting to my readers; however, the names are essential to the historical record and I have chosen not to change them. Nor did I give the various Marguerites fictional names, for they too are historical figures. I hope I have sufficiently distinguished among them to avoid confusion. I have also added a list of the book's most important historical characters and their relationships at the beginning of the novel in an effort to help the reader.

It is my sincere hope that those who read this book will find in it a new reason to love and explore Jekyll Island and the marvelous Georgia coast, which is so rich in history.

QUESTIONS FOR READING GROUP DISCUSSIONS

1. What characteristics attract Marguerite and Christophe to one another?

2. Is Marguerite's decision to leave Marie Clarice behind in the temporary care of her grandmother understandable? Why or why not?

3. What is the most important goal that Marguerite and Christophe share? Do their motivations and goals change throughout the novel? If so, how?

4. Do you know anyone who, like Marguerite, has tried to weave together two or more families? Have they been successful? If so, why? If not, what has caused them to fail? What do you think it takes for two families to become one?

5. How does Christophe's attitude toward his oldest son change from his birth until his adulthood? What provokes this change initially? What seals it? Do you think it is justified?

6. Does Christophe draw clear distinctions between his attitudes toward his children and his stepchildren? Explain.

7. Why does Christophe come to consider Henry his "good son"? Do you agree with him?

8. How do Marguerite's and Christophe's attitudes toward slavery differ? What evidence do you see of these differences?

9. Does the character of Marguerite seem to change when her Boisquenay grandchildren arrive in Georgia? If so, can you explain the change?

10. Why do you think Amélie chooses the younger son in marriage when given a choice?

11. Compare Marguerite's and Christophe's attitudes toward love and forgiveness. Which one do you think is right?

12. Do you find it odd that none of Christophe's sons or grandsons is named for him, given the time period and the propensity for family names? *Note in the list of characters at the beginning of the book that even the child born the year after his grandfather's death is not named for his grandfather but rather for his father.*

13. Does the life of a coastal planter seem a desirable one to you? Why or why not?

14. Why do you think some of the du Bignon slaves choose not to leave when the British invade Jekyll Island and offer them the opportunity?

15. Compare the relationships of Christophe and Joseph to Maria Theresa and explain her reaction to each one. Do you think such relationships were common at the time?

16. Why do you suppose Sans Foix is able to live successfully as a free black man in Georgia?

17. What do you think causes Maria Theresa's apparent physical decline?

18. Why does Christophe question himself concerning the terms of his will? Do you think he comes to the right conclusion?

19. Do you agree with Marguerite that no one is "all good or all bad"? If you agree, choose a character and see whether or not you can apply this statement to him or her. Do you think the character would agree with you?

20. Who in your view is the strongest or most memorable character in the book? Justify your choice.

ABOUT THE AUTHOR

JUNE HALL McCASH has written thirteen books of nonfiction, historical fiction, and poetry, many of them about the Georgia coast. She first discovered Jekyll Island with her late husband in 1983, and it has been a major part of her life ever since. She has written four books about the history of the island and has been twice named Georgia Author of the Year for her historical novels.

Currently a full-time writer, McCash holds a Ph.D. and M.A. from Emory University and an undergraduate B.A. from Agnes Scott College. She is a professor emerita from Middle Tennessee State University, where she was chair of the Department of Foreign Languages and Literatures as well as the founding director of the Honors Program (now Honors College). She has been a fellow of the American Council on Education and the National Endowment for the Humanities, as well as recipient of her university's Distinguished Research and Career Achievement Awards. She was also honored by Agnes Scott College in 1996 with its Distinguished Career alumna award. She divides her time between Murfreesboro, Tennessee, and Jekyll Island, Georgia.

CPSIA information can be obtained
at www.ICGtesting.com
Printed in the USA
BVHW051209191222
654535BV00008B/432